WHEN I'M
DEAD

WHEN I'M
DEAD

A BLACK HARBOR NOVEL

Hannah Morrissey

MINOTAUR
BOOKS
NEW YORK

First published in the United States by Minotaur Books, an imprint of St. Martin's Publishing Group

WHEN I'M DEAD. Copyright © 2023 by Hannah Morrissey. All rights reserved. Printed in the United States of America. For information, address St. Martin's Publishing Group, 120 Broadway, New York, NY 10271.

www.minotaurbooks.com

Designed by Omar Chapa

Library of Congress Cataloging-in-Publication Data

Names: Morrissey, Hannah, author.
Title: When I'm dead : / Hannah Morrissey.
Description: First Edition. | New York : Minotaur Books, 2023. |
   Series: A Black Harbor novel |
Identifiers: LCCN 2023018033 | ISBN 9781250872340 (hardcover) |
   ISBN 9781250872357 (ebook)
Subjects: LCGFT: Detective and mystery fiction. | Thrillers (Fiction). |
   Novels.
Classification: LCC PS3613.O777928 W47 2023 | DDC 813/.6—dc23/eng/
   20230417
LC record available at https://lccn.loc.gov/2023018033

Our books may be purchased in bulk for promotional, educational, or business use. Please contact your local bookseller or the Macmillan Corporate and Premium Sales Department at 1-800-221-7945, extension 5442, or by email at MacmillanSpecialMarkets@macmillan.com.

First Edition: 2023

10 9 8 7 6 5 4 3 2 1

For Mam.
Who doesn't flinch at the stories I write.

WHEN I'M
DEAD

1

ROWAN

You'll love me more when I'm dead.

The memory of her daughter's words makes the hair on the back of her neck stand up. Or perhaps it's just Black Harbor and the way she can't help but feel chilled to the bone whenever she finds herself skulking in its shadows. Eighteen years in this purgatory; Rowan would have thought she'd be used to it by now.

It could be that there are some things you never get used to: babies in dumpsters, brains smeared on sidewalks, junkies lying on the lawn, their last needle offering a stiff salute from their basilic vein.

Dead girls in gullies.

Shards of white glint on the river rocks, little snowflake fractals. But it's only mid-October in Wisconsin, which means it's too early for anything but hoarfrost. The broken triangles are teeth, knocked out of the skull of her daughter's best friend.

Madison Caldwell lives just around the bend, a handful of houses down.

Lived.

Rowan shines her flashlight on the corpse. It stares up at a starless sky, head nesting on tendrils of blond hair. The skin is snowy and soft; the eyes float in pools of plum-colored bruises. Crouching low, Rowan flutters the eyelashes and receives no response. She presses two fingers to the victim's neck, then, and feels nothing. After she lifts them, her prints stay there in white, blanching the skin. Next to them is a red mark. Rowan squints and leans closer. A hickey?

She turns the victim's head and examines the other side. A second mark peeks from beneath the hood. With her work phone, she snaps a picture of each injury, and hears the sound of leaves shuffling as an evidence technician crouches to place a yellow placard by what appears to be a set of house keys. No chance they belong to the killer. They wouldn't get that lucky.

The scene is crawling with law enforcement. There are ten officers with flashlights and black memo pads, including the four members of the Violent Crime Task Force. At least two officers must have gone to notify the parents. It's a responsibility usually reserved for a sergeant or lieutenant, but they're too shorthanded to be concerned about formalities. A fifteen-year-old girl is dead. Someone has to tell her parents.

Rowan raises the handheld recorder to her mouth. "Time of death, October 19, 2039 hours, mechanical asphyxiation," she says, when suddenly, the dead girl draws a breath.

A scream catches in Rowan's throat. She doubles back, scuttling like a crab. The sharp rocks in the gully dig into her palms. Her flashlight rolls away from her, its light diffusing to bathe the entire area in a halfhearted haze. She watches the victim's chest cavity expand, the head tilt back slightly, and listens to the whisper of air that fills the lungs and fades to silence. There is no muscle movement for an exhale. The postmortem breath will stay there, trapped like oxygen in a balloon, until Liz, the forensic pathologist, cracks open the rib cage and weighs the organs in flat metal trays.

Which could be days from now. The county medical examiner's office is overwhelmed and understaffed. Only in a place like Black Harbor is the line for the morgue longer than the queue for a Chick-fil-A drive-thru. Too many bodies, not enough of them warm.

"You get spooked or what, Winthorp?" Kole's voice is nearly drowned out by the waves that slam into the sunken piers. Lake Michigan is less than a hundred feet east.

"Yeah." Rowan scrubs her palms against her thighs. She looks up to see him handing her a fresh pair of black latex gloves. "Thanks. I hate when they do that."

"What? Draw one last breath of this noxious air?"

Rowan nods. For a second there, she feared it was Lazarus syndrome, a phenomenon where someone can be clinically dead—no heartbeat, no circulation, no brain activity—and suddenly come back to life. It's called ROSC: return of spontaneous circulation. She's seen it twice.

She looks at Kole, who chews the inside of his cheek. He guessed correctly because he hates it, too. There isn't one person in this field—from patrol officers to medical examiners to investigators—who can honestly say that interacting with a corpse doesn't unnerve them at least a little bit. Anyone who does is a liar. Death makes existentialists of us all.

That isn't to say there's nothing reassuring about them. No matter what you do—a poke, a prod, a bone saw through the cranium—you can't hurt them. The worst has already happened. As a medical examiner, Rowan's job is simply to pick up the pieces and zip them into a polyethylene bag.

But this one is different. This is Madison Caldwell. Just yesterday, Rowan waved to her as she rode her bike past their house. And hadn't she been over not all that long ago, singing karaoke and doing whatever teenage girls do, before Chloe decided to cross over to the dark side?

"Relax, she won't bite," says Kole when he notices Rowan tiptoeing cautiously. "What time do you think it actually happened, 18, maybe 1900 hours?"

"Sounds about right," replies Rowan.

The time of death recorded on the death certificate will be 2039 hours, which is the time she observed the victim was not breathing and did not have a pulse. However, the stiffening of the limbs and the way the blood has settled, pulling color from the victim's face and pooling at the back of the head and shoulder blades, indicate that the girl was killed at least two hours ago.

She pauses. Chloe left the house around that time to walk to the school's performing arts center. She had to be there early for hair and makeup—though she's been in character for weeks now, hiding beneath stormy clothes and stark slashes of eyeliner. "I'm a method actor," she said defensively, when Rowan had gaped at her transformation, because from her perspective, her blond, sun-kissed daughter had gone into the bathroom and an hour later, an emo teenager emerged. Her hair was dark as midnight, her fingernails beetle-black. A faux leather choker severed her neck. Everything about her had simply darkened, as though whatever flame had burned inside her the past fifteen years had suddenly been snuffed out.

Rowan didn't recognize this girl. She didn't like her.

She was moody and antisocial, and brimmed with an umbrage that made her seem more like Chloe's shadow than Chloe herself.

A seed of dread plants itself in the pit of Rowan's stomach. *What if Chloe is nearby, her body broken and strewn across the river rocks, too?*

No. She can't be. Earlier this evening, Rowan had watched from the kitchen window as Chloe took to the walking trail that stretched from their quiet lakeside neighborhood of Belgrave Circle to Monroe Academy. And hadn't they just seen her dazzle onstage as Lydia Deetz, the angsty adolescent character who identifies more with the dead than the living?

She must have taken a page out of Rowan's book to have been so convincing. Long has Rowan mused at how calming it must be to be dead. No more guilt, no more feeling like you're not enough. You just . . . are. You have no obligation to anyone but to let them sink you in the ground or burn you to ash.

The call came just before intermission. She remembers the death phone buzzing between her and Axel. They'd slipped out into the hall and she'd pressed her ear to his cheek as together, they listened to Kole's voice recite the details of the scene: "Homicide . . . female, white . . . Patrol found her . . . asystolic . . ." Then, he mentioned the name of their small neighborhood nestled near the lake's crumbling edge. She'd inhaled sharply and texted her best friend, Marnie, asking her to give Chloe a ride home.

Axel pocketed his phone. "Rock Paper Pistol for who's gotta be the bad guy?"

Rowan tucked the black rose bouquet in her armpit. They shook hands—down, up, down—and then broke apart. Axel pointed at her open hand with his index and middle fingers, thumb cocked. "Pistol shoots paper."

And that was how she ended up face-to-face with a brokenhearted Chloe, who looked so mature and melancholy in a red lace dress, mascara-dyed tears streaming down her cheeks as Rowan broke the news that Mom and Dad would not be watching the rest of the musical. Not that it was the first time they'd had to leave in the middle of an event, nor would it be the last. People had a nasty habit of dying in Black Harbor, and Chloe was cursed with having both a medical examiner and a homicide detective for parents.

"Sweetie . . ." She set her hands on Chloe's shoulders. Something glimmered in Chloe's ears, she noticed—safety pins. A pained, insistent voice gnawed at Rowan's brain stem. *I don't know you,* she thought. *Where is my bright, darling girl?*

"Where's Dad?" Chloe stood on her tiptoes trying to see over Rowan's shoulder.

Rowan sucked her teeth. If she had a nickel for every time Chloe asked for Axel. "I'm sorry, honey. But listen, it happened close to home, and—"

"So it's someone we know?"

"I want you to get a ride home with Marnie, okay? I'll text her and let her know to wait for you." Marnie was here. She'd seen her jet-black hair and Burberry scarf in the third row, sitting next to Sylvia Halquist. "Chloe?"

Around them, people moved in fast motion. Stagehands pushed brooms and carried props overhead. The main actor, in a green wig and pinstriped suit, chugged a Red Bull. Mr. Cutler skirted around him, yelling at someone to put their phone away. "There are no cell phones in *Beetlejuice!*" And yet, Rowan and Chloe were in their own bubble.

Rowan suddenly remembered the roses. The cellophane crinkled as she handed them to Chloe. They seemed a cheap consolation now. "These are for you. We love you so much, Chloe. You're killing it, you really are. But work—"

"Do you?"

Rowan paused. She felt her brows knit. "What?"

Chloe sighed. Her pointed bangs made everything about her look barbed, scary. And then she uttered seven little words that cut Rowan to the bone. *You'll love me more when I'm dead.*

The accusation razes her still. She feels scraped, empty inside as she maneuvers around the corpse of someone else's daughter. They will make it right, she promises. By the time she and Axel get out of here, they could still have time to curl up on the couch with Chloe and watch a movie.

"So, how'd he knock out her teeth?" A cloud of vapor issues from Kole's mouth as he begins asking the first of a million questions that thicken the air.

"He?" Rowan raises a brow.

"Statistically, you and I both know this was a male."

While she hates to default to statistics, she knows Kole is right. Of the hundreds of homicides she's worked, nine times out of ten, the guilty party is male. And this death reeks of a male aggressor. Giving the body a quick scan, she notes the victim's jeans are still fastened, her jacket still zipped. But then there are the marks on her neck, near her collar. Rowan creeps closer and pulls the hood of the victim's sweatshirt aside, revealing the inch-long abrasions.

"Hickeys?" Kole kneels beside her and she catches a whiff of his cologne—woodsy and clean—too subtle to mask the stench of decomp all around them: the foliage, the fish carcasses caught in the rocks, the body of Madison Caldwell.

"Could be." Rowan squints. "Or choke marks. Which would make sense, considering the trauma to her mouth is postmortem."

"How can you tell?"

She cups the victim's chin and puts her other hand on top of the head, tilting the skull for a better perspective. The mouth is transmogrified into a broken cavity, sharp little pegs stuck like shrapnel in the gums. No blood. "I'd guess they used a hammer," she says. "Or a rock. Something to deliver blunt force."

"Let's hope it was a rock," says Kole, and Rowan agrees. A hammer hints at premeditation. She watches his gaze slide toward the darkness, where thousands of rocks litter the creek bed, and she knows what he's thinking: finding the murder weapon will be as impossible as finding a certain needle in an opium den.

"So, he strangled her to death, then smashed her teeth out? Is that what you're telling me?"

"That's what it looks like." Rowan considers the corpse again. She was someone's daughter, this empty vessel, now stiffening with rigor. "Have you notified her parents yet?"

"Fletcher and Hayes are at the house now. It's only a matter of time before they try to cross the tape." Kole turns, his jaw parallel with his shoulder as though to affirm they aren't about to be ambushed by hysterical parents. But he and Rowan are alone. The other officers and investigators, including Axel, are a ways up the bank, processing the scene. Yellow evidence placards mark possible DNA, footprints, and anything the killer might have left behind. At the top of the hill, crime scene tape cuts a fragile division between them and the rest of the world. The local news van is parked on the street thirty yards from the little stone bridge that Madison's body lay beneath.

"I thought you were typically the one to tell the family," says Rowan.

Kole shrugs. "Someone has to stay and command the scene. We're suffering a deficit in manpower, if you haven't noticed."

She's noticed. The entire city has noticed. Since incurring massive budget cuts, the police department is down forty-two sworn officers from the year prior. They hardly have enough investigators to conduct search warrants anymore. "Axel might have mentioned it," she says. With a sigh, she turns back to the body. "I'm gonna bag her hands." The narration is unnecessary, but speaking out loud helps her focus on the task in front of her. She isn't a mother who disappointed her daughter yet again, but a medical examiner with the job of bagging up someone else's.

"That's a good idea." Kole coughs, the crisp fall air infiltrating his lungs. Or is it the coal dust from the mine only a few miles away? Rowan can feel it, too. They probably all have black lung disease by now, anyone who lives within a ten-mile radius of Black Harbor. The city is intent on killing them one way or another.

Reaching into her kit for the paper bags, Rowan can't help but wonder what Madison's last words to her own mother were. Did she die regretting them?

Rowan slides the victim's left hand into the opening, cinching it at the wrist and cringing as though her thoughts have been projected on the ground for Kole to read. But he is no longer beside her. She didn't even hear him walk up the bank. Axel enters her work space. He's breathless. "Hey, I tried ringing Chloe but she hasn't answered. You told her to get a ride with Marnie, yeah?"

Rowan pauses. The evening has been a blur. Yes, she sent a text to Marnie. But had she heard anything back, or even glanced at her phone since? She checks it now.

Her internal temperature plummets. A red exclamation point glows next to the message she'd sent Marnie, asking her to wait for Chloe and take her home. Beneath it, the text: Not delivered.

"Row?" Axel's voice sounds far away.

Her hand shakes when she holds the phone for him to see. She watches an eleven form between his brows, then relax. "I'm sure she took her home," he says. "You told Chloe to get a ride with her, didn't you? When you went backstage?"

"I did, but—" Rowan bites her lip. He didn't see Chloe, the tears brimming in her eyes. He didn't have to be the one to walk away from her, leave her with a bouquet of black roses. He didn't have to be the bad guy.

He never does.

"But what?"

She is already calling Chloe. It rings four times and goes to voice mail. The lines between Axel's brows return.

Next, she tries Marnie, who answers on the second ring. "Hey Rowan, where'd you two scoot off to? Missed you at the end of the—"

"Did Chloe come home with you?"

"What?"

"Chloe. Did she ask you for a ride home?"

"No, I—I saw her walk out into the commons. She was taking pictures with a group of kids when I told her congratulations." A pause. "Did I miss something?"

Rowan sighs. She hates doing this. Because what she says next will make Marnie feel guilty, even though none of this is on her. She didn't know. She never got the message. It's all on Rowan. "It's okay, Marn. There was a death call and Axel and I both had to leave at intermission."

Silence on the other end. Marnie is used to death calls; she's an ICU doctor.

"I told Chloe to get a ride with you, but—"

But she didn't. How did she get home? She wouldn't have walked, would she? She thinks of the trail at night, pitch-black and rife with danger. There are coyotes in this part of Black Harbor, not to mention the occasional human predator.

"I'm so sorry." She can hear the apology in Marnie's voice. "Do you want me to go over there and check on her?"

Rowan swallows. "No, no. I'm sure she's there. I'm gonna run over there right now, actually. We're just on the other side of the circle."

She hears shuffling and knows that Marnie has gone over to her window to peer out. They live next door to each other. "I see the lights. Who is it, Rowan?" Her voice wobbles.

I'll talk to you later, she means to say. But she doesn't say anything at all. Fear spurs her body into motion. Rowan treks up the hill and in a matter of seconds, her fast walk has become a run. With her heart pounding, her feet kick up a pile of leaves that have been raked against the curb. Her hands, still encased in black latex gloves, are blades slicing the air. She feels as though she's careening through a tunnel. The darkness closes in around her, its fabric punctured by the orange flickering lights of the season. Ghosts with pillowcase bodies hang from the tree branches.

It's less than a half mile from one end of the circle to the other. She cuts down Hennepin Street, which spits her out in front of their white brick colonial. A pair of jack-o'-lanterns glow on the front porch steps, welcoming her home. Or warning her to stay out?

The door is locked. *Good girl,* she thinks as she shoves her hand into her pocket and fishes out her keys. Shadows fill the interior like smoke in a bottle. Fry's barks echo off the walls. His nails clack on the floor as he runs to greet her, the intruder, and spins a lap around her feet.

Chloe is probably asleep. She might have passed out on the couch or she could already be upstairs. Rowan wanders into the kitchen, her eyes conducting a cursory search of the cereal bowls from this morning left in the sink "to soak" and the bag of cheesy popcorn on the countertop. Around the corner, the living room is empty.

"Where's your sister, huh?" Rowan asks the French bulldog. She tucks him under her arm like a football and heads up the stairs, quiet though, because Chloe must have gone to bed.

Her room is on the right side of the landing, down a narrow hall that boasts her school portraits from 4K through tenth grade. All the different versions of Chloe smile at her—toothless Chloe, pigtail Chloe, preppy Chloe, goth Chloe. The most recent one bears almost no resemblance to the others. It's as though she made it her mission to look as different as possible, to eradicate every golden thing from the girl before.

She knocks softly on Chloe's door. There's no answer. No blade of light leaking through the crack to indicate Chloe is even awake.

Her ears prick at the click of the door disengaging from the frame when she pushes it inward. The room is bathed in a cool, desaturated haze. Moonlight strikes the comforter, filling the space between each crease with dark shadows. Chloe's Bubby, a frayed, love-worn rabbit, slumps in front of the pillows. Above, a black-and-white poster of a young Winona Ryder smirks.

The edge of a pillowcase ripples, and suddenly, Rowan is aware of the sound of the wind rustling the leaves outside, the *shush* of the waves curling along the shore. This time of year, Lake Michigan sounds like the ocean. Her breathing becomes shallow. Slowly, she turns her head to look at the wall. A shadow dances. It belongs to a little gauzy ghost that hangs from a hook in the ceiling. It dances, as though someone is blowing on it.

The window is open.

Fry kicks against her, launching himself out of her hold.

Downstairs, the door slams. Axel has followed her home. His footsteps wander in the wake of hers: the kitchen, the living room, up the stairs.

She thinks it's him, at least. The footsteps are too heavy to belong to Chloe.

Goose bumps stipple her flesh. Her knuckles are bone-white as she grips the windowsill. She leans halfway out, her gaze sweeping across one end of the yard to the other.

"Chloe!" she screams. "Chloe!"

Next door, a light pops on in Marnie's house. A gust of wind barrels in off the lake, ripping tears from Rowan's eyes. She screams again. "Chloe!"

The only answer comes from the waves crashing into the half-sunk pier. She leans farther when suddenly, a pair of arms locks around her waist, wrenching her back into the room and away from the darkness that has swallowed her daughter.

Her cheek hits the hardwood floor. Her body instinctively curls, like a hand closing into a fist, as the dreaded blossom inside her sprouts thorns and she feels herself being torn apart from the inside out.

Chloe is gone.

2

AXEL

Rowan is a wreck. He hates to leave her but he has no choice. Chloe is missing. Her best friend, Madison, is dead.

"If we find the killer, we find Chloe," Kole says as they stand in the intersection of the rooms upstairs. The sergeant's words are almost drowned out by the sounds of searching, but Axel hears him loud and clear. It plays in his head like a mantra. *If we find the killer, we find Chloe. If we find the killer, we find Chloe.* He doesn't like that the subjects of that sentence are in such close proximity to each other.

His house has been taken over by law enforcement. It feels surreal, being on the other side of things. In Axel's thirteen years in Investigations, he's searched hundreds of homes. But tonight—having his own space be shredded and sorted—is a first. He stares into Chloe's bedroom and watches as they manhandle her things—opening trinket boxes, emptying dresser drawers, flipping through books—and his heart rips a stitch. What comes to mind is all the kids' rooms he's searched throughout his career. Rooms that belonged to wayward kids, dead kids, missing kids. How many of them had he rifled through while the parents looked on, as distraught and frozen as he is now?

His thoughts flit to the Caldwell household, where Riley and Fletcher concurrently lead the search in Madison's bedroom. Her parents will be in the living room, probably, consoling their other children, and waiting, helpless and hopeless. Their daughter is dead. She was murdered less than thirty yards from their front door and now there is nothing to do but cooperate so the cops can find her killer and bring him to justice. Albeit there's no magic list when it comes to searching, Axel knows that in this case, they are looking for two things: anything out of the ordinary, and anything that links Madison and Chloe as having been at the same place at the same time—concert tickets, receipts, pictures—anywhere they might have met someone. Beyond that criterion, they will take her computer along with any and all tablets to comb through her search history and deleted files. Madison's cell phone was collected at the scene.

Kole's voice, quiet but firm, brings him back. "You know you can't work this case."

Axel sets his jaw. He knew that was coming, which was why he'd had his retort queued up. "Sir, with all due respect, over my dead body am I going to sit on my hands and trust someone else to find my little girl."

Kole sniffs. He shifts his stance and crosses his arms, his elbow grazing the handgun on his hip. "I knew you'd say that. Which is why I've already decided I'm going to let you do this, as long as you understand one thing."

Axel tears his gaze from Chloe's torn-apart bedroom and locks eyes with Kole. He swallows and hates the way it probably makes him look afraid.

"From this moment on until we find Chloe, you and I are connected. You won't so much as take a piss without me knowing about it."

Before Axel can nod that he understands, Kole taps him on the arm and jerks his head toward the stairs. "Go check on your wife. I'm going to get a team together for Monroe."

They're here now. The school looks like an oil painting, the way the dingy brick blends with the backdrop of a polluted night sky. Spotlights shine on the entrances, an easy deterrent for characters with a mind for breaking and entering.

Axel waits for Kole to get out and slam his door, then does the same. Sergeant Mackhorn, head of the School Safety and Security Division, emerges from a dark SUV. They're met by Principal Werner, who clearly threw a winter jacket over her pajamas. Her silk head wrap catches the light.

"Sorry to wake you, Mrs. Werner," says Kole.

She shakes her head and although she presses her mouth into a tight seam, her chin still quivers. "I'm sorry we're all here," she manages. Her eyes move to take in each of them. When she gets to Axel, she squeezes his arm. "Anything I can do to help you find her, you all just let me know."

Axel nods. Tears sting his eyes and he lets himself pretend, for a second, that it's the autumnal bite in the air, not the claws of raw emotion scratching at him. That would mean he's scared. And why would he be scared when he knows they are going to find Chloe, safe and sound and probably just asleep backstage?

"Who's got keys?" asks Kole. He's already crossing the empty parking lot. Once inside, the school is as quiet as a crypt. Axel peers into the glass box of the administrative office, where he goes to sign Chloe out for dentist appointments and if she ever needs to go home sick. It houses the principal's office, too, but Chloe only landed herself in there once. She's a good kid.

More officers show up. They conduct the briefing right in the vestibule. Kole passes around Chloe's latest school portrait, taken just over a month ago. Axel hardly recognizes her as his daughter; rather, she is what his daughter morphed into for her part in *Beetlejuice: The Musical,* with black chin-length hair and smoky eye makeup. She promised she would change back when the play was over this weekend. He hopes she makes good on that promise.

"She was last seen wearing a red lace costume dress." Kole recites the description Rowan had shared with him to activate the Amber Alert. "Red fishnet tights. Combat boots. May or may not have been carrying a bouquet of black roses."

Axel feels pockmarked by their pitying gazes. But there's no shade, because just as surely as everyone recognizes his involvement in the investigation as a conflict of interest, they also recognize that, if the tables were turned, they would be here too.

Sergeant Mackhorn takes over, delegating areas to search: the bathrooms, the theater, any stairwells she could be hiding under. He pairs the officers together, leaving Axel and Kole to search the girls' lockers. Principal Werner accompanies them with a master key.

"Do you know if anyone's been giving Chloe a hard time lately?" Kole asks as they walk.

Principal Werner hums as she thinks. Finally, she shakes her head. "No. Chloe Winthorp is . . . has always seemed to be, at least . . . a well-respected student. She's certainly more reserved, especially this year it seems. But when she's in the right company, she really lights up. Which . . ." She swivels to Axel. "I'm sure you know."

"So, Chloe's a quiet student who keeps to herself?" Kole clarifies.

"Yes, from what I've observed anyway. Which was why I was quite surprised to see her cast as lead in the musical. She's a talented actress, but . . ." She shivers animatedly. "There's enough adrenaline in that stage fright to last me a couple million years."

"Talk about her being more reserved," says Kole, and Axel is glad the sergeant is the one asking the questions.

Principal Werner pauses, choosing her words carefully. But her expression betrays her. *Surely you've noticed,* it says. "Well, she's certainly a bit more withdrawn this year than she was last year. I don't know if changing her physical appearance is a representation of that or—"

"She's method acting." Axel hears himself repeat Chloe's words by heart. His tone sounds more defensive than he means it to.

"Yes, that's her story and she's sticking to it." Principal Werner sighs and offers a slight, close-mouthed smile as though to slough off some of the tension. "Here's Miss Chloe's locker."

The locker before them with the paint chipping near the top vent unmistakably belongs to his daughter. A handmade poster made to look like the front of Beetlejuice's black-and-white-striped suit is taped to the door. Pasted to it in an off-kilter fashion is a purple cut-out star with *CHLOE* written in Sharpie. Doing a quick cursory search, Axel notices several other lockers with similar posters. They must belong to the other cast members.

"I'll warn you, a lot of students hardly use them. They're allowed to take their backpacks to class now, so they just carry their books everywhere they go."

"We're not looking for books, Mrs. Werner," says Kole.

She inserts the key. Axel holds his breath, praying that Chloe, herself, could even be stuffed inside—the victim of a cruel prank. But, when the door comes apart with a metal twang, she isn't there. He exhales, releasing any pent-up hope, and bends to sift through what can only be described as debris. Crumpled and folded papers tumble onto the recently waxed floor. He opens one to read the message scrawled in black pen.

Chloe the Hoe-y.

His lips move as he reads. Screwing up his face, he opens another one. It's a crudely drawn image of a female figure sitting on a male figure's lap . . . on a stage. Above them, a marquee sign flashes: *Chloe Gets Extra Credit*. The figures are labeled *Chloe* and *Mr. Cuddler*.

"Is that supposed to be Mr. Cutler?" Axel whispers. "The drama teacher?"

Behind him, he hears a sharp intake of breath. In his peripheral vision, he sees a horrified Principal Werner. A loud *crack!* splits the quiet as Kole smashes his fist against a locker.

3

ROWAN

Midnight creeps in like an unwanted houseguest. Rowan's sanity frays with every second that elapses without news of Chloe.

It isn't the worst thing, she reminds herself. The worst thing would be that Axel and Kole return to tell her they discovered Chloe in the same state as Madison Caldwell—strangled to death and discarded in the woods or a dark stairwell.

She and Marnie sit on the front porch steps between jack-o'-lanterns whose flames flicker as faintly as her hope is waning. Marnie draws circles on Rowan's back. The police have finished searching her house for now. They left with Chloe's computer, iPad, and fingerprints lifted from the windowsill.

The neighbors' cameras didn't reveal anyone entering the house by way of the front or back doors. No one traipsed across the leaf-strewn lawn or up the asphalt driveway on which a younger Chloe used to roller-skate and create chalk comic book strips. Which raises the question, if Chloe had come home after the play, how had she gotten in and out of the house, undetected?

The sugar maple.

The answer surfaces in the murky waters of Rowan's mind before she can finish asking herself the question. Chloe could have climbed in and out of her bedroom by way of the sugar maple—a towering tree with a canopy of bright burnt-orange leaves that stands between her and Marnie's yards. But what reason would she have had to come home secretively? She's used it a few times after coming home from school and realizing she'd forgotten her house key.

She is overcomplicating this. The simplest answer is that Chloe never made it home. She must have opened her window before she left for the play and forgotten to shut it.

Tears prick Rowan's eyes. She drags her shirtsleeve across her face to catch them before they fall as she thinks of Chloe taking the walking path. Alone. In the dark. She must have felt so abandoned, so—

You'll love me more when I'm dead.

The tears flow freely now. She hides her face in her hands. Marnie pulls her closer; the fresh scent of her friend's strawberry-mint shampoo mingles with her unsavory thoughts as she considers the mystery of Madison Caldwell's murder. What are the odds that Chloe would just happen to go missing the same night her best friend is murdered?

Slim to none. The girls were targeted.

Finally, Rowan emerges and drinks in a breath of the crisp autumn air that already tastes like winter. She closes her eyes, feeling all the muscles in her face twitch as she tries not to break down again. But, what began as a singular blossom of dread has multiplied. She is so filled with fear that it's hard to breathe.

Inhale. Exhale. Focus.

Mentally, she retraces her steps from a few hours ago, when she'd gone backstage to tell Chloe there had been a death, and that she and Axel had to leave. Faces blur in her memory. She recalls stagehands dressed in black and toting various props. Kids flopped on old, worn furniture, snapping selfies and reading lines. The boy in the striped suit and neon-green wig. Mr. Cutler yelling about there being no cell phones in *Beetlejuice.*

A shudder courses through her. Perhaps she had encountered her child's abductor then without even realizing it. The timeline adds up. Madison was killed between the hours of 6 and 7 p.m. The play started at 7 p.m. Chloe and all cast members had to be there an hour early for makeup. Which means someone could have killed Madison on their way to the school, then taken Chloe on their way out.

Axel will begin interviewing the students tomorrow. He'll know to ask whether or not anyone had been late for makeup, among other questions. It wouldn't be proof of guilt, but it could be a start, a lead.

"I'm so sorry, Row," Marnie apologizes for what cannot be less than the hundredth time. "I should have looked for you guys afterward, made sure Chloe had someone."

"It wasn't your job, Marnie." Rowan sniffs. The undelivered text message she'd typed to Marnie, asking her to give Chloe a ride home, burns the backs of her retinas.

It's a shame their girls aren't better friends. Chloe and Libby are the same age. They must have some classes together, go to the same sporting events? But from little on, Chloe and Libby had established a mutual avoidance of each other. Rowan asked Chloe once, when she was around the age of five or six, why she didn't want to play with Libby, to which Chloe simply replied: "She's weird. And she stares."

Rowan couldn't blame her. She's noticed it herself, as more than once she's caught Libby staring. It's unsettling, to be completely honest; it feels as though this sixteen-year-old is peeling back her layers to see what lies underneath.

Rowan and Marnie sit in silence broken only by an eventual shushing sound. They both look up as a black Impala pulls into the drive. Scarlet leaves swirl in front of the grille and settle back to the pavement. Kole gets out first, then Axel. Their faces are wan and serious. Rowan's gaze is pulled toward the brown bag Axel carries at his side. Her brows knit as she tries to make out the shape of what's hidden within its kraft paper walls.

"This was found on the walking trail." Axel's voice is raw. It holds an edge Rowan's never heard before. He hands the parcel to her, which she accepts and lays across the steps. Gingerly, she unsheaths it, then draws a sharp breath.

Lying across the flagstone are a dozen black roses, thorns and all.

4

LIBBY

Libby Lucas knows what happened before she even reads the notification on her phone. Madison Caldwell is dead and Chloe Winthorp is missing. In their little neighborhood of just sixty-seven residents, it's unnerving to say the least.

Last night, she watched from her reading nook as police searched Chloe's room. They were there for a good three hours, dusting for fingerprints and digging through drawers. All of Belgrave Circle was a light show of alternating red and blue. Now it's barely 6 a.m. and all is dark again. Quiet. You'd never guess that a mere twelve hours ago, a girl had been strangled and left for dead in the gully.

Madison Caldwell is dead. Chloe Winthorp is missing.

The staccato statements repeat on a loop as her brain short-circuits. It doesn't seem real—any of it. In all of Libby's sixteen years on this earth, in this circle, she's never experienced the death of a peer. The neighbor, Ms. Starkey, died a couple summers ago. Libby's mother used to tend to her plants while she visited her sister in Florida for the winters. But Ms. Starkey was in her nineties, and that made her passing more expected. It was almost as though it was an afterthought, actually, Libby muses as she remembers walking by the house while movers marched in and out, hauling furniture onto the lawn for an estate sale. "Oh, Ms. Starkey must have died." Her mom said it as nonchalantly as one might say, "they're calling for rain on Tuesday," and Libby told herself that was just one more thing she would probably come to understand when she's older—how humans can be as indifferent to the end of a life as they are to a weather forecast.

This one feels different, though. Madison Caldwell is young. People will not be as quick to write her off. Because if Madison Caldwell could be murdered, so could their kids. It's tragic, titillating, and ironic. Never has Belgrave Circle felt more alive than it does now after the death of one of its own.

No one's found Chloe yet. Not to Libby's knowledge. But, her mom is best friends with Chloe's mom. If anyone's going to be among the first to hear anything, it will be her.

She sees a lot of things from her bench beneath the tall turret window in her bedroom. Her parents built it as a quiet place for her to study, but the study Libby conducts is most often not confined to books—the exception being her favorite graphic novel series, *Crestfall*. Instead, she observes the neighborhood below. Rowan's yard is a smattering of red and golden leaves to her right, the fire pit brimming with them so it appears to be ablaze. To her left is the street where people walk their dogs and their kids; they'll come from across town to take a stroll in her crescent-shaped community, meandering down all the side streets and stone bridges. Behind her—

Libby sucks in a breath and holds it. Her right hand presses against her chest, as though she's trying to calm her racing heart; instead, she clutches the heart-shaped locket she only recently remembered she had upon finding it in the drawer of her nightstand. It's silver with raised filigree that she imagines to be a code written in braille, the key to unlocking all her secrets.

The cops are parked outside Reeves Singh's house. It isn't part of the circle, but behind it, one of the many identical single-story houses that form her neighborhood's outer shell. The backyard is dusted with blood-red leaves that cling to the soccer goal. Every night for as long as she can remember, she has watched Reeves practice his footwork and launch the ball into the net. Except last night when she'd gone to the play. Where had he been?

A light turns on in the kitchen, illuminating the space above the

Singhs' sagging deck. Even from her perch fifty yards away, Libby can tell that Reeves's house on Rainbow Row does not have marble countertops or updated cabinetry, staples for the dwellings of Belgrave Circle.

Libby scrunches her brows, wondering what the police can possibly want to talk to Reeves Singh about, and then it dawns on her. He is—was—Madison Caldwell's boyfriend, and quite possibly the last person to have seen her alive.

If there is such a thing as a golden couple at Monroe Academy, Reeves and Madison were it. Both were as beautiful as walking statues, especially Reeves with his strong jaw and chiseled athletic physique. Madison sang soprano in the choir and danced at halftime shows, sequins shimmering like starlight. The way they fit together was as satisfying to watch as peeling the skin off a mouse in one piece.

Several times already this semester, Libby caught herself staring at the ropy veins that twined in Reeves's forearms. He noticed her once, in the seventh-hour history class they shared, and a dimple dented his cheek. Libby squinted then and pursed her lips as though she'd just sucked on a lemon, forcing herself to find Uzbekistan on the world map on the wall behind him. Her face suddenly scorching, she promised herself she would never do it again.

But she lied. Even as she recited the oath in her mind, she knew she would never stay true to it. Rather, she amended her promise to be that she would simply never stare at Reeves Singh again *and get caught*.

He would never catch her from up here, never feel the weight of her gaze as he sinks ball after ball into the net. Or when he sits shirtless on the back deck while his mother cuts his hair.

The memory makes her cheeks start to heat up again. She licks her lips as her wandering eyes find purchase on Reeves being walked out of his front door, a cop on either side of him, and her breath hitches. Her hand flies to the silver locket around her neck and she leans even closer to her window, the chill wicking the warmth from her face, to zero in on Reeves's shrinking figure. Her gaze travels down to his hands, as though searching for blood, but she knows as well as anyone that there was no blood at the scene.

She watches as Reeves gets into the back of an unmarked car. A woman with braids shuts the door on him, then gets in behind the wheel. A man with a mohawk ponytail sits down in the passenger seat. Reeves's parents and his sisters stand at the edge of the yard and remain there even as the car pulls away.

Libby tries to swallow but her throat is too dry. She leans away from the window, so the back of her skull rests against the wall. She draws her knees up toward her chest and just sits there, a vacant stare plastered on her face.

They took Reeves Singh.

Monroe Academy's golden boy.

Why? What could they possibly have—

She checks her phone and scrolls for news. Madison's and Chloe's names and faces are everywhere, but there's no mention of Reeves. Yet.

What the articles do mention is how the missing girl and the murdered girl were best friends. But Libby knows the truth. She remembers lying in the dark, she and Chloe so close their foreheads were nearly touching, as Chloe wept and told her every terrible thing Madison had done to her. About the Snapchat and the rumor that threatened Chloe's dream of becoming an actress and of leaving Black Harbor. Tears well in her eyes at the memory. She wipes one away and watches as the water fills the artful, recessed swirls of her fingerprint. Libby puts it in her mouth. Tasting salt, she prays that she didn't leave any trace of herself on Chloe's window.

5

AXEL

Kole knows something. He's been cagey ever since they discovered the drawings in Chloe's locker. A subsequent search of Madison's revealed no items of interest.

Rather, it was what was missing that snagged Axel's attention. Unlike Chloe, it appeared as though Madison actually used her locker. On the inside of it was a collage of cut-out photographs. There she was, smiling on the soccer field with who must be her boyfriend, a dark-haired boy of about seventeen. He was tall and tan, wearing a royal-blue jersey and white shorts marked with grass stains. In another, she and a girl with an Afro, who Axel recognized as Sari Simons, held hands while roller-skating. A black-and-white strip showed a film reel of Madison and the same boy kissing.

But there were no photos of Chloe. Two girls who had been friends since kindergarten.

Sari Simons had only come into the picture (literally) about a year ago, when she and her dad moved from Cape Canaveral. She's as "army brat" as they come: fiercely independent, mature beyond her years, and transient. She's been over to the house a handful of times with Madison.

"You familiar with any of these kids?" Kole asked from over his shoulder as they searched Madison's locker.

Axel shared what he knew about Sari. "Her dad's a general in the army. It's just the two of them, I think."

"He leave a lot?"

"Once a month?" Axel tried to remember what Sari had told him about her father's training schedule.

"She stay with family while he's gone, do you know?"

Axel shook his head, then shrugged. "She must stay with the Caldwells. I see her around our neighborhood quite a bit."

It isn't just Belgrave Circle where he's seen Sari; it's everywhere. She's a nomad, always out walking, always wearing a camouflage jacket, always carrying a purple star-printed backpack which, he imagines, has all her little life packed inside.

"Maybe she saw something."

"Maybe."

"What about this kid?" Kole gestured to the boy on the soccer field. "Looks like Madison's boyfriend."

Axel considered the photo again and after a moment, recognition dawned on him. "He lives next door," he started, and corrected himself. "On the other side of Belgrave Circle."

"In Rainbow Row?"

Axel cringed upon hearing the derogatory, yet widely accepted, nickname of the adjacent neighborhood. Rainbow Row was named for the garish spectrum of free government paint slapped on the houses. It had been called that for as long as Axel had lived there as a child—for longer than he'd been alive, even—when his father and dozens of other tradesmen came to work at the tannery. Besides the abandoned factory, Rainbow Row is all that remains of the Hedelsten Hides & Leather Goods Tanning Company. Just over a hundred years ago, Jim Hedelsten himself, commissioned the building of fifty single-story homes in a community within two miles of the tannery. There was—and still is—a bus stop at its only outlet. Narrow one-way streets discourage through traffic, which lends to Rainbow Row's reputation of trapping its residents.

For years, the tannery has been in the possession of Bennett Reynolds, a venture capitalist who recently confessed to coercion, blackmail, and murder. Upon his death, the property was sold at auction for pennies on the dollar to an anonymous buyer who pledged to revitalize the building and its surrounding community. Last Axel heard, it was going to be a mixed-use development—whatever that means.

"We need to talk to him," Kole said, already texting Riley.

"Who?" Axel had too many trains of thought going on.

"Him." Kole tapped the picture of the boy in the blue uniform.

"You talk to him. I'll talk to *him*." Axel waved the sketches from Chloe's locker.

Kole laughed. "Not a chance in Hell. I don't need you busting up a teacher because of some stupid drawings. They're kids, Axel. They're shits."

Rage boiled beneath Axel's skin. Kole was minimizing the importance of these sketches. They weren't just "some stupid drawings"; they were allegations. Of his minor daughter being inappropriately involved with an older teacher, someone who Axel *knew* she had been spending more and more time with as of late with the upcoming musical: before- and after-school practices, weekend rehearsals, things of that nature.

Now, hours later, following the search of the entire school and canvassing nearby premises for cameras, he is still thinking about the sketches. Self-loathing seeps into his bloodstream. He's a fucking cop. How could he have been so trusting? How could he have been so blind?

He hasn't shown the sketches to Rowan yet. He was about to stop home and check on her when Marnie texted him to let him know she'd fallen asleep on the couch. He wanted her to stay that way as long as possible, temporarily escaping the reality that they are living their worst nightmare.

Their daughter is gone. Missing. Maybe dead.

No. He cannot allow himself to think like that. Chloe's alive. He will find her, no matter if he has to turn over every leaf and stone in this godforsaken place.

He's upstairs at the Black Harbor Police Department. It's been a while since he's been in the Investigations Bureau with its cream-painted cinder blocks and endless grey filing cabinets, now that he spends most of his working life either incognito on the streets or holed away in the secret headquarters of the Violent Crime Task Force. He grabs the carafe and pours himself a warmup. Coffee hisses as it hits the heating plate.

Then, he joins Kole in the viewing room, a deep narrow recess that offers a front-row seat to the goings on of Interview Room #1.

"I don't know why we're here and not at Cutler's house." Axel's voice is a low growl. His heartbeat hastens, whether from the sudden jolt of caffeine or the prospect of willfully entering into a confrontation with his direct supervisor.

"Who would you like me to send over there, Axel?" The question has a bite of condescension to it. "We're not exactly teeming with talent, here."

Axel sets his jaw. In all of his years in law enforcement, he's never seen the Black Harbor Police Department stretched so thin. Crime, on the other hand, is up threefold. Violent crime has never been more rampant, and yet, even in this environment, Madison's death and Chloe's disappearance still manage to hook everyone's attention.

Because they weren't in a gang. Or selling drugs or themselves on the street corners—actions that might make them victims of a violent crime. Rather, they were simply two high school girls minding their own business. Axel's mind inevitably flits back to the sketches and derogatory nickname: *Chloe the Hoe-y*. Had she been minding her own business? Or had his little girl been stirring up trouble in someone else's?

He shakes the thought out of his head.

Kole is still waiting for an answer. He raises a brow.

"We don't need four investigators on one kid," he argues. "I could go to Cutler's house. Ask him a few questions."

"That's ironic, because that's absolutely out of the question."

Axel jerks his head toward him. "Nik."

Kole stares forward. "Axel." Silence slips into the sliver of space they generously call a room. The only sound is Kole drawing a breath. "We find the killer, we find Chloe. As far as we know, Reeves Singh was the last person who saw Madison Caldwell alive. We'll talk to Cutler soon enough. But for now, how about you buckle up, shut up, and watch the show."

Reluctantly, Axel turns away from the sergeant and looks straight ahead, through the pane of acrylic glass. Reeves Singh sits at a stainless-steel table across from Investigators Riley and Fletcher. There's an unopened bottle of water in front of him. He stares at it like he could telekinetically knock it over.

Riley is the first to speak. Her voice is gentle enough, yet laced with a warning not to cross. "Reeves, thank you for agreeing to come talk to us this morning. I know it's early."

Reeves doesn't look at her. His head bobs slightly.

"Listen, we won't beat around the bush, okay? We're sorry for your loss. I understand Madison Caldwell was your girlfriend."

His head bobs some more. He clears his throat as though to say something, but decides against it.

"How long did you two date?"

From where he stands approximately ten feet away, Axel watches Reeves's shoulders rise and fall. Finally, the kid pushes his dark hair out of his eyes. "Fifteen months. We started going out the summer before freshman year."

"And you're a sophomore now, is that right?"

He nods.

"How would you describe your relationship? Were you serious about each other?"

Reeves seems to freeze at this question, but for the muscles twitching in his jaw. He takes a deep breath before he speaks again, and Axel knows he's chosen his words carefully. "She was more serious than I was, I think. Madison wanted to be together forever. At least, that's what she always told me. But, I . . ." He trails off, letting the thought hang there, incomplete.

"It's okay," says Riley. "Most high school relationships don't last forever." She shares a glance with Fletcher, who hasn't spoken yet. He sits beside her, forearms extended across the surface of the table, hands folded into one big fist.

"Did you two ever . . . have disagreements about that? Or anything?"

Whether it's the question that does it, or the stark lighting, or Riley's intense gaze, Reeves wilts. His shoulders slope; his chest hollows. He slumps a little in the chair, and every last bit of golden warmth evaporates from his skin. "Sometimes." He is hesitant, as though Riley wields a bar of soap to wash out his mouth should he say the wrong thing.

"When was your last argument? Approximately?"

Now, Reeves is still. Axel watches a vein pulse in his temple. Shadows dance across the lower region of his face as he clenches his jaw shut.

"We have Madison's phone," offers Fletcher. "We can read every message exchanged between the two of you since last summer."

Reeves considers him for a moment, the whites of his eyes burning bright. His gaze flickers to Riley then, who cosigns Fletcher's statement with a nod. "Pretty recently," he admits. "A couple of days ago, I guess."

"Over texting or in person?"

When he doesn't answer, Fletcher reaches into his pants pocket and produces an iPhone with a coral-colored case. He sets it on the table, and leans toward it slightly to read in a monotone.

It's so unfair, Reeves.

Grow up.

Why are you defending her?

I'm not. I just don't know why you're acting this way.

You know she only got the part because of her stupid baby teeth.

Fletcher looks up from the phone. He and Riley both set their sights on Reeves.

"What's that about?" asks Riley.

In the viewing room, Axel's breath catches. Chloe has retained baby teeth. Her two front incisors never fell out. He noticed it bothered her as she grew older; the way she often kept her mouth closed when she smiled. Could Madison have been texting about Chloe?

When Reeves doesn't answer, Fletcher adds: "That last message was sent at 5:53 p.m. Madison was strangled to death sometime between the hours of 6 and 7 p.m. Maybe a little earlier."

"I didn't do it."

"No one's saying you did."

"But you brought me here to the police department. And you're interrogating me—"

"We asked you to assist with our investigation," Riley cuts in. "To which you agreed. You're free to leave at any time; however, we think you want Madison's killer brought to justice as much as we do. Without you, Reeves, we can't make that happen."

Good save, thinks Axel. Asking Reeves to simply "assist" with the investigation means his parents don't have to be present.

Fletcher switches tactics. "Listen, Reeves. Madison is dead. You're not doing her or anyone any favors by lying by omission here."

"I'm not lying."

"You're holding out on us." When Reeves throws a questioning glance at Riley, Fletcher adds: "Investigator Riley ain't gonna save you. She's harder than I am."

Reeves looks up at the ceiling, as though pleading for a higher power to get him out of this situation. When nothing happens, he sinks lower in the chair and crosses his arms over his chest.

"Reeves," Riley says gently. "Investigator Fletcher is right. You're not doing Madison any favors by keeping something from us. On that same token, nothing you say can hurt her, either. In fact, anything you tell us could help us find her killer. Where were you last night between the hours of 5 and 7 p.m.?"

"At soccer practice."

"Which is at the school?"

"Yes, ma'am."

"Until when?"

"I stayed after for some extra footwork and to burn off some stress." He tips his head toward the phone as though to indicate the conversation between him and Madison. "I think I hit the trail around a quarter to seven. It was just after seven when I walked into the house and my mom already had dinner on the table."

"And you were home the rest of the night?"

"Yes."

Fletcher scribbles some notes and Axel knows he's planning to interview at least the soccer coach and a few of Reeves's teammates, to corroborate his story and confirm his whereabouts. If Reeves was at practice until nearly 7 p.m., chances are slim that he had anything to do with Madison's murder. He steals a look at Kole to his right and can't help but glare. They should have been at Cutler's already, making him squirm.

"Did you see anyone on the trail while you were walking home, Reeves?" Riley asks.

"A few people. They must've been headed to the play. I thought I'd run into Madison, but . . . well . . ."

"Were you nervous about the possibility of crossing paths with her, after that text exchange?"

"A little."

Riley taps the stainless-steel surface next to the phone. "Believe it or not, this is a good thing. It means Madison was alive at 5:53 p.m. You've already helped us immensely, Reeves, by having this conversation with her. Just help us a little more, please. What did Madison mean when she said she only got the part because of her baby teeth?"

Reeves sighs, then swivels his head from one side of the room to the other, his gaze holding on the two-way mirror. If Axel didn't know better, he'd swear the boy could see him. "Madison used to say that the only reason Chloe got that part of Lydia Deetz in the *Beetlejuice* play over her was because she still had her baby teeth, so she looked young. Which is dumb because I think that character's like fifteen anyway. It was just a reason for her to pick on her."

His daughter's name is a punch in the face. Axel takes a step forward, so his fingertips press just beneath the pane of glass. He holds his breath to better listen.

"For Madison to pick on Chloe, you mean?" Riley clarifies.

Reeves nods. The ends of his hair look sweaty. "It's kinda why I wanted to break up with her. Madison got really . . . mean. After she started hanging out with Sari, it seems."

"Who is Sari?" asks Fletcher.

"Sari Simons. She transferred to our school last year and . . . I don't know."

Axel watches as Fletcher scratches the name on his notepad.

"You don't care for her?"

Reeves shrugs. "She acts like the rules don't apply to her. And to be honest, I think the only reason she really took to Madison was because Madison had money—at least her parents do—and the two of them could kinda do whatever they wanted."

"You think Sari was using Madison?" Riley asks, a brow arched.

"Maybe a little."

"Did Madison ever say anything to you about that?"

"She mentioned it offhand once or twice, but I could tell it was after she and Sari just got into a fight or something. They always made up, though. They'd have an explosive argument one morning, be clawing each other's eyes out, and that afternoon, they'd be best friends again. Lately, it seemed ganging up on Chloe was the only thing that brought them together."

Axel clenches his teeth so hard they creak. Sari Simons is lucky she isn't here. He'd wring her neck himself.

"But they were all friends, weren't they—Sari, Madison, and Chloe?" asks Riley. "In fact, I thought Madison and Chloe had been best friends since kindergarten, according to the girls' parents, anyway."

"They were," agrees Reeves. "Until the beginning of this year."

"What happened at the beginning of this year? Chloe got the part in the play?"

"Yes, ma'am. Madison didn't like that."

"And that's why she and Sari 'ganged up on her' as you put it?"

Reeves takes a deep breath. "Yeah." He pauses. "And, I think it was Sari's way of stealing Madison all to herself. She, like, worshiped the ground Madison walked on, and that made Madison think everyone else should, too."

Fletcher lifts his legal pad and slides out a couple of loose-leaf papers that Axel recognizes as the sketches from Chloe's locker. "Does this look like Sari's handiwork to you? Or, do you recognize these drawings at all?"

Reeves hesitates. His gaze lifts from the papers to consider both Fletcher and Riley. "I don't want to get my DNA on them," he says, and Axel can practically hear the gears whirring in his mind. The boy is genuinely afraid they'll frame him. Or that they will lift his prints and match them with another set. The ones on Chloe's windowsill, maybe. He narrows his eyes, the edges of his vision darkening to blot out everyone but Reeves Singh. Suspicion deepens. Fletcher is right. Reeves is holding out on them. And he's about to get a rude awakening, because soccer star or not, lying to detectives is a game he cannot win. They always uncover the truth.

"Relax, Reeves," says Fletcher, exasperation tinging his voice. "That's why we took your prints earlier. So we can rule them out of shit like this. Plus, you're on video." He jerks his thumb to the little red light that Axel knows is just above the two-way mirror. Reeves turns to look, his gaze scaling the wall, and again, Axel swears the boy can see him. Perhaps it's just that Axel wishes he could see him, see the death stare he's drilling into him. Because if he's lying to save his own hide or some-one else's, and it's keeping them from finding Chloe, his dead girlfriend will be the least of his worries.

"It's okay, Reeves," Riley assures him in a soothing voice. It's the one she employs when talking to child victims. It's also reason #899 why Riley the Reaper is so dangerous. She can make anyone feel safe, to the point where they believe that confessing to their crime was their own idea.

Slowly, Reeves pinches the pages and flips through them. He traps his bottom lip between his teeth. "No, but . . ."

Axel doesn't know whether or not Riley and Fletcher realize it, but they both lean slightly forward.

"It could be anyone, I guess. I mean . . . it was a known fact that Chloe and Mr. Cutler were . . . I don't know. A thing?" He winces as though the investigators' expressions tell him he's said entirely the wrong "thing," and hands the papers back.

If Axel were drinking coffee, he'd have sprayed it all over the glass.

"Explain," says Fletcher.

Reeves sinks even lower. His hands are underneath the table now, fingers ripping at the calluses on his palms. "Everyone knows that Chloe is Mr. Cutler's favorite. It's just one of those things. People always talked about them sleeping together and stuff." A deep rouge plumes in his cheeks.

"Did Madison talk about it?" asks Riley.

He shoots a guilty look at Madison's phone as though apologizing for diming her out, and that's all they need to know.

Without turning her head, Riley throws a glance at Axel as though to warn him to stay put and not go flying to Cutler's house. She asks Reeves: "Are you sure it was just a rumor?"

"I hoped it was, but . . ." The boy trails off. Now, he begins to pick at the label on the water bottle as though hidden underneath is a safe word that will end this interrogation.

"You said you *hoped* the notion of a relationship between Chloe and Mr. Cutler was just a rumor," says Fletcher. "What did you mean by that?"

Reeves remains fixated on the soggy label. "My parents are probably worried about me. I should get home."

"Reeves." Riley leans forward and touches his arm, even though he hasn't started to get up from the table. "Remember: you can't hurt anyone by telling us what you know or what you've heard. And anything you share with us will stay right here in this room."

A lie, Axel thinks, but it might give the kid some peace of mind.

"Is there any doubt in your mind," she presses, "that the alleged romantic relationship between Chloe Winthorp and Mr. Cutler was anything more than a rumor?"

It takes him forever to answer. He stares dumbly at the table for a moment and the scraps of the shredded label. Then, he heaves a sigh as he divulges the last little bit of everything he's been keeping close to the vest. "It's just . . . I don't know why anyone would take it so hard if it wasn't a little true. But I do know that if anyone had a reason to want Madison dead . . . it was Chloe."

FRIDAY, OCTOBER 20

6

ROWAN

The whine of the door opening rouses her from sleep. Rowan's eyes rip open. She immediately jams her knuckles into them to rub away the feeling of sand beneath her eyelids. She looks around. Amber light spills into the living room. What time is it? How long was she out?

A heavy stone of dread sits in her stomach, weighing her back down, as a broken reel of images pummel her memory—Chloe in her red lace dress, walking alone on the trail; her mascara- and tear-stained cheeks; black roses crushed on the asphalt. So, she had at least made it out of the school. Had she discarded the roses on her own, or had she dropped them during an attack?

The door softly connects with its frame. Entering through the back hall and into the kitchen are the sounds of Axel's measured footsteps. He's trying not to wake her; she can tell, but his effort is futile. Fry jumps off the couch and begins to bark and spin on the hardwood floor. She sits and stretches, reaching her arms first in front of her then toward the ceiling.

Had she heard only one set of footsteps, or—

Rowan whips around to peer over the back of the couch, every nerve in her body suddenly charged with the hope that Chloe will be beside him. She isn't though. Axel looks completely wilted. His dark jacket washes him out and purplish shadows encircle his eyes. His hair is mussed, like what happens when frustration compels him to put his head down and rake his fingers through it.

"Kole sent me home," he says, unsolicited. He sighs and it steals all the wind that's left in his sails. "Said I should try to catch a few hours of sleep."

"I'm sorry," Rowan says. "I didn't mean to fall asleep."

"I'm glad you did." Axel comes to sit next to her. She tugs her knees up toward her chest to make room for him. He sits facing forward with his forearms resting on his knees, head bowed and hands clasped, like he's waiting for a verdict.

Outside, birds sing. A woman in a red jacket walks her snowy-haired labradoodle. She doesn't live in Belgrave Circle, but Rowan sees her walk around this time every morning. It must be about 8 a.m., then. The woman stops to talk to the neighbor across the street, Ellen Hargrove. They pause for a moment, still as figures in a painting. Inevitably, the dog walker's head turns and she looks into Rowan's window.

"Any . . ." she starts, but the rest of her thought is lost. Any *what*? *Any news? Any updates? Any word on where our daughter could be?*

Axel is silent for a long while. She doesn't want to press him and yet, every second is another twist of the invisible screw in her chest.

"They interviewed Reeves Singh," he says, finally.

"Who are *they*?" Rowan asks.

"Riley and Fletcher. Kole and I watched from behind the mirror." He pauses, giving her time to visualize. "He says that if anyone had reason to want Madison Caldwell dead . . ." He swallows. His jaw goes slack for a few seconds, as though his tongue cannot simply form the words for what he has to say next. Slowly, Rowan reaches for his hand and folds her fingers over his. Axel wets his lips and drinks in a deep breath. "He said that if anyone had reason to want Madison dead, it was Chloe."

"What?" The statement is shocking, to say the least, and seemingly out of the blue. "But Madison and Chloe have been best friends since . . ." Rowan thinks back. The reel of Chloe's life speeds backward as she remembers. ". . . kindergarten."

"Have they?"

She doesn't like the way he looks at her out of the corner of his eye.

Doesn't like the way she feels challenged, under the microscope. "She was just over a few weeks ago with Sari."

A muscle in his face twitches. He's biting back something sarcastic; she knows it.

"What, Axel?" There's an edge to her voice. "You don't think . . ." She shakes her head. The action is involuntary. Her body is short-circuiting. "You're not telling me that you think our daughter killed Madison Caldwell. Or had something to do with her death?"

"I didn't say that."

Rowan narrows her gaze at him. He is too calm, which means he has already considered every corner of this scenario, probably on his way home from the police department. She, on the other hand, has not had that luxury. Pausing her emotions, she wills logic to take over. "Reeves Singh is Madison's boyfriend," she says, and suddenly recalls the marks on Madison's neck that could have been caused by either strangulation or a steamy make out session. "Of course he wants to point suspicion away from himself."

Axel nods. It feels like the first time since he walked in that they're agreeing on something. "I know," he says. She doesn't realize her hand is still on top of his until he moves his thumb back and forth to caress her palm. "But Reeves has an alibi. He was at soccer practice until almost seven o'clock yesterday, then he ate dinner with his family. Kole is corroborating his story now."

"He's interviewing the soccer coach?"

"And everyone on the team. And Reeves's parents. If it checks out . . ." He shrugs.

Rowan knows what happens if Reeves's alibi checks out. He goes free. There will be nothing to keep him in Black Harbor, nothing to stop him from running across state lines and going into hiding before police unearth any damning evidence against him. Nothing to keep him from killing again.

Axel reads her mind. "You think it was him, don't you?"

Now it's her turn to let the long seconds of silence chip away at him as she sifts through everything she knows. Belgrave Circle is safe. She knows all of her neighbors—doctors, lawyers, city council members—and yet, people do wander in. She thinks back to the woman in the red jacket who she saw walking her dog just a few moments ago. Outsiders come here all the time, accessing their quiet, strollable community via the street or the trail that cuts behind Marnie's house through Rainbow Row where Reeves Singh lives, all the way to Monroe Academy.

"You don't?" She answers Axel's question with another question. "Don't tell me you're on Reeves Singh's side." A dark, staccato laugh escapes her, and she watches as his jaw goes slack again.

"We have Madison's phone," he says.

"Okay, and let me guess. Chloe was sending her death threats?"

"She was teasing her, Rowan."

Rowan raises a brow. "Chloe was teasing Madison?" Chloe wasn't always a spoonful of honey, but Rowan had never known her to be outright mean to anyone.

"No. Madison was teasing Chloe. About her baby teeth. Saying that's the only reason she got the part in the play, or whatever. Apparently, they'd been competing for it."

She's quiet for a moment. She knows why he's bringing up the baby teeth, of course. Last night, Madison's teeth were busted out of her skull and scattered in the gully. Still, she says: "Well, it sounds like Chloe's the victim, here. Madison was bullying her."

"Row." He squeezes her shoulders.

She used to love when he looked at her like this, staring into her eyes so intensely like he was trying to read her mind. They used to make a game of it. *What am I thinking about?* Rowan would ask, fighting back a smile.

You're thinking that you want . . . ice cream for breakfast? Matching tattoos? That you want me to take you upstairs and—

But this isn't a game. Their daughter is missing, her best friend is dead, and allegedly there had been some bad blood between the two of them.

"Remember the last time someone jacked her up about her teeth?"

"Oh, come on, Axel. You are not serious." Of course Rowan remembers. How could she forget the day the principal called her to report Chloe had dumped her mashed potatoes on Colton Nichols's head during lunch? They'd punished Chloe by taking away her TV privileges for the night and giving her a stern talking-to, but what else was there to be done? The boy had been in the wrong. He'd started it, after all, and hadn't his actions been more damaging than Chloe's? Sticks and stones and all that . . .

He says nothing, and she knows he's waiting for it to sink in, the realization that the teeth are a connection, not a coincidence.

"It doesn't mean anything," she says, finally.

"Not definitively, no," Axel agrees. "But Row, we can't disregard the fact that Madison was harassing Chloe maybe only moments before . . ." His voice trails off.

A chill seeps into Rowan's blood. Chloe left around 5:45 p.m. last night. Had it been exactly that time? No, she doesn't remember. But she saw her turn right out the front door and head toward the trail. She would have been at the school around 6 p.m. Surely the school's cameras will show that. She is about to tell Axel as much, when he says, "There's more."

Rowan frowns. "What do you mean?"

He exhales heavily, and she knows that whatever he is about to say, he's been holding back since the second he walked in the door. "Do you know Chloe's drama teacher, Mr. Cutler?"

She nods. "Of course."

"*How well* do you know him?"

Rowan frowns. "I don't know. How well do we know any of her teachers, Axel? It's not like we barbecue with them on weekends."

"I know. It's just—"

Fucking say it already, she wants to scream. *What* about *Mr. Cutler?* Nevertheless, she bites her tongue.

He shifts to take his phone out of his back pocket. She watches as he maneuvers to his camera roll and views the recent photos. "We found these in her locker."

Rowan pinches the screen to zoom in. The sketches are crudely drawn, depicting what are hardly more than stick figures, but the acts they are engaged in are undeniable. She observes Mr. Cutler's signature sports coat and Chloe's safety pin earrings in one, not to mention the figures are labeled *Chloe the Hoe-y* and *Mr. Cuddler.*

Before she can dismiss it as kids being cruel, Axel adds: "According to Reeves, there were rumors floating around the school regarding a sexual relationship between Chloe and Mr. Cutler. Rumors that Madison may have initiated." There's a distance in his voice, now; she can hear him compartmentalizing, separating himself from the subjects in this story. He could be talking about anyone's daughter.

It pisses her off. Rowan's breath is ragged. "You're not saying . . ." Yes, he is. He's insinuating that Chloe killed Madison Caldwell, all because she'd perpetuated a rumor. "There's no way. Madison was bigger than Chloe," she says, picturing her petite daughter. "She couldn't have taken her down like that."

She recalls the scene. Madison Caldwell suffered no bullet holes or knife wounds, no perimortem injuries but for the chafe marks on her neck. A toxicology report will reveal whether or not there were drugs in her system, but as it stands to reason at this moment, the person who killed her probably did it with their bare hands.

"Not alone," he says as suddenly, a notification appears at the top of his phone screen. Rowan squints as Axel takes the device from her. "Fuck." The word is a sharp whisper.

"What?" Rowan edges closer.

"Kole just interviewed one of Reeves's teammates who crossed paths with Chloe on the walking path, sometime around six last night."

"And?" Rowan frowns. "What was she doing?"

Axel looks afraid to meet her eyes. When he does, she sees how all the shards of blue in his irises break apart to reflect their shattered life. "She was running."

7

ROWAN

Swirls of multicolored soaps make a psychedelic pattern on her windshield. Pink bleeds into blue and is muddied by a squirt of yellow. Axel was passed out on the bed when she left, still wearing his clothes from last night. She needed to get out of the house and the ringing silence trapped within. So she came here, to the car wash. It's where she always goes whenever she feels the weight of the world pressing down on her.

It's also the only place she can escape the feeling that she is being watched. For years, she's been distracted by the odd prickling sensation on the back of her neck, an unexplained moment where her arm hair stands on end and she catches a glimpse of something fleeting in her peripheral vision. It's just Black Harbor, she reminds herself. The city has a way of inhabiting you versus the other way around.

The sound of rushing water is calming. If she closes her eyes, she can almost convince herself she is somewhere else, living in a reality where her daughter is not gone.

Perhaps even living in a reality where she never had a daughter.

It's an unforgivable thought for a mother to have, and yet, she cannot stop it from tumbling through the impossible maze that has become her mind. But is it worse than considering her own child capable—even culpable—of murder? That's where Axel's wrong.

Chloe is anything but perfect, but she isn't a killer. She can't be. And yet, the apple never falls far from the tree.

Rowan snaps her eyes open as her vehicle jolts forward on the mechanical track. She reaches toward the glove compartment and pops it ajar. The laminated carton peeks at her amid proof of insurance and fast-food napkins. She snags it and dips her fingers inside. A cold dread hits her when only one cigarette falls into her hand.

She remembers the days of chain-smoking a pack in one sixteen-hour shift just to stay awake, back when she did her residency at Divine Savior Children's Hospital more than twenty years ago. But when she migrated from her small town of Saltsburg, Pennsylvania, to Black Harbor, Wisconsin, she made herself a double-edged promise: she will smoke only one cigarette a year. When the pack is gone, she's gone.

Axel has known about her plan to pack up and leave this coal-dusted, crime-ridden city ever since they first got together. They used to lie awake at night and fantasize about leaving the way most couples dream about traveling somewhere exotic. She fears his sincerity eroded with each year that drifted by, however. He'd been a cop for seven years when they met. He was mobile, still, not vested with the city. They could have gone anywhere. But then, just over two years later they had Chloe—and Black Harbor offered them each a steady job, a retirement plan, and all the overtime they could want. Now, Axel has twenty-five years on, and at forty-six years old, she cannot ask him to start over.

She did once. She didn't get far.

She wishes now that she had pushed harder. That she had shared with him her fears about staying here, about being found out. He knows her history but he does not know the extent of her worry, of the persistent paranoia that gnaws at her nerves every waking moment of every day.

They can never leave now—not when Chloe is still here, dead or alive.

Chloe's last words cut through the noise of the car wash. Tears fill Rowan's eyes. Is it true? Does she love her daughter more now that she has become a mystery, her whereabouts a puzzle to figure out?

Regardless of how she would answer that, she has unearthed the truth to something else, and that is the fact that she would rather have her daughter be dead than behind this murder.

Axel seems to be the opposite. Although, he isn't opposed to entertaining the idea Chloe could be involved with a teacher. Rage warms her blood. There is no way. It's a rumor . . . nothing more.

He texted her from upstairs after he'd gone to bed. The Identification Department submitted results for the prints discovered in Chloe's bedroom. The only prints on the window belonged to her and Rowan. She didn't text anything back to him. She knows what it means: that Chloe may have left on her own.

Madison's autopsy is scheduled for 10 a.m. tomorrow. Rowan recalls the curious marks on the girl's neck. They could not have been the work of Reeves Singh's lips, as his alibi has been confirmed. He was at soccer practice at the time of the attack. He never wandered into Belgrave Circle, according to his teammates and his mother who saw him at the dinner table that evening.

Still, it stands to reason that Reeves may not have been the only one making out with Madison. Teenagers cheat on each other all the time. Who is to say the Caldwell girl had not engaged in some clandestine meeting down in the gully that turned ugly?

No one. Yet. The autopsy results might prove otherwise. Until then, Rowan plans to continue on that path of suspicion. Because if Madison had been cheating on Reeves, perhaps Chloe had witnessed it and threatened to tell. She was never one to stand by and do nothing while another person is being wronged.

She inherited Axel's empathy.

Rowan's vehicle crawls along the track but her mind whirs a million miles a minute. A hypothesis like that would also explain why someone came for Chloe—to silence her.

The bear claw releases her tire. Rowan and her vehicle are spit out. She rolls forward and doesn't tap the brakes until she is inches from sliding into traffic. Stopped on a slant, she closes her eyes again as a rattling exhalation escapes her lips. When she opens her eyes again, it is only to look down at the corner of the newsprint all but hidden inside the cigarette carton. Gently, she slides it out. The paper is as thin as a butterfly's wing; the smudged words remind her of Chloe's eye makeup. Next to them, a black-and-white image of a girl makes her throat go dry. She feels her mouth twist, bowing into a frown, her chin quivering. Knowing is a knife slowly turning in her chest. After all this time, the universe has come to collect.

8

LIBBY

Twin shocks of white run parallel until they converge at the base of the animal's skull. Libby runs a gloved finger over the ends of the pearlish hairs as though tempting a flame. The skunk's hide is flattened and stuck to a board with minutien pins to keep the limbs from curling up. The only tools she needs are set to the side: a scalpel, a pair of bone-cutting shears, and an evisceration spoon—great for removing eyes and soft tissue.

She's pleased with her progress so far. When she found the animal on the side of the road its fur was bloody and matted. Now that she's brushed it, it looks as though it could have been someone's pet.

Taxidermy class is held in the woodshop room, with large square tables and concrete floors. It's taught by Black Harbor's lone taxidermist, Mr. Deschane, who teaches at Monroe as an adjunct. Rumor has it that he works here for the extra money so he can pay prostitutes. More than once, she has wondered what degree of truth there is to that. If there's one thing she's actually learned at school, it's that rumors are like fingerprints: everyone has their own special set, and like it or not, they are part of our identity. Libby's gaze drifts from her work to Deschane sitting behind the actual shop teacher's desk. He drags his forearm under his nose as though to catch a drip. When he turns her way, she diverts her attention to Gabe Krause, her table partner who works with his face half-buried in his T-shirt. Others do the same or similar with neck gaiters pulled up to their eyeballs. The smell is still so thick she can taste it, a medley of piss and vinegar.

Yesterday, she punctured her skunk's scent gland—because the universe felt her peers could use another reason to ridicule her. Mr. Deschane set out bowls of vinegar in an attempt to knock out the potent ammoniacal reek, but it seems to have just added another layer of complexity to the stench which, if it were a candle, Libby imagines would have a name like *Roadkill Rendezvous* or *Scent Gland Soirée*.

Across from her, Gabe taxidermies his family's late house cat. The pink collar with a jingle bell rests on the table, waiting to be fastened around the animal's neck once he's stuffed the hide with cotton and sewn it all up.

Libby looks around, noting the progress of the other students. They're in the middle of a small mammals unit. Zachary Davis's squirrel looks like it went through the lawnmower, limbs broken and pointing every which way. Kayden Thompson is sewing two rabbit heads together on one body; it actually looks quite good, Libby thinks, if you're into macabre art. She could see the finished piece in a gallery or in an exhibit where they keep things in jars and insects pinned to foam core.

In a class of twelve, Libby is—shocker—the only girl. Which is fine by her. While still merciless, boys are less cruel and quick to wit than the girls. The boys entertain themselves with Neanderthalian imitations and call her Neck Roll; they tease her for reading graphic novels about Vikings and Valkyries. But girls are far more cunning. Their insults are like termites that burrow under her skin and into her brain, turning her against herself.

Cedar dust peppers the surfaces of the tables and sticks to everything—her hands, her hair, her clothes. Thankfully, this is her penultimate class of the day. She only has to stink for forty-two minutes of world history, then she can air out on the walking trail. No. She has to take the road home, on the other side of the school, she remembers. The trail is still taped off and off-limits until investigators have what they need—including intel from students.

Classes are in session, which means almost everyone the police need to talk to is corralled in one place. They can just go from classroom to classroom and pluck people at will. Her heart skips at the thought of being summoned for an interview, and she can't shake the feeling of being a cow trapped in a holding pen, waiting to be slaughtered.

Ask me what I know, she dares. *Ask me what I saw.*

"Hey, Neck Roll, fork over some cotton, would ya?" Gabe holds his arm out expectantly across the table.

The nickname hardly fazes her anymore and yet, her proud smile at her handiwork vanishes as quickly as it had come. Like following an evolutionary chart, Libby can trace its transmogrification, not that its origin is all that wholesome to begin with. Last year, when she brought a dead squirrel to Deschane's taxidermy class, her peers started calling her Necro, short for necrophilia. Eventually, they realized they could kill two birds with one stone, and jeer at her weight as well. So, Neck Roll she is.

She tells herself she doesn't care, and yet more often than she's comfortable admitting, she has caught her reflection in the mirror and brought her hands up to her neck, palpating and attempting to smooth the skin.

Kids are cruel. And creative.

It's probably why she's so drawn to dead things. Unlike the living, the dead don't poke fun at her. Or judge her. Or tell her where she needs to go to school and what she needs to do with her life. With graduation encroaching, her parents have become obsessed with HGTV and living vicariously through couples on the hunt for their "affordable" beach home on some destination island: Aruba, Hawai'i, St. Thomas. As soon as they can both retire and her ailing grandparents have passed, Libby knows they will move in a heartbeat.

But they're waiting for her to chart the course. They want her to follow in either of her older brothers' footsteps: graduate at the top of her class, then go off to Harvard and become a lawyer like Sterling or a neurosurgeon like Jackson after eight years at Johns Hopkins and another five in residency. They will come along, telling all their friends they're supporting their daughter, when really, she's just the vehicle for them to live out their dream of leaving Black Harbor behind forever.

She shoves the bag toward Gabe. Suddenly there's the sound of heels clicking on the shop floor and Libby isn't the only female in the room anymore. The woman is beautiful, Black, and her silver badge clipped to her belt denotes she is with the BHPD Investigations Bureau. Her name is Investigator Amanda Riley, she tells Mr. Deschane, and, "Is Libby Lucas available?"

Using the process of elimination, Investigator Riley makes eye contact with Libby, locks in. Libby slumps in her chair, willing herself to become invisible. Her heart pounds and her throat goes dry. She coughs and chalks it up to the cedar dust. Her arms cross over her torso, wrapping her up like she's a danger in a straitjacket, and she feels her hands fill with soft, fleshy rolls. Her size makes hiding a challenge. She is pinned to her stool as surely as her skunk is pinned to its board.

She knew her turn was coming.

"Libby." Mr. Deschane's gruff voice severs the awkward silence.

Libby snaps to.

Mr. Deschane raises a brow, then gives her a half smile that he probably means to be reassuring. As if she's scared.

Or rather, as if she should have a reason to be scared.

"Should I—" She gestures to her deflated skunk.

"I'll take care of it," he offers. "Just go."

Libby grabs her tablet and her history book, a ten-pound slab of dictionary-thin paper that could stop a bullet.

"Smell ya later!" Gabe calls after her. A chorus of laughter follows her exit.

"You know, I remember high school boys having BO," says Investigator Riley, "but I don't remember it being *that* bad when I was in school."

Libby almost cracks a smile. "It's me," she admits. When Riley gives her a puzzled look, she adds: "I punctured my skunk's scent gland the other day."

"The other day?" Riley reels back in surprise. "And it's still that . . . pungent?"

Libby nods.

They pass the turnoff for the English hallway. It's a straight shot through the cafeteria, which is coming up on their right. There are only two places they could be going: the auditorium or the music room. She hears the cacophony of horns, denoting that band class is obviously in session, and knows they're going to the auditorium.

"So taxidermy class, huh?" Investigator Riley is making small talk. Libby has watched enough crime shows to know this is what they refer to in the business as "building rapport."

She plays along. "It's an elective."

Riley grimaces, revealing a glimpse of teeth that are bright white. "And you don't mind . . . touching dead things?"

"I love dead things," Libby says faster than her filter. She wishes she could stuff the words back in like stuffing cotton into a hide. "I mean . . . taxidermy . . . it's fascinating."

"Why?"

She pauses to think before she speaks this time. "Because it's a little like magic, I guess. You get to take something that's dead and bloody and make it look alive again."

Investigator Riley looks skeptical, but seems to approve. "All right, maybe you could show me a thing or two sometime. Lord knows I could use a little magic now and again."

Halfway down the hall now, Investigator Riley pulls open a door that's flush against the eggshell wall, almost invisible. The door swings outward, inviting them into a mouth of darkness. A short staircase leads them backstage, where a strong overhead light washes out everything beneath it, including the man seated on the worn velvet couch.

Axel Winthorp stands to greet her. Despite his signature widow's peak and strong, square jaw, Libby almost doesn't recognize the man who lives just twenty feet from her. It's weird seeing him in professional clothes, a silver badge clipped to his belt. He looks official and authoritative—a stern older brother, perhaps, to the affable neighbor she has known practically her whole life.

Sympathy settles in the pit of her stomach, raises the hair on her arms as she shakes his hand as though they are strangers meeting for the first time. Here is a man who's come over for barbecues and birthday parties, shoveled their driveway while they were out of town, and even driven her to school on more than one occasion when it was raining buckets—his words. She'd sat in the back of his truck, then, beside Chloe on the bench seat, their knees softly knocking together with every bump in the road. She remembers the way she felt on those rare occasions: like a normal high school girl catching a ride with her friend.

If she and Chloe had ever been friends, that is.

"It's good to see you, Libby. Not under the circumstances, of course. Please." The furniture is arranged in a makeshift living room— two armchairs, a couch, and a coffee table upon which Libby sets her things. Axel gestures for her to take the olive-green armchair opposite Investigator Riley.

She does, her eyes never leaving him. *This is it,* a niggling voice whispers in her brain. *He's going to tell you they found your fingerprints on Chloe's bedroom window. You're fudged.*

Axel lowers himself back down to the couch, leans forward with his hands lightly clasped in front of his knees. She watches his nostrils flare. He wrinkles his nose. "You're not smoking weed, I hope."

"Skunk," Riley explains for her. "She punctured its scent gland in taxidermy class."

"Ah." Axel gives a knowing nod in a *say no more* manner. "I once skewered my squirrel's stomach. That was a mess."

"You took taxidermy, too?" Investigator Riley looks like she might throw up.

Axel shrugs. "Of course. It's an elective."

Libby feels a lightness swim through her. Calming her blood, easing her bones. She can do this. She has talked to Axel a million times before. Well, maybe not a million. But maybe close to a hundred in her lifetime. So, why should today be any different?

"That old guy still teaching it? Debush or Deschane . . . ?"

"His son," says Libby. "Dale."

"I think they're all named Dale."

"You people up here. Bunch of hillbillies." Riley rolls her eyes.

"Up here," Axel repeats, then talks out of the side of his mouth to Libby. "You'll have to excuse her lack of culture. Investigator Riley is from *Chicago.*"

Libby smiles because she knows he is being ironic, although at the same time, she knows this is a tactic. He is likening her to him, the two people in the room born and raised in Black Harbor. So Axel is playing Good Cop today.

Bad Cop is all bark and no bite. She simply provides a foil for Good Cop, so Libby will naturally be endeared to Axel and want to answer his questions. She also knows that Good Cop is the one you need to watch out for. Not because he bites, but because he has a nose that can smell a lie a mile away. She watches him closely, her gaze trained on his mouth, watching as his lips open and stretch to form words, like a paper fortune teller. She feels her own mouth moving, as though this is a waltz. He's leading.

"Thanks for meeting with us today, Libby," starts Axel. "We were hoping we could ask you a few questions about Madison Caldwell."

She almost exhales with relief—he didn't mention the windowsill!—until she remembers the things she saw and did that night, the impulse that took over her. "Okay." It takes everything in her to stop those two syllables from rattling.

"As you, no doubt, have heard, Madison Caldwell was killed in the area of Belgrave Circle last night between the hours of 6 and 7 p.m."

Libby nods to show she's following along.

"Had you seen her at all yesterday?"

"Um . . . just in Spanish. And I think at lunch." With an annual enrollment of approximately four hundred students, Monroe Academy was not a terribly large school. Still, besides sharing one class period together, she and Madison rarely crossed paths. They didn't run with the same crowd. Madison chummed with Reeves, Sari, and until recently Chloe; Libby chummed with no one. Not at school, anyway.

"When's Spanish?" asks Axel.

"Third period. Between 10:15 and 11?"

"Did you notice anything off about her, perhaps? Was she quiet or sad or anything?"

"Umm . . ." Should she tell them she's cultivated a habit of never really looking directly at her peers? All anyone needs is the tiniest reason to make fun of her, and meeting someone's eye is reason enough for them to jeer and slip into some brutish imitation of her. Especially Madison. Convinced that Madison would read her face like a book, she avoided that girl's gaze like she was Medusa. Because if she didn't, Madison would discover her secret, and she couldn't do that to Chloe.

She promised she'd never tell.

"No." Libby shrugs. "She seemed normal, I guess."

"Describe *normal*," prompts Investigator Riley.

Libby explains that Madison was socializing before class started, and when the bell rang, she leisurely strolled to her seat in the right-hand corner of the room. She was as attentive as she usually is, which wasn't very, and occupied her time sketching in her notebook. "I didn't see what she was drawing," she adds, when she notes a shared look between Axel and Investigator Riley.

"It seems like Madison was a pretty popular girl," says Axel, to which Libby agrees. Then, he asks, "Did she have any enemies?"

The question reminds her of the time Jack Zellner lobbed a walnut at her head. She had seen it coming almost in slow motion, and yet, she couldn't get her shit together to dodge it before it clocked her in the temple. She wobbled on one foot for a few seconds, flailing her arms but catching only air, and fell hard on her butt. Instead of helping her up, several kids walked by, squealing and pointing at a crack in the sidewalk they swore hadn't been there before.

Axel's query knocks her off-kilter. Not quite as hard as the walnut, but off-kilter all the same. She doesn't flail this time; instead, she locks eyes with him and muses at the storm of reluctance that brews behind his irises. He knows the answer, but he doesn't want to hear it, she realizes.

It's the same storm she noticed in Chloe's eyes Thursday night. The musical had just ended and Chloe was taking pictures with her cast-mates. Still wearing her red lace dress and clutching a bouquet of black roses, she dared a look in Libby's direction and Libby knew, without even having to verify, that Rowan and Axel had left.

She made a fist and rubbed it in a circular motion across her chest. *I'm sorry.* A dimple dented Chloe's cheek as she offered the slightest smile in return.

That was the last time Libby ever laid eyes on Chloe Winthorp.

"You're quiet, Libby," states Axel. "What are you thinking about?" His voice is softer now. Encouraging but not pushing. He's good at playing Good Cop. "Was there anyone who didn't like Madison Caldwell? Who might have wanted to hurt her?" He leans forward so that his forearms rest atop his thighs. His knuckles are chapped. She homes in on them; they're striated with thin cracked little rivers of red that remind her of the gully where Madison Caldwell's body was found, all these little avenues cut into the silt, converging toward the lake.

She swallows and holds her mouth half-open for a moment. Breathes. Bites her lip. "No one *really* liked Madison Caldwell."

The detectives both sit up a little straighter as though this statement has breathed some new life into them. "What about her friends?" asks Investigator Riley. "Sari Simons or Chloe Winthorp? Or her boyfriend, Reeves Singh?"

Funnily enough—well, not funny—is that the three people she just mentioned are all people who are not at school today. Sari was no surprise. Her best friend was murdered last night. She probably spent the day sobbing under her covers and scrolling through memories on her phone. As for Reeves, Libby had left for school by the time police brought him home—if they ever did, that is—and Chloe remains a mystery.

"Libby?" Investigator Riley's voice prods. "You said no one liked Madison, but she had friends, didn't she?"

Libby shrugs. Her face feels as though she's just face-planted into a sizzling frying pan. She promised she wouldn't tell, and yet, her heart is pounding in her throat like it was Thursday night when she—

"You know, like, Regina George from *Mean Girls*?" The question is a projectile word vomit. She should stop talking, but there seems to be a short circuit between her brain and her body, like when she got clocked with the walnut.

When Investigator Riley and Axel both nod, she adds: "She was kinda like that. People just pretended to like her. Now that she's dead, everyone will act like she was their best friend when really, secretly . . . they're glad she's dead."

"Are you glad she's dead, Libby?"

The bell rings to announce the end of seventh period. Libby drags her backpack across the floor and picks it up.

"Stay," commands Investigator Riley.

"You're fine," says Axel. "Not feeling one hundred percent sadness over someone's death is okay, by the way. Especially if that person had been tormenting you. I'm sure it can even feel a bit like a relief." He pauses for a beat, and then: "Had Madison been causing problems for you or someone you know? Maybe not just for students, but maybe a teacher?"

Libby stares past his shoulder as she shakes her head. She has already said too much. She promised she wouldn't tell. And Libby keeps her promises.

Axel leans forward again. He's close enough she can smell his cologne, see the beads of sweat glistening at his hairline. Her stomach churns. "We have reason to believe that the same person who killed Madison Caldwell also took Chloe. If you have any idea who that person is, you have an obligation to tell us."

Libby looks from one investigator to the other. Then, she feels her lips stretch and the air hit her teeth, and the skin by her eyes crinkles as she closes her fist over her locket and reminds herself that some things should be kept inside.

9

AXEL

On paper, Cutler is clean. He has no record with the Black Harbor Police Department or neighboring jurisdictions, as far as Axel can tell. But absence of evidence is not evidence of absence—the golden rule of investigations, though Kole would challenge him on that.

Everybody lies. His sergeant's voice echoes in his head. Axel has always hated that grim perspective, but after nearly a day of neither hide nor hair of Chloe, he's beginning to adopt it himself. Teenage girls don't just disappear into thin air. Someone has to be lying.

It might even be Kole. He was supposed to interview all the teachers today while Axel and Riley teamed up to take on the students. But Cutler, conveniently, wasn't there when Kole made the rounds.

Kole is protecting Cutler and Axel doesn't know why.

But he's going to find out.

He unlocks his phone and scrolls through the camera roll. The crude drawings discovered at the bottom of Chloe's locker glare at him, daring him to pick them apart. Earlier today during her interview, Libby Lucas mentioned that Madison Caldwell had been sketching during Spanish class. He needs to compare notes with Kole. Perhaps the Spanish teacher saw what Madison had been working on.

It's a shot in the dark, but then, that's all he has right now. If the rumor was as widespread as it seems to have been, any number of students could have harassed Chloe with these drawings, whether tormenting her in class with them or stuffing them into her locker. Swiping back and forth through them, he observes that they don't appear to be the work of just one hand.

Scarlet leaves cling to his windshield wipers. He listens to the whispers they etch in the glass, whispers that condemn him for the things he should have known.

Chloe was involved with an older man. A man older than him, even. Mark Cutler is fifty-one. He has a wife and an adult daughter, and a grandson from what Axel dug up online. He found articles of Cutler winning Monroe Academy's Teacher of the Year award, a photo of him at a parade holding the hand of a little boy in a blue jacket. The caption beneath read: *Local teacher, Mark Cutler, attends Black Harbor's Winter Festival Parade with grandson.*

He has no social media as far as Axel can find, which means he cannot follow or befriend Cutler with the VCTF's burner account. It doesn't raise a red flag. Axel knows that teachers generally do well to avoid opening a portal between their personal and professional lives. Most cops—at least his generation—don't have social media for that reason. The same cannot be said of the general public. So many confrontations could be circumvented if people just kept their personal lives off the internet. Instead, they act as if having social media is a God-given right.

Someone back at the police department will be combing through the girls' computers now, scrolling through their online accounts, saved pictures, and hidden files. He wonders what they will find. Hate-fueled messages from Chloe to Madison? An online diary?

He can't help but think about what Reeves Singh said this morning: . . . *if anyone had a reason to want Madison dead . . . it was Chloe.* But then, what had Libby said? That no one really liked Madison Caldwell. His Spidey senses tell him there is more to that story. He will catch Libby at home today, hopefully, while she's alone, taking the garbage out or checking the mail, and engage her in a casual, neighborly chat.

Suddenly, a message from Rowan floats on his phone screen.

> Where are you?

At work, he replies, which is true. His work can be anywhere, even here outside Mark Cutler's residence. His house is on a dead-end road, tucked away at the edge of the woods, on the other side of which Axel knows is Monroe Academy. The windows are dark and opaque, reflecting black mirrored evergreens and birds that float against a stark sky. He checks the time. It's 3:18 p.m. Cutler should be home soon. He'll watch him pull into the drive, then he'll get out and run circles around him before he even has a chance to get his bearings.

He wonders if Rowan is home or if she's gone to Marnie's. She could also be at the car wash. It's where she goes when she's anxious, says it's the only way to quiet her thoughts. He is thankful for that; there are worse ways to self-medicate. And they're all too accessible in Black Harbor.

Everyone has their remedies. Jiujitsu is his. He spars at Silva's Academy downtown two to three times per week, crime permitting. Riley got him into it. She's been going since she got hired at the PD. It gives her an edge on guys who think lady cops are just playing dress-up. For Axel, it's about the release, an opportunity to shed his skin as a homicide detective and slip into a gi, in a place where no one cares who or what the hell he is. Until the death phone rings, that is.

Axel drinks coffee out of his thermos and focuses intently on the hunter-green house across the street. It's a tri-level, given away by the staggered stories and two-car garage underneath what might be a living room or a dining room. A backdrop of evergreens looms behind it. Could Chloe be in there, her body lying in a shallow grave not twenty feet from Cutler's backyard?

No. He shakes the image from his head.

Chloe is alive. And she's not a killer.

She used to talk about him a lot—Mr. Cutler. It's when she stopped talking about him, he realizes, that he should have grown concerned.

It's as though she'd picked up on his fatherly disapproval, his dislike of her having a friendship with an adult male, teacher or not. He never outright told her he didn't like it, but Chloe was sensitive. She picked up on a lot of things.

Axel rolls down his window to listen. For what, he doesn't exactly know. He twists the volume dial on his stereo all the way counterclockwise. The cool air wicks the warmth from his skin. He sucks in a breath through his teeth and it pricks at his gums.

He holds it for a beat, listening.

And listening.

Then he hears it: a warble coming from Cutler's backyard. Axel leans into the open window, his ear open to the night. The warbling continues in a series, then a cackle pierces the quiet.

Laughter? Who is outside laughing? He imagines Cutler's wife, bundled up in a flannel jacket, clutching a cup of coffee and talking on the phone. It's possible. His own mother used to talk on the phone at all hours of the day, sitting on the front stoop and stubbing out cigarettes while she gossiped with her best friend. It was her way of filling the silence after his dad died.

The cackle is quieter this time. It isn't Chloe, and yet, he has half a mind to walk around back and see who it is. Maybe they'd have a scrap of information to share about his daughter.

So far, nothing has come of the Amber Alert. Someone called in to report a dark-haired female matching Chloe's stature, but when patrol responded, they determined the subject to be a thirty-three-year-old sex worker. The walking trail has yielded no more clues. Police have combed every square inch of it stretching from Monroe Academy to Belgrave Circle and beyond—but it's the most trafficked strip of asphalt in Black Harbor. Monday through Friday, hundreds of footsteps travel back and forth to the school, and kids have a habit of dropping things: soda bottles, empty vape cartridges, key chains, scrunchies, student ID cards, you name it. A patrol officer discovered an earring with a speck of blood on it, which seemed morbidly promising, but neither Axel nor Rowan could identify it as belonging to Chloe, and besides, it was gold with a jade stone; she'd been into punching silver safety pins in her earlobes before she disappeared.

The cackling stops. All is quiet again.

He exhales and turns on the radio. The banter of the radio show fills the interior of his car.

". . . *disgusting! I can't choose!*"

"*Elle, you have to! Come on, hair for teeth or teeth for hair.*"

"*Ugh, fine! Teeth for hair, obviously.*"

"*That's the right answer. See, it wasn't that hard.*"

"*Do I use the same toothbrush for both?*"

Talk of teeth sends Axel back to the gully where Madison Caldwell's body was discovered with hers knocked out. He wonders if Chloe could have suffered the same fate.

No. Chloe is alive.

But perhaps she wasn't meant to be. It's possible she was meant to be killed that night, too, which is why they are looking for connections between the two girls, shared experiences they might have had where they met someone they shouldn't have. Someone who wanted to do them harm.

The school is an obvious connector.

And the neighborhood.

Both girls attended Monroe Academy. Both girls lived in Belgrave Circle. One girl is dead. The other is missing.

He considers the possibility that Chloe escaped her would-be murderer and is on the run. She could be hiding somewhere, anywhere. *It's safe now,* he wants to broadcast to her. *You can come home now, Chloe. Please come home.*

But is it ever truly safe? If the world itself is a dangerous place, Black Harbor is its core, a stagnant cesspool where bad people come in and never leave. And why would they? Rent is free or cheap and there aren't enough cops to take them all. Paddy wagons see more action than public transportation around here.

Another message from Rowan appears. What should we do for dinner tonight?

Madison Caldwell's autopsy is tomorrow morning, he remembers. His heart rate spikes, suddenly, at the notion of discovering a new lead.

Chins, he texts. I'll pick it up.

It might be a lie, because if Cutler comes home, Axel is acutely aware of the possibility that he might not. No one hurts his little girl.

No one.

10

LIBBY

Dinner was grilled brussels sprouts and chicken piccata. Libby made an effort to eat most of the little charred cabbages with the hope that her mother wouldn't say anything about the capers she strategically scattered to make it appear as though there were less on her plate than when it had been set in front of her. It's the texture, mostly. Soft and fleshy; biting into them feels like eyeballs exploding between her teeth. The salty aftertaste doesn't help.

She did the dishes while her parents made espresso like they do every night. They drank it out of ceramic Wonderland-sized cups. Her dad looked especially ridiculous sipping from his, Libby thought, like he was playing tea party with a child.

She never played tea party—not even when she was small. Rather, she was always outside catching bugs to study them, observing how they moved and whether or not they made a noise when she plucked their legs off.

They never did. At least, she never heard anything. It begs the old adage: if there's a scream and no one hears it . . . did it even happen?

Madison Caldwell screamed the other night, but it seems Libby was the only person in the world who heard it. Perhaps everyone in the neighborhood assumed the noise was a rabbit being preyed on by an owl.

Upstairs in her room, now, she watches Reeves Singh in his backyard.

He's hardly more than a silhouette, backlit by the fluorescent light shining from the porch. A sound like a firecracker exploding makes her snap to attention as he skips forward and launches a soccer ball into a net.

There are nine more balls all lined up like a firing squad. With expert footwork, he goes down the line and kicks one after another.

Crack! Whoosh!

Crack! Whoosh!

The net makes a sibilant sound, a surreptitious hush demanding she remain a silent observer. Libby can do that—creep on the neighbor boy who may or may not have killed the girl next door.

The court of public opinion has already convicted him. The allegations are everywhere. You can't turn on your phone or the TV without being hit with a denunciatory headline.

Killing for Sport: High School Soccer Star Slays Girlfriend

Murder at Monroe Academy: One Student Dead, One Suspect, One Missing

Lovers' Quarrel Turned Deadly? Inside the Murder of Madison Caldwell

He will never unbury himself from this. Even if he is proven innocent, these accusations will follow him like a shadow quenching his golden light. And while she feels bad for Reeves—really, she does—she cannot help the swift, infinitesimal smirk that twists her mouth. It's so slight it would be imperceptible to anyone not watching her closely, studying the way her features morph in sync with the thoughts zipping back and forth behind her eyes. Thoughts in the vein of: *Oh, how the mighty have fallen . . .*

It isn't fair for her to think like that, though, she realizes as suddenly, something like nostalgia hits her, and she remembers when they used to walk to school together now and again, not saying much or anything at all. Libby blames herself for that. The first time their paths had converged—her freshman year—Reeves had smiled and said, "So, come here often?"

The joke tickled her just right, not to mention it was so unexpected that Libby laughed, spewing a mess of half-chewed apple. Mortified, she quickened her pace and sped ahead, and never spoke to him again. Which was just as well, because then Madison Caldwell started walking with him and if Libby ever saw that their paths were about to converge, she would stop and tie her shoe so they could walk ahead of her. She didn't need her day starting off with letting her classmates count her back rolls.

Crack! Whoosh!

The final ball careens into the goal. Just as it does, Reeves looks up toward her window. She ducks as though he's just aimed an air rifle at her, and falls off her bench seat. Her body crashing to the floor causes a thunder her parents would have to be deaf not to hear.

On cue, her mother calls: "Libby! Everything okay?"

Crawling on hands and knees, Libby makes her way to her bedroom door and cracks it open to shout down the stairwell. "I'm fine! Just . . . lost my footing when changing into my pajamas!"

"Okay, dear! Love you!"

"Love you, too!"

Her mom is kind of an I-love-you whore. She says it all the time— unsolicited, unexpected, and unconditionally—as long as Libby acts accordingly and goes off to college to become a doctor or a rocket scientist like a proper young lady.

No more taxidermy.

Right . . .

It seems a year has passed since she was pulled out of Mr. Deschane's class to talk to Axel and Investigator Riley. But it was only a few hours ago. Her stomach drops when she thinks of what she told them.

No one likes Madison Caldwell. It's true. But should she have played it safer than that? Or perhaps she should have told them more.

We have reason to believe that the same person who killed Madison Caldwell also took Chloe.

In the end, she gave them nothing. She sat there mute until Axel suggested she return to class and maybe they could pick this back up later, if anything came to mind.

A little fire burns inside her now, tempting her to go next door and tell him how wrong he is.

No one took Chloe.

Chloe left all on her own.

Libby knows this with as much certainty as we know an asteroid killed the dinosaurs.

While no one saw it with their own eyes, there is enough evidence to basically cement the theory as fact.

For Libby, all the proof she needs is the text Chloe sent her after the musical. It was late; Libby was riding home with her parents, sitting in the bucket seat when her phone screen illuminated.

> Dead People: 9,997 Chloe: 0

I'm sorry, Libby texted back, remembering the forlorn look on Chloe's face while she'd been posing for pictures after the play. She recalls having noticed Axel and Rowan sneak out during intermission. They sat at the end of a row, Rowan holding a bouquet of black roses. Should I come over?

Chloe never responded to Libby's text, though, and less than an hour later, they heard Rowan tearing her voice to shreds as she cried out into the dark.

Crack! Whoosh!

Libby makes her way back to her window, and resting her forearms on the bench seat, slowly pulls herself up to peer out. Reeves's lineup is reassembled. He kicks the next ball into the goal.

She imagines him sitting in a spartan interrogation room this morning, detectives drilling him with questions as aggressively as he is now drilling those soccer balls. He didn't show up at school today, and yet, he can't have given himself away, she reasons. He's here, not in jail.

Unless they put a bracelet on him. Would they do that? She squints but can't see for sure.

Chloe wanted Madison dead. That was no secret. At least it wasn't between them. Libby knows everything about Chloe—her hopes, her dreams, her fears—and vice versa. That's how you secure a friendship: by telling each other things you'd never want anyone else to know. Because when the wrong people know your secrets, they become weapons of mass destruction. It's because of the secrets they shared that Libby also knows Chloe is connected to Madison's murder.

Could Reeves be the boy who had stolen her clandestine friend's heart? There was someone. Chloe had told her once, when they lay in her bed staring up at the little twirling ghost that she felt, strangely, like she might be a little bit in love.

If Libby didn't know better, she might think she was jealous of this nameless person who seemed capable of distracting Chloe even when he was nowhere near. It was all Chloe had wanted to talk about in her final days, between bouts of complaining about Madison and Sari.

Reeves makes sense.

Him killing Madison makes sense.

Perhaps Madison had gotten in the way of him and Chloe being together. It also explains why she would have slut-shamed Chloe with those drawings and that awful prank. Jealousy over Chloe getting the part of Lydia in the play was a cover-up for the real reason she turned on her former best friend.

Libby sighs. It always boils down to a boy.

Chloe is small. Although Madison was thin, she was a good head taller. Chloe wouldn't have been strong enough to take down a girl her size. She would have had help.

Libby's gaze drifts back to Reeves. She studies him, her focus following the muscles that strain beneath his tight long-sleeve T-shirt. Envisioning his arms stretched out, hands closing around Madison Caldwell's throat, there's one more thing she knows about Chloe.

She didn't act alone.

SATURDAY, OCTOBER 21

11

ROWAN

Death is a stench you don't forget.

Nor do you ever get used to it. Musty, acrid, and pungent all at once, the sensory assault makes Rowan's eyes water and her nose run. She's heard the thing about Vicks VapoRub—putting a swipe of it under your nose—but that's only for actors and people who aren't going to last on the job. Plus, the menthol makes her crave a cigarette, of which only one remains. Then she has to leave. That's the deal.

She's in the morgue, gowned up from head to toe. Formaldehyde masks the cadaverine and putrescine, a stinging odor formed by the decarboxylation of lysine. An exhaust fan overhead hums, further diffusing the compounds.

The corpse lies naked on the table, waiting to be cut, peeled, and fileted with the assortment of stainless-steel tools that rest on the surgical tray. Rowan stares at the body. Now two days deceased, it looks smaller than it did in the gully, and younger. *She*. Axel's voice echoes in her head. Why he insists on giving pronouns and names to corpses is a mystery to her. For Rowan, it's just easier not to. This is not Madison Caldwell; rather, it's the body Madison Caldwell left behind.

A tag is looped around the decedent's toe.

Case No. 23-58313
Name: Madison Olivia Caldwell

```
Age: 15 | Sex: F | Race: W | Weight: 125
Height: 5'7"
Place of Death: Black Harbor, WI
Date of Death: 10/19/23 | Time of Death: 2039
hours
Cause of Death:
```

The necropsy will determine the cause of death, though if she were a gambling woman, Rowan would bet all her chips on murder. Coldness slips down her throat and pools in the pit of her stomach, like she's swallowed a shard of ice. She imagines a tag like this on Chloe's unidentified body, stored in a mortuary cold chamber who-knows-where. JANE DOE, it would read. She pushes the image out of her head. She needs to focus on finding answers, because what she learns during this examination could lead to a discovery of Chloe—dead or alive.

They thought they found her yesterday. Someone called the number for the Amber Alert to report a girl curled up on a bus stop bench who matched Chloe's description. Police arrived, but it wasn't her. Axel later told her it was a sex worker wearing a tacky red dress.

Peering through a plastic face shield, her eyes take in the pale canvas before her. The hands are clean of defensive marks, no cuts between the fingers, fingernails intact. But then Rowan's gaze travels up the rectus abdominis, up the sternum and across the clavicle to the fresh abrasions on the neck. She squints and leans closer to better study the chafing marks. "What do you think these are?"

She hears the whisper of non-woven fabric as Liz, the forensic pathologist, leans over to look. "Manual strangulation," she says without hesitation, and turns the victim's head. She draws a sickle shape in the air with her finger, following the curve of a rash. "Petechiae of the ear."

Through the fog on the inside of her shield, Rowan observes a smattering of round, pinpoint spots near the jaw.

"Blood flow was obstructed, causing the blood vessels in the skin to rupture above the area of constriction." Liz tilts the head again. The petechiae are on both sides. "Look, it's in the eyes, too."

She pops open one of the eyelids and Rowan notes constellations of red that bleed into one another like a watercolor.

"Petechial hemorrhage of the lower left palpebral conjunctiva . . ." Liz mutters. Rowan watches as she scribbles notes on her clipboard. Shadows cut beneath Liz's cheekbones, making her cheeks look hollow. She has the porcelain skin of someone who never sees the light of day, every inch of her smooth as bone. She's pretty in a creepy way, and Rowan imagines Chloe would have been enamored with her, especially during her character study of Lydia Deetz. The light from above glances off Liz's face shield.

Liz is a forensic encyclopedia. Over the years, Rowan has stood shotgun on hundreds of autopsies with her, watching her expertly define causes, manners, and mechanisms of death. Her findings have led to solving otherwise unsolvable cases, including one this summer when police discovered a skull fragment in a man's garage. Liz recognized it as the missing sphenoid bone of an unidentified specimen dredged up from the river in 2016. A positive ID of the killer led to positively identifying the victim, a thirty-eight-year-old woman who'd allegedly gone on a date and never returned. She was drugged with Rohypnol, smashed into pieces, wrapped up in a black garbage bag, and tossed off the bridge. Axel was on that case, Rowan remembers. The guy was a painter. The pressure washer he used to clean flaking paint off home exteriors was the same one he used to clean the victim's blood off his garage floor. Liz was interviewed about the case, and when asked how she put it all together, she simply said: "I like jigsaw puzzles."

It's quiet but for the constant whirring of the exhaust fan. Rowan watches Liz as she opens the victim's mouth and peers inside with a penlight. Cracked teeth poke out of the gums like stalactites. Gently, she curls the bottom lip and pulls it taut. The sound of subtle curiosity escapes her.

"What?" Rowan leans forward to look.

"You see those?"

Rowan tilts her head. "Umm . . ."

"Here." Liz extracts the gel pen from her lab coat pocket. She unscrews the tip. Rowan watches as the filter comes free in her hand. Liz snaps it in half. Then, she does something Rowan has never seen before: she pours a thin strip of ink along the inside of the lip and smears it with her finger. When she's finished, she folds the flap down for Rowan to see.

The word "BITCH" is scratched in fine lines. Filled with ink, it looks like a tattoo.

"I'd wager a guess she didn't do this herself," says Liz.

Rowan agrees. The letters are too straight, the loop of the *B* perfectly closed. "What do you think they used?" she wonders out loud. She thinks maybe an X-Acto knife, but the lines don't look deep enough.

Liz sucks her teeth. Her right eyebrow arches as she considers the thin, shallow cuts. "A needle probably, or a safety pin."

Suddenly, Rowan feels light-headed. The edges of her vision darken as she thinks of Chloe's tearstained face the last time she spoke to her— and the safety pins that glimmered in her ears.

12

AXEL

Riley sits in the narrow window seat, her back up against the light-colored brick. From his desk, Axel can see her eyes flicker as her gaze roams the bleak city. It looks miniature from here on the third floor of the lighthouse, and he likens it to one of those Dickensian Christmas villages, if it had been broken in a move and left to collect dust for a decade or however long it might take for someone to take pity on it and fix it up. Glue the shingles back on the rooftops, screw in new light bulbs.

She pauses her sweep of Black Harbor to stare at him. "You want to talk about it?"

Axel looks over his computer. All he can see of Fletcher are the tops of his shoulders; they're hunched so high his head has disappeared. Aside from helping with Chloe's case, he's in the throes of working a triple-jurisdiction robbery and kidnapping, so Axel cuts him some slack for his terrible posture. Kole is in a meeting with the DA regarding an old case that's finally gone to trial. On his way out, he ran through his checklist. "We still need to talk to a couple faculty members: Mark Cutler, Amelia Kazmaryck, and Eddie Taylor . . . I never trust a guy with two first names."

"Nikolai Kole," Riley recited slowly. "Isn't that kinda two first names?"

Kole flashed a smile. "Just do as I say. Oh, and a couple more students. If Sari Simons thinks she's skating away without talking to us after her two friends were—" He caught himself from speaking Axel's worst nightmare into existence.

"Yes, boss." Riley sent him off with a salute.

Now it's just the three of them in the lighthouse where the Violent Crime Task Force has set up shop. Whiteboards covered in coordinates and crime scene photographs stand in front of each curved wall, boxing them in. Their desks are clustered together in the center. Axel works across from Riley, Kole across from Fletcher. Work space is limited, but it's more room than they had in the bureau. They've been here for the past three months, since Kole convinced the City to let them use the watchtower as their hideout, instead of dumping a dime of taxpayer money into reconfiguring any part of the BHPD.

"Do you want to talk about it?" Riley asks.

"No." Even to himself, his voice is barely audible over the waves that crash against the east side of the lighthouse. Whether the "it" Riley is asking him to talk about is in regards to what Reeves Singh mentioned earlier about Chloe wanting Madison Caldwell dead or the fact that his daughter's absence is driving him crazy, he doesn't want to put it on her. He's never liked people who shoulder their grief onto someone else. And he damn well isn't going to do it to Riley; he likes her too much. "I just want to find her."

Riley nods. "I know," she says quietly. "We will."

A muscle spasm tugs on the left side of his mouth. The fact that she didn't say they'll find Chloe alive isn't lost on him. In fairness, though, he hadn't mentioned the word, either. Another rule of investigations: never make a promise you can't keep.

Steam rises from Riley's mug of Earl Grey, creating the deception that it's a ribbon of smoke billowing from one of the factory stacks below. But the tannery is defunct now, and has been for thirty years. Perhaps not for too much longer, though. Anywhere else, a piece of real estate like that, as ramshackle as it might be, would go for a hefty amount. But in Black Harbor, a hardscrabble city that's eroding more and more by the minute and where a bullet with your name on it might be right around the corner, they're lucky to scrape up even bottom-dollar bidders. Whoever the anonymous new owner is, Axel hopes they've got half a mind to turn it into something that can transform the city.

He's grateful for the window and the illusion that it creates of him looking at something, when in reality, the city below could be on fire and he wouldn't even know it. He stares blankly, his mind sorting and turning the jagged pieces of the past two days, as though he's gluing together a glass mosaic.

Chloe is still missing.

Madison Caldwell is still dead.

And of all the rocks they've turned over, there could be thousands more yet to go.

His phone rings. It's May Peters, the bureau secretary. "Hello, May."

"Investigator Winthorp, a young woman is here to see you."

"Can you get her name for me, May?"

She hardly finishes saying it when Axel ends the call. He looks at Riley, who is already standing.

She tosses back the rest of her Earl Grey like it's a shot of whiskey.

Sari Simons is at the bureau and she's ready to talk.

The girl sits on the pebble-grey couch, knees together, white Vans bouncing so rapidly her heels are going to rub holes in the plinth base. Axel's eyes are drawn to them, scanning for flecks of blood. At this point in the investigation, everyone is a person of interest.

Her face is tearstained, the whites of her eyes bloodshot. For the record, she was crying before she even entered Interview Room #3.

She wears her hair in an Afro with a blue velvet flower. Long, slender prisms hang from her earlobes, catching and reflecting the dim light from the window. They remind him of fishing lures.

He knows her fairly well. It's been a while, but she used to come over to his house, always tagging along with Madison Caldwell. Sometimes he'd come home from work and the three of them would be on the couch eating pizza, or up in Chloe's bedroom singing karaoke.

Riley and Axel sit perpendicular to Sari, a shared coffee table between them. Axel leans forward, feeling awkwardly slouched, swallowed by the secondhand armchair. "Thanks for coming in, Sari."

For the first time, Sari makes eye contact with him. Her pupils are deep, dark wells of mystery. Her bottom lip quivers, offering a glimpse of braces.

"You know, you're allowed to breathe," says Axel, noticing the girl's barely taken a breath since sitting down. She exhales and he watches her shoulders fall slightly. Shifting, she tugs on her drab army jacket and wraps it tightly around her, as though to keep herself from falling apart.

"So, are you a cat person or a dog person?" he asks.

Sari regards him quizzically, but answers: "Cat."

"I can tell." He points his chin at her jacket, and Sari's cheeks flush.

"My cat, Pickles," she says as she starts brushing off the white fluffy hairs. "He sheds like a mother—" she catches herself—"like crazy."

"I feel your pain," acknowledges Axel. "Fry always sheds like there's no tomorrow." He hooks a thumb at Riley. "Investigator Riley here can't relate. She doesn't have any pets."

"I do enough shedding all on my own," assures Riley, absentmindedly picking a long black hair off her button-down.

Sari almost smiles. She seems a bit looser now. Even her curls look less tightly wound. Axel takes an opportunity to study the backpack Sari brought in with her. He stares at it, as though doing so intensely enough will activate X-ray vision. It's a JanSport with a cosmological print—a purple-and-blue ombré with dots of white. He's seen it before, slouched on the bench in their entryway. Sari doesn't seem to go anywhere without it. He and Rowan share the sense that she probably lives out of it more than a kid should have to.

"Your dad dropped you off?" he asks, though he knows the answer.

"He's away at training. He doesn't know I'm here."

Axel frowns. "How'd you get here?"

"I took an Uber."

An Uber. He forgets there's such a thing in Black Harbor. Times have certainly changed. From little on we're taught never to get in cars with strangers. Now there's an app for it.

"What did you come to tell us, Sari?" Riley leans in a little. "Is it about what happened to your friends, Madison and Chloe?"

At the mention of their names, Sari's eyes glisten. Tears shine on her long lashes, falling like raindrops as she nods.

"This is a safe space," Riley says, her voice soft and soothing. "You can tell us anything." She stands and remains crouched as she hands Sari the box of tissues.

Sari plucks two and crumples them in her fist. Her tongue darts out between her lips, then, priming them for what she came here to tell them. But for whatever reason, the words don't come.

"Why don't you start by telling us why you weren't at school yesterday," suggests Axel.

The girl stares at him, aghast. He might as well have just asked her to tell them her favorite way to skin a cat. A question Libby wouldn't flinch at, he thinks. Rather, she'd probably start up a PowerPoint.

"My best friend was *murdered*," says Sari. Her voice is thick with phlegm, and her tone suggests that one's friend being murdered is the trump card to trump all trump cards.

"Right." Axel clears his throat and swallows back some of his anger toward the girl. So far, what Reeves Singh alleged about her instigating problems between Madison and Chloe is hearsay. She wasn't there to defend herself or point the finger back at him. Although he's always thought Sari to be a bit of a brat, he realizes that while he is dealing with the tragedy of his daughter's disappearance, she, concurrently, is dealing with the fact that another friend is gone indefinitely.

There is no hope for Madison Caldwell.

But there is still hope for Chloe. Though, he's acutely aware of it waning as the seconds tick by. "I'm sorry. I'm sure this is extremely hard for you."

Sari nods. Tears splash onto her jeans and darken the denim.

"So you stayed home yesterday? You didn't go anywhere?"

She nods again.

"I just slept and . . . watched TV. I hoped that every time I woke up, it would all turn out to be a bad dream." Her face crumples to mirror the tissues wadded in her hand. She sniffs and takes in a breath so deep, her shoulders rise toward her ears. The long silver earrings are prisms catching the grey light.

"Sari, how did you find out?" wonders Riley.

The girl shakes her head and stares at the edge of the coffee table, as though she needs an anchor point for her gaze but doesn't want to look directly at either of them. "Everyone was talking about it."

"Who's everyone?"

"From school. Someone Snapchatted a video of the cops out in her neighborhood. Red and blue lights. Caution tape. You couldn't see anything, but then I googled it and . . ." She traps her bottom lip between her teeth and drinks in another lungful of air. ". . . there it was. Something about a fifteen-year-old female found in the gully in Belgrave Circle. It didn't say her name but I knew. I knew it was Madison."

Axel wouldn't have thought it was possible for her frown to deepen, but it does. Even the corners of her eyes are pulled toward the floor.

"How did you know it was her?" asks Riley.

"Because I texted her and she didn't respond. Which was unlike her. She *always* texted me back immediately, unless she was with Reeves, and I knew she wasn't because he was at soccer practice. We were supposed to meet up and walk to the play together, but . . . when she didn't show I knew something was wrong. I mean . . . I *thought* something could be wrong . . . but then I also thought she might have met up with Reeves and maybe she texted me to let me know but her message didn't go through or something."

"Would her meeting up with Reeves have been a bad thing?" asks Axel. "Were you ever concerned for Madison's well-being when she was with him?"

Sari purses her lips and stares even harder at the table's edge. "No. I mean, they got into arguments sometimes, but . . . to be honest, Madison was the more aggressive one."

"What do you mean by *aggressive*?" Riley's pen is poised.

"Like . . . she'd always get her way." Sari shrugs. "Even if Reeves disagreed at first, he would always come around to doing what she wanted in the end."

"Can you give us some examples of that?"

Sari sniffs. Axel notices how she sits with her knees knocked together, toes pointed in toward each other, heels hovering three or four inches off the floor. She shares with them, then, about different times Madison convinced Reeves to pay for things even though her parents gave her an unlimited allowance and he spent his weekends bagging groceries, or to badger his uncle into letting him drive his Mustang convertible for Homecoming. "And the Snap," she says, locking eyes with Axel for a fraction of a second before tearing away. "She got him to send it to the whole soccer team, which helped it go viral."

Riley and Axel frown. "The Snap?" asks Riley.

"Snapchat," clarifies Sari. "The one that . . ." Her voice falters. If she'd had any bit of an edge when she first sat down, she's lost it now. Axel swears he can see her pulse quicken in her neck. "You know about the rumor, don't you?" She pauses, waiting for them to fill in the rest.

But Axel cannot say it out loud. "Why don't you tell us," he suggests.

Incredibly, Sari looks disgusted. And a little haughty. If Chloe truly hated this girl, Axel can see why. He hears a soft razing sound as his fingernails scratch into the grooves of his jeans.

"Rumor has it that the only reason Chloe got the part in the musical was because she was, like, sleeping with Mr. Cutler." She cringes as though waiting to take a punch.

Axel feels all the air go out of his lungs. Seeing the crude sketches labeled *Chloe the Hoe-y* and *Mr. Cuddler* in Chloe's locker was one thing. Hearing Sari say their names in the same sentence is quite another. It leaves him hollow. After a few seconds, he unballs his fists and glances at his palms where his nails have pressed little crescents into his flesh. He looks up to meet Sari's rueful stare. "Was it true?" he asks, dreading the answer.

To his immense relief, Sari shakes her head. "No. I don't think so."

He squints at her, thinking about what Reeves Singh had said in his interview yesterday morning. *I don't know why anyone would take it so hard if it wasn't a little true.* "How do you know?" he presses.

Sari's face is a stone, at first, with delicate features etched into it: a tiny scoop of a nose, a pair of perfectly spaced almond-shaped eyes, and a chin with the shallowest cleft. A single teardrop slides down her cheek. "Because I started it."

Axel and Riley wait and watch as Sari reaches for her backpack on the floor. The zipper makes a soft, high-pitched whine. Plunging her hand into the compartment, she withdraws a black long-sleeve T-shirt on the front of which are three rows of white letters that read STRAIGHT OUTTA REHEARSAL. Axel squints, processing the familiarity of it. He's seen this shirt before, and he knows where as soon as he takes it from Sari. Down the sleeve, in the same white lettering, is the name WIN-THORP.

"This is Chloe's shirt," Axel says, to no one in particular. "How did you get it?"

Sari begins to sob. She slouches and covers her face with her hands. "We stole it," she says, her voice thickening again. "From her bedroom. We came over to do karaoke and . . . yeah."

"Who stole it?" asks Axel. "You and who?"

"Madison."

"Madison Caldwell?"

Sari nods.

Axel is shaking his head. "Because you were planning to do something with it?"

She begins to sob again. Finally, she straightens up, exhales. The severe frown returns. "I was trying to help Madison." Dabbing at her eyes, Sari explains how Madison was upset by Chloe being cast as Lydia Deetz in the *Beetlejuice* play. "She came up with a million reasons why Chloe had been cast over her—"

"Baby teeth," names Axel, unable to hold back. "She said Chloe looked young enough for the part because she still has her baby teeth."

"Oh, yeah." Sari throws up her right hand, a motion that suggests tossing the ridiculous criticism out there. "Which doesn't even make sense because that Lydia character is, like, our age anyway."

A switch has flipped in Sari. Suddenly, she seems less sad about Madison's tragic death and more desperate to save her own skin. If Madison was truly manipulative with Reeves Singh, Axel wonders what resentful things she might have coerced Sari into doing throughout their friendship. "Whose idea was it to take the shirt?" he asks.

"Madison's," Sari blurts, and it's clear the confession has been on the tip of her tongue for quite some time.

"What about the Snapchat? Whose idea was that?"

Shamefaced, Sari slowly raises her hand. "I was all in at that point. I figured . . . go big or go home, I guess. If we were going to start a rumor, we were going to *start a rumor*." Her eyes bulge in cadence with the last three words.

When Axel and Riley are quiet, Sari takes the opportunity to add context. "Madison wanted that part so bad," she emphasizes. "*Beetlejuice* was, like, her favorite movie of all time. She loved Halloween. And for Chloe to—" She catches herself so as to not speak ill of the dead, Axel suspects. Not that Chloe is dead, but perhaps Sari thinks she might be.

"Chloe did, too," he says. He can't stop himself. The chance to talk about his daughter—about something beyond the fact that she is missing—is too tempting to resist.

"What?" Sari pauses. She looks confused, as though she'd forgotten he was anything more than a sounding board.

"Loved Halloween." He remembers making little ghosts with Chloe when she was young out of scraps of a white bedsheet and Styrofoam balls. They hung them from the sugar maple in the backyard, and Chloe named them all: Franklin, Jessica, Maria, Johnny, Davie, Moe. There had to be a dozen or more that she knew by heart because each one had a different face. And then one day a gust of wind came and blew them off the branches. They disappeared and Chloe made up a story about how they'd passed on, except for one that landed on the flat part of the roof by her bedroom window. Franklin. She took him inside and hung him from a hook in her ceiling. And so he became her guardian ghost, watching over her on nights when Axel and Rowan would get called away to investigate a crime scene. He's probably still there, now, twirling lazily in the moonlight and dancing with dust particles, wondering where the girl who sleeps beneath him has gone.

Although he hears Sari's confession, it doesn't immediately register. A fictitious reel plays in his mind of Chloe being groped by some middle-aged man, someone she was supposed to be able to trust, and he can't help but start to sort out which pieces are true and which are constructed solely out of jealousy and other petty emotions. Chloe wanted that role of Lydia Deetz more than anything in the world. It was being recorded for her reel, the one she would eventually show talent scouts and use for her admission to the Juilliard School in New York. To what ends would she have gone to attain it?

The unfortunate truth about rumors is there is always a sliver of truth to them.

"Hey." Axel leans toward her. As much as it pains him to, he says: "No one hates you for what you did, Sari. You wanted to support your friend. So, you helped her facilitate a rumor about Chloe sleeping with the drama teacher to get the part. Is that right?"

Sari nods. Her tongue slips out to catch the tears that crest the cupid's bow of her lips.

"High school stuff," he adds dismissively. "You didn't mean for anyone to get hurt."

Sari shakes her head.

"Can we see it?" he asks. "The Snap?"

"They disappear in twenty-four hours," Riley starts to explain, when Sari reaches into her jacket pocket and produces her cell phone.

"I have a screenshot," she says. Axel watches as she thumbs through apps and scrolls through her camera roll to find a certain screenshot. She surrenders it to him and closes her eyes.

The photo shows a brown leather messenger bag with what he recognizes as Chloe's shirt partially tucked inside. It looks staged, obviously the work of high school girls rather than seasoned con artists. The white letters of her last name are wrinkled but legible. A cartoonish stamp overlays the photo, like a sound effect in a comic book. *Daddy Issues.*

Axel's stomach twists. He swallows, his mouth dry. He wants to speak, but all the air has gone out of him.

Riley seems to pick up on it, that this interview needs to end. "Thank you, Sari," she says professionally. "Is there anything else you need to tell us?"

Sari bites her lip so hard it starts to bleed. She drags her head up and meets only Axel's eyes. Her voice trembles when she says: "Mr. Winthorp . . . I'm afraid your daughter is going to kill me next."

13

LIBBY

Despite one of its windows being boarded up still and the whole exterior being the color of dirty snow, Gallagher's Garden Center is the nicest place in town. Of course, these are the imperfections one notices when one comes here probably fifty Saturdays a year—not to browse the perennials or to sip lattes in the café, but to man the nursery.

Or rather, "woman" the nursery, in Libby's case.

From the road, the building looks like a wedding cake, its triple-tiered center flanked by greenhouses. Libby has always admired how their geometric, cataractous walls have a way of blending into the sky, no matter what kind of day it is.

Fall mums offer fireworks of orange, sunshine, and plum. Some of their blossoms are wide open to welcome the world, others are closed like tiny fists. There are racks of them and a BOGO sign that screams ONE FOR YOU AND ONE FOR YOUR MUMMY!

She walks toward the cascading rows of pumpkins in front of the entrance. There must be a whole patch's worth of them in wooden boxes and stacked on straw bales—smooth ones and warty ones, some that are perfectly orange and others that are zombie-grey. Leaning, she touches the back of her hand to one. The flesh is matte and cool; she used to wonder if this is what a dead person's face feels like, but now she knows for certain that it isn't.

"Morning, Libby." Caroline, the cashier, greets her cheerlessly. Her

chin is tucked into her neck; she doesn't bother to look up from thread-
ing a price tag onto a Halloween wreath.

"Good morning," says Libby through a smile. It's a full Duchenne
smile, the kind that crimps the skin by your eyes into crow's feet and
has the power to elevate one's mood. They learned about the different
kinds of smiles in AP Psychology a few weeks ago and since then, Libby
has been trying it out.

It seems to be working. She does feel happier.

Or, this may be her body tricking her mind into simply thinking she
is. She can practically feel the dopamine and serotonin surging through
her bloodstream now, two cracked capsules whose happy little chemicals
are dissolving into her.

Her mom says that people can always hear if you're smiling or not,
which is why you should always answer the phone with a smile. She
also says that Gallagher's gift shop is for white ladies from Chicago who
are too rich for Black Harbor, but not rich enough to dock a yacht on
their own shoreline, so they "summer" here until Labor Day, wearing
fake grins and white pants and jangling their chunky Pandora bracelets.
Thus, the reason Marnie Lucas never steps foot on that side of the store,
except maybe to grab a bottle of wine after dropping Libby off.

The wine rack is behind the cashier's counter, boasting columns of
red, white, and seasonal blends. Libby's eyes land on a copper-colored
vintage labeled *Hallowine*. She remembers sampling it once from her
mother's glass and immediately making a face. It tasted like licking the
basement floor.

Which she's never done, by the way, but one can infer.

Even though Caroline doesn't look at her, Libby knows she can hear
the inflection in her tone, the singsonginess of the *ee* sound in "Good
morn*ing*." Her head turns so her gaze can stay locked on Caroline, watching until her coworker's mouth curves upward in response.

Smiles are, in fact, contagious. That's another thing she learned in
class.

The smells of the café wrap her up in a warm, sugary hug. Maple
syrup and pumpkin spice mingle to create a spellbinding concoction
that she's sure will lure customers to the menu board. Wending her way

toward the nursery, Libby says hello to Octavia in the café and continues on back, through the aisle of resin statues: gnomes, fairies, and this time of year—skeletons.

She is happy here, at Gallagher's. Her coworkers, with the exception of seasonal help, are older. They have crepey necks and sunspots and a little extra weight in their midsections, which means they don't judge her as harshly as her peers at school. Except there was that one time when Kim from Home Decor told her she'd probably have a boyfriend if she lost twenty or thirty pounds. Libby couldn't smile her way through that one.

Even though she noted, as Kim waddled away, how her ass shifted like a giant, gelatinous pendulum, it still stung as much as if someone like Madison Caldwell had said it. It also stung because it was probably more than a little true.

Sliding glass doors open up to a living menagerie. Perennials, evergreens, and shrubs fill the space. Libby often imagines maneuvering through here like spelunking in a verdant cave; the hanging spider plants and English ivy are the stalactites and the dracaena bushes are the stalagmites, their spiky shoots piercing the well-oxygenated air. And then there are the cacti and the succulents, of course, behind her little station.

Today, however, it looks like a blood bath.

"Holy roses," Libby breathes.

"Some guy ordered them in," calls Heather, her manager. She totes a watering can down the aisle of ferns. "He'll be here sometime this weekend to pick them up."

"Oh. Okay." Libby sidles behind the desk, cluttered with water bottles and chipped ceramic planters repurposed into pen and safety pin holders. There's a jar of little glow-in-the-dark pumpkin charms. Eluding Heather's gaze, she takes one and slips it into her pocket, then ties her apron around her waist.

Another shot of dopamine spikes her blood.

"Can you plant roses this late in the year?" she wonders. It seems like a death sentence with winter encroaching.

Heather shrugs. "Sure. They're heartier than people think. And actually, these are Aurora. They're bred specifically for Canadian climate conditions . . . i.e., here, i.e., Hell frozen over."

"On a warm day," supplies Libby.

Heather nods appreciatively and keeps watering.

The entire left side of the nursery is bathed in red. Although when she gets close, she sees that they are actually a very vibrant pink, a brush stroke in the sky just before the sun goes down. Libby wanders over to the pallets of roses, gently pinching the silky petals of one, and cannot help but think of the ones her mom said were found crushed on the walking trail.

Chloe's roses.

But hers were black. She saw Rowan holding the bouquet wrapped in cellophane when she and Axel first walked in and took their seats. Then, after the play, she saw Chloe with it, white knuckle–clutching the thorny stems as she fought the urge to cry, forcing a smile—a full Duchenne—for pictures instead.

"Just be thankful you're back here and not out there selling pumpkins," says Heather, already exasperated. "We hit a lull right now, but it's been a shit show all morning. Why everyone has to wait til the last freakin' minute . . ."

But Libby isn't listening to her. Instead, she stares at a skull planter, a Venus flytrap exploding from its cranium. She studies the way it grins at her with teeth that are so perfect and porcelain. Remembering Madison Caldwell's teeth scattered in the gully, she grins back.

14

ROWAN

Rowan rolls out onto the street, water droplets clinging to her windshield. At this rate, she'll use up her punch card by midweek, if not sooner.

She will never be clean. That much is apparent. No matter how many times the bear claw locks onto her tire and pulls her vehicle through a gauntlet of soaped-up scrub brushes, the filth of Black Harbor will remain. It's deep-set and everywhere, like lymphatic cancer. There's no cutting it out, no blasting it into atoms too infinitesimal to matter.

Moments ago, she closed her eyes and meditated, inhaling and exhaling a series of calming ocean breaths to the rhythm of the brushes. The word *BITCH* glared angrily at her, as though it had been scratched on the insides of her eyelids instead of Madison's lip.

Liz believes it's the killer's handiwork, done very last. After the strangulation. After smashing the victim's teeth with a rock.

"Like a signature?" Rowan wondered.

Liz peered at her through the fog that had collected on the inside of her face shield. She lifted it to breathe. "I guess we'll see, right?"

The chill that seeped into Rowan's bloodstream, then, was so frigid, it felt as if someone injected a syringe of liquid nitrogen into her bone marrow. She knew what Liz meant: that if more bodies popped up with slanderous words carved into their skin or the inside of their mouths, they could be dealing with something far more sinister than a crime of passion.

"Police suspect a male aggressor," she mentioned, remembering what Kole had said Thursday night at the scene. *Statistically, you and I both know this was a male.*

"Yeah." Liz pouted thoughtfully. "They were definitely larger—at least large enough to overpower our victim, who's fairly tall. But honestly . . . it's anyone's game. Whoever strangled her knew what they were doing, I can tell you that."

Her insides thawed just a bit. Chloe was smaller than Madison. She wouldn't have been able to overpower her. Unless she'd had help. Rowan dismissed the notion as hastily as it had come.

But, the safety pins. The cuts were too superficial to be from anything much more substantial. And lately, Chloe had taken to wearing them all the time, pierced through her ears or the cuffs of her sweatshirts, even stuck through the knit fabric of her stocking hat.

"As in . . . they've done this before?" she asked, returning to the conversation.

"Or practiced. You know, humans aren't all that hard to kill. One wrong kink of the neck and we're"—she snapped her fingers—"kaput."

The low, vibrating yawn of her garage door lets her know she's home. She was so lost in thought, she doesn't even remember driving the short distance from the car wash to Belgrave Circle. Her body has switched to autopilot. Dread gnaws at her brain stem. That's when bad things happen.

It's why all this has come about. She knows it without a shadow of a doubt. Her past has come back to haunt her in true karmic fashion.

Slowly, Rowan presses the brake to pause in her driveway. The front porch is empty, the jack-o'-lanterns she and Chloe carved last week gone. Her vision blurs. Her jaw quivers as she fights back tears and remembers the quiet conversation they'd had while plopping handfuls of guts into a mixing bowl. How the tip of Chloe's pink tongue peeked between her lips while she carved the faces of the tragedy and comedy masks on the gourd's curved surface. They had names, Chloe informed her: Melpomene and Thalia, though now she can't remember which is which.

Why would someone take them? She checks her mirrors to see if their smashed bits are strewn in the street, but it's only copper- and rust-colored leaves that collect in the curtilage.

Rowan parks in the garage. The engine purrs. Exhaustion settles over her like a weighted blanket, and she feels suddenly as though she could fall asleep. It reminds her of when Chloe was a baby and the only way to get her to nap was to take her for a drive or set her bassinet on the dryer. There was some magic in the subtle vibration coupled with Rowan's singing that soothed Chloe to sleep. "Skidamarink a dink a dink, skidamarink a doo . . ."

With a shaking hand, Rowan reaches for the glove box.

Click.

The door falls open and the cigarette box she'd stuffed precariously back inside yesterday morning tumbles out. She doesn't go for the cigarette this time. Instead, she pinches the corner of newsprint and draws it out. Holding it taut but gently, she studies it.

On the right-hand side is a black-and-white thumbnail image of a girl. She's forever fourteen, if Rowan remembers correctly, with a heart-shaped face and long, straight hair. Rowan caresses the picture with the edge of her thumb. "I'm sorry," she whispers. "I'm so sorry."

The tang of salt awakens her taste buds. A glance in the rearview mirror reveals trails of tears streaming down her cheeks, disappearing into the seam between her lips and into the folds of her scarf. She can't stand to look at herself. Her gaze falls back to the obituary, and she's trapped in a simulation wherein "I'm sorry" are the only two words that remain of her vocabulary.

She doesn't know whether she's apologizing to Chloe or to the girl she killed eighteen years ago.

Katelynn Diggory was admitted for laryngeal surgery after recurring bouts of strep throat left the girl's vocal cords badly damaged. Rowan was the attending anesthesiologist. The procedure of opening the airway and repairing the laryngeal framework took seven and a half hours, during which Rowan monitored and administered the anesthetic.

However, that meant she'd been working for twenty-six hours—awake for almost forty, as she'd been studying for exams. She'd already smoked an entire pack of Marlboros and her ride on the nicotine train had come to a crashing halt. She fell asleep right where she stood, and when she awoke it was to the high-pitched shriek of a flat line on Kate-lynn's heart monitor.

"I'm sorry," she whispers again. The air is thin and insubstantial. She can hardly get enough oxygen for a full breath. A pressure squeezes her temples, and in her mind, Katelynn's face merges with Chloe's, until she cannot determine which girl she is seeing.

The familiar heaviness takes over her now. Keeping her eyes open is too strenuous, even sitting upright seems an impossible task. She slumps forward, her cheekbone nestled into the curve of the steering wheel. The newsprint flutters out of her hand, and an indeterminate amount of time later, she is wrenched back into the waking world by the cacophony of slamming doors and her husband shouting at her to turn off the engine.

15

AXEL

"Thanks for coming by, Marnie."

Axel walks her out. Marnie opens the back door and pauses with one foot on the flagstone, the other still in the entryway. "Just keep her hydrated. Hot lemon water or some more of that ginger tea to help with the nausea. No coffee or soda or anything that's a diuretic. And make sure she sleeps, Axel. You, too."

He called Marnie as soon as he got Rowan inside. She came to as he carried her into the house, so she wasn't completely dead weight, at which time an oddly placed thought chose to present itself. As he supported Rowan with one arm and opened the door with the other, his memory told him that this was the first time he had ever carried his bride over the threshold. They hadn't even done it drunkenly on their wedding night, or when they leased their first apartment together, or when they bought this house in this quiet, presumably safe neighborhood. They never heeded traditions like that, viewing them instead as some kind of archaic conformity. But had he known that carrying her over the threshold was inevitable, he would have done it earlier, when she was fully conscious and the moment might have been romantic. He jostled her as he nudged the door aside with his foot and felt her arms tighten around his neck. She wasn't just holding on to him, she was clinging, the way a drowning person might cling to a buoy.

Marnie sounded like a dispatcher over the phone. She was cool and collected, speaking in a tone as easy as though he'd called to tell her that one of her packages had been delivered to his porch. "How long ago did you find her? Is she awake? Okay, good. Talking? Check her pulse and count how many beats per minute. I'll be right over."

She came bearing gifts: a tin of ginger tea and lemon wedges stored in a Tupperware container, and one of those cool gel compresses. A check of Rowan's vitals revealed she would more than likely be fine, despite a high probability of waking up with a headache.

"Row?" Marnie rubbed two fingertips across the top of her hand. "How ya doing?"

"Marnie?" The slightest smile peaked Rowan's mouth, which then curved into a frown to match the lines that appeared in the center of her forehead. "What are you—"

"You passed out, sweetie. Tsk tsk. Didn't your parents ever warn you not to sit in the garage with the engine running? You're lucky Axel came home when he did."

She's on the couch, now, half asleep with reruns of a '90s sitcom playing on the TV. The canned laughter feels like a taunt or a joke made in poor taste. It makes Axel want to punch his fist through the drywall.

"No caffeine, no alcohol. Got it," he says to confirm he understands. "Ginger tea and lemon." He smiles as if to say, *I got this*.

Despite Marnie's twenty years of practicing modern medicine, she fosters a healthy balance between Eastern and Western philosophies. He's always admired that about her, the ability to think independently and take agency for herself and her patients. Too often, people are one extreme or the other. Marnie's appreciation for both, however, gives her a critical edge, a way of seeing things others might miss. But now, he has uncomfortably become the subject of her perspicacity—a germ squeezed between two glass slides, being scrutinized under her microscope.

"Get some sleep. Seriously." Her eyes fix on the dark pockets under his. Her gaze feels like two prongs of a Taser hooking into his skin.

"I will," he promises, though unsure whether or not he can make good on it.

Marnie peers past his shoulder, as though she's a rifle with a hinged scope that can see around corners to the living room where Rowan rests on the couch. "She's lucky she made it home, first. If she'd have fallen asleep on the road. *Dios mío*."

"I know." It was the first thought that registered in Axel's mind, after he confirmed Rowan was alive, of course. "Thanks again. I can't tell you what it means to have you next door while we're going through this."

"I'm so sorry, Axel." Marnie's face pulls into a frown. Propping the door open with her hip, she takes his hands in hers. "Sometimes I just . . . I want to say something but I don't know what to say."

Staring down at their hands—his folded in hers—he nods. "We'll find her," he says. He tries to smile but it feels like a grimace the way it stretches his face. He can feel his bottom lip receding from his teeth.

"Without a doubt," agrees Marnie.

It's in this moment that Axel realizes exactly what they are: two people lying to each other in an effort to keep the world from collapsing just a little while longer.

Everybody lies. Kole is right about that.

She offers a sympathetic smile and rubs his shoulder. "I'll see you. Let me know if you need anything, okay?"

"Okay."

"I'm just dropping Libby off at the Compound, but other than that, Daniel and I will both be home all night."

"The Compound? You mean that haunted house complex?"

"Oh, yeah. That old warehouse on Pruitt. I think it was textiles or something back in the day."

"Everything was textiles or something back in the day."

"Minus the old tannery."

"You're right." Axel summons to mind the hulking yet sagging struc-ture of Hedelsten Hides & Leather Goods Tanning Company. Its walls bow out and it has a lean to it, like some kind of brick slug that, as he watches it from his station on the third floor of the lighthouse, gives the illusion of creeping slowly but surely down the hill. "Funny they don't make that into an attraction. That place is actually haunted, yeah?"

"I think so . . ." Marnie purses her lips on the last syllable, resulting in an almost query-like inflection. "That girl . . ." She shakes her head.

"They ought to tear the place down, to be honest. It's just an eyesore now. And a hazard."

"What isn't in this city?"

"Touché." Marnie blows out a breath.

Axel stands awkwardly, wishing he knew how to prolong the conversation. In this moment, it's almost as if he's returned to his old life, the one that wasn't jagged and wrong and upside down, the one in which he had even the slightest inclination to talk about trivial things like vacant buildings and the ghosts of industry past. But in this new life, he doesn't, so he changes the topic. "She goes by herself?" he says, putting the conversation back on Libby. "To the Compound?" A lightbulb flickers in his brain. Perhaps he could meet her there, pick up where their interview left off.

Marnie shrugs. "She meets up with friends there, I think. You know Libby, though. She's not afraid to go through those things alone." She shivers animatedly, as though the mere thought gives her the heebie-jeebies.

The funny thing about Marnie's statement is that Axel really doesn't know Libby. In fact, his interview with her yesterday was the most he'd ever spoken to her. He wonders if she told her parents about it, to whom, oddly enough, Libby bears hardly any resemblance. Personality-wise, that is. She has dark hair and rich, silty eyes in common with her mother; her dad's height. But, that's where the similarities end. The girl has a *lurchiness* about her, a furtive expression and andante shrinking inward that suggests she's always trying to disappear from the space she inhabits.

The elephant in the room desperately wishing it were a mouse.

She's sullen and demure. Of the handful of interactions he's had with her—the girl is usually up in her room if ever he and Rowan go over—he's noticed she has a habit of staring. At his mouth, specifically. More than once, he's caught her lip-syncing his sentences, and every time he does, it reminds him of a guy he interviewed a few years ago, who was eventually found guilty of murdering his parents with a hatchet while they slept.

Not that he thinks Libby is a murderer. But she is a bit bizarre.

The taxidermy thing is weird, he admits, to someone like Riley who didn't grow up in Black Harbor. But he took it himself, as an elective back in the day, and if Libby derives enjoyment from stuffing cotton into animal hides, he doesn't see the harm in it. There are a lot worse things she could be doing. At least she isn't keeping company with Sari Simons. That girl is trouble.

He almost tells Marnie to not let her stray off-site, but then reconsiders; he's in no position to lecture anyone on keeping track of their children. Besides, on the penultimate Saturday before Halloween, the area will be teeming with kids. It doesn't exactly afford the same opportunity for a killer as a quiet trail or gully.

A lump lodges in his throat as his memory conjures the image of Chloe's black rose petals scattered on the asphalt walking path. His ears burn and his eyes feel raw even though he has yet to shed a tear. He knows he should follow Marnie's advice and get some sleep.

Except, he has something else in mind.

16

LIBBY

"Don't tell your mother."

Libby plunges her blue plastic spoon into a thick swirl of custard to the tune of her dad's warning. They are the only two people on the veranda, seated at an octagon table and bathed in the glow of Ponticelli's fluorescent sign that boasts the flavor of the day: PUMPKIN SPICE CHEESE-CAKE.

He only says it for good measure; he knows she knows better. Just as Libby knows why they eat their ice cream out here, chilled from the inside out, instead of getting it to go on the way to the Compound—easier to destroy the evidence. It isn't she who will get Dr. Mom's lecture about her weight or the unnecessary sugar intake, it's her dad.

Libby drags a finger across her lips, pulling an imaginary zipper, to give him peace of mind. She won't tell.

"Good girl," he says, and despite the cold, Libby feels her cheeks warm. Moments alone with her dad are rare. Moments of her receiving praise from him are rarer still. It isn't that he doesn't love her. It's just that they have very little in common. He connected better with her brothers growing up for obvious reasons—they're all men, for one, and two, they all have "normal" interests, such as computers and baseball and searing steaks on a grill. They even look like him, sharing a strong jaw and high cheekbones, a mouth that either curves into a severe, con-templative frown or a sincere smile.

Libby has none of these attributes. At fifty, her dad looks like he's carved from marble. She looks down and can't deny the fact that her gut resembles a roll of raw bread dough, the way it rests atop her jeans. She's soft.

Libby takes another bite of custard. It's rich and creamy, fragrant with nutmeg and cinnamon and everything that makes pumpkin spice. She catches her father's eye. He grins, mischief dancing in his eyes. She grins back.

For all their differences, Libby has even less in common with her mom. She's rigid and petite, beautiful and angular. While her brothers are a perfect blend of both of their parents, Libby cannot understand how her mom plus her dad equals her. More than once, she's legitimately wondered if she was switched at birth.

"Listen." Her dad's voice pulls her back to the here and now. "I know you're sixteen and you think you're invincible . . ."

Libby feels her brows knit, like someone is pinching the skin between them.

". . . and your mom and I don't want you to stop living your life and having fun and whatnot. But you have to be on high alert, okay, Lib?"

Okay, Lib? Her lips move silently in sync with his. She nods to show she understands, but continues to watch his mouth, anticipating what he might say next.

"Libby, look at me."

Her jaw tightens. She drags her gaze up to meet her father's eyes.

"Someone is out there killing girls your age."

Girls. He said *killing girls.* Plural. Dimples stipple her chin. She takes a breath and scrapes another spoonful of custard. "I don't exactly fit the bill, Dad." Hearing the statement as it leaves her lips, it almost sounds as if she's pouting. Like she's not good enough to be killed like straight-A-student Madison Caldwell or Little Miss Steal-the-Show, Chloe Winthorp.

He obviously believes Chloe is dead, then. Is that what her mother believes, too? And yet, how many times already has Libby heard her mom comforting Rowan, assuring her that they will bring Chloe home?

She never specified dead or alive, she supposes.

Semantics.

"What do you mean, you don't 'fit the bill'? Those girls were sixteen, Libby, like you. They went to Monroe Academy—like you—and lived on Belgrave Circle—again, like you."

Fifteen, she thinks, but doesn't correct him. Born at the end of August, she's the oldest girl in her class. More than once, she's wished her parents would have sent her to school a year earlier. Maybe then she'd be able to blend a little better, though she doesn't know that a year would make all that much difference. Kids are mean in any grade. But, being that much closer to graduation by now would have been nice.

Libby stabs her spoon into her custard. It's softened too much to hold it upright. The utensil slowly, pathetically falls forward until it rests against the edge of the plastic dome lid. She sighs and straightens her posture. She fixes her father with a serious stare. "Those girls were a lot smaller than me, Dad. Easily overpowered." She pauses and looks down at her soupy ice cream, her appetite gone. "For once, me being fat plays to my advantage."

"Honey, you're not fat. Please don't—"

"—tell it like it is?" Libby finishes his sentence for him. "Mom's right. Don't think I can't hear you two through my bedroom floor."

Her dad's face falls. A muscle in his neck twitches as he, no doubt, replays the most recent argument he and her mom had over their teenage daughter's weight. No more salty snacks in the house. No added sugars. No soda. *Look at the nutrition label, Daniel. The first listed ingredient is corn syrup!*

Restrict. Restrict. Restrict.

The only snacks at the Lucas household are unsalted chickpea puffs and bags of apple slices. She honestly cannot remember the last time she had pizza that wasn't made with cauliflower crust or drank something that wasn't sweetened with agave or stevia.

The Winthorps always have the best snacks. Pudding cups and cheesy popcorn. Cherry Pepsi. And all the cereal she and Chloe could eat. How many evenings in the past month alone had they carried bowls of Count Chocula up to her room and sat pretzel-legged on her bed, eating and watching *Friends*?

They call me Neck Roll at school, Libby almost tells him, but she thinks better of it. She will see her peers soon enough as they all huddle into the haunted house together. All she wanted was to enjoy a clandestine cup of custard with her dad and she just ruined it by bringing up her weight. She hates whenever her mom does this, and now she's gone and done it herself.

But he brought it up, didn't he? He made it seem like she could be a plausible next target for whoever killed Madison and Chloe. How little he knows about the girls in the neighborhood—including his own daughter, she thinks a little guiltily.

They finish their custard and discard their cups in the overflowing garbage bin. It's a quiet drive the rest of the way to the Compound, with Libby's dad speaking only to tell her to make sure her "Find My iPhone" feature is activated and to text him when she's ready to leave.

Now, she waves as he pulls away in his black sedan. She knows he will just go park in the lot and read his Kindle. As soon as she turns, her personal space is invaded by a face covered in white, cracking paint. Eyes red and black, like a pair of bull's-eyes, severed by matted tendrils of polyester hair. The colored contacts are a nice touch, she muses as the ghoul stalks off on stilts that make them over seven feet tall; the eyes are usually a dead giveaway.

The air is thick and smells like rotten eggs. It clung to her as soon as she got out of the car, permeating her hair and clothes. A fog of fake smoke obscures the grounds, but she can see the haunted house complex just ahead, a line snaking out from it like a tentacle or a tongue. Strobes flash, elongating shadows.

Her heart skips. Reeves Singh is in that line.

There are only two kids behind him. Libby jogs to the end, confident she can squish in among his group. The flannel tied around her waist waves behind her like a cape. Catching her breath, she nonchalantly positions herself beside them as a bloodcurdling scream tears from the entrance. The people closest back up like a herd of sheep, as though whatever elicited such terror is coming for them next.

Reeves talks to his friends as if she isn't there. In her sixteen years on this planet, Libby has learned one defining truth about herself, which is that she is an oxymoron. Fat *and* invisible.

It makes eavesdropping easy.

". . . can't pin anything on you," Kayden Thompson says. "So you got in an argument, so what?"

Reeves shoves his hands in his jeans pockets. He heaves a loud sigh that rattles from his chest. He's probably been crying a fair amount. Madison was his girlfriend. He loved her once, even if they fought a lot. "It was just . . . bad timing."

He shakes his head.

"You don't think they're looking into you as, like, an accomplice?" asks Derek Janssen. "Like maybe Chloe wanted Madison dead and you helped?"

Listening to her own hypothesis being spoken aloud by someone else, Libby feels validated. Perhaps there had been something between Reeves and Chloe. Just hearing the way he says her name hints at some stowed-away emotion, and Chloe had mentioned a crush, once.

Reeves shrugs. "They didn't say that, but . . ."

Kayden snorts. "As if they'd tell you."

"Especially if you're a suspect," adds Derek.

Reeves appears to shrink at the word "suspect."

The line moves. They shuffle forward. A demonic clown cuts through, forcing them to abruptly stop. Libby stands on tiptoes to peer at the bobbing heads, and imagines them all to be apples in a barrel waiting to be sucked up by the mouth of some giant monster. Any minute now, a giant Cyclops will take the top off this tent like lifting the lid off a kettle and sink his teeth into one of them. She notices Sari Simons's Afro perched atop her signature camouflage jacket and cosmological backpack. Who is she with? She squints to see and bumps into the boy in front of her.

Reeves turns. "Oh, hey, Libby." He tries to smile politely, but it's obscured behind a mask of melancholy.

"Hi," she mumbles, and immediately realizes she spoke the word into her chest.

"You come with anyone?" Reeves asks, his eyes automatically scanning the crowd.

"Oh, yeah. My cousin is just, um, in the bathroom."

"Who's your cousin?" pesters Derek.

"She doesn't go to our school," says Libby. She catches a surreptitious glance exchanged between the boys, but they don't press. They might suspect her of lying, but good luck proving it.

The line moves forward again. "Better tell your 'cousin' to shit or get off the pot, Neck Roll," Kayden jeers. His last syllable is cut short when Reeves elbows him in the ribs.

Attempting to read Reeves's lips, she can't quite make out what he says to him. But it looks something like, *Leave it be.*

She almost allows a small smile to creep out, when she suddenly wonders whether or not the "it" Reeves was referring to was the situation itself, or her.

Semantics.

Sticks and stones.

They're all the same.

Another shriek hurls toward them. It's so loud, Libby swears it blows her hair in front of her face. Instinctively, she huddles closer to Reeves. When they plunge inside the ramshackle building, he lets her clutch a handful of his jacket so she doesn't get lost in the pitch black.

The temperature plummets a whole ten degrees, if not more. She went spelunking once, with her parents on a family vacation to Mexico. It feels a little like that, with the cold, dead air and the inability to see your hand if you hold it two inches in front of your face.

"Shit, it's dark!" Kayden commentates.

"Thank you, Captain Obvious," scoffs Derek.

A door slams. Libby's ears perk. She clings a little closer to Reeves as the two boys in front jump. A sibilant hiss swims through the air, raising the hairs on the back of her neck.

"Sssss . . ." goes the noise in the dark. "Sssssstay with ussss . . ."

"Forever! Forever! Forever!" comes a singsong chant.

They turn a corner into a dimly lit room where porcelain dolls have come to life. One has her face cracked down the middle. Another is missing an eye. "Come play with me!" She dances over to Libby. Her dress is torn and bloodstained. A teddy bear's head hangs from a rope around her neck. "What's your name, ssssweetheart?"

Libby shakes her head.

"It's Libby!" shouts Kayden.

"Libby! Libby!" The dolls begin to march and sing. "Libby's going to stay with us forever! Come back, Libby! Libby!"

It's more disturbing than it is scary. Still, Libby holds tightly to Reeves. He doesn't seem to mind. Rather, he seems relieved about the fact that he isn't bringing up the rear, his back exposed.

Somewhere in another room, the whine of a chain saw severs the air. Libby hurries forward, desperate to keep up with the boys. They make their way through the haunted labyrinth, wandering into a cellblock where undead prisoners drag their shackles and rap their chains against metal bars. Next, a movie theater shows a black-and-white zombie film to an audience of corpses who suddenly stand up and begin traipsing after them.

"Run!" Kayden yells.

He takes off, Derek hot on his heels.

"Come on!" Reeves grabs Libby's wrist. It's the closest thing she's ever experienced to holding hands, except for the nights she and Chloe lay in bed and made up stories about Franklin the ghost. Reeves's hand is cold, but warmth emanates through his grip. A shiver shoots up her spine as the chain saw gives another shriek. It sounds like the night is unzipping itself.

They come to a screeching halt at the edge of a precipice. The drop could only be a couple of feet, but with shadows as dark as an oil slick, it feels vast. A swinging bridge stretches across it. Suspended above are dismembered body parts drenched in fake blood.

Boards creak when Derek steps onto it. Kayden follows. Libby ducks to avoid a bloodied torso swinging her way when suddenly, a hulking figure appears at the other end of the bridge, chain saw wielded overhead. The ground falls away beneath her as he steps all his weight onto it.

"Go back! Go back!" one of the boys cries.

Libby scrambles backward and feels solid ground beneath her again as she jumps back onto the precipice.

"This way!" Reeves yanks her to the left. They run through a mesh tarp that reeks of mildew and old spray paint. The cacophony from the swinging bridge fades. The temperature drops another ten degrees.

"Is this still part of the attraction?" Libby wonders aloud. Just a little way ahead, a red EXIT sign glows. She catches a glimpse of Reeves. Sweat drips from his dark curls and shines on his forehead. She can feel her own perspiration beading above her lip. Her shirt sticks to her back.

"I think so?" Reeves goes to explore. Gravel crunches under his sneakers.

"Watch out!" Libby pushes him back a step before he trips over a dummy. It's grotesque with its eyes gouged out, mouth open in mid-scream.

Then she notices the camouflage jacket and the blue flower barrette.

17

AXEL

Riley lies on her back, Axel between her legs. His hands are on her hips, her ankles wrapped around his torso. She rises in a crunch position and sweeps his left hand away. It slaps the mat as he falls forward, into her, and in a fluid motion, she releases her ankles and snakes an arm over his shoulder and under. With her right hand, she grabs her own left forearm, drops her hips, and pulls his arm tight against her chest. His face grinds into the mat that smells of cleaning chemicals and sweat. He fights to straighten his elbow, to escape the pain that's burning in his shoulder, but she curls her hand and twists. She recrosses her legs, securing him in a traditional kamura—also known as a double-joint arm lock.

He taps.

Now, he sits on his knees, facing her, fighting to catch his breath. "That was much better," he says, finally.

Riley is stronger than she looks. While not necessarily a petite woman, she is tall and lean. A sprinter in her college days, she's a 130-pound bullet of sinew and muscle. "Thanks," she says, breathing hard. "I misplaced my thumb early on, should have been pressing it into your arm from the beginning, but . . ."

"But you corrected it, and that's what matters."

Riley is one of only two female practitioners at Silva's Jiujitsu Academy. She's vastly outnumbered, but as a double minority at the police department—female and Black—she's no stranger to it. She drags the sleeve of her gi across her chin to catch the sweat. "You want to switch?"

Axel smiles and holds up one finger. "Give me a second, I'm old." He flashes her a self-deprecating smile.

Riley rolls her eyes and delivers a friendly punch to his shoulder. This is her twelfth year in the sport; she's competing for her black belt next month. It was she who got Axel into it. She invited him to enroll when he left Patrol and came upstairs, and years later, he finally took her up on it. He's a blue belt now. Not awful for six years of training, but nothing to write home about, either. He'd be further along if he wasn't constantly ditching practice for a major crime incident, or hunting down killers. Not that Riley didn't do the same, but she doesn't have a family to absorb the rest of her time and attention. The gym is her second home, the bureau her first. Or the lighthouse, since the VCTF moved out there.

If we find the killer, we find Chloe. The memory of Kole's hard-edged voice melts into the youthful soprano of Sari Simons saying, *Mr. Winthorp . . . I'm afraid your daughter is going to kill me next.* The thoughts race separately on an infinity knot–shaped track in his mind until they collide.

If we find the killer, we find Chloe.

But what if they are one and the same?

No. He shakes his head violently. Chloe is not a killer.

"You okay?"

Riley noticed. Of course she noticed. "Yeah, just . . . had some sweat in my eye." With a grunt, Axel lowers himself onto his back, trading places with Riley. She kneels between his legs, and opens her mouth to speak. He knows what she's going to say before she says it. Years' worth of long nights of searching residences and guarding prisoners at the hospital together will make you that way.

It's those same long nights spent on watch together that stir up rumors. While he'd like to think that the police department is comprised of rational-minded individuals, not one of them can seem to rationalize the fact that his and Riley's relationship is anything but romantic. Friendly, yes. Trusting, yes. But romantic? Never. He loves Rowan. Always has, and always will.

But lately he's begun to wonder if Rowan hasn't caught a whiff of the rumors. She works closely with the people spreading them, after all. He feels it in her sideways glances sometimes, when he comes home later than expected or grabs his gym bag. He's considered bringing it up, getting ahead of her concerns by addressing them point-blank and reassuring her that she has nothing to worry about, and yet, he knows that will only make him look guilty.

"So, what's the deal with Sari Simons? She telling the truth?"

Dread draws his muscles tight. They don't usually talk shop while sparring, but time is of the essence. Back-seat quarterbacks would criticize them for sparring in the midst of a homicide investigation, but Axel needs to blow off steam and get his head right after . . . everything.

The scare with Rowan.

The obituary she's apparently kept after all this time.

And what Sari Simons told him just a few hours ago. How she and Madison started the rumor about Chloe sleeping with the drama teacher. How there had been bad blood between the girls in the weeks leading up to Madison's death. And how, now, she's afraid she'll be the next to die.

"About what?" he asks.

"All of it," Riley says. She inhales to catch her breath. "It isn't a virus. Being exposed to a murder victim doesn't mean you're gonna get it next."

He and Riley drove Sari home after the interview. It appeared she was telling the truth about her father being away at training. No one was there except for a cat that sprang effortlessly onto the back of the couch and meowed at them from the other side of the picture window. Sari keyed her way into the back door. It yawned to reveal a dark, vacant entryway.

"You shouldn't be alone," Riley said. "You have any family you can stay with? An aunt, or . . . ?"

"They're all back in Florida. I used to stay with Madison whenever he was gone, but . . ." She re-shouldered her backpack, the straps hanging down and grazing the sides of her thighs.

Axel couldn't meet Sari's gaze, then. He stared down at the scuff marks on his shoes. She was in danger, maybe, because of his daughter—also maybe—and there was nothing he could do to protect her. Her father was out of town, her best friend dead, and there was no place for her to go but remain inside the walls of this cold, uninviting house. She was as safe here as she was anywhere.

"Well . . ." Riley did that thing where she sucked in her lips. "We would advise you to stay inside. Lay low for a couple of days if you can, okay? When will your dad be back?"

"Tomorrow night."

"Okay. We'll plan on making contact with him then. In the meantime, we can send a patrol unit as often as we're able, if that's all right with you?"

Sari nodded. "Yes, thank you."

Axel frowned, fighting a cringe. *As often as we're able* might easily mean once or twice. It was Saturday and drawing close to darkness. Black Harbor could either be dead quiet on nights like this, or Armageddon.

Riley gave Sari her business card. "Call if you need anything, okay?"

The girl nodded again, her tight, springy curls bouncing.

It seems a lifetime has passed since then. "I think so," Axel says after a beat, finally answering Riley's question. "Otherwise, I don't know why else she'd incriminate herself . . . for starting that rumor."

Riley scoffs. "Maybe to incriminate your daughter?"

"You think she's lying?" He locks his ankles around her torso, squeezing below her ribs. She shoots her left arm toward his neck to grab the collar of his gi. He weaves his right arm underneath and twists into a side-crunch, locking Riley's arm in place. She taps the mat.

They sit, facing each other. While he hates to default to Kole's coldhearted philosophy that everybody lies, the fact that Sari could have been lying creates a pinprick of hope.

Chloe is not a killer.

"It's just . . ." Riley chooses her words carefully. "The girls around here seem to have a flair for the dramatic."

She's right. It isn't the first time Axel and Riley have found themselves untangling teenage drama. There was that incident on Hoffman Drive last year that resulted in a near-fatal game of Spin the Bottle when one party broke the bottle over another party's head. That was a doozy and a half to figure out, especially since everyone fled the scene for fear of getting underage drinking tickets, leaving the two violent parties locked in a sudden death struggle.

Not to mention, knowing his own daughter with her method acting and mood swings, Axel cannot disagree. He returns to the rumor. Sleeping with a teacher. Not only could a lie like that have ruined Chloe's reputation, it could have shattered her dream of getting into Juilliard. And consequently, her dream of leaving Black Harbor in the dust.

A sinking realization occurs to him: no wonder she had withdrawn. Dyeing her hair black was just the beginning. She started wearing sweatshirts that were two sizes too large, often sitting on the couch or on her bed with her knees tucked in, head sunk in like a turtle in a shell. She pushed safety pins through her earlobes and listened to music that sounded as though it was recorded in basements with screaming girls and out-of-tune guitars, and whenever he dared to ask if something was wrong, she always gave him the same answer: she was getting into character, doing everything a modern-day Lydia Deetz would do.

For weeks leading up to her disappearance, Chloe had kept up the ruse of the goth character she was portraying so well that Axel and Rowan grew concerned that something sinister might have been going on. Perhaps they should have heeded their instincts.

A ruse. He wishes that's all any of this is. That he will go home after this and Chloe will jump out of a closet and yell, "Boo! I tricked you!" like she used to do when she was young and they played hide-and-seek.

Now she's all grown up and playing a game of killing spree.

No.

Chloe is not a killer.

Chloe is not a killer.

Chloe is not—

"Hey." Riley squeezes his bicep. She waits until he gives her eye contact, then says: "Chloe is out there, Axel. We are going to find her. And there's no fucking way in this hell she's killing off her classmates.

Okay? Sari Simons is going to be just fine. We'll make contact with her dad tomorrow and—"

"Well, well, well, Gordo, look what the street sweeper dragged in. Bueller and Walking Dead have finally decided to show up to class."

Axel hears Orca's wry voice mocking his and Riley's sporadic attendance as of late.

The jiujitsu community is relentless when it comes to naming its members. Despite their often derogatory nature, the nicknames and the anonymity they afford is what Axel loves most about this place. The ability to shed your hard outer shell and leave it at the door like a discarded suit of armor to grapple barefoot and barefisted with others who are doing the same. They exonerate themselves from the weight of their public personas, whether they be janitors or CEOs, doctors or homicide detectives. Because at Silva's, who you are outside of these walls holds no weight whatsoever inside them.

Axel's truancy earns him the parallel to Ferris Bueller, and according to an academy-wide census, Riley resembles the machete-wielding character from *The Walking Dead* series. No matter what sphere she is in, Riley cannot shake the invisible cloak of death. They've called her Riley the Reaper at the police department for as long as he can remember.

"Don't you two ever get tired of each other?" Orca smiles, showing pointed, spaced-apart teeth, thus the moniker. Although he joined the academy after Axel, he's already a purple belt with two stripes.

Gordo used to be more portly, which is why his name means "fat" in Portuguese. He might be a barber, a suspicion formed from the straight razor tattoo on the inside of his wrist, but for all Axel knows, he could be a cop from another jurisdiction.

No, not a cop. Cops can always sniff out other cops. It's how they hold themselves, the ego that puffs out their chests and makes them stand up straight, the unflinching eye contact. Gordo is not a cop. No way, no how.

"Let's have a go," Gordo says to Riley. "One soon-to-be-black-belt to another. You can leave ol' Bueller behind for a roll or two."

Riley starts to look guilty, but Axel nudges her with his foot. If she wants to progress and truly improve her technique, she should spar with someone who knows what he's doing—someone who can live and breathe jiujitsu every waking moment of the day, like Gordo. Not someone who has to leave early every night to answer the death phone.

Riley leaves with Gordo and Orca, and Axel is glad for the alone time. The truth is, after what Sari told him, he needs a minute to indulge in some serious self-loathing. How could he have let himself get so far out of touch with Chloe? He had no idea she was suffering from such a devastating rumor. Suddenly, his ears burn hot, his hands tighten into fists. He will interview Cutler in the morning. And if there's a shred of truth to the rumor, he'll kill him.

18

ROWAN

Sari Simons is one of those bodies that doesn't look real. It looks like something out of a graphic novel—lying supine and encased in a camouflage jacket, skin pale and dusky. The two front teeth peek out from the edge of the top lip that has lost its color. It doesn't help that the crime scene is a haunted house, wherein Rowan had to trek through a forest of hanging artificial body parts to get here.

Kole wasn't exaggerating about the eyes. They're gone, a pair of gaping cavities in the middle of the girl's skull. She crouches carefully, leans to hover over the victim's face, but everything in her peripheral vision floods her focus. Her gaze flits to footprints and fingerprints and smears of fake blood. Everywhere. *Shit.* With so much scene contamination, they have better odds of winning the lottery than they do of finding the killer's DNA.

As is the nature of all scary things, the place looks less threatening with the lights on. Torn black tarps are draped over plywood partitions, and warnings like TURN AROUND and GET OUT are clearly the work of teenagers. Masks lie on picnic tables, empty and shapeless. A crinkled granola bar wrapper catches the reflection of a strobe light. The cocktail of death and spray paint makes her head swim.

"Will someone pull the plug on that strobe?" she asks. "It's giving me a headache." That isn't the whole truth. It's *worsening* the headache she had before—the one she brought upon herself after a good old-fashioned carbon monoxide poisoning. The same one she was so close to sleeping off before her phone ripped her out of a REM cycle. Finally, the incessant flashing stops.

"Thank you," she breathes.

She closes her eyes and feels them flicker. Just twenty minutes ago, her ringtone woke her up from a dead sleep. She answered the unidentified number to hear Sergeant Kole.

"Winthorp," he growled. "We got another one."

"A what?" *Where was she? Was this one of those lucid nightmares?* She coughed to clear the hoarseness from her voice.

"Another teenage girl. Appears to be a homicide. At the Compound, 216 Pruitt Avenue."

"I'm on my way." She swung her legs over the edge of the couch, disturbing Fry, who leapt onto the floor and sauntered over to his water dish.

"Rowan." His utterance of her first name gave her pause. She was "Winthorp" to most cops, with the exception of Axel, of course.

A long pause followed, until she said, "Nik?"

Kole exhaled, causing the line to crackle. "We've never seen one like this before."

Now, she stands inside the shell of an old warehouse, her shoes and shins caked in gravel dust, staring at a corpse whose eyes have been plucked out of its skull. The sight can only be described as horrifying and gruesome. Rowan whips around, slamming into someone.

The woody, amber scent of Axel's cologne mixed with sweat infiltrates her senses. It soothes her, and for a moment, she dreams she could slip back into sleep. She wants to bury her face in his sweatshirt, feel his lips plant a kiss on her forehead, but this is neither the time nor place.

"I know," he says quietly, shaking his head.

"Did you find them?" Rowan asks.

"Her eyes?"

"Not yet." Entering their vicinity, Riley answers for him.

"An animal could have taken off with them," suggests Axel, and Rowan agrees. Coyotes have been known to lurk around these parts. They're mangy things, half the size of coyotes elsewhere and starved. But, with the Compound teeming with people for the Halloween season, she doubts any coyotes would have gotten too close. Not to mention, if that were the case, there would most likely be other injuries to the body. Bite marks, scratches—of which Sari Simons has none.

"Or the killer did," she offers.

Gloved up, Rowan lifts the girl's wrist. It's still warm and flaccid. Watching her, she imagines she can see the muscles stiffening, the fingers of her left hand curling into a claw as rigor encroaches. The body won't turn cold for another six or seven hours yet, though. We lose a degree and a half of body temperature for the first hour after death, and one degree for every hour thereafter, until we match the atmospheric temperature. Textbook, of course, Rowan thinks, as she takes the girl's reading. There are factors that can manipulate the numbers, such as dying on a cold slab of concrete or decomposing under a beating sun. Neither applies here.

She reads the thermometer. The digital numbers show 97.3. Assuming Sari started out with a base temperature of 98.6, she couldn't have died more than an hour ago.

Rowan touches the victim's neck for a pulse, despite knowing there won't be one. "Time of death . . ." She turns her wrist to read her watch. "Saturday, October 21, 2250 hours. I don't suppose the ice cream scoop was left behind, was it?" She says it to no one in particular, and yet a retort cuts through the crowd of sworn personnel.

"Shut up, that isn't what he used." She hears the whisper of Kole's leather bomber jacket as he bends toward the corpse for a closer look. "Is it?"

"I mean . . . it's possible," she says, noting the lack of blood indicates the injuries are—

"Postmortem?"

She nods.

"Fuck," says Kole, and Rowan knows it is not because the postmortem mutilation means that Sari Simons did not suffer the torture of her organs being carved out of her skull, but because he knows that just two nights ago, another girl was found with her teeth knocked out in a manner that was also determined to be postmortem.

He points his chin at the mutilated body. "What other marks does she have?"

Sliding her fingers under the collar of Sari's camo jacket, she exposes the marks she feared would be there. "These are perimortem." She points to a graze on the girl's neck. It looks like a burn, almost, or—

"Rope burn?" Kole echoes her next thought.

But Rowan is already shaking her head. "There aren't any ligature marks, though."

She leans over the body to peek at the other side where a corresponding injury glares at her. Extracting a ruler from her bag, she measures each abrasion. "About an inch and three quarters," she mutters, then palpates the throat. "Hyoid bone is still intact."

"So, she wasn't strangled?"

Rowan shrugs. "I didn't say that." She recognizes the landed-on cause of death for Madison Caldwell. The marks on Sari Simons's neck look similar, but are they the same? She will have to compare photos back at the office.

She continues to deliver her report in real time, gently turning the victim's head from side to side. "And . . . the eyes, obviously, they're—"

"MIA," offers Kole.

"Yes." Continuing to deliver her report, she leans over the corpse and peers into the bloodless orbital cavities. Her gaze roams the areas around them, then. "Petechiae," she notes, waving an index finger over the jaw, near the ear. "Madison Caldwell had that, too."

Kole nods. He will no doubt have seen the preliminary autopsy report from this morning. Therefore, he will know that the cause of Madison Caldwell's death was strangulation and that she had not one, but two postmortem injuries: the teeth, and the word carved inside her mouth.

BITCH.

It's all Rowan sees when she closes her eyes now, as though the five letters are scored on the insides of her eyelids. Although she's loath to admit it, she is too afraid to peel down the dead girl's lip and see if another ugly word is carved into the soft meat.

Why? Because she might recognize Chloe's handwriting?

Kole makes a slow circle around the corpse, like a wolf surveying a fresh kill. "So, he grabbed her . . . probably from over here." He walks to a faux wall and kicks it. The black tarp bows inward. "Then he dragged her back here. Strangled her. And scooped out her eyes." Kneeling now, he looks up at Rowan. His irises are cold and colorless. They pin her in place and stare at her so intensely, she swears he can see her skeleton.

Her heart crawls into her throat. She draws her hand up to her neck to hide her quickening pulse from him.

"But with what?" Kole persists. "An ice cream scoop would be too dull."

"I was mostly kidding about that," admits Rowan. A poor time for a joke, she knows, but, call it a coping mechanism or whatever you will, at this point, morbid humor is just part of her makeup.

"Mostly," he repeats, sounding thoughtful and not sarcastic as she might have expected. "'Tis the season for sharp objects, right? Pumpkin carving and all that. Everyone's got knives and shit."

"It had to have a good edge," she says, thinking out loud. "Whatever instrument the killer used had to be . . . made for this kind of thing."

"Like a surgical tool?"

"That would be my guess."

"And my guess would be he didn't really know what he was doing." He points with a black gloved hand. "That's a hack job if I ever saw one."

Rowan follows his finger that points at the torn flesh around the injuries. "Or they were working fast."

"Or that." He sighs, his breath issuing a plume of vapor. "Ah fuck, Rowan, why do we live here?"

"No better place to be if you're a cop, right?" Rowan repeats a line she used to hear from Axel, whenever he'd come home all electrified after making an arrest or testifying on the stand. Those days are long over. Now, he's utterly defeated. A husk of the man she married.

"I used to think like that, but now I don't know," admits Kole. "Dead kids everywhere you turn. Not my cup of tea." He sighs again, and draws himself back up to his full height. "So, why'd he take them? A ritual? Something satanic, maybe?"

"Revenge."

Both Kole and Rowan step aside to give Axel the floor.

"Revenge?" Kole raises a brow.

Axel doles Rowan an apologetic look, then explains to them both that, mere hours ago, Sari Simons had sat in Interview Room #3 and confessed to staging and circulating a photo that, for all intents and purposes, destroyed Chloe's reputation at Monroe Academy. "They stole Chloe's shirt out of her bedroom," he narrates, and Rowan feels a quiet rage simmering inside her. ". . . stuffed it in the drama teacher's bag." He goes on to share what Sari told him at the end of her interview. "She said, 'I'm afraid your daughter is going to kill me next.'" He pauses to draw in a deep breath.

"And you let her go?" Kole's voice crescendos with each word. "To, what, just wander around town? Did you at least tell her not to get murdered?"

"We took her home. Her dad's gone for military training until tomorrow night. She had nowhere else to go. We had Patrol checking on her every couple hours. Last they reported, she was at home, alive and well, when they stopped around 1900 hours. Must've slipped out after that."

Kole splays his hand over his eyes and squeezes his temples. Either he's suddenly experiencing shooting pains in his skull or he simply finds this conversation excruciating. As badly as he might wish for there to be a rebuttal, however, Rowan knows there isn't one. With no family in Black Harbor, and her best friend dead, where, but home, would Sari have gone? They cannot keep her at the police station. They're not set up for it, and besides, they have a murder and missing persons investigation to conduct, not to mention all the other crimes that don't magically stop, like turning off a faucet.

Rowan runs through everything Axel has just shared. "You think that Chloe had something to do with this? Or Mr. Cutler?"

Axel clenches his jaw as all eyes land on him. His expression is glazed as though he's set himself on cruise control. He has split himself in half; the detective searching for an answer remains out front while the father searching for his daughter disappears somewhere inside of him. He wets his lips. "Maybe both," he answers. "Why else would it be these two girls, so soon after that rumor was started?" The silence that falls is suffocating. Finally, he adds: "It's also possible that Cutler has Chloe and he's . . ."

"Saving her for later?" Rowan finishes when he can't.

"Right."

"What about our witnesses?" interrupts Kole. "The kids who discovered her?"

"They didn't see anyone," Axel says. "But . . . Libby said Sari had a backpack with her."

As Kole turns to confirm there's no backpack anywhere near the body, Rowan's brows knit together. "Libby? As in Marnie's Libby?"

"And Reeves Singh."

"Oh fuck you," says Kole, turning about face. "Reeves Singh found her?"

"And Libby Lucas. Our neighbor." He draws an imaginary line between himself and Rowan, who checks her phone. There are three missed calls from Marnie and a text: Headed to the Compound. Are you out there already? Tell Lib and Daniel I'm OMW.

"Shit." Rowan's gaze ricochets off the walls like a racquetball. "Marnie's here?"

Kole looks from Axel to Rowan. "So you know her well."

"She's my best friend's daughter," says Rowan. "We've been neighbors for . . . sixteen years?" Yes, Libby was a newborn when they moved next door.

"Good." Kole tilts his head toward the exit, where Reeves and Libby both wait on the other side with Investigator Riley. "Go find out what she's lying about."

Rowan watches Axel's face scrunch in confusion, and feels hers mirroring it. "Why do you assume she's lying?" she asks.

"Because everybody lies, Winthorp. Her withholding information is obstruction, same as a bold-faced lie. She's at the scene of this crime with the BFF of Thursday night's dead girl. She lives ten feet away from your daughter, who's gone missing. You can't tell me she doesn't know more than she's letting on."

Rowan flinches at the sensation of something tugging at her heartstrings. *Missing.* Chloe is still missing, a mystery, and no one but Rowan can fathom why this has happened.

It's karma. Comeuppance. The universe teaching her a lesson.

Earlier today, she sat in her poisoned car, lamenting over the obituary of a girl long dead. A girl she killed.

An eye for an eye. That's the only reason Chloe is gone.

She took someone else's daughter. Now the universe has taken hers.

It isn't Libby that Kole's got dead to rights. It's her. She is a liar for this information she's withholding and yet, it will do nothing for the investigation besides close the lid on it. Even if this is all because of her, it doesn't change the fact that she is desperate to find her daughter, karma be damned.

The word "revenge" is bitter on her tongue. She turns to Axel, shaking her head. "You think Chloe did this." The rage inside her burns hotter. "You actually think our daughter—our fifteen-year-old, one-hundred-pound-soaking-wet daughter—killed her friends."

"They weren't her friends." Deep lines of latitude crease his forehead. "Friends don't . . . steal each other's clothes and spread rumors like that."

"Oh, okay, I get it. Chloe was a victim of bullying; therefore, she must be a murderer. Real good detective work, Axel. Tell me, does the City give you a bonus for jumping to irrational conclusions?"

Kole steps between them, but Rowan leans back and walks around him.

"I just . . ." Axel swallows, gathering his bearings. "Sari Simons told me she thought Chloe would kill her next. And here she is . . . less than eight hours later." His chest heaves. His breath is ragged. "Is it possible that just maybe, Chloe could have—"

"Don't," she warns.

He strides toward her, closing the distance between them. The air around them is charged. "Rowan, listen to me!" Axel grabs her bicep, forcing her to look at him. *Here it is,* she thinks, as Axel opens his mouth to speak again. His incessant need to solve this case trumps protecting their daughter's memory. He's throwing her under the fucking bus. Accusing her of murder when she is not here to defend herself.

Because she's fucking dead.

Oh God. The trueness of that sentiment has all the force of that hypothetical bus careening into her. Chloe is dead, her body buried beneath someone's porch or hidden away in the one place they haven't yet looked.

Her bottom lip quivers. A whimper escapes.

"Row, the truth is that our daughter is out here, and she could be ki—"

She slaps him. The crack is satisfying, like an ax splitting a block of wood. Her whole palm tingles.

He lets her go, pressing his hand to his cheek as though to keep it from falling off his face.

"Chloe is dead!" she yells, and is mortified by the screech of her voice. She doesn't recognize it as her own. It's shrill and desperate, and more than a little psychotic. "Whoever is killing these girls is sending us a message!"

"A message for what, Rowan?"

That is the ever-burning question. The one whose flames lick the back of her skull, charring her skeleton while she sleeps, while she eats, every waking and sleeping moment since Chloe has been gone. Turning her into smoke and ash with a silhouette so fragile, the barest touch would cause her to splinter, to snap like a piece of used-up charcoal.

She knows the answer. She's just too afraid to speak it. Saying it makes it real, makes it something she cannot rescind or redact like blacking out names in a police report. It doesn't matter, anyway, because the truth is that, regardless of what human guise this killer may wear, it's karma.

Karma killed her daughter.

Because Rowan killed someone else's.

"Come on." Kole's voice is quiet, but stern. He touches her arm and she swats him away. Stomping toward her kit, she yanks out a polyethylene bag and lays it on the cement. There's only one saving grace for tonight, and that's zipping up the victim before she gets too stiff.

SUNDAY, OCTOBER 22

19
AXEL

Light pollution blots out the stars. Axel's gaze cuts to his rearview mirror where he watches twin clouds of steam spew from the power plant's cooling towers at the edge of the county. They curl and twist in a whimsical dance before dissolving, the way snowflakes melt on asphalt. The sky is a bruise-colored backdrop, torn at the edges by the tree line's craggy silhouette.

The cloud factory—that's what Chloe used to call it. Whenever they passed it while driving home, she would hold her arm out the window, point like E.T., and draw, as though she could command the direction of the vapor. For years she believed she could, believed that it was she who created the chubby Pegasus and the tombstone shapes. When did she stop?

Probably when he and Rowan stopped paying attention. Over the years, they've both gotten so wrapped up in their own work that he wonders, now, if Chloe ever felt abandoned. She must have. There's a fresh death at least once a week in Black Harbor, which means, for Rowan, that there are autopsies to attend and reports to write. For him and the Violent Crime Task Force, the crimes they investigate span every brutal variety, from gang fights to civil disputes turned deadly; shootings, stabbings, you name it. And they are constant.

He is never home. That's what he realized sometime around

midnight when he lay on the floor of the VCTF office, determined to get a few winks on a makeshift bed of Mylar blankets, his jacket wadded up for a pillow. Even when he is home, physically, he isn't present; his mind always has a million tabs open, mentally crawling through nooks and kinks and crannies of whatever cases he's currently working.

Which was why he couldn't lie there a second longer. If ever there is a case to work himself to the bone on, it's this one. His daughter is out there, somewhere. She could be in danger, or worse—dead.

With the blankets rolled up and tucked beneath his arm, Axel paused on his way to the cabinet. There was a light on in the old tannery. Apparently, whoever bought it was getting an early start on restoring it. Or maybe they're living in it?

He squinted and let himself be lured toward the window as if by some magnetic force. Here in the lighthouse, three stories above the ground, he could see the rooftop where it appeared renovations were already underway. Even with his eyes having adjusted to the dark and what faint light shone from the tannery's window, it was hard to discern exactly what it was, but it appeared to be a greenhouse or garden in the making.

That would be wise, he thought. Some sort of sustainable, eco-friendly initiative would probably go a long way as far as securing grants for whatever project the new owner has in mind. If only they could find a way to tack some solar panels onto the PD—maybe then they could get a dime to spruce the place up. At the very least, they need a new boiler system. The building is constantly having hot flashes, ice-cold one moment and stifling the next. Not that he and the rest of the VCTF have to deal with that much anymore.

These thoughts all followed him down the stairs and out to his vehicle, five miles down the road, to where he now sits. And watches. His eyes drift back to where they were before the clouds in the rearview wafted into his peripheral vision. The house across the street is a black hole, pitch dark until suddenly, a light flips on. Axel adjusts in the driver's seat, leans forward for a slightly closer look. He has studied the residence on real estate websites enough to know that this is the master bedroom. He waits. In a moment, someone passes in front of the window. It's a man, judging by the build.

Cutler.

Fifty-one years old. Married with one child—a daughter who's grown and out of the house. Caucasian. Occupation: teacher at Monroe Academy.

More specifically, he was Chloe's drama teacher. And maybe more.

Her confidante.

Her co-conspirator.

Her captor.

Axel watches to see if a second person rises and meanders in front of the window. According to the background check he conducted in Onyx, Cutler is married, but Axel knows as well as anyone that what Onyx says and what actually is are sometimes two very different things. Cutler is married on paper, perhaps, but his wife may be living somewhere else. Not that he would blame her. In fact, he wishes he could talk to her, find out what she knows about her husband's doings.

He's been watching the place for the past two hours, ever since he woke up with a start after falling asleep at his desk, the space bar imprinted on his forehead. He couldn't go home last night, not when he and Rowan are so divided. She's on one precipice, and he's on another, an ocean of "what ifs" roiling between them.

In his mind, there are only two distinct possibilities: either Mark Cutler killed Madison Caldwell and Sari Simons alone, or Mark Cutler killed Madison Caldwell and Sari Simons with Chloe's help.

He knows where Rowan's head is at. She would rather believe their daughter to be dead than guilty. But, at least if she's guilty and they find her, they can get her help. No. He's lying to himself and he knows it. He knows what happens to kids like that. She will spend her days sedated and sitting in front of a cement wall, drooling into a Dixie Cup.

That's not the life he dreamed of for his daughter. This isn't the life he dreamed of at all, for any of them.

Axel chews his thumbnail. He drags the sharp edge of it across his lip as he stares intensely at the hunter-green home, as if it might sprout legs and walk off. He bounces his foot. His coffee thermos is empty now, and he has to pee, but he can't leave. Not when Cutler could be coming out any minute.

He bites and rips a small chunk of skin off with his nail. The metallic tang of blood fills his mouth as he continues to watch and stew about his and Rowan's disagreement last night. His cheek stings with the tactile memory of her slap, and yet, that isn't the worst part. The worst part is that he had felt the weight of all her resentment behind it.

It was true that they dreamed of leaving Black Harbor one day. Who didn't? They wanted to live in a place where the crime rate was only average, where cars weren't hot-wired and stolen out of driveways. Somewhere that little girls weren't discarded like broken dolls and murder was kept to a minimum.

Wanting something doesn't mean you can have it, though. Axel learned that during all his years growing up in Rainbow Row with two brothers, a sister, and parents who made just enough between them to keep the lights on and mouths fed. They were all gone, now. His siblings had their own families and lived scattered across the US. His parents were both dead by the time he was thirty. Chloe never knew them.

At the age of twenty-one, he entered the police academy after graduating with a degree in criminal justice from the local community college. He walked a beat for twenty years, responding to domestic abuse calls, dead babies, shots fired, and dog attacks. When Chloe was three, he got promoted upstairs to the Detective Bureau so he could get off nights and start pulling more overtime to keep the family afloat.

Peace and quiet come at a cost. Tuition at Monroe Academy is twenty grand per year, and their mortgage on Belgrave Circle is close to three thousand dollars a month; add taxes and sundry essentials such as groceries, phone bill, internet, and more, and Axel is staring down the barrel of sixty-plus hours a week for the rest of his career.

While they desperately want to leave, they can't afford to, not when he's vested with the City and has several years before he can draw from his pension. Rowan knows this and yet, it never stops her from counting down the days on an imaginary calendar. Sometimes he'll roll over at night and catch her staring up at the ceiling, her eyes vacant, and he swears she's scheming ways to disappear.

It's always the following morning when he wants to tell her to just take Chloe and go. Away from Black Harbor. And when she gets to whatever place finally makes her happy and at peace, to text him the address so he can send a monthly check and visit on holidays—if he can get the time off.

People in Black Harbor have a penchant for murdering one another on holidays.

Despite her knowing that they cannot reasonably leave the crime-ridden city that signs both of their paychecks, Rowan still blames him. The slap said it all, like, *See, I told you we should have left. Now Chloe is gone and it's all your fault.*

She'd slapped him not noticing how close he was to breaking all on his own. Cracking under the pressure of providing for his family—and failing miserably.

He recalls the screenshot on Sari's phone, of Chloe's shirt in a man's messenger bag and the words *Daddy Issues* taunting. Do Chloe's peers really believe that she has daddy issues?

He considers the stereotype: a female needing attention from an older man because she allegedly has a troubled relationship with her own father. And then he thinks of all the times he's picked Chloe up from school and asked about her day, how many evenings they listened to Bon Jovi and CCR on vinyl together. The weekends they spent skipping stones off the pier and walking Fry through the neighborhood. But it had been a long time since they'd done any of that. At least a year for sure, but even before then. When he thinks of his evenings, he sees a faceless suspect sitting at a stainless-steel table in Interview Room #1, the empty stare of a cadaver peppered with bullet holes; he sees negligent caregivers and neighbors of the deceased and the lies that tumble from their lips. When had he let work become more of a priority than his daughter?

The dead can wait. They're not going anywhere. Unfortunately, it's taken him until now to fully comprehend that.

The worst thing about a lie is there's always a kernel of truth to it. Perhaps Chloe had sought comfort in another man, a father figure of sorts. Mr. Cutler was her drama teacher. During the school year, especially during play season, she'd spent more time with him than she had with either Axel or Rowan. Perhaps even more time than either of them realized.

Axel rolls down his window. The early morning air is crisp and cool. His frustration and anxiety begin to evaporate just a little, and then his ears prick to the strange cackling sounds he remembers having heard before. He squints, his eyes roaming Cutler's yard for shadows and silhouettes with their heads thrown back in laughter.

A louder noise booms as the garage door peels upward. Axel watches as the brake lights of an SUV flash red. A blur of sneakers race across the opening as a boy in a blue hockey jersey runs to claim shotgun. A dark-haired man is staring down at something in his hands—keys or a phone, maybe?

Axel opens his door and steps out. The moment he's been waiting for has finally arrived. He slams his door and the sound is masked by the lake slamming into the shoreline less than two blocks away. It swallows the sound of his footsteps, even, but Cutler has already seen him by now.

They make eye contact. Axel stares hard at the man who knows something about his daughter's disappearance. It isn't that cold out, but Cutler totes a navy parka under his arm, rolled like a sleeping bag. His face is pinched, like an invisible hand is twisting his nose, twisting his whole face into a deprecating sneer that Axel can't stand.

"Papa, who—" the boy starts.

"Get in the car, Michael," says Cutler. "I'll be right there."

The boy is obedient. He shuts the vehicle door.

"Your grandson?" Axel asks, even though he knows it is.

"Yes," answers Cutler. Axel steals a few seconds to scrutinize the man's jet-black hair, the wrinkles that fan out from his eyes but are not yet deep creases in his skin. Two longitudinal lines cut across his forehead. He's mapping him, committing his face to memory. File > Save. "Been waiting long?" Cutler juts his chin toward Axel's Impala.

"Long enough to watch a few episodes of *The Wire*," admits Axel.

Cutler doesn't smile or flinch. Instead, he says, "Listen, I know you're here to rough me up about—"

"No one's roughing you up."

"You're here to interrogate me—"

"You're not a suspect. No need for an interrogation."

"—and I already told—"

"Hey!" Axel raises his voice. "Mark, right? I'm not here to interrogate you." He sighs and feels his resolve crumbling. "Father to father, right. Is Michael's mother your daughter?"

Cutler nods.

"If she ever went missing . . . how would you feel? What would you do? You'd look everywhere you could for answers, right? Talk to everyone who knew her to try and piece things together."

Cutler says nothing. His gaze falls on the ground.

Axel can feel the air wicking the moisture from his lips and every inch of exposed skin.

He doesn't want to ask the questions he's about to ask. But he has no choice. He didn't spend the last four hours sitting on this house not to. "Were you close?" The words are awkward, breaking as they leave his tongue. "Chloe was your student. But was she more than that?"

"God no," says Cutler. There's a tinge of disgust in his tone. "Not like—those girls were just making problems for her. With that picture."

"What picture?"

Cutler stares at him, tilts his head. "I'm sure you've got it saved on your camera roll, Detective. No need to play dumb."

"The one of Chloe's shirt sticking out of your messenger bag."

"Yeah, that one." Cutler sighs. "There was nothing lewd or lascivious going on, I promise you. She just used to come talk to me sometimes. During lunch or before class."

This is news to Axel. He imagines his daughter sitting on a desk, swinging her legs back and forth and clutching her books to her chest. She's in her goth getup—plaid skirt and black razed tights, plastic choker slicing her neck. "About what?" he asks.

Cutler shrugs. "Anything. TV shows, what happened in so-and-so's class, things of that nature."

Axel feels his brows inching toward each other. "Why'd she come talk to you? She had friends."

Cutler's mouth curls into a sardonic smile. Axel resists the urge to slap it off. "Friends, sure. The same friends who started that rumor?" Cutler searches his face, his eyes scanning Axel up and down. "Listen." He slips into a softer tone, one he's no doubt used with Chloe. "I think she turned a blind eye sometimes, only because we all, to some degree at least, want to be accepted by our peers. Even if we don't necessarily like them or want to be like them." Cutler pauses, as if deciding whether or not he should go for it. "Walk with me for a second, would ya?"

Axel takes a look around. Cutler's house is sequestered against a backdrop of evergreens. They sway in the wind, their branches reaching toward him like thousands of arms ushering him into their darkness. Had Chloe gone in there? Had she gotten a ride from Cutler after the play, followed him around back like Axel is about to do?

There's a rustling noise, and the sound of quick feet tearing at the dirt. Voices are warbled, like trying to speak underwater, and he recognizes them from when he sat watch the other day.

Curious and a little afraid, if he's being honest, Axel follows Cutler around the side of his house. His heart launches into his throat when he sees it: what looks like a child's playhouse is in the backyard, attached to some kind of man-made enclosure. Chicken wire stretches across each panel. Axel peers inside to see a row of nests.

"I turned Michael's old playhouse into a chicken coop," says Cutler. He says it like a man who doesn't take on a lot of home improvement projects. Like stapling chicken wire to a couple of 2x4s is the epitome of honest work.

"Innovative," notes Axel. "You want me to collect eggs or what?"

Cutler ignores the sarcasm. Instead, he bends down over a five-gallon pail and slides off the board that sits across it.

He watches as Cutler reaches inside it, then, and grabs a chicken by the foot. It's white and speckled with black, with the bluest eye Axel's ever seen. The bird doesn't struggle. It's frozen stiff. "This is Penguin," says Cutler.

"I hate to break it to you, but Penguin's dead."

"Yes, as of yesterday."

"How?" There's a rustling noise, accompanied by the sounds of talons scratching in dirt. Axel looks over at the coop where three white chickens have come out to watch.

Cutler turns the bird in a sort of macabre rotisserie until Axel sees the naked torn flesh. The bloodied hole where the other eye is missing. "You might notice Penguin doesn't look like the others. Chickens aren't the brightest animals, but they noticed it eventually—that she was different—and when they did, they tore her apart."

Axel considers Cutler, this man who holds a dead, mangled chicken upside down with chapped hands. This man whom his daughter had confided in, whom she'd probably spoken to more than she had Axel in the days leading up to her disappearance.

"Jesus, what don't they eat?" Axel asks, noting the skeleton of a watermelon rind and scraps of scrambled eggs.

"I wouldn't fall down in there," warns Cutler. "They'd peck you clean."

"Yeah?"

Cutler shrugs. "It'd take 'em a while, but sure. They're raptors, after all." Then, he does something that makes Axel's stomach turn. He opens the latch and tosses the stiff carcass of Penguin inside. The three hens swarm it.

"You've heard the saying *fox in the henhouse*?" Cutler's voice is muted by the feeding frenzy. "Sometimes the fox is just a distraction. The hens are so concerned with the proverbial predator, they fail to recognize that the real danger is among themselves."

Over the cacophony of the chickens, Axel can barely hear the sound of tires shushing on the pavement. Someone has parked on the asphalt driveway. Assuming it's Cutler's wife, he waits for the sound of a woman's voice, but hears a deeper one with a serrated edge instead.

"Mark, good to see you again." Suddenly, Nikolai Kole stands shoulder-to-shoulder with Axel and gives him a less-than-friendly nudge. "Time to go."

Forge Bridge is a charred, blackened skeleton that stretches from bank to bank. There's no telling how it begins or ends. Evergreens shoot up on either side. Against a pale sky, their needles look like ink from a blown-out tattoo. Aspens with titian tops add splotches of lurid color to the landscape. In a week they'll be naked, their trunks stripped to resemble bones that have been licked clean by Black Harbor.

Axel sits in the passenger seat of Kole's SUV. His own vehicle sits empty in a nonexistent parking space to his right. The yellow lines have completely faded, decimated by time and weather.

A bracelet is looped around Kole's rearview mirror. It's made of black cord and plastic beads, the kind of tchotchke you'd find on vacation at a souvenir stand. White beads stamped with black letters spell the name HAZEL and Axel knows better than to ask. She's one of the few people who left Black Harbor of her own volition, and rumors say she took a piece of Kole with her. The sergeant never talks about the transcriber, but Axel knows from experience that sometimes the people we don't talk about are the ones we miss the most.

They've been sitting in silence for almost five minutes when Kole finally speaks. "Cutler's not our guy."

Axel clenches his jaw. A fire builds inside him. His ears are hot. He imagines the tips of them are as red as branding irons. "How'd you know I was there?"

"I got eyes and ears everywhere, Winthorp. Plus, his grandson called me."

Axel thinks back to approaching Cutler's garage. He must have given Michael his phone with instructions to call Kole as soon as he got in the car. Which means he knew there was going to be trouble.

"Why would he have—"

"I already checked into him. He's squeaky clean. His A-name's got nothing but a couple of speeding tickets."

"That's not 'squeaky clean,' then," argues Axel.

"It is for Black Harbor." The silence returns, creating a barrier between them. Kole shifts in his seat to better face Axel. "Trust me, he's not our guy."

Axel stares at him hard. He feels his eyes narrow as they block out everything but Kole. What he has to say is all that matters right now. Kole takes the intensity as a prompt to explain.

"I got a call from Brewer," he says, mentioning the name of the school resource officer. "He told me about this rumor that was circulating, about a teacher and a student, and wanted me to look into it, which I did. I talked to Cutler, scoured his record every which way to Sunday, spoke to a couple of his colleagues, and closed the book."

"Without consulting me."

"Damn straight."

"How could you do that?" Rage claws its way out of Axel's throat.

"I just told you how. I interviewed a few teachers at Monroe to get a read on him. No one had jack to say about him, beyond the fact that he's a nice guy, family man, cares about his students, blah blah blah."

"*Why* then?" Axel changes course.

"To protect you." Kole lets the statement simmer between them for a few seconds, before firing: "Tell me you wouldn't have gone apeshit if you found out there was scuttlebutt about a teacher defiling your little girl."

Axel sucks in a breath so deep, his chest strains against the fabric of his shirt. "I would have," he admits. "But still, you should have—"

"No." Kole shuts him down. "I did exactly what I should have done. What I had to do. You remember Dylan, right?"

Axel nods. He thinks he knows where this is going. Investigator Dylan was fired from the Black Harbor Police Department six years ago for tampering with an investigation regarding his own daughter dealing drugs. "I moved the heroin from Sarah's music box to her boyfriend's dresser drawer." Kole taps his middle finger against his sternum, taking all the blame. "He was a drug-dealing, lowlife piece of shit anyway. I thought it would give her a chance to get clean, back on the straight and narrow. Instead, it made things a whole hell of a lot worse. She turned on her own father and accused him of planting the drugs. Dylan fell on the sword and was exiled from the PD, and Sarah went on to make dear old dad proud when she became the Candy Man, peddling pills to kids and catalyzing an epidemic of overdoses." His gaze flicks back to Axel. "So, don't tell me what I should have done when I learned the hard way what not to do."

Axel swallows some of his anger. He believes Kole, that he did what he thought was in Axel's best interest, and yet—

"You're my second-best homicide detective, Axel. I can't afford to lose you. Especially now."

Axel can't help but smile a little at the jab. He knows Kole favors Riley; they both do. And yet, here they are, putting their heads together to solve a double murder and a missing persons case.

"Absence of evidence isn't evidence of absence," he remarks. Just because they haven't found clues pointing to Cutler having been at any of these crime scenes doesn't mean he wasn't there. It doesn't mean he didn't kill those girls.

"Trust me, I know," Kole agrees. "But indulge me for a moment."

"Okay." Axel continues staring through the windshield. Silver clouds skate across the sky. It's almost calming.

"What do the victims tell us?"

Axel feels his brows knit. "The autopsy for Sari Simons isn't scheduled until later," he says.

"You need an autopsy report to know that the girl was murdered?"

"No."

"Good. What else do we know about her?"

Axel swallows. Grotesque images of Sari's sightless eye sockets, mouth open in a silent scream, and the angry marks on her neck flash through his memory. "She was probably strangled."

"And then . . ." Kole prompts. When Axel is quiet, he adds: "Don't overthink this, Winthorp. What did the killer do after he strangled her?"

"He cut out her eyes."

"Very good. Now, what kind of person does that?"

Finally, Axel turns to him. "What do you mean?"

Kole's stare could turn him to stone. "Kills them quietly and then mutilates them."

Axel shakes his head. He hadn't thought of it like that before. "Someone who's . . . angry?" He doesn't realize how every sound around them has quelled to create a quiet so intense it's suffocating until the name Kole gives steals the air from his lungs.

"Someone like Libby Lucas?"

"Libby?" Axel frowns. "You're serious?"

"She's an outcast. You mentioned once that your own daughter didn't want to be friends with her because she's strange. You don't think she gets teased, maybe has some pent-up aggression?"

"Maybe, but . . ." Axel shakes his head in an attempt to part his colliding thoughts. There could be merit there. She was evasive in her interview with him and Riley on Friday, and last night, she'd been at the murder scene of Sari Simons.

"I got a call from Patrol about an hour ago . . . I'd literally just fallen asleep. Anyway, I was confident we were looking for a male aggressor, but . . ." He leans toward Axel as though he's going to whisper in his ear. Instead, he reaches for the backseat and retrieves what looks like a little black CD binder. He hands it to Axel, who studies it. "This was wedged in a pallet and partially obscured by a tarp about ten yards from the body."

The zipper groans as Axel drags it along the track, and the case unfolds to reveal an array of sharp objects: scissors, scalpel, bone shears. A tag above an empty compartment identifies the kit as: PROPERTY OF LIBBY LUCAS.

"I'm guessing whatever goes there was the spoon or scalpel or whatever used to gouge out Miss Simons's eyes." Kole points to the vacant slot.

Axel is shaking his head, all these shards of evidence forming a mosaic in his mind. The busted teeth. The gouged-out eyes. Libby's taxidermy kit. "So, you think—"

"I think you should interview Libby Lucas again. Find out why the hell she would bring a taxidermy kit to a haunted house."

Axel gnaws at the hangnail that's now a pulsing pain in his thumb as he considers all of Libby's potential excuses. She might say she forgot she had the kit on her, although it's too big to conceal in a pocket and Libby didn't have a backpack. Sari Simons did, which, as far as he knows, is still missing. She might claim it isn't hers and that someone wrote her name on it as a plant; however, the fingerprints on the tools could tell them otherwise. Or, she might simply deny any knowledge of how it got there, in which case—

"Listen," says Kole, interrupting his thoughts. "Everybody lies, Axel. And everybody has a tell." He pauses for dramatic effect, long enough for Axel to swivel his gaze away from the bridge and back to him. "Your ears get red, did you know that? Riley runs her tongue across her teeth. You mean to tell me you've lived next door to that girl for practically her entire life and you don't know her tell? Because if that's the truth, then I failed as your supervisor."

Axel sits quiet for a moment, thinking back to the interview with Libby. How had it only been two days ago?

We have reason to believe that the same person who killed Madison Caldwell also took Chloe. If you have any idea who that person is, you have an obligation to tell us.

He remembers telling her that before she was dismissed on Friday, remembers her staring at him with those ink-black eyes, her mouth twisting into a grimace. He remembers her hand creeping toward her throat and closing around her locket.

And then she smiled.

20

ROWAN

Grief is a pier, ruined and sunk by the waves of Lake Michigan, like the ones near her house. It is that pier that crushes Rowan's chest, pulverizing her sternum and spine until they transform into shrapnel like the zebra mussel shells that turn the sand white and sharp. Grief is the weight of that 22,500-square-mile basin of water that swallows the pier. And it is all on top of her.

Sometimes, she wonders if finding nothing is worse than finding something. She contemplates how long she can go on existing in this purgatory of not knowing, and yet, there are moments when she knows without a shadow of a doubt that Chloe is dead, her body lying busted up and broken somewhere just like her friends'. And if she's being horribly, despicably honest with herself, she wants to believe it, because somehow it seems easier than living with an open hole in her chest. If Chloe is dead, she could start stitching the hole back up. But if she isn't, if her daughter is out there somewhere, alone and afraid, or worse—not alone—the hole will eat at her like acid tanning a hide.

Only . . . Madison and Sari weren't her friends, were they?

Not according to the story that Axel shared, anyway. It sounded as if Sari and Madison were a couple of mean girls on a mission to butcher Chloe's reputation and make her life at Monroe hell.

The killer is trying to link their murders to Chloe—and Axel is falling for it. A stinging sensation prickles her palm at the memory of her hand smacking her husband's face. She looks at it now, as though her palmar flexion creases will be embossed by his razor stubble.

They've neither spoken nor seen each other since. He didn't come home last night; Rowan imagines he spent it canvassing the area—gathering witness statements, checking for security cameras—and concocting more harebrained hypotheses that paint Chloe as a psycho killer. If that's the tune he's going to sing from now on, then he can just stay gone for good.

She knows he's probably with Riley. And while it bothers her, she doesn't have the mental or emotional capacity to deal with it right now. She's got work to do.

The morgue is never a welcome sight, especially on a Sunday. A Sunday autopsy means that what they're dealing with is dire, and Rowan doesn't know for the life of her how they are going to stop this motherfucker.

He's murdered and mutilated two—maybe three—girls within two days. Maybe more.

A cactus of dread takes root and blooms in the pit of her stomach. What's to say there aren't other fresh corpses decomposing in riverbeds or abandoned lean-tos?

Peering through a plastic face shield, Rowan's eyes take in the colorless canvas. An old bruise stains the left thigh, another the right forearm. Sari played rough, her dad told police. She liked to jump into a game of Ultimate Frisbee and she wasn't afraid to start a wrestling match with someone twice her size. Therefore, it's reasonable to assume the bruises were a result of innocent child's play. Her hands are clean of defensive marks, no cuts between her fingers, fingernails intact. But then Rowan's gaze travels up the rectus abdominis, up the sternum and across the clavicle to the fresh abrasions on the neck. She squints. Some kind of chafing? Madison Caldwell had the same marks.

"What do you think these are?"

Liz leans over to look. "Manual strangulation," she says without hesitation, and turns the victim's head.

A constellation of angry spots stipple the skin along the jaw. Rowan notes it in the pinna of the ear, too. Petechiae. It means there was bleeding under the skin. Pressure built in the venules and capillaries, and in areas of little connective support tissue, causing the vessels to rupture. Like when pipes burst in the winter.

Normally it's in the eyes, too, but . . . well.

Liz reaches over her to grab a scalpel.

"What do you make of this?" Rowan asks.

"Of what?"

Rowan's hand is a blade as she gestures to the empty eye sockets.

"Oh." Liz's shoulders rise and fall as she takes a steadying breath to collect her thoughts. "I think we've got one sick son of a bitch in our neighborhood. I found sisal fibers on her clothing when I undressed her, by the way."

Rowan frowns. "Sisal fibers? Like from a rope?"

"That's typically where they come from. It was a very small sample, but noteworthy, I thought."

Noteworthy indeed. She doesn't remember Madison Caldwell having sisal fibers on her, but then, it's possible they were missed. Not that using a rope to strangle someone is so unorthodox it could lead to the positive identification of the murderer, but it's a clue they didn't have before.

Wearing blue gloves, Liz's long-fingered hand slices a Y-incision that starts at the shoulder and extends to the pubic bone, intersecting at the sternum. Blood beads along the cut, but minimally with no heartbeat to pump it out.

The autopsy is clockwork. The crack of bolt cutters notes the beginning of the thoracic evisceration. Liz inspects the viscera for tumors, adhesions, fluid, and organ damage while Rowan's mind drifts back to last night and the conversation with Axel. Her gaze scans the body from bottom to top. The toe tag awaiting its cause of death entry, the ribs that have been cracked open. The nonblanchable lividity that looks like the victim's whole backside was dipped in red wine. The abrasions on the neck. The depthless eye sockets.

She shifts two steps to the right for a closer look. The skin has been scrubbed clean. There are no stray specks of dirt or flecks of blood. It makes it all appear even more vile. What kind of monster tears into flesh so young and otherwise flawless? Flaps of skin hang ragged. They look like wrung-out mop strings. Rowan cringes.

Whoever did this was angry, she thinks, and for the first time throughout this investigation, a solid answer slides beneath her. She finds her footing. The strangulation was the work of an expert. She notes the parallel chafe marks on the victim's neck, the petechiae. Sari must have lost consciousness and gone to sleep within seconds. Even if she had screamed, she was in a haunted house. Everyone had been screaming.

The eye-gouging, however, was an act of impulse, just as smashing Madison's teeth had been. Rowan hovers over the sightless cavities where the orbs have been plucked from the skull. Plucked . . . or scooped? What kind of tool would the killer have used to remove them? She thinks back to her initial crack about the ice cream scoop, and wonders if she hadn't been too far off.

The holes bore into her, unblinking. Rowan feels unnerved. Her skin starts to crawl and she almost expects the corpse to draw a breath, like Madison Caldwell's did down in the gully the other night. Rowan shuts her eyes and imagines the horrific violence Sari Simons must have endured in her final moments.

She was probably alive when he cut into her.

Now that she has a firm foundation—cause of death: practiced, mutilation: impulse—a new question threatens to rock her. How is Chloe connected to this dead and ruined little girl?

Sari Simons was small. But scrappy. Chloe could not have overpowered her. Not alone anyway.

Stop.

Rowan clenches her jaw. Forces herself to breathe in and out through her nose. Chloe is not a killer. And yet, Axel is so desperate to find their daughter alive that he is willing to entertain the idea that she is. Apparently, he'd rather have her be a murderer than dead. At least if she's dead, no one can hurt her anymore.

Tears well in her eyes. Her throat feels tight. She turns her attention back to the body on the table. The absence of defensive marks is interesting, if not telling. She's only given a moment of reprieve when the dread slips back inside her, this time pooling at the base of her skull and trickling down her spine. Sari knew her attacker.

Statistically, you and I both know this was a male. She recalls Kole's assessment at the crime scene of Madison Caldwell, and finds herself, perhaps for the first time in her life, clinging to statistics. Last year, nearly twelve thousand murders were committed in the US, approximately nine thousand of which were the work of male offenders. The remaining three thousand were credited almost fifty-fifty to female offenders and unknown. Besides, the Violent Crime sergeant has solved hundreds, if not thousands of cases in his time. She has no reason to doubt him.

Suddenly, it smells like vomit, and Rowan knows that Liz is sorting through the stomach contents.

"Pop-Tart?"

"Hmm?" Rowan looks down to observe a partially digested Pop-Tart.

"Looks like some kind of Halloween edition." Liz picks up a piece and sifts through the crumbs in her hand. "Orange frosting. There are even little bat sprinkles. I think. These shapes always look like blobs anyway."

"Cute," says Rowan. Breathing through her mouth and fogging up her face shield, she moves toward the victim's head, studying the marks on the neck again.

"Do you think it was the same guy who killed Madison Caldwell?" she asks, wondering if Liz will contradict the masculine pronoun. She feels a fleeting shot of relief when she doesn't.

"A lot of similarities," Liz admits.

"And the eyes . . . ?"

"Evisceration spoon." Her response is matter-of-fact, like she's a game show contestant. When Rowan furrows her brows, Liz adds: "It's a surgical tool used during enucleation procedures. You can remove an entire eyeball from the socket without cutting into it, like popping a nut out of its shell."

The imagery is visceral, but then, there is little about either of their jobs that isn't. While their professions are similar in that they each deal with determining the cause and manner of death of persons who have died violently or unexpectedly, Rowan has come up with a simple way to differentiate them: she works on the outside, Liz works on the inside. Liz also had to complete three years of pathology residency beyond medical school.

"Would Streuthers have one?" She mentions the name of the local funeral home. "An evisceration spoon."

"Maybe." Liz sets the liver in a metal tray and marks the weight on her clipboard. "Or a surgeon. Or a taxidermist. They're always taking the eyes out of shit. Taxidermists, I mean. Surgeons, not so much. Hopefully."

Rowan swallows. All this talk of eyes has her acutely aware of her own. They start to sting.

"I've never seen anything like this," Liz admits. "Whoever did this has some deep-seated issues."

Rowan says nothing, but thinks: *Don't we all?*

21
LIBBY

The nursery is a blood bath, still, as the roses remain precisely where they were when Libby left last night. Whoever ordered them will be here today, then. She best not water them, or they will pee all over their new owner's vehicle.

Meandering past them, Libby wields her watering can and wanders down the aisle of Dutchman's britches (her favorite), picking off a handful of dried, curling leaves as she goes.

She could have stayed home today. Her parents asked if she wanted to, even offered to call in on her behalf. They've never done that before. Keeping your commitments is a core value in the Lucas household, though Libby supposes it isn't every night that one of them trips over a dead body.

Freshly dead, too.

Sari was still warm when Libby fell on the dirt floor next to her, her body pliant. She can still see her as vividly as though they're lying next to each other now—the gouges where her eyes should be, her skin torn and twisted. The image haunted her all night, even though Libby isn't necessarily scared of death the way most people seem to be. It's life that she loves.

Reaching into the pouch of her apron, she sprinkles fertilizer into a potted delphinium.

Dead things are empty things.

Taxidermy is therefore the art of illusion. With cotton and some glass eyes, she could make Sari look alive again. Not that she wants to . . . but she could.

Her phone buzzes in her back pocket. Libby's heart skips and an unsettling feeling drags her stomach toward the floor. She checks it and discovers a text message from her mom. Love you, Lib. Have a good day, ok?

Love you too she thumbs back, and shoves the phone in her jeans pocket again.

She exhales. For a second there, she was afraid it was Reeves. She woke to a Snapchat from him this morning, a three-word query to which she didn't know how to respond, so she didn't.

How are you?

Besides Chloe and her parents, no one's ever asked her that before. Certainly not a boy, and certainly not one of Reeves Singh's social status.

How is she?

Traumatized? Afraid? Fine?

She's all and none of these things. What is that, then? Indifferent? Confused? Suspicious?

He could be a killer, you know, her internal voice nags.

"Oh, I know," she replies. Libby snaps her head up, checking to see if anyone overheard. But she is alone in the nursery as far as she can tell, unless someone is lurking behind a ficus.

Which, someone is.

"Know what?" the stranger inquires, though as he approaches, she sees he isn't a stranger at all.

"Oh, hi, Mr. Taylor." An ember flares in her cheeks. "I was just . . . talking to myself."

He smiles. Always a kind, close-mouthed smile with him. A non-Duchenne smile, the one that doesn't quite reach the eyes.

"Are you here for pumpkins?" she wonders. "They're out at the front." It's become her default greeting to people who wander back this way this time of year. No one's interested in aloe or echinacea; IT'S FALL Y'ALL, as the many painted signs remind her.

"Actually . . ." Mr. Taylor points to the potted rosebushes. "I'm here for those lovely ladies."

"Oh . . ." Libby's brows shoot up toward her hairline. "So you're the mysterious rose . . . buyer." She's so dumb. Her cheeks warm again and she busies herself with getting a cart to help him bring them to his vehicle.

"Indeed I am." He's nice to play along. In his thirties, Mr. Taylor is one of the younger teachers at Monroe Academy, and therefore, one of the most notorious student-crushes. It isn't that he's terribly attractive—though he'd be out of Libby's league for sure—but he has a job and a house and a car and he isn't bald, although he keeps his hair shorn close to his scalp. More than that, however, it's the air of mystery that trails him like a shadow. He never talks about his personal life. No one knows if he has kids or a wife—or a partner at all—and Libby supposes that's actually the way it should be. Teachers shouldn't be airing their dirty laundry in the classrooms, not like Ms. Allouez, the recently divorced chemistry teacher who allegedly had students destroy her wedding photos over Bunsen burners.

"Are these for Sweetest Day?" she asks, because she has to try. Sweetest Day was yesterday, but people will come in for belated gifts all week.

"I didn't know that was a thing." Mr. Taylor chuckles as they load the last of the sunset-pink roses onto the flatbed. Libby takes the handle and follows him out to his vehicle.

"When you work in a garden center, you learn that every day is a special occasion."

"That's kind of a nice way to look at life in general, isn't it?" He winks, and she so badly wishes she could believe him. But after tripping over Sari's dead body last night, she just can't get behind it. Nevertheless, she smiles, a non-Duchenne to match his from earlier.

"Are these for you, or . . . ?"

"My sister, actually. She's always wanted a rose garden. And I thought . . . well, what better time than now?"

June, Libby thinks, but doesn't say it. Maybe he has a shelter to protect them from the frost. But these are Aurora, Heather had said. They're heartier than most. She shares that little factoid with him, pleased with herself for retaining it.

"Aurora? Well, how 'bout that. That's her name."

"Your sister's?"

"Mm-hmm. I'll have to let her know; she'll be amused, I'm sure." Mr. Taylor slams the hatch.

Libby can just barely make out the roses on the other side of the tinted glass.

"Thanks, Libby. I'll see you in class tomorrow."

So he doesn't know about Sari Simons yet, she thinks, and it isn't her place to tell him. He will find out on the news soon enough, whenever police release their statement.

Back inside, her mind is a Rubik's Cube, wringing and twisting this way and that, trying to unlock an answer. She compartmentalizes what she knows.

Reeves's DNA is on Madison. He allegedly admitted to having had contact with her at school Thursday afternoon. Smart on his part, reasons Libby. That way, police are inclined to ignore his fingerprints.

Furthermore, they had been fighting. They were always fighting, it seemed, their few amiable moments existing between arguments. It honestly would have struck her as odd if they hadn't been fighting up until Madison's death.

And Sari. This one is so obvious it's almost laughable, because Reeves *led* her right to the body last night. They hadn't been lost at all. How easy would it have been for him to have killed Sari and hidden her in the haunted house?

But she had seen Sari in line, hadn't she? She'd seen her barrettes and her cosmological-print backpack. Unless . . . her mind had been playing a trick on her. We see what we want to see. That isn't a phenomenon. That's just a fundamental truth about being human. Perhaps her memory is filling in its own gaps, coloring the reality she wants to believe.

Another theory slithers into her mind.

Chloe.

What if she had been there last night? What if she killed Sari and ordered Reeves to bring Libby to the body? But—

"Libby?"

She whirls around, her hand flying open and tossing fertilizer onto the concrete floor.

Axel Winthorp looks like an apparition the way the light obscures him. "Do you have a few minutes to talk?"

Libby sinks her teeth into her bottom lip as she mouths a single syllable. *Fudge.*

22

AXEL

Libby doesn't speak. Her hand snakes upward to clutch the heart-shaped locket that rests just below the suprasternal notch of her collarbone.

Suprasternal notch. Axel almost rolls his eyes at himself for just thinking of the medical terminology for the dip between clavicles. After eighteen years of working and living with Rowan, she has the scientific name for everything embedded in him. It's a valve he cannot just shut off.

"Here," he offers, and maneuvers the Impala around the back of the garden center. He parks near a collection of old spools where there are no passersby. "Is this all right?"

Libby's tongue sneaks out to wet her lips. Still not making eye contact with him, she nods. He hears her exhale again, and knows that she is trying to calm herself.

"How are you?" he asks. He might as well have slapped her. She blanches at the question, as though it's one she doesn't hear often. Or ever.

"I'm fine," she says. They are the first words she has spoken since he collected her from the nursery, when she silently followed him through the aisles of fertilizer and garden decor, past the café and out the front doors to the parking lot where his Impala waited.

"Listen, Libby," he starts. "I know you've got to get back to work, so I'll cut to the chase. Is there anything you want to tell me about last night?"

"Last night?" Faint stitch marks appear above her brows.

Axel fights an eye roll. Teenagers. Their number-one defense is feigning aloofness. "The haunted house. You found Sari Simons." He takes a deep breath. Jesus, this is harder than he thought it'd be. Marnie and Daniel are not going to be thrilled when they find out he cornered their daughter for an interview, without their consent.

Not when, *if*, he reminds himself. And he's fairly confident that this conversation will never rear its ugly little head in the Lucas household. After all, it's in Libby's best interest if her parents don't know what she's been up to.

His exhale fogs the windows. "Remember?"

He watches the muscles in her neck convulse as she swallows. Her chin touches her shoulder as she looks away from him, and a spot of condensation appears on the window where her forehead hovers less than an inch from the glass. She clutches the locket, and he knows she is contemplating another lie.

"I know you didn't hurt Sari," he says. "I'm just trying to put the pieces together to find out who did, to stop them from hurting anyone else."

The stitches in her brows deepen. She opens her mouth as though appalled he would even think such a thing. He knows, then, that the time has come to reach into the paper evidence bag by his feet and reveal the black taxidermy kit. "Investigating officers discovered this near the body," he states. "It's missing a tool."

A shadow passes over Libby's already dark eyes and stays like a storm cloud. She stares at the black case as though it might snap its jaws and lunge at her. She wets her lips again, but doesn't speak.

He waits. He has all day.

"Do you have any idea how it got there?" he asks.

She shakes her head and a seed of frustration bursts inside him. His right eye twitches.

"Fri-Friday," she stammers. "I went to talk to you during taxidermy class. You told me to leave my stuff."

"And you never went back for it?"

She swallows. It appears to take great effort. "I didn't think of it until now. But no, I guess I didn't."

It could be a lie, but in the moment, relief floods through him. This is all so much easier if Marnie and Daniel's daughter is not a killer.

The relief is short-lived, however. Perhaps their daughter isn't, but his—

He won't go there. Not now when he has Libby alone with her back up against the wall. He remembers two days ago, when he and Riley sat with Libby backstage and asked her about Madison Caldwell. No one really liked Madison, isn't that what she had told them? And after that, she would divulge no more.

But maybe now—now when he had something of hers found at the scene of a second murder, something that might have contained a tool that very well might have mutilated Sari Simons—she would talk.

"Someone . . . must have taken it," she reasons. Her elbow digs into her thigh. She leans forward and touches her fingertips to her hairline, catching tiny beads of sweat.

"Could Sari have taken it?" he asks.

Libby huffs out a breath. "It's possible. I don't know why she would have, but . . . she didn't mind causing trouble just for the sake of causing trouble."

That, he knows, is true. Sari would probably still be alive if she'd listened to him and Riley and stayed at home when they told her not to go out. She should have—

No. He's not about to victim blame.

Sari wasn't perfect. But that doesn't mean she deserved to die.

"Investigator Riley reported you were there with Reeves Singh. Is that true?"

Libby nods. Her lips soften into a natural pout. "We didn't go together, though. My dad dropped me off."

Axel checks that off his mental list. Daniel dropping Libby off at the Compound corroborates what Marnie told him yesterday afternoon.

"But, he . . ." She trails off as though she's just stepped on precarious ground.

Axel latches on. "He as in Reeves?"

She nods. "He led me right to her. We got lost . . . I thought. But then . . . there she was." Her mouth goes slack and her eyes frost over, and he knows she is reliving the moments of last night, moments she probably hasn't truly processed yet.

"Did you notice your kit or any of your tools near her then?"

Avoiding eye contact, Libby shakes her head.

"You said Reeves 'led' you to Sari's body. Do you think that was intentional?"

"I don't know."

"Do you think he might have killed her?"

"I don't know."

"But he was with you the whole time, wasn't he?"

Libby opens her mouth to speak, and stops. He's got her there. It's time to check something else off his list, too.

"Forensic results have returned from the lab and they discovered something that, I have to admit, piqued my interest."

Libby, whose gaze has drifted to the other side of the parking lot where a rogue shopping cart is being pushed by the wind, turns toward him again.

"Why were your fingerprints on Madison Caldwell?"

The darkness lifts from her eyes as all the pigment drains from her face. Her skin becomes translucent, a mirror reflecting the overcast sky. He thinks she's about to remain silent, when she says: "Reeves's were, too." She flinches as though hearing how it sounds, like they'd tag-teamed Madison.

Axel watches her intently. She hadn't been expecting him to come out with that, and now he can see the thoughts racing frantically behind her eyes as she wonders what all he knows.

He doesn't know much, that's the truth of it. But she doesn't know that.

"Are you admitting that your touch DNA would be on Madison Caldwell? Did you have contact with her on Thursday, Libby?"

"No."

"Then how would your prints get to be on her?"

Libby is shaking like a leaf. "I don't know."

Axel pauses for a moment, then leans slightly closer to her. "Why did you mention that Reeves Singh's DNA would be on her? Did you see him with her that night, perhaps?"

"Everyone knows that," states Libby. "That's why the cops came to talk to him Friday morning."

"When was the last time you saw Reeves on Thursday? What was he doing?"

She shrugs. "We have algebra together. Fifth period."

"When did you walk home?"

"Like three-fifteen?"

"Did you see him then?"

"No."

"Did you see Madison?"

"No."

"Libby, here's the deal. Reeves and Madison were in a relationship. He admitted to having had contact with her that day. From everything you've shared with me, you and Madison weren't exactly gal pals. Unless you were in gym class together or you played a game of tag football, there's no reason your prints should have been on her."

She's a mouse snapped in his trap. Squirming, at his mercy. She knows that if she doesn't give him whatever she's been holding back, he'll tell her parents about her taxidermy kit. Their house and lives will be turned upside down as completely as his and Rowan's.

Finally, Libby takes a breath. "I was . . . collecting." Her teeth sink into her lip again, forbidding her to speak further.

Axel feels his brows knit, his eyes squint. "What do you mean 'collecting'? Collecting what?"

The spot on the window vanishes only to reappear three times its size. She says nothing, though.

"Libby."

She won't look at him.

"What do you collect? Did Madison Caldwell have something of yours?"

The movement is so slight, it's almost imperceptible as she shakes her head.

Finally, she's given him something. A single bread crumb on a morbid trail. He can't let it go now. "Did you *want* something of hers?"

She swallows again. Axel watches closely as her thumb slides against the back of the locket. He switches gears. "It must have sentimental value, your locket. I noticed you wearing it the other day."

Libby pauses like a deer that's just heard a twig snap. Slowly, her fingers slide away from it, and he gets a good look at the silver filigreed heart.

"Chloe used to have one," he lies. "She kept, well—" He smiles down at his hands, now clasped in his lap, before bringing his stare back to Libby's face and holding it on her. His mention of Chloe has caught the girl's interest. "Maybe you can tell me what you keep in your locket, then we can decide together whether or not Chloe was so . . . out of the norm."

He sees the gears turning behind her eyes. Still, she shrinks back, trying to disappear through the thin crack in the door.

"Unless there's something you don't want to show me," he says. "In which case, I'll have to ask your parents for permission. And then whatever you're keeping so close to the vest, Libby—they'll know, too. If you show me, now, I promise it'll stay just between us."

Minutes elapse. Axel watches the clouds overhead. They darken as they roll across the sky, east toward the lake. Raindrops slap against his windshield, and he thinks about how they look like tiny, shallow incisions in the glass.

Finally, when he thinks she's about to try to wait him out, she brings her hands around to the back of her neck and unhooks the necklace. The chain dangles from her fist as she extends her arm toward him and drops the locket into his palm.

Both feet are on the floor again. She leans forward and hides her face in her hands. "Do I need a lawyer?" she asks.

Axel cracks open the locket. The hair on the back of his neck rises. Resting in the heart-shaped frame are two broken triangles that he knows, without a shadow of a doubt, are Madison Caldwell's teeth.

23

ROWAN

She's in her vehicle, backing out of the garage when she taps the brakes. She stares at the backyard. Scarlet leaves blanket the ground and form a ring around the sugar maple from which they fell. Chloe used to climb that tree. She said she could see everything from up there—the lake, the lighthouse, the broken pier to the east; Forge Bridge and the police department to the west. North was a deader-than-a-doornail downtown and just south of them, across the yard, was Rainbow Row with its neighborhood of crack houses.

"Don't call them that," Rowan scolded her once, when Chloe had been seven or eight.

"What?" Having swung down from the lowest branch, Chloe stared up at her with big turquoise eyes that glistened with curiosity and innocence. A swipe of dirt marked her cheek. "Crack houses?"

Rowan raised a brow. "Yes."

"But that's what Daddy calls them."

Rowan was aware. And for all intents and purposes, the one-story homes coated in flaking government-issued paint probably did harbor crack cocaine and other contraband. But there were probably a few that housed good people trying to stretch a dollar, old tannery families who'd lost their living when the place shut down. That's the thing about places. You're allowed to speak ill of them if you grew up there. "And what's the rule about things Daddy says?" she quizzed.

Chloe dug the toe of her sneaker into the grass, then looked up at Rowan with an exaggerated cringe. "Not to repeat most of them."

Rowan spit-shined the dirt from her daughter's face. "Good girl."

"But what should I call them, Mommy?"

After thinking for a few seconds, she decided on: "Row houses. It means they're arranged in a row and they share the same sidewalk."

Chloe pursed her lips, pondering this new nomenclature. "Row. Like your name?" When Rowan nodded, Chloe threw her arms around her neck. How she smelled like a child back then—Froot Loops and earth and fresh air. "I like that. It makes them less scary."

When Chloe released her, Rowan held her hands, keeping her at arm's length. "Why are they scary, honey?"

Chloe drew in a breath. Her eyes shifted from one shoulder to the other, as though to ensure no one was listening. She lowered her voice to a whisper. "Because they look like broken teeth, don't you think? Sometimes at night I dream about them. That I'm up in the tree and the city is really this giant monster and the crack hou—I mean, row houses—are its teeth and it swallows me up. And then everything gets dark and I try to scream for you and Daddy except I can't. I can never scream in my dreams."

The chill Rowan feels now is the same as the one she felt back then. She frowns and feels gravity pulling at her mouth. A tear slips down her cheek and splashes on the back of her hand. Had Chloe's nightmares been a premonition? That one day Black Harbor would swallow her up and she'd be lost forever, unable to speak or scream?

The dead can't scream.

Chloe is dead. She knows it and yet, she swears sometimes she can feel her pulse in everything she touches. Even the cold steering wheel feels as though it's got a telltale heart beating inside. Her eyes slide to the glove box where she knows is the obituary of Katelynn Diggory and one last cigarette.

She could leave now. And maybe she should. Leave her life in Black Harbor in the dust, but Rowan knows better. Our pasts always know where to find us. The sugar maple shrinks in her windshield as she backs the rest of the way out of the driveway, and after a few minutes, the faded pink channel letters on the side of the Shop-and-Save's pitched roof flicker a Morse code message to her. She pulls into an empty space next to the cart corral and shifts into park. Sitting behind the steering wheel, she watches the uninspiring scene laid out before her with the same muted interest involved in watching a low-budget film of someone else's life.

A black plastic bag tumbles end over end across the pockmarked and pitted asphalt. It floats toward the street and eventually snags on a tree branch where she knows it will be abused by the elements until it disintegrates as completely as skin decomposing over bones. Nothing ever gets too far in Black Harbor. That's how she knows Chloe is still here.

Now, standing in the candy aisle and ogling the bright-colored bags, she feels exposed. She has no business putting out a bowl of sugar-coated anything. In fact, she's fairly confident that she could advertise full-sized chocolate bars, and no one would dare approach her porch. Except, perhaps, whoever stole her jack-o'-lanterns.

Humans are pie charts, divided into two compartments: logic and emotion. The splits aren't always equal. In fact, they rarely are. She knows that her pie chart is 95 percent logic and 5 percent emotion. The logical part of her knows that Chloe isn't coming back. But that tiny emotional sliver is what's compelling her to buy these pumpkins and carve new faces into them. Because if she is alive, maybe the flames flickering inside them will guide Chloe home.

With her gourds in tow, she pushes her cart. It clangs against another. Rowan jumps back, her hand smacking against her chest. "I'm so sorry," she starts, when recognition makes her pause. "Oh, hi, Mr. Taylor."

Eddie Taylor retreats a step, dragging his cart with him. He offers a soft, forgiving smile. "Don't worry about it." A pause. "It's good to see you, Mrs. Winthorp."

"Please, Rowan is good."

"Eddie's good for me, then." He winks, and she gets the feeling that he is practicing for the day he bumps into a pretty, single woman in the grocery store. He certainly isn't unattractive himself, with brown hair that's been buzzed short, a square jaw, and eyes the color of cobblestones. Upon first meeting him at parent-teacher conferences a few weeks ago, she'd guessed him to be in his mid to late thirties, though here in a hoodie and sneakers, he looks even younger.

She doesn't envy single people in Black Harbor. Well, rewind. She doesn't envy single people who don't want to be single in Black Harbor. Pickings are slim to none. If she hadn't met Axel while on the job, she probably never would have met him at all.

It's crazy how, every now and again, all the elements of the universe shift into alignment for two people to meet. If she hadn't experienced it for herself, she might never believe it could happen.

"Stocking up on Halloween candy?" he asks rhetorically.

"Oh." She laughs a little. "I like to be prepared. Pretty soon all that will be left are Smarties and saltwater taffy."

"Right," he agrees. "Trust me, if I hand out that stuff, the kids won't let me live it down until next year. Maybe not even then." He reaches past her and grabs two big bags of assorted candy.

Rowan goes for the bag of special-edition orange and purple Sour Patch Kids. She stares at them longingly. "These were Chloe's favorite. The zombie ones." She doesn't mean to say it out loud, and yet maybe she does. Just as Eddie Taylor is practicing his pickup game, she is trying out past tense for size. "I always called her my Sour Patch kid." Tears well in her eyes. She dares not blink, lest one spill down her cheek. "She could be so sour sometimes, so impossible, and then when you were at your wit's end with her, she'd turn around and be so sweet." She swallows. "Teenagers, right? I guess I'm preaching to the choir. I had one teenager to contend with while you've got hundreds."

"Except I get to send them all home at the end of the day," he says with a smile that's off-putting in a way. Although he's otherwise handsome, his teeth are sharp and spaced apart. It looks almost like a veneer job left unfinished, as though the dentist filed down all his teeth and forgot to put the caps on.

Dolphin teeth, that's what Axel calls ones like that. He mentioned a guy in his jiujitsu class. What do they call him? Orca? It just goes to show that despite the fact that we all have insecurities, humans are cruel by nature and we never really grow out of it.

Rowan begins to shrink away and it seems he quickly realizes what he's done—shown her a glimpse of his unpolished, unfiltered self—because he clamps his mouth shut as though in apology. A blush colors his cheeks. Rowan instantly feels bad. Who is she to judge? She knows that to call herself a hot mess right now would be flattery.

She watches guiltily as he selects a bag of Sour Patch Kids off the shelf. "They're my sister's favorite, too," he offers quietly. "The zombies." He doesn't open his mouth again, just gives a parting nod and moves down the aisle.

An hour later, after stopping at the garden center on her way home, Rowan sits on a trash bag on her kitchen floor. Its corners are taped down to protect the hardwood, though she imagines the look all of this would elicit from Axel: two eviscerated pumpkins, a Sharpie, a plastic carving kit . . . and a partridge in a pear tree.

Not that she expects or even wants him to come home anytime soon.

A knock sounds at the back door. She can discern by the soft, one-knuckled rap that it's Marnie.

"Row?" she calls down the entryway.

"In the kitchen."

"Trick-or-treat . . ." Marnie enters with caution, her footsteps a slow cadence across the hardwood. A contemplative expression steals over her face when she observes Rowan on the floor, holding a butcher knife.

Rowan glances from Marnie to the knife, and sets the knife down on the garbage bag beside her. "Sorry, I'm just—"

"Carving pumpkins, I hope?"

"Yes."

"Why?" Marnie edges nearer. She's wearing purple scrubs and brandishing a bottle of cabernet. Her black hair is tied back, but she has a bit of a helter-skelter thing going on. She had as late a night as any of them, and still, she went to work. Although, there's a fundamental difference between their patients, Rowan thinks. Marnie's are alive. Requesting someone to reschedule their craniotomy isn't at the top of her want-to-do list.

Rowan's shoulders fall. Her gaze sweeps the mess on the floor and she shakes her head.

"Row, what is it?" Marnie kneels down to her level.

It seems so stupid now that she's about to say it. But, never in their sixteen-year friendship have she and Marnie ever judged each other. She tells her that someone stole her pumpkins off her porch. It's the only rational explanation that has come to mind since this morning when yesterday, upon returning from the morgue, Rowan noticed the empty steps. She stared for a moment at the little spots of condensation, the only telltale sign they'd ever been there at all. She turned her head right, then left, checking the yard and the driveway to see if the gourds had sprouted legs and walked off on their own. They hadn't.

"And they didn't show up smashed down the road or anything?"

Rowan shakes her head. "I know it's stupid," she says as she rips open the cardboard packaging of the orange carving kit, "but Chloe loved carving pumpkins." She smiles a little. "I think she'd carve them all year round if she could."

Marnie smiles back. It's tinged with pity. Rowan can tell by the way her lips press tightly, forbidding any wrong sentiment from escaping, the twitch of her carotid artery. Her eyes look liquid—wet, black puddles of paint set in the middle of a crestfallen portrait.

In the past couple days, Rowan has gotten used to the piteous stare, the one where people retract their lips and slant their eyes so far they resemble a pair of Dalí's melting clocks, but she has yet to get it from Marnie. This particular look is reserved for strangers and acquaintances, for people who know *of* you but nothing *about* you. Simply wearing the expression makes Marnie appear slightly alien, as though she is Marnie's twin instead of Marnie herself.

"No, it isn't stupid," assures Marnie. Then, she adds dismissively: "Probably just kids. Quiet as it is back here, it's easy to forget we're still in Black Harbor. Sometimes."

Rowan knows that by *back here,* Marnie means their little neighborhood at the edge of the lake. She never forgets, though, not when she meets her daily exercise goal by crawling around crime scenes and wrestling dead weight into body bags.

She sniffs and gives Marnie a sad, slight smile. "So, is this your Halloween costume, or what?" Side-eyeing her friend, she waits for the glare.

Despite having studied at Johns Hopkins, completing her residency

at Stanford, and practicing medicine for more than twenty years, patients still ask to see "the real doctor" when Marnie greets them. "Honestly, the chauvinism of society—"

"—is astounding." Rowan finishes her catchphrase for her.

"This dick today, I'm in there gloving up, already got the lines
drawn on his forehead where I'm gonna cut, and he asks, 'When's the
doctor coming in?' Are you fucking kidding me right now, sir? I have a
bone saw. Not the time to piss me off." She turns and fixes Rowan with a
deadpan stare. "Is it because I'm a woman, or because I'm Latina?"

"C, all of the above," says Rowan matter-of-factly.

Marnie waggles her index finger at her. "How do you know everything about everything?"

While it isn't true, Rowan's flattered. As a medical examiner, you
need critical thinking skills, common sense skills, and a good nose for
bullshit, like when the decedent's cousin tells you he found the guy dead
at the bottom of the stairs—he must've fallen—but the skull fractures
are consistent with a hammer and the body isn't even stiff yet.

Dead bodies don't lie.

Perhaps it's more accurate to say that Rowan's profession requires
her to know not everything, but a little bit about everything. Not to
mention, she had a previous life before becoming a medical examiner.
Before Black Harbor. Axel is the only one who knows, but he doesn't
know the extent to which it influences every decision she makes.

Marnie sets the wine on the counter and hangs her jacket on the
back of the stool. "So, what's for dinner?"

Rowan thinks about her freezer drawer full of toaster strudels and
microwaveable meals she bought for Chloe. They were rarely all home at
the same time, and whenever they were, Rowan preferred not to spend
her time sweating over a stovetop. Dinner at the Winthorp household
was very much a "fend for yourself" concept.

"You brought it." She nods at the cab.

Marnie's off to fetch the wineglasses. She knows her way around
Rowan's kitchen, not only because she's been here more often than any
other houseguest, but because Marnie is the type of person who is so
confident, so competent, it's like all she has to do is simply believe she

knows what she's doing, and she does. Of all the things Rowan admires about Marnie—her brains, her naked-faced beauty—she wishes for that one to rub off on her most.

The cork coming unstuck makes a satisfying sound. "Two things," prepares Marnie, as she pours the blend into a stemless wineglass. "How was the autopsy and what's Axel up to? Why didn't he come home last night?"

"That's three things," says Rowan.

"Two and a half." Marnie slides the glass across the counter to her. "I live like ten feet away, in case you haven't noticed. He didn't come home last night, did he?"

"Oh, I've noticed," says Rowan, thinking of all the various times she and Marnie have serendipitously caught each other's eye from their kitchen windows, or how in the summertime, they'll have every intention of doing yard work but, instead, end up leaning against their respective sides of the fence passing a bottle of wine back and forth until it's too dark to mow. "And no, he didn't."

They cheers to nothing and each take a sip.

"We got into a fight," she adds. "At the crime scene."

Marnie swishes the varietal in her mouth thoughtfully. "I heard a bit of it."

Holding the knife again, Rowan pauses. She finds her reflection in it and notes how unwell she looks. Unhinged. A tear slips down her cheek.

"Oh . . ." Marnie moves closer and before she knows it, she's leaning into her like she did on the porch steps when Axel presented Chloe's crushed roses. Amidst all the pain, Rowan feels a surge of gratitude for her friend. Marnie is always on her side. "He thinks Chloe—" Suddenly, with the force of a storm, a sob bursts from her lips. She can't go there. She can't—

Marnie's touch is cooling as she makes small circles on Rowan's back. "It's okay. Let it out."

She feels crushed, still, under the weight of her grief. But just as the tide recedes from the broken pier now and again, the pressure lessens. She can breathe—a little. Tears pour forth because somewhere inside her a dam has ruptured.

Marnie wraps her arms around her, and Rowan feels her pieces slowly coming back together. A curtain of her sable hair falls over Rowan's face. Finally, she exhales a ragged breath and draws herself up a little straighter. Marnie's embrace relaxes but doesn't let go.

"He thinks Chloe could be . . . k-killing her classmates. But not my little girl, Marnie. Not my little girl." Rowan's mouth pulls down in a frown and she's shaking her head.

"How could he think that?" Marnie's tone is incredulous, validating Rowan's feelings. Indeed, how *could* Axel think that of their daughter? Why would he spend all his energy turning over every rock in Black Harbor searching for Chloe, only to hand her over to the police? If that's the case, she's better off staying gone.

Perhaps even better off dead.

You'll love me more when I'm dead. Chloe's last words ring in her head like tinnitus.

Marnie squeezes her hand. "You can talk to me, Row. I'm your best friend. Nothing leaves this kitchen, okay?"

Rowan takes a minute, then she tells Marnie everything. Well, perhaps not *everything*. There are secrets Rowan has kept drowned so far beneath the surface, she's even hidden them from herself. Until the other day, when the newsprint peeked out at her from the cigarette carton.

She tells her about the rumor and the drawings Axel and Kole found in Chloe's locker.

"Wait. Cutler?" says Marnie. "As in . . . the drama teacher?" She pries the top off her pumpkin. They both sit on the trash bag now, wine in one hand, knife in the other. Adulting at its finest.

"Yeah," replies Rowan.

"Hmm." Marnie chews the inside of her cheek.

"What?"

"I've heard some things. I don't know how true they are. You never know around here."

"What kinds of things?"

"Well . . ." Marnie leans close as though she's forgotten they're alone in Rowan's kitchen. "He married one of his students, I'm pretty sure."

A bolt of shock forces Rowan upright. "What? As in his current wife?"

Marnie shrugs. "That's what I've heard. Had to be almost thirty years ago, I'm sure. She was a senior in high school when they met. He was her teacher. Allegedly they didn't *do* anything until after she graduated, but you know how that goes."

Indeed, Rowan is all too familiar with exactly how that goes. She allows a brief reminiscence of her own high school days, when her parents would have sworn on each other's graves she was a virgin at least until she went off to college. It isn't like she screwed the whole football team or anything like that; however, a golden little Sandra Dee she was not.

She waits for Marnie to ask whether or not there could be a kernel of truth to the rumor of Chloe and Mr. Cutler being involved in some sort of off-limits, illegal sexual relationship, but Marnie knows when to stay behind the caution tape.

Rowan sorts the tools from the pumpkin-carving kit. There are five in total: a carving saw, a small detail saw, a scooper, a poker, and a long-handled spoon. Rowan picks up the spoon, twirling it between her fingertips, and imagines using it to remove an entire eyeball from its socket, like popping a nut out of its shell as Liz mentioned.

She thinks of Sari Simons and the twin cavities in her skull. Would Marnie have any experience with a spoon like that? As if Marnie can read her thoughts—and Rowan often suspects she can—she says, "Jesus, these look like the tools Libby uses in taxidermy class."

Suddenly, a *pop!* like the burst of a flash illuminates the dark corners of Rowan's mind. Everything is so starkly lit for a fraction of a second, it's blinding, disorienting. "What did you say?"

"This kit," repeats Marnie. "I had to buy something like this for Libby's taxidermy class." She pauses, then, as though realizing what she's just insinuated. Marnie takes a drink of her wine and asks: "Did I tell you she came home *reeking* like skunk the other day? Apparently she ruptured its scent gland . . ."

But Rowan isn't listening. She's thinking. About the fact that Marnie's daughter was found at the scene of a murder last night. And, unlike Chloe, Libby is no pipsqueak. She easily could have hurt one or both of those girls. And not just any girls. Girls who had probably tormented Libby similarly to how they tormented Chloe.

And not just any murder. Sari had been mutilated, her eyes gouged out of her skull in haste. It would take a specialized tool to do it, one possibly from a taxidermists' tool kit—a course Libby happens to be taking.

". . . I'll be burning candles for a month."

Rowan forces a smile to hide her suspicion. Could Libby have killed those girls? Could she have killed Chloe?

She slides her tongue between her teeth then, and steadies her hand as she sinks the blade into the orange flesh of her pumpkin, cutting a pair of isosceles triangles in the center. The sharp chunks pop out and roll on the black expanse of the trash bag, conjuring the memory of Madison Caldwell's teeth glinting in the gully.

"Who teaches that?" she asks nonchalantly.

"One of the Deschanes. I think they're all named Dale."

"The taxidermist?"

"As an adjunct or something. He was a grade ahead of me in school." Marnie is so progressive and put together, Rowan often forgets she's Black Harbor born and raised. If it wasn't for her aging parents who now reside at the assisted living facility, she'd be long gone. Selfishly, Rowan is glad her best friend is anchored here. At least while her parents are still alive. It must be odd living in the same city all your life, running into people you went to high school with at the grocery store or tending to them as patients. Of course she would know the Deschanes. Deschane's Taxidermy is one of those fixtures of Black Harbor. A fourth-generation business, it's as much a part of the landscape as Forge Bridge.

"How is Libby?" Rowan asks.

"She's . . ." Marnie swirls her wineglass. She stares into the liquid as though she's reading tea leaves. "I sent her to work today because I didn't know what else to do. I figured it was better than having her just sit in her room and think about . . . everything. She's been through a lot. I fear what effects this might have on her." Her voice fades as she no doubt compares her own situation to Rowan's. At least Marnie has a daughter whose future she can worry about.

"Is she showing any signs of being traumatized, or . . . ?"

"I mean, she's distant, but she's also Libby. I'd honestly be more worried if she was bubbly."

Rowan sucks her teeth. Marnie's right. Distant and withdrawn is Libby's usual countenance.

"Can you tell me anything about these deaths, Row? I know it's confidential, but . . . we're in the dark here. And these are our children." She shakes her head and a piece of black hair comes loose from her bun. "I'm starting to lose my mind. All I know is that last night, my daughter went to a haunted house and tripped over the body of another one of her classmates. The third in a matter of two days. What if someone is out there preying on our daughters—" She catches herself and claps her hand over her mouth.

It's too late.

She knows what she's done—counted Chloe as a dead body—and yet, she doesn't know the guilt Rowan feels about all this. After all, she was a mother, once. Is she still? Are you still a mother when your only child dies? Or does your mom license get revoked? She's always believed people should have to obtain a license to be a parent. You need one to drive a vehicle, to get married. Why don't you need one to have a child? Seeing as many shaken babies as she has, newborns addicted to heroin and cocaine, will jade a person to that ideal. She just never, in a million years, would have predicted that she was exactly the kind of person she was referring to.

Who loses their child?

Someone who never deserved her.

"They might be," is all Rowan manages to say.

Marnie stares blankly at the countertop for a long time. Finally, she says, "I hate this place."

Rowan lifts her glass and softly clinks it against Marnie's. *Don't we all,* she thinks for the second time today.

She downs the rest of the cab in one gulp.

24
LIBBY

nec·ro·phile [nek-*ruh*-fahyl]

1. a person who is sexually excited by or attracted to dead bodies
2. a person who is excited or fascinated by death or killing

Libby identifies with the latter definition. It's important to establish absolute clarity that there is no sexual attraction whatsoever between her and dead bodies. She is simply fascinated in the same way that pluviophiles love the rain and bibliophiles love books. They're not trying to boink them.

Thwump!

The shingles' teeth raze the soles of her sneakers, but, as always, Libby sticks the landing on the Winthorps' rooftop. Allowing herself to fall forward, she uses her hands to climb up the subtle slope to Chloe's window.

Libby looks over her shoulder, ensuring that Rowan and her mother are still preoccupied and paying no mind to anything she might be doing. In this light, the windows of her own house are black and reflective; she can see herself on the opposite side of the sugar maple. From this distance, she looks like a figurine, a little troll someone might shove into a fairy garden.

It's starting to rain. The sprinkles are cold little kisses on her skin. It feels good, actually. She closes her eyes and allows herself the brief fantasy of a boy's lips touching her cheeks, her forehead, her chin. A boy like Reeves Singh?

Oh God, no.

Gross.

Reeves Singh could be a murderer. At least, that's what she pitched to Axel just a few hours ago, when he interrogated her outside Gallagher's Garden Center. It's the reason he let her go, too. He could have booked her for obstruction, but Libby knows as well as Axel that she is more valuable to him outside than in.

Libby grips the window frame and pushes upward. The latex gloves, compliments of Gallagher's, prevent her from leaving prints. They came in handy—no pun intended—for her crime scene rendezvous.

Which, now that she thinks about it away from Axel's intimidating stare, she was wearing when she collected Madison's teeth. She couldn't have left any fingerprints—

Unless—

He's bluffing, her logic chimes in. *That was all a scare tactic and you fell for it.*

Bluff or not, he knows about the teeth. And the cops have her taxidermy kit. She's fudged. Unless—

The window slides upward. Her ears prick to the sound of it moving along its tracks. It's so quiet up here, two stories above the ground, that she turns her head, slowly, to make sure no one's come outside to see what the noise is about, like she did the night Madison Caldwell was murdered.

She remembers it all so vividly, the way the black silhouettes of the trees blotted out the moon and stars, and how the temperature instantly dropped ten degrees or more, enough to freeze the hairs in her nose. The darkness was so intense it was depthless, disorienting in a way that made her question whether or not she was still in Belgrave Circle, less than a block away from where she'd heard the shrill cries of an animal meeting its end.

She was upstairs getting dressed to go to the musical when she

heard the ear-splitting sound of what she thought was a rabbit being
eaten by an owl. She shoved her feet into a pair of sliders, grabbed a
hoodie, and hurried out her bedroom window, down the branches of the
sugar maple, and across the yard. Running toward the sound, she hoped
she'd get down there soon enough to scare off the raptor and have a body
to resurrect with cotton and borax.

She was tired of stuffing squirrels and field mice.

There was so much you could do with a rabbit.

The flashlight on her phone lit the way. The rocks made a precarious
path, and more than once she nearly lost her balance. One rolled under her
weight. She stumbled, her phone flying from her grip. It landed faceup,
the beam of the flashlight illuminating the gully. A gasp tore from Libby's
throat as she saw what—or rather *who*—the screaming had come from.

The dead thing before her was indeed not a field mouse or a squirrel or a rabbit. It was Madison Caldwell. She lay on her back, her neck
turned unnaturally to the side, tendrils of golden hair veiling her face.
She stared at Libby with blue, doll-like eyes. Her mouth was a ruined
thing, painted red. Shards of white clung to her face like scraps left from
paper snowflakes.

Libby didn't think; she just acted. She scooped up a few of the teeth
and shoved them in her pocket. And she did something that was perhaps
even more surprising: she touched her, traced Madison's jaw with the
edge of her thumb. She was still warm, and more delicate as a corpse
than she had seemed alive. As a flower kept in the dark, she etiolated.
The rosiness began to fade from her cheeks and her eyes glazed, like frost
stealing over a garden. She was a braille book, begging to be read, her
frailty evident beneath Libby's fingertips. It was then that Libby under-
stood a universal truth.

We are fragile things.

No different than the woodchuck struck by a car, or the squirrel
devoured by a hawk. She knows that wolves will kill over territory, that
rabbits will eat their young if they're stressed or lacking protein in their
diets. And yet, are humans the only animal that will kill each other for
sport? This wasn't the work of a coyote or even a bear. The marks on

Madison's neck said otherwise, and there were no gashes from claws striping her body, no puncture wounds.

She couldn't say how much time passed while she marveled at Madison's transformation—seconds or minutes, only—but she snapped to her senses when the sound of a twig cracking split the quiet. She ran, then, leaving Madison in the gully. An officer would discover the body soon enough, she reasoned. Back here, a patrol car crawled by every hour.

She was right. The whispers had started before everyone had dispersed from the school's performing arts center. Police activity had been observed on Belgrave Circle. The charge that hummed in the air was not born of urgency, but rather curiosity as they wondered which elderly resident had fallen down the stairs or suffered a heart attack in their La-Z-Boy.

Naturally, that curiosity morphed into true terror when they realized that Madison Caldwell had been murdered and Chloe Winthorp was missing.

In Chloe's bedroom now, Libby moves on cat's feet. Her mom and Rowan are downstairs in the kitchen, carving pumpkins, it looked like? She'd rather have waited until her mom went home, but this can't wait.

Being caught with Madison's teeth in her locket made her a person of interest. Subsequently, Axel revealing that her taxidermy kit had been located at the scene of Sari's murder might have made her a suspect.

Until she mentioned her theory about Reeves.

His DNA was on Madison. And he was at the haunted house complex, same as her. He could have walked by Mr. Deschane's room any time on Friday and stolen her kit.

Had he even been there Friday?

One of his friends could have taken it. There are over four hundred students at Monroe Academy, and probably two dozen faculty members, which means there are that many possibilities.

Libby's kit being on-scene doesn't prove anything, and Axel knows it. That's why he had to let her go. She just prays he doesn't tell her parents. If they find out she went to the gully instead of reporting a murder, and stole Madison's teeth, she'd be deader than the skunk whose hide she nailed to a board in Mr. Deschane's class on Friday.

Still, it doesn't make her a murderer.

Reeves truly might be, though. She will see if she can peel back his layers, get him to talk, but first, there's something she has to take care of.

Her mind is a manic merry-go-round as she is careful not to upset the meticulous order of things in Chloe's room: the pillows that are just a little crooked on the bed, the comforter folded like a dog-eared page of a book. She hasn't been here since Thursday night, before she knew Chloe had vanished. She'd read the text message on the way home, Chloe sharing that her parents had, once again, chosen work over her.

Should I come over? Libby texted, but Chloe never responded. She climbed out her bedroom window and shimmied onto the sugar maple to climb into Chloe's room, except Chloe never showed up. Then, she heard the door slam downstairs and knew something was wrong. Panicked, Libby left the way she'd come in, forgetting to shut the window in her haste. She'd just made it into her own bedroom when she heard Rowan scream.

Franklin, the little fabric ghost, spins languidly in front of the smirking Winona Ryder poster, and for a fraction of a second, Libby is taken aback by how much Chloe really did resemble her while method acting for the *Beetlejuice* production.

No wonder Madison hated her. It wasn't just that Chloe stole her part. She killed it.

Oh, Chloe.

A wave of melancholy rushes at her. It knocks her off her feet, onto the bed. The mattress springs creak under her weight, but not protesting, just yawning, perhaps, after not having held a body these past few nights. She, herself, wants to be held. So badly. By Chloe, the only person in the world who made her feel as if she belonged. Who didn't judge her for wanting to stay in Black Harbor after graduation and breathe life into dead things, the same way Libby didn't judge Chloe for wanting to leave and pursue her dream of acting.

Most people do. Want to leave, that is. And Libby always knew Chloe would. She just didn't know it would be so soon. That their secret sleepovers would be cut short by an untimely vanishing. That's what she's taken to calling it. It sounds less final than "disappearance," or "tragedy." There is something more ethereal to the word "vanishing," something about it tougher to pin down. It gives Chloe's absence an almost mystical quality, like she vanished intentionally and will return when she is ready.

And when will that be? Libby wonders. When all the girls who wronged her are dead?

She remembers the night Chloe showed her the Snapchat. Libby already knew about it. A miracle in itself; she was only ever contacted via the app when her classmates needed help with their homework. But that day, she had received the Snap from Sari Simons, had seen the *Daddy Issues* caption dancing on the screen in real time, unlike when Chloe showed her the static image later that night.

The worst part, Libby thinks now, is that, despite the circumstances of the message, she had felt a sense of giddiness, of excitement at being included. That, for once, she hadn't been the last to know about whatever scandal ran rampant through their school.

Chloe knew Sari and Madison were behind the whole thing. Madison had been seething with jealousy ever since she landed the part of Lydia Deetz. Chloe had cried to Libby about it, feeling stupid about how she'd let Madison and Sari into her bedroom, had thought they were having a good time singing karaoke but really it had all been a ruse, premeditated for the girls to steal a shirt from her closet and plant it in Mr. Cutler's bag.

Chloe cried. Libby remembers it being the first time she had truly shown her naked vulnerability, and she held her, imitating the way her mother used to hold her when she was younger and didn't understand why the other kids didn't want to play with her. She stroked her hair that felt like a doll's after the box dye had coated it with chemicals and told her that this would pass. That Sari and Madison would get bored and move on to other targets. That by tomorrow, no one would give the faintest fuck about that stupid Snapchat.

Wishful thinking.

Chloe separated from her, then, and went to her bookshelf. Libby watched from the bed, her eyes having adjusted to the dark enough to see that Chloe was holding a yearbook. She took a Sharpie from a coffee mug that held pens and markers, and rejoined Libby. The annual was spread open between them. It made Libby think of all the crime shows she'd seen, when a victim's chest cavity is opened up on the autopsy table. Chloe flipped the pages, and when she reached Monroe Academy's sophomore class, she drew an *X* over the portraits of Madison Caldwell and Sari Simons.

She pressed so hard, her knuckles glowed white.

Now, sitting on the bed, Libby leans so her nose hovers less than an inch above the pillow and sniffs. Gummy bears, that's what Libby told Chloe she smelled like, once, in a fleeting moment of bravery. She knew it was silly and yet, she wanted to tell Chloe. She'd had this sudden compulsion to speak her mind—a feeling she'd learned to tamp down in front of most people—but Chloe was different. She pressed her lips tight after Libby said it, and then what did she do? She laughed. It wasn't a jeer or a scoff, but a genuine giggle. Libby felt like the funniest person in the world.

Chloe had that effect on her. She made her brave. Whenever she saw her in the halls at school, Libby would straighten her posture and walk a little taller. And when she saw the little glowing lights around Chloe's bedroom window, she felt . . . invited. Chloe was her shot of golden courage. And now she was gone, a star snuffed out in the vast night sky.

And Libby was utterly lost without her.

Gingerly, she kneels in front of Chloe's bookshelf. She thumbs through the spines of young-adult novels and classics like *Frankenstein* and *Fahrenheit 451* they'd had to read for school until she finds the yearbook she's looking for.

She cracks it open. Then, taking a Sharpie from the cup, she flips to the sophomore section and scribbles out the portrait of the girl Chloe forgot.

MONDAY, OCTOBER 23

25

ROWAN

Rowan sloughs to the fridge and grabs the carton of heavy cream. She pours a splash into her coffee and watches it swirl like a tongue of smoke before dispersing, changing the whole thing to a lighter shade of brown. This is her favorite part of the day. It might be the only good part, she considers as she raises the mug to her lips and looks out at the backyard.

The leaves that litter the ground are turning from scarlet to russet. Some are already black and shriveling; blood clots scattered in her yard. A sparrow perches on the edge of the birdbath and pecks at flakes of ice. A light sheet of frost blankets the lawn, transforming the grass into slivers of glass. She knows if she were to go out there, it would sound like she was stepping on Christmas ornaments.

Turning to face Marnie's house, she takes another sip, closing her eyes as the hot liquid travels down her throat, simultaneously calming her nerves and waking them. The kitchen light is on. Shadows move past the window. Marnie must be getting ready for work. Like Rowan's, her schedule is often without rhyme or reason, entirely dependent on when people's lives decide to take a turn for the worse.

It's why they're such good friends. Well, that and the fact that Marnie has the kind of manners that prohibit her from ever showing up without a bottle of wine. Rowan feels the tug of a dimple denting her right cheek. The smile is subtle and short-lived. Their friendship is over after this, she knows, once the news breaks that Libby is killing her classmates.

Who else could it be?

According to Axel, Libby admitted to disliking Madison Caldwell, who lived only a few houses down. It aligns with the word that was scratched into the inside of her lip: *BITCH*. No such signature was discovered on Sari Simons during the autopsy yesterday morning, but Libby being a practiced taxidermist doesn't help the girl's case.

Had she done Chloe the same way? While Rowan had never witnessed any blatant animosity between them, they had never gotten along—despite her and Marnie's encouragement. Especially in the earlier days, when the girls were young. But perhaps their antipathy ran deeper than dislike.

A sour taste fills her mouth when she falls into wondering what, of Chloe's, has been removed. Her ears? Her nose? Her tongue?

Rowan closes her eyes, willing her imagination to stop conjuring horrific images of her daughter. She wishes she could talk to Axel. Find out what he knows, if anything more than she does. But they're not exactly on speaking terms at the moment. His suspicion of Chloe's guilt is an irreconcilable rift between them.

Above the ringing silence, the walls whisper. It's unintelligible. She cannot make out what they are saying, but they are there, insistent. The register lowers; it rumbles beneath her now, pricks her toes through the soles of her slippers, as though the floor is a breeding ground for thorns. She feels a sharp, sudden pain in her foot that causes her to jump. Coffee slops on the hardwood, catching her robe that she threw on over her pajama pants and tank top when she rolled out of bed just twenty minutes ago. It can only be a fraction of a second later that she watches the mug go the same way. It shatters into a porcelain mosaic.

Rowan falls into a crouch and starts picking up the pieces. She sees it before she feels it—a scarlet slit in the web of her hand. The blood is bright and free-flowing. She springs back up and turns on the faucet, thrusting her hand under a stream of cold water. Suddenly, a question bursts out of her mouth, a question she's been keeping inside because she doesn't want to hear the answer.

Because she already knows the answer.

"Why?"

Why is this happening? Why did my daughter have to disappear?

Blood pulses in her temples. She swallows, bracing herself for the walls to reply. She can feel it building, can hear the roll that precedes the thunder. She has to get out of this house.

She turns the water off, then sprints across the dining room. Her robe catches on a chair. She yanks it free and the chair topples over. If someone were to see her, they would think she was running from an intruder.

And perhaps she is.

Our pasts can be intrusive, a wrench thrown into our lives at the absolute worst possible time. But is it ever a good time to be the subject of retribution?

Her past is flooding back with a vengeance.

Eighteen years ago, she killed someone's daughter.

Now someone has killed hers.

A cold sweat coats her skin. Fire shoots through her hand as she grasps the door handle, pushes down, and she's out. The crisp morning air is a hand hell-bent on choking her. Rowan propels herself off the front porch, catching her foot on the second-to-last stair. She tumbles to the grass, blades all crunching beneath her. The frost feels like saline pumping into her skin, and for a moment, she lets herself believe that it is. She could just lie here and close her eyes and forget . . . everything.

All is quiet now.

The past that has come to haunt her is shut inside her house. How long until it learns to open doors? She inhales and listens for the scraping of the latch. All is still, quiet. She cracks an eye open, ensuring the door remains tight to the frame. It does, but . . . something is missing.

Slowly, Rowan sits up. Her back is damp. Wet leaves cling to her legs and elbows. Her gaze sweeps the porch where two discs of condensation mark the stairs in place of jack-o'-lanterns.

"Son of a bitch." The curse is sharp under her breath.

Quick as though yanked by a fishing line, her head turns toward the street. Against a George A. Romero–inspired sky, a backdrop of orange and grey, she can just make out the silhouette of a figure ambling away.

Rowan rolls to her feet. Inching her toes all the way back into her slippers, she stands and starts to jog, her robe billowing behind her like a terry cloth cape. Suddenly, the sound of a fan or an engine comes from overhead. She looks up, expecting to see a low-flying small plane, but instead sees an echelon of Canada geese flapping their wings in unison as they head south. She slows to watch them, envious of their escape, then breaks into a run toward the figure down the street.

Her footsteps pound in sync with the blood thrumming in her eardrums. The cold air enters her bloodstream as she inhales, chilling her from the inside out. It smells like the inside of a pumpkin, sweet and vegetal. "Wait," she calls, breathless.

The person does not turn around. They're wearing a stocking cap and a black parka.

"Wait!" Rowan calls again, and coughs.

Still walking, the person looks back over their shoulder. Rowan slows her gait to avoid slamming into the back of them. Her heart sinks.

It's Tom Hargrove, the town treasurer. One hand grips the leash of his Yorkshire. He fixes Rowan with a curious stare. "Rowan?"

Rowan fights to catch her breath. She bends forward with her hands pressing into her knees. "I'm sorry, Tom."

"Is everything all right?"

She almost laughs. Nothing is all right. Not one damn thing. Girls are being murdered and mutilated, and her husband is determined to prove their daughter's guilt just so he can prove her to be alive.

"Rowan. You're bleeding." Tom looks appalled. His bottom teeth are miniature piano keys, slender and straight. The dog stares at her with the same expression.

"Oh." Rowan raises her hand and holds it about a foot from her face, giving the wound as much concern as if he'd alerted her to a mosquito. "Just, uh, I dropped a mug."

"Do you need me to call someone?"

"No, no. I'm fine. It looks worse than it is." She forces her most glowing, reassuring smile. "I'm gonna go bandage it up." Her mind tells her body to pivot, but it doesn't heed the command.

Tom eyes her suspiciously. "You sure I can't . . . You must've run out here for some reason?"

Rowan shakes her head. "Really, Tom. I'm sorry. I thought you were someone else."

"Who?"

She laughs, though it sounds more like a bark. The dog tilts his head. "It's stupid. Just . . . someone's been stealing the pumpkins off my porch. I don't know if you and Ellen even put pumpkins out, but—"

Tom's white brows knit, the movement of his forehead pushing up the brim of his brown cap. "Yeah, ours are gone, too. The first time it happened, I had the grandkids carve us up a couple more and I set them out, but I noticed this morning that they're gone again."

Be it this particular conversation or because this is the first conversation she's had with anyone about anything besides murder, Rowan has forgotten the throbbing in her hand. "And nothing else is taken or messed with?" she wonders.

"Not so far as we can tell. I got half a mind to sit out there dressed as Freddy Krueger and scare the bejeezus out of them, whoever's doing it."

Rowan allows a small smile. "Let me know when and I'll join you."

"All right then." He swallows, as though unsure she can handle more. "The neighborhood watch group is pegging a woman. She looks half-starved, a little drugged-out maybe."

Rowan feels the familiar creases in her forehead. "We have a neighborhood watch group?"

Tom stares at her with a look that asks *Where have you been?* "On social media," he says. "People post about the goings-on around here. Usually it's just 'saw a car parked by the lake with no plates,' or 'the raccoons got my bird feeder again.' Benign stuff like that. Until recently, of course—" He catches himself. A puff of air issues from his mouth. It hangs between them for a moment. "Have you heard anything?" he asks. "About Chloe?" He speaks in a low voice, as though his neighborhood peers have their ears pressed to their windows, eavesdropping on their conversation. His wife among them. Ellen Hargrove is one of those people who wears a look of disapproval as naturally as others wear a smile. Maybe she reserves it only for Rowan, though.

Rowan swallows the lump in her throat. She shakes her head and a strand of blond hair falls in front of her eyes. "No. Nothing. I mean . . ." She exhales, too, and wishes desperately that she had a cigarette. She taps each of her fingers on her right hand against her thumb, digging the nails into the flesh. "I hear a lot of things, but not about Chloe."

"I'm sorry."

"It's—" The immediate response is automatic, but she has nothing more to say.

"Do you have social media?" Tom asks, his tone helpful now.

"Never touch the stuff." She says it like someone refusing a drink. She's seen the zombifying effect social media has on society. It takes people out of the present and freezes them in time, comatose but for the ability to scroll, while life goes on around them. She's seen careers that took decades to build ruined over a Facebook post. All it would take is a night alone and a bottle of wine and Rowan has no doubt she would slip up. Her goal is to keep people at arm's length. Why would she ever offer anyone—let alone hundreds of people—a glimpse behind the scenes of her life?

"Well." Tom pats his jacket pocket. "I don't have my phone with me or I'd show you."

"I'll ask Marnie."

"Do that." Tom's eyes hold Rowan for a moment, working his jaw as though he's chewing his next words. "I heard there was another one. Another little girl . . ." He pauses as though waiting for her to fill in the blank.

She doesn't. Instead, she is painfully aware of blood dripping from her hand and staining the road. "Yes," she replies, because what is the point of lying about it? He has grandkids. He should know that there is a killer at large. "I'm afraid I can't share anything about the—"

He waves away the notion as though dismissing a trail of smoke. "I understand. It's just . . . well . . . there isn't a chance that any of this has unearthed clues about Chloe's whereabouts, has it?"

Rowan freezes. How can he ask so flippantly? If she knew where Chloe was, does he really think she would be out here, crazed and wearing only a bathrobe, bleeding onto the asphalt and desperate to solve the stupid mystery of who is stealing her pumpkins?

She doesn't recall answering him. All she knows is that some silent moments must pass, because when she comes to herself again, she is still standing in the middle of the street, staring vacantly at the space Tom once occupied. Turning in a slow stupor, she walks back to her house. The cut in her hand screams, and all she hears is the sound of her slippers dragging across the blacktop, over the lawn, through the leaves, and back to her doorstep—and the condemning whispers that are no longer dormant.

She understands what they're saying now.

An eye for an eye.

26
LIBBY

"Seriously, Row, you're lucky you don't need stitches."

Her mom's parental voice echoes from the kitchen. It's usually accompanied by a rhetorical question, such as when she asks Libby, *Do you really need* that much *peanut butter?* Or *You scraped that off the side of the road, didn't you?* But Rowan is an adult and not her daughter, so maybe that is what makes the difference.

Their house is decorated in cool tones—dove-feather greys and whites, and blues the light shade of Araucana eggs. The color palette is calming and quiet. Except Libby doesn't feel calm at all right now. Her heart hammers. She can hear it in her eardrums, her blood pulsing to its beat as though there's a raging club inside her and she's not even invited. Why is Rowan here? And why is her mom hovering over her, pressing a bag of frozen broccoli into her hand?

"What's up?" Libby screws her fingertips into the corners of her eyes, scraping out the crusts of sleep. It's early and there's no school today. It was canceled for obvious reasons. So, why has her mother called her to come downstairs at—she looks at the clock on the microwave—7:18 a.m.?

Whatever the reason, it can't be good. Her chest tightens when she remembers sneaking into Chloe's room yesterday. Perhaps Rowan knows.

She didn't leave the window open again, did she?

No. She's sure she didn't. But there could have been a footprint—it was raining, after all—or a strand of long, black hair left on the bed-spread. She needs to be more careful.

Rowan drags her gaze to her. Her eyes are wet and sunken into pools of purple. Libby furrows her brows as she looks at Rowan's hand. "Is everything all right?"

As far as rhetorical questions go, this one takes the cake for dumbest ever. Of course nothing is all right.

"We need your phone," says her mom.

Her stomach drops. "My phone?"

What if they see the texts between her and Chloe from Thursday night, and all the messages that date back to last year? She never erases them. In fact, sometimes she lies in bed and scrolls through old conversations to remind herself that she does have one friend in this world, despite what everyone believes.

She did, anyway.

"Your social media, Lib. Please."

With a shaking hand, Libby lifts up her T-shirt and pulls her phone out of the waistband of her sleep shorts. She hands it over as though she's just been caught with it in class, but her mom doesn't take it. "Can you log on to your Facebook or whatever?"

"Supposedly, there's a neighborhood watch group," explains Rowan. "For Belgrave Circle."

There's something about the way Rowan is looking at her that makes Libby more uneasy than she was when she first came down. She doesn't know if medical examiners use magnifying glasses or microscopes, but she feels like a germ being scrutinized beneath one right now.

"Okay." Libby searches groups and types in Belgrave Circle Neighbo—

"There it is!" her mom exclaims, pointing at the screen.

It's too early for loud noises. Flinching, Libby clicks on the group and brings up the page. "What are you looking for, specifically?" she asks. If she's confident and competent, perhaps they won't take her phone and try to do it themselves. Who knows what they might push or unlock. She straightens her posture and keeps a firm grip on her phone. She's got this. She's in control.

"A woman is taking pumpkins from people's porches," Rowan explains. "There might be some footage or a forum or something."

A knock sounds at the front door. Libby and her mother exchange a look, each questioning the other on who it could be. Her dad is already gone to work.

"I'll get it," Libby offers. It gets colder as she nears the door. The morning chill seeps in through the windows, tiny fractures in the glass, the hair-thin space where the pane meets the sill. She peers through the peephole and her internal temperature drops to match that of her surroundings.

Fudge.

Axel Winthorp is standing on her front porch. He looks right at her, as though the fish-eye lens magnifies her eyeball. Reluctantly, and with all the horrible potential reasons why he could be at her house right now at this hour a melee in her mind, Libby opens the door.

"Good morning, Libby," he says, his voice hoarse. "May I come in?"

She steps aside and feels as though she's just let a vampire into her house. He's pale and sallow, and walks with a hunch as though he dragged himself out of a grave to get here. She looks outside as she shuts the door behind him and notices his black Impala parked in his driveway. She wonders if her kit is still in the backseat with her silver locket and if the vehicle is unlocked.

"Oh. Hi." Her mother's voice is breathy, surprised at Axel's sudden appearance.

"Hello, Marnie. Rowan. I, um, stopped home to shower and whatnot and you weren't there. I thought you might be over here."

This is awkward. They've been fighting; Libby can tell by the way neither wants to meet the other's eyes. She observes how Rowan wraps her cardigan around herself tighter. A muscle twitches in her jaw. She looks ashamed and stares down at the bag of frozen vegetables in her lap.

"Did you hurt yourself?" Axel moves closer. While Rowan explains that she dropped a coffee mug, Libby takes the opportunity to recede to the outer edges of this unorthodox gathering. She doesn't need to be here when Axel changes his mind and brings up the topic of the locket and whose teeth are where. She can sneak upstairs and put pants on, then climb out the window and just wander a bit. Return when her mom cools down.

But her phone is still on the countertop. She can't go too far.

If she could just—

Toast. She'll start making toast. And while she's buttering her bread, she will nonchalantly slip the phone back into her waistba—

"Can I get you some coffee, Axel? I was going to make a fresh pot." Her mom whizzes behind her, already grabbing another mug from the cupboard.

"No, thank you, Marnie. I was hoping I could talk to you about something."

"Oh." A startle. "Of course."

Fudge. Oh fudge. Oh fudge.

Libby grips the edge of the island, bracing herself. It's too late to run now. In the next thirty seconds, everyone will know about her gruesome hobby. She collected Madison's teeth. It's not as if they were still in her skull when she took them. It isn't a crime and yet—

It's obstructing, Axel made sure to tell her yesterday. She could be charged with concealing information that could have helped the investigation. But she didn't see anything. She already swore that to him. And if she gets him dirt on Reeves Singh, she'll be free as a bird.

Which is why she needs her phone back. Desperately. Like Thing from *The Addams Family*, her fingers dance across the countertop and grab the device. She scrolls frantically, searching for anything that could derail this conversation. Then, something silver flashes. As adept as a cat locking onto a laser dot, Libby's gaze darts to Axel's hand that's half out of his pocket. He's holding her locket chain.

"Oh!" Libby cries. The grown-ups in the room all startle. "Is this who you're looking for, Rowan?"

She pauses on a grainy fish-eyed video of what appears to be a person in a drab, olive-green jacket and a maroon stocking cap. The post is captioned Porch Pirate Stealing Pumpkins!!

The time stamp on the video is 22:14:03, just a few minutes after 10 p.m. and plenty dark. They watch intently as a bony woman approaches the porch, then gathers the glowing jack-o'-lanterns one at a time and deposits them in a stroller. With the gourds in tow, she ambles on, probably to the next house.

Libby reads the comments. While some people express sympathy, others are judgmental and/or fearful.

She must be mental.
Wouldn't be surprised if she turns out to have killed that Caldwell girl.

As she continues to scan the thread, she sees a comment where someone suspects where the woman—who's been coined the Pumpkin Lady—stays: that old haunted house on Winslow Street.

She knows that house. There isn't a soul in Black Harbor who doesn't. A girl was kept there once and tortured, pimped out by her aunt. Just last year she became an important piece to solving the twenty-year-old mystery of Clive Reynolds's disappearance. Rumor has it she left and never set foot on Black Harbor soil again. Good for her.

"Play it again." Axel's voice is suddenly in her ear. She taps the play button and he leans closer. The cold October air clings to him. "Oh my God." His words are hardly more than a whisper.

"What?"

Her mom comes to watch as Axel presses play a third time. "That's the Glencasters'," she says, noting the red bricks and the pair of teal planters.

Axel taps the screen to pause the video. The woman is frozen mid-bend and Libby sees it, too. On her back is a purple, star-speckled bag. "That's Sari Simon's backpack," she says.

27

AXEL

The house on Winslow Street is the definition of derelict. It's owned by the City, which means they don't need a warrant to search it. Axel doesn't know why they don't just tear it down. It's unfit for human life, this dilapidated shack with the leaning walls. It looks as though a great gust of lake-effect wind barraged through, and the house is crumpling in on itself to brace for another. A woman died here, Axel knows. She fell on the ice and split her skull on the asphalt. His eyes flick to Kole on his right. The sergeant stares at the ground as though he can still see the stain.

Axel, Riley, and Kole approach the house. Fletcher mans the perimeter with patrol officers Jiminez and Matlin. Kole inches to the front and they divide into a V, like a formation of birds flying south for the winter. They wait, holding their breaths and listening. Axel stares hard at the house and the house stares back. The windows on either side of the door resemble empty, far-apart eyes. The doorway is a mouth open in a silent scream. A ragged sheet hangs from a corner, twirling languidly. From a few blocks away, he hears the muted klaxon of a car alarm and the waves crashing against the pier. There's a low roar, too. It mingles with a sibilant hiss sometimes, and he knows it is only the incessant score of Black Harbor. It used to scare Chloe at night; she was convinced it was some monster lying in wait, and she wasn't wrong. He knows the haunting air belongs to Forge Bridge, which isn't far from here, its rusted rungs and railroad ties groaning and whispering, beckoning people to its edge. Closer, he hears frantic scratching and skittering. Cockroaches in the walls. They might be the only reason the place is still upright.

Axel draws his gun and hears Riley do the same. Kole carries his 9mm at his side, index finger resting against the slide. It's the first thing they teach at the academy: only put your finger on the trigger when you're going to pull it.

Kole sets his foot on the bottom stair. A piece breaks off. Rotted. He continues on up, muttering, "Jesus Christ, this place is just a bunch of termites holding hands."

Axel's heart pounds against his rib cage as he prepares to follow. What if Chloe's here? What if she's been hidden away in this vile, decrepit place all this time, right under his and Rowan's noses? Guilt shreds his insides. How could he ever forgive himself? How could Chloe ever forgive them for not finding her, for not spending every minute of their waking lives turning over every brick and leaf and stone until she's home?

He's trying to. God knows he is. He might very well have gotten somewhere with Libby Lucas before this bend in the road diverted him off course. She collected Madison Caldwell's teeth the night of her murder. It's weird and it's creepy, but it isn't a crime. And she's a juvenile. Even if he charged her with obstruction for not sharing this information earlier, no detention center would ever hold her. Besides, she is more valuable to him outside than in. She can work on Reeves Singh while he keeps his sights trained on Cutler.

Once he finds out what this lady is doing with Sari Simons's backpack.

Kole tosses a quick glance over each shoulder. Axel locks eyes with him and nods. When Kole turns around again, he points his gun at the hollow doorway. "Police!" he shouts. And again: "Police! Come out with your hands up!"

Nothing. The only movement is the grey sheet, still twirling. As it moves, Axel can see a faded yellow stripe of spray paint. A gang symbol maybe, or something Wiccan. Kole walks up another stair, then two more. "Police!" he shouts. He's standing on the porch now, just six feet in front of the cavity.

Suddenly, Axel sees them. So dirty that they match the sheet, are two bony feet. "Nik!" he whispers.

Kole pauses, and Axel knows he cannot turn around, cannot turn his back to the entrance.

"Look down!"

Kole does and skips a step back. Her skinny silhouette is now made plain to them. Once Axel sees her, he cannot unsee her, this skeletal thing reaching, reaching—

"Police, stop!" He trains his gun on her. His finger grazes the trigger.

The movement stops. A breeze blows the sheet just enough to reveal a pair of eyes glowing wild and bright and hungry in the pitch of the hovel. "No harm," she says. Her voice crackles, like a record that's collected dust from disuse. *"Arrêter,"* she says, though the word is whisper-quiet. Slowly, she places her hands on top of her head and retreats inside.

Kole follows in her wake, leading Axel and Riley into the leaning structure.

Her name is Celeste Cyzon and she's from Montreal, according to her profile in Onyx. She's been in Black Harbor for ten years, the past four spent either in and out of group homes or homeless. At forty, she looks much older; the deep creases in her forehead and fine lines around her mouth are those of someone twice her age. Her skin is reminiscent of a tanned hide, callused and copper-colored, though it's lost its richness. Icy-blue eyes and naturally pouty lips tell Axel she must have been beautiful before whatever cataclysm brought her here to the house on Winslow Street. It had to be something momentous, he knows, because you don't just wake up one day and find yourself wearing rags and squatting in an abandoned house of horrors.

He wonders what lies in the gulf that separates him from her. How much time do you have to spend brokenhearted and destitute to lose yourself completely? Thinking of his pathetic makeshift bed sprawled on the third floor of the lighthouse, he realizes that perhaps it's not a gulf that separates him from the Pumpkin Lady. Perhaps it's more of a gully, like the one Madison Caldwell's body was found in.

Axel looks around. Wax is hardened to the floor, petrified into wraithlike fingers reaching toward chalk pentagrams and shattered crack pipes. There are needles and wads of tinfoil with blackened ends, crumpled cans of malt liquor and a fogged bottle of vodka. Dried-up condoms look like a snake has shed its skin and could still be slithering about. Strange enough, there are no pumpkins.

Not a single grinning face.

"No English," Celeste repeats for the third time since they entered her dwelling.

"¿Hablas español?" asks Kole.

She shakes her head.

"They speak French in Montreal," says Riley.

At the mention of her home, Celeste's eyes brighten. "Oui," she says. "Yes."

"Hold on," Riley commands both Axel and Kole. She marches out of the house and down the stairs. Her footsteps dissipate then, returning less than a minute later when she reappears with the young, blond twentysomething that is Officer Matlin.

"She took French in high school," says Riley. "And she's a lot closer to it than any of us."

Kole squints at Officer Matlin, and Axel suspects they're thinking the same thing: she looks barely old enough to hold a beer, let alone a perimeter.

Officer Matlin acknowledges them both with a polite nod, then crouches to meet Celeste at eye-level. "Parlez-vous . . . ?"

Celeste is hunched over a pile of what appear to be random things—half-melted candles and fast-food wrappers, a tattered red scarf, and a baby doll missing an eye that reminds them all of Sari Simons—but Axel knows these are probably all of her earthly possessions. The backpack leans against the stroller, which he observes has a cracked wheel.

Celeste tilts her head. The movement is jerky, like a bird, and Axel wonders how long it's been since someone has spoken her home language to her.

"We're here to help you," Matlin enunciates slowly. "Um . . . us"—she taps her chest and motions to Kole, Axel, and the two officers—"help you." She gestures to Celeste. "Um . . . *je suis là pour t'aider* . . . I think. Me help you. *Oui?*" She nods, prompting Celeste to do the same.

She does. Her eyes narrow, though, and she tilts her head again. *"Pourquoi?"*

She looks scared, Axel thinks, and suddenly, he is afraid of her scuttling away. Matlin must sense it, too, because she hastens to the point and gestures to the backpack. *"Le sac,"* she says. "Belongs to you?"

Slowly, Celeste nods. But then her brows knit and she chews her lip.

"Tell her it's okay," says Riley. "We're not going to take it from her. But ask how she found it."

Matlin speaks what must be calming words, because Celeste appears to relax. Axel feels his own heart rate slow now that it seems their best lead isn't about to dart out a window.

"Vous découvrez . . . le sac? How did you find it?" Matlin presses on.

Axel uses the voice memo app on his phone to record the conversation. With the little French she knows—which is more than the rest of them combined—Matlin may only be catching every third or fourth word. They can send the recording for translation.

Celeste tells them that she went to the Compound last night. "She said she likes seeing the costumes," Matlin translates. "The flickering lights. The energy."

Axel can see it. For someone who lives a rather hermetic life, this time of year must provide ample entertainment. He can also see what Celeste is not saying, which is that she probably also goes there to scavenge. All those kids teeming about means discarded candy and dropped belongings, maybe even a dollar bill or two skittering across the flattened grass.

"She was walking around the back of the building, when, through a split in the wall, she saw a hand on the ground. Lights were flashing. She went to investigate, and discovered the body of a young girl." Axel catches *"les yeux,"* which he knows to be "eyes." She discovered the body with the eyes already cut out, then.

"What time?" he asks.

"A quelle heure?"

Celeste thinks. "Um . . . *je ne sais pas.*" She shrugs and proceeds to tell them it was sometime at night.

"And *le sac?*" Riley asks, tilting her head toward the JanSport backpack with the cosmological print.

Celeste stares at Riley like a child about to be punished for wrongdoing. She lowers her gaze, then, and mutters something to Matlin.

"What did she say?" Kole leans in.

Matlin turns away from Celeste to regard Axel, Kole, and Riley. "She says the dead girl didn't need it."

Silence settles. It's heavy as a weighted blanket, but cold as a covering of snow.

Axel crouches beside the young patrol officer, so he stares at Celeste eye to eye. "Did you see anyone else?" he asks.

"Autre personne?" relays Matlin.

They wait. The silence settles heavier. It feels like the roof is caving in, the ceiling coming to rest on his shoulders. Axel watches Celeste intently, and finally, she nods. Then, she takes off her pilled cap to reveal a scalp of close-shorn hair. Flecks of silver sparkle in it. She points to her temple, then to Axel, and back to her temple.

"Me?" says Axel, to which she shakes her head. "A cop? A man?"

She nods.

"Okay, a man."

She taps her temple.

"With grey hair?" Axel turns to Kole and sees the shadow that passes over the sergeant's face. It's because he knows Axel had him, just as he knows he made him let him go.

Cutler.

28

ROWAN

Bells jingle against the glass when she walks in. Deschane's Taxidermy shop smells like urine and dust, a hint of tobacco. A transparent stream of vapor spews from an essential oil diffuser in a poor attempt to mask the musk of a man who probably came with the place. She imagines Deschane to be ancient, all leathery skin and white hair, with dentures that are too white and sharp, like the ones he fits into his dead animal skulls. His shop's been here since 1931, as much a fixture of Black Harbor as Forge Bridge.

The shiver of the bells sends a corresponding tremor down Rowan's spine. Her fingertips tingle as she reviews her current suspicion: Libby Lucas is larger than most girls her age. She's larger than most boys, too. If Reeves Singh could be a viable suspect, why not Libby? Throughout this investigation, she has not even tried to conceal the fact that she disliked the victims. And then there's the matter of the evisceration spoon.

Which is why she's here. She waits at the front, her ears pricking as a new sound enters the environment: the low thunder of footsteps. Her gaze roams the shop, peering through the dozens of stuffed animals and boxes of buckshot to try and steal a glance of who she's come to meet.

"Hello, what can I do ya for?" It's an automated response, Rowan knows, because he stops abruptly when he observes that she is not his usual customer.

Neither is he what she expected. Broad-shouldered and bearded,

this Deschane is a good twenty years younger than the one she was envisioning. He smiles, showing teeth that are definitely originals; they're
a little crooked and stained from probably thirty years of coffee and
tobacco.

"Um . . ." Rowan inhales. It fills her chest and makes her stand up
straighter. "Hello, Mr. Deschane. I'm Rowan Winthorp, the medical examiner for Sulfur County." She offers her gloved hand, which he shakes.
His grip is strong. The diamond from her wedding ring cuts into her
finger.

"Dale Deschane. But you already knew that." He looks uncertain.
She notices his stare move over her shoulder to take a look at her car
parked outside. "You with the police?"

A nervous smile cracks Rowan's face. It's out of character for her.
She doesn't usually get nervous while on the job, but then, this is unoffi-
cial business. A medical examiner's investigation tends to stay with the
body. *Bodies,* in this case.

She decides to stick with the truth. "I investigate deaths. You might
have heard, we've had a few of them recently."

Deschane retracts his lips. He strokes his facial hair that looks like a
doe's tail with a white streak down the middle. His eyes are a cold grey,
the color of the lake on a sunless morning. "If you're looking for dead
things, you've come to the right place. But I don't know if I deal in the
kind of dead things you're looking for."

Slowly, Rowan peruses his shop. She avoids eye contact, not wanting him to catch a glimpse of her gears turning. How would Axel read
this man, she wonders. He seems closed-off; she notes how he stands
with his arms crossed and feet shoulder-width apart. But he's not alto-
gether unkind. She did just waltz into his store and start talking about
murder, after all. She touches the snout of a stuffed badger, then taps the
eye. "These are glass?"

"Sure are." He takes a few steps toward her.

"Do you always remove the eyes when you . . . taxidermy something?"

"Yes, ma'am."

"With what?"

Deschane tilts his chin and narrows his gaze. "Depends. Usually a screwdriver, maybe a spoon to scoop them out. Scissors to cut the fatty tissue clinging to the skull."

She stopped listening at *spoon*. Her heart skips. "Can you show me? The tools you use, I mean."

Deschane squares his stance again. "Listen Miss Winthorp, do I need a lawyer or something? Or do you need a warrant?"

Rowan clenches her jaw. She doesn't correct him on the prefix. In fact, it feels kind of nice. It makes her feel young. Untethered. Before Black Harbor was anything more to her than a faraway, destitute city at the edge of the lake.

Deschane's eyes are locked on her, holding her in place.

"No. It's just . . ."

"It's just that there are little bunnies turning up around town with their body parts cut off and you thought you might start with the most obvious choice, the taxidermist, right?"

Rowan says nothing. Her whole body stiffens as though affected by rigor. Her cheeks burn and tears sting her eyes. Dale Deschane is a red buffalo plaid blur. She feels so stupid. She should never have come here. But she's as desperate to prove her daughter's innocence as she is desperate to stop the killer from snagging their next target.

"How do you know about all that?" she asks. Nothing about the crime scenes and mutilation has been disclosed to the news. Unless something leaked, which wouldn't be surprising.

"I might spend a lot of time talking to dead animals, but I don't live under a rock. You'd have to be deaf, blind, and dumb not to know what's been going on. Lots of rumors going around. And by your reaction just now, I'd say there's some truth to them."

Rowan's moved on to a rabbit now. She pinches its little cottontail. She had one with this same coloring when she was young, except it had floppy ears. What a terrible existence it must've lived, she thinks. Kept in a cage outside, sucking water from a metal spout and chewing tasteless pellets. It lived and died in captivity, all for a little girl's amusement. She never let Chloe have one, no matter how many times she asked. "Wild things can't be kept," Rowan always reminded her. "You'll kill it."

"You didn't come here to accuse me of killing little bunnies, did you?" Deschane's voice is disembodied. As hairy as he is, he's quite camouflaged in this menagerie of stuffed carcasses. Ironically, the question sounds like an accusation.

"No," says Rowan a touch too quickly. She yanks her hand away from the rabbit as though the tail has become a flame. She thought she heard him say it before, but this time the word "bunnies" is unmistakable. Her ears prick to the sound of the large man's footsteps. The old floor creaks beneath his weight. She's easy prey, she realizes. Every hair on her body stands on end as she thinks of the marks left on the girls' necks. Is that where he pressed his thumbs when he choked them?

She imagines Axel reviewing the security camera footage after she's dead and bagged up. Once he gets over the mortification of her murder right here in Deschane's Taxidermy shop, he will rack his brain wondering how she could have been so stupid to wander into a killer's den.

Because Deschane is a killer. Her eyes dart from one dead animal to the next. He killed all of these or most of them. Or his family did. Killing is in his blood.

"You know, I grew up in this shop." Deschane is circling her. She can feel his atoms disturbing the stagnant air, closing in. Her chest tightens. Her arms are stiff at her sides. She's as petrified as a deer in an open field. "My dad owned it and his dad before him. So, in three generations, no medical examiners or beautiful women have ever set foot in here. And here you are killin' two birds with one stone."

"I—" She what? She's sorry for coming here? Apologizing would insinuate she's accusing him of murder. And she isn't. She's just looking for answers. "I—" She's stammering now. She has no recourse, no tactful way to escape.

And then Deschane says something that makes her knees go weak: "You look like you could use a cigarette."

They stand out back behind his shop, letting the building block the wind. Rowan takes her first drag in over a year and feels suddenly awake, her head cleared. She blows out a puff of smoke, some of her anxiety with it.

"I know who you are," says Deschane.

Rowan's breath hitches. She sucks in the anxiety she just exhaled. It hits her tenfold. She coughs like a rookie smoker. "I should hope. I introduced myself a few minutes ago."

"You're the mom of that little bunny who's gone missing. I recognize the name. Winthorp." A pause settles between them. "I'm sorry," he adds.

Rowan is not good at responding to comments like this. She never knows whether to nod or shrug or say thank you, so she usually does nothing. Except to Deschane, she asks: "Why do you call girls *bunnies*?"

Deschane takes a long drag and lets it out. "Because girls are prey." He says it so matter-of-factly that Rowan flinches. He side-eyes her. "Tell me I'm wrong. Tell me that in the last few days, we're not dealing with the wrongful deaths of two or three girls who all attended Monroe Academy. In a school of four-hundred-and-some students, that's inexcusable. And undeniable."

"I hate that," Rowan says.

Deschane shrugs. "It's a fact. You don't have to like it for it to be true."

The silence is back. One by one, Rowan sees the corpses of each victim: Madison. Sari. And Chloe, the question mark. *You'll love me more when I'm dead.* Is that a fact, too?

"I've seen her," says Deschane. "Not recently, but . . . recent enough, I suppose."

"Who?" Rowan is zoned out. There are a handful of names he could say. But he says the one that matters most to her.

"Chloe. She's never taken my class, but . . ."

"You teach there?" Rowan feigns being dumb.

She's not very good at it, because Deschane smiles and says, "You already knew that. It's an elective. I'm there every afternoon, Monday through Friday. The shop closes at one during the week."

"How was she when you saw her? What was she doing?"

Holding his cigarette between his index and middle finger, Deschane scratches his head. A ribbon of smoke curls upward, disappearing into the overcast sky. "It was kind of abrupt, wasn't it? Her transformation. One day she's like this ray of sunshine, all blond and skipping down the halls; and the next she's a storm cloud, dressed in black, safety pins punched through her ears. I thought something was up, but . . ." He swats dismissively at nothing. "Kids are weird. Especially high school ones." He pauses, his thoughts catching up with his mouth. "Sorry, I didn't mean to offend your daughter by calling her weird."

"No, it's fine," Rowan replies on impulse. "It was weird . . . Seeing her change so fast like that. She told us she was method acting."

"I thought maybe something was going on," Deschane offers. "I'd heard things."

Rowan nods, and she can tell by the look he gives her that he knows she's familiar with the rumor. Thankfully, he doesn't rehash it. She doesn't have the mental fortitude for that right now.

"But what can you do? You learn quick not to stick your nose anywhere it don't belong. Especially as an adjunct. Besides, the cops were investigating it."

Rowan's forehead knits. This is news to her. Axel never shared anything about an investigation. Did he know about the rumor of Chloe and Mr. Cutler this whole time? Despite the cold, her blood begins to boil.

Deschane doesn't need to know she's rocked, though. She'll deal with the shock later. "What do you mean about being an adjunct?" she asks. "The full-time teachers are . . . standoffish, or what?"

He grins. "That's putting it nicely. Look at me." He pivots away from her and gestures at his body from neck to knees. Rowan's gaze drifts even farther down to his boots that are so worn, the steel toes are visible. Deschane sniffs. "I'm not exactly Monroe Academy–chic here. They like to make it known I'm on their turf. Only reason there's a taxidermy class at all is because my granddad's one of the school's founding fathers. We used to have money, I guess, back when the tannery was up and runnin'. Every now and again I grab a shovel and start diggin' in the back forty. Hopin' I'll find where he buried his treasure."

Rowan knows what it feels like to be the black sheep. She used to get it a lot when she first started out as a medical examiner. The cops didn't take her seriously. They acted as though she—a woman—belonged literally anywhere but their crime scene. Even the women cops.

"Bunch of elitist pricks." She doesn't realize she's spoken out loud until Deschane snorts.

"That's putting it nicely, too. There's some characters in that school for sure," he says.

This piques Rowan's interest. "Like who?"

You're going to say Cutler, aren't you? Come on, say his name.

Deschane flicks his cigarette and squishes it into the asphalt. "Meet me out for a drink and I'll tell you all about 'em."

Rowan stops breathing. Her heart skips, not in a good way. It's been ages since she's been asked out; she's out of practice. But this is not a date or anything like that. It's one drink in exchange for information. A transaction.

Axel. What will she tell him?

She waves him away as though he's nothing more than a cloud of smoke. He never came home last night. God knows who he's with, doing God knows what.

He was probably with Riley. It's always Riley.

Texting him. Calling him. Sparring with him. For a while now, Rowan has wondered if she's in the way of something. Taking one final drag, she drops her cigarette to the ground, too, and corkscrews it with the ball of her foot.

She doesn't have time for that right now. First, she will find Chloe. Then, she'll worry about picking up the pieces of her marriage. Because right now, Deschane is telling her he knows something that could help her clear her daughter's name and nail a killer.

For a second, she is yanked back to Thursday night, when she faced the terrible disappointment in Chloe's eyes and when she warned her that she would love her more when she's dead. But there had been something after that, hadn't there? Chloe's lips had moved to form words, but . . . she never said them. What had her daughter been trying to tell her?

Rowan drags her gaze to meet Deschane's which, frightfully, never strayed from her. She shouldn't do it and yet, she has no choice. She cannot keep pining at the window and carving pumpkins until Chloe comes home. She has one singular, double-edged mission now. Find Chloe, nail the killer.

Here she goes again, killin' two birds with one stone when she says: "Beck's. Six o'clock."

29

AXEL

"No more talking to this guy at his house." Kole fixes Axel with a hard look before turning to Riley. "Now, he comes to ours."

The three of them are in the bullpen at the BHPD; the lighthouse isn't set up for interrogations. It isn't busy. Most day shift investigators work Monday through Friday until 3 or 4 p.m., with the exception of two who work a rotating schedule—as though criminal activity can be forced into the hours of a normal workweek, and two detectives are enough to manage the unruly overflow. When he first came upstairs from Patrol, Axel snorted at the ridiculousness of it, but over the years, he has come to understand how futile their jobs are. The way crime surges in this city, command might as well tell them to mop up Lake Michigan. It's never going to happen, just like crime is never going to ebb. Honestly, who cares when they do it?

The emptiness of the bureau strikes a chord of melancholy. He remembers when this place was teeming with hungry investigators, hunting killers and searching houses. It wasn't all that long ago. The budget cuts coupled with a hostile landscape drove a lot of people—from white shirts to patrolmen—into early retirement, and a current hiring freeze keeps new recruits from coming in. The fact that the police haven't even had a contract in three years doesn't add any lipstick to the pig, either.

Cutler answers on the second ring. He's on speakerphone. Kole's voice betrays none of the seething animosity any of them feel toward him as he asks him to come in for an interview. "Some new information has come to light about some of your students," says Kole. "We think you could help us work through some stuff, maybe put this whole thing to rest."

It isn't a lie. Not yet.

They do want to interview Cutler about his students—particularly the dead ones who happen to be the same girls involved in the rumor.

Kole ends the call, then slides his phone into his back jeans pocket. He leans against the wall, feet crossed at the ankles, as casually as though he's waiting for a pizza to arrive, not a murder suspect.

"What's the plan?" asks Riley.

"Switch interview." He says it so confidently that Axel has to wonder how many times the sergeant has done this, especially in his detective days. "We lure him in here with an interview, let him get comfortable, then we surprise him with an interrogation and get him really uncomfortable." His eyes light up at that last part. Breaking people is his forte.

A realization strikes Axel, sharp as a needle. It fills his veins with a cold sensation as it sinks in. What if it's true? What if Chloe's *daddy issues* ran so deep, she sought out a relationship with her older male teacher? What if he got her pregnant, and she's been hiding this whole time, waiting until it's safe to come out and explain?

Oh Jesus.

She's only fifteen. But it would explain the baggy clothes. The change in her mood. Her sudden disappearance. It's the first time the scenario has entered his mind and it's so plausible, he almost faints. He leans forward and lowers his head. His chair scrapes across the floor. With his elbows pressing into the tops of his knees, he clasps his hands across the bridge of his neck. A shiver runs up his spine. Riley presses her hand flat against his back, smooths it up and down.

"You all right, Winthorp?" Kole's voice grounds him, pulling him away from speculation and transporting him back to the here and now. The nausea starts to lift. Axel lets out a deep exhale and straightens up. He nods.

"The good news," says Kole, "is you're not invited to the interrogation. Riley and I will take the lead."

Axel nods again. It's for the best. If he were in the same room as Cutler, he would lunge at him and strangle the living daylights out of him. A cross-collar choke would do the trick. He imagines himself shooting his left hand into Cutler's shirt collar, then crossing underneath with his right, and using his forearms to squeeze the life out of his carotid arteries. He'd be rendered unconscious in ten seconds, brain-dead twenty to thirty seconds after that.

The fantasy is sickly satisfying. He wonders if the sergeant can see the movie playing behind his eyes, because Kole fixes him with a piercing stare that warns simply: don't.

It's just after 2 p.m. when Cutler comes upstairs. Riley leads him to Interview Room #1, apologizing in advance for the harshness of it. "Our soft interview room's occupied," she lies. Cutler says that's fine, because what else is he going to say? Axel sits behind the two-way mirror. He watches Cutler take a seat at the stainless-steel table. It's bolted to the concrete floor, after a previous person of interest picked it up and threw it across the room.

When Kole enters, he brings a bottle of water and sets it on the table in front of Cutler, pulls up the chair across from him. Riley sits to Kole's left, farthest away from the mirror.

"Thanks for coming in, Mark. We really appreciate it," says Kole. "Especially on such short notice."

Cutler presses his lips into a tight seam. He's wearing the same blue hoodie as yesterday. Axel matches the emblem on it to the one on his grandson's hockey jersey. "Well, I'm kind of 'off' for the foreseeable future." He makes air quotes, then clasps his hands, resting them on the surface of the table.

"Right," says Kole. "I heard they closed the school for this week at least. Smart decision. Lots of kids up in arms about missing Homecoming or whatever it is goes on this time of year?"

"Homecoming was actually a couple weeks ago," states Cutler, and Axel remembers that Chloe had chosen not to participate. Lydia Deetz would not have gone to a school dance where kids swayed awkwardly to basic bitch music and then ditched to guzzle alcohol at after parties only to wake the next morning with baby's first hangover. Instead, she stayed home and watched horror movies with Fry, rolling her eyes at the caravans of kids who came to Belgrave Circle in their poofy Starburst-colored dresses to pose for pictures by the lake.

"My bad," says Kole. "It's been a while."

Cutler lifts a shoulder. "To be honest, if Homecoming were yet to happen, I doubt the kids would care at this point if it got canceled. Especially the girls. They don't want to be next."

The statement reminds Axel of Sari Simons. Just two days ago, she sat in Interview Room #3 and confided her fear of becoming the next victim, and she was right.

"Do you think there is real danger to them?" asks Riley. "If you had a teenage daughter, would you let her out past dark these—"

"God no," says Cutler prematurely. Overcompensating? "I've even warned my own daughter to stay indoors and she's an adult." He shakes his head. "It's terrible what's happening. Just . . ." He shakes his head.

"We can't ignore the fact," says Riley, "that the girls whose deaths or disappearance we're investigating are all students at Monroe Academy. Have you noticed anyone suspicious? Someone hanging around school grounds or near the walking trail who perhaps shouldn't be?"

Cutler doesn't answer. His eyes move back and forth like he's reading something. Finally, he looks up at Riley and Kole again. "You said 'deaths.' Have there been more?"

"Sari Simons was murdered Saturday night," explains Kole. "Her body was discovered at the Compound—that haunted house complex on Pruitt. She was strangled and mutilated, similar to Madison Caldwell."

If there was any light in Cutler's eyes when he first entered the room, it's gone now. "Jesus," he breathes.

"What do you know about Sari?" asks Riley. "Was she a good student? A good kid?"

The sigh that Cutler heaves takes so much air out of him, he slumps in his chair. "She wasn't *bad,* but . . . I'd be reluctant to characterize her as *good.*"

"Do tell." Kole's command is firm, though not unfriendly.

The seam of Cutler's mouth splits apart. He wets his lips with his tongue. "I'm fairly certain she and Madison Caldwell started that rumor," he says finally.

Riley tilts her head as though she has not the slightest inkling what he's talking about.

"Care to educate Investigator Riley?" asks Kole. "She's coming *in media res*. That's a theater term, yeah?"

It's a lie. Riley's been on this case since the beginning, but this way, they'll get Cutler to share his story for the record, and so they can start poking holes in it.

"In the middle of things," translates Cutler. "Sure." He exhales. "A few weeks ago . . . It was September. Yes, because school had just started and we'd just announced the cast for the play."

"What play?" prompts Kole.

"*Beetlejuice: The Musical*."

"Wholesome," notes Riley.

Cutler smiles, despite himself. "We had a vote. The kids picked it."

"They're Black Harbor babies," says Kole. "Disturbing and macabre is baked into their DNA."

"Right," agrees Cutler. "Chloe Winthorp was cast as one of the leads."

"I hear she took it very seriously," says Kole. "Her role."

Cutler nods. "She did. Chloe was a method actor through and through. Even in other plays, when she got cast in more supporting roles, she never broke character. I worried about that a little with this one, but . . . I'd be lying if I said I wasn't curious to see what she was made of."

"What do you mean by that, exactly?" asks Kole.

"Lydia Deetz is a dark character," explains Cutler. "She's deeply troubled, over-sexualized . . . Chloe wasn't like a lot of the other girls at Monroe. She was fragile. Sometimes emotionally distant, other times overly emotional. Part of that comes with being a teenager, I get that. But there was more at play, too."

"Such as what?"

Cutler is calm as he fixes Kole with a hard stare. On the other side of the mirror, Axel leans forward to better listen.

"I'm not a doctor, but I think she was dyslexic." The word is a monolith that steals every molecule of oxygen out of the air. Its magnetic force pulls Axel to the glass, so he can study the subject who wields it. He's never heard that term before in regards to Chloe.

"Dyslexic," repeats Kole. "Is that, like, when people transpose their words and whatnot?"

Cutler nods. "It's a visual processing disorder. People have difficulty reading and spelling. They might transpose similar sounding words or letters, like *b* and *d*, for instance." He glances at Riley as though wanting her to validate his definition. She stands stoic, her gaze trained on him. "It can be stressful and anxiety-inducing," Cutler continues, "resulting in social isolation, depression, and unhealthy obsessions. Especially if it goes undiagnosed."

"Was Chloe ever diagnosed?" asks Kole.

Behind the glass, Axel shakes his head, although he can't tell if it's in response to Kole's question or in disbelief. Chloe couldn't have a— what did Cutler call it—a visual processing disorder? He and Rowan would have known about it. They would have gotten her help—

"No," says Cutler. "I tried reaching out to her parents several times about it, though. I sent emails that went unread, I tried to set up a time to meet after school, but . . . well, I guess I got a glimpse of what Chloe's life was like."

"What do you mean by that?" Kole's question is innocent enough, but it incites an angry edge to Cutler's voice.

"They were never around." He says it so simply, as though it's a fact and not a teenager's dramatization. "They left her alone a lot, and if they showed up to her events, they almost always left early. I know they're homicide cops or whatever, but Jesus. The dead can wait a minute, yeah?"

Kole looks somber and Axel knows what he's thinking. He's thinking that they're all guilty of it—of saying you'll be somewhere and then getting yanked onto a scene instead. Of missing holidays and family get-togethers. Of eventually just ceasing to commit to anything that isn't work, and yet having the audacity to get irritated or hurt when the invitations stop coming your way.

"She told you she was left alone frequently?"

Axel feels a twinge of amusement, knowing that this is where Kole turns it around.

"Yes."

"And that bothered her?"

Cutler nods. "I know it did."

"How do you know that?"

Cutler pauses, fixing Kole with a stare that grows colder with each passing millisecond. "Listen, I know that anything I say in this room can and will be shared with Chloe's father. He's probably sitting on the other side of that glass, watching this whole conversation." He tilts his head toward the two-way mirror. "Just keep him over there and we won't have a problem. But yeah, she did tell me her parents worked a lot. It was sad; I felt sorry for her. She used to tell me the only way they'd start noticing her was when she was dead."

The last sentence is a barb in Axel's chest. He remembers, as a child, his dad always being gone at the tannery. The loneliness and the frustration he often felt over him not being there, but at least his mom was home. Chloe didn't even have that. Both her parents had chosen their careers over her.

As harsh as it is, he has to admit there's truth to what Cutler is sharing. How many nights had he and Rowan left Chloe to her own devices? He always thought she'd just whiled away the time in her room, drawing or singing or watching TV. Apparently, she'd spent it missing them and sinking into a depression so deep, perhaps she couldn't claw her way out.

And an unhealthy obsession. Hadn't Cutler mentioned that?

"When would she tell you these things?" Kole asks.

Cutler sighs. "Whenever we were alone, I guess."

The image of Cutler—a fifty-one-year-old man—alone with his fifteen-year-old daughter spikes Axel's blood.

"I met with her twice a week before school," explains Cutler. "We'd work on reading and writing. Specifically spelling. She was really self-conscious about that." He shrugs. "I graded her papers differently than the other students, focusing more on the context and the ideas she was supporting versus her spelling and grammar. I thought I was doing right by Chloe, helping her this way, but in retrospect, I wonder if I hadn't been adding fuel to the fire."

His voice breaks and climbs an octave with the last four words. Axel almost feels something other than hatred for him, but then he remembers: Cutler is an actor.

"They thought you were giving her preferential treatment?"

Cutler sucks his teeth. "Yeah. And then they started talking. Or texting or Snapchatting, whatever. I guess that's how kids communicate these days."

"You're talking about the rumor?"

"Yeah." Cutler's exhale is ragged. Clearly agitated, he slides his elbows across the table and scrunches his hair. It's dark and strewn with silver, just like the Pumpkin Lady indicated.

"You mind filling Investigator Riley in on what happened?" Kole asks.

Cutler straightens. He bites his bottom lip before speaking. "Madison Caldwell and Sari Simons—two girls in Chloe's class—planted Chloe's shirt in my messenger bag. They took a Snapchat and put some text that said *Daddy Issues* on it and circulated it around the school."

Riley takes a deep breath as though taking it all in. "Insinuating that you and Chloe Winthorp were having a . . . sexual relationship?"

"Yeah, I guess so." He opens his mouth to say more, but stops. His shoulders visibly rise and fall. He shakes his head. "If they had any idea how much trouble this caused me . . . My career. My marriage." He pauses. His jaw hangs slack as though he can't believe this is his life. "They found out about my wife. How we met when she was a senior in high school and I was her teacher. It was wrong, I get it, but . . . I was only four years older than her and we never dated until after she graduated. For Christ's sake, we've been married for almost thirty years. But that doesn't matter to people. All they care about is the headlines. The 'drama.'" He breaks out the air quotes again.

"Who's they?" asks Kole. "The people who've been digging into your past?"

Cutler turns his hands palms up. Even from where he sits, Axel can see the condensation they leave on the table. "Everyone, it seems. Now my wife won't come home. She's staying with her sister until this blows over. *If* it blows over." He looks up at both Kole and Riley. "Do you know how isolating it is when no one believes you? I mean, fuck. You were the only person who did at first"—he gestures to Kole—"and then the others started coming around. Not everyone, but . . ." He pauses for a long time. "They called me Mr. Cuddler. Still do. I mean it's like being back in high school, myself, again, with kids whispering behind your back. Some things never change, right?"

Axel knows the feeling. He's spoken to correctional officers and guards who work in the jail. It's like being in jail eight, ten, twelve hours a day, every day. They're trapped inside those concrete walls right along with the inmates. Same goes for teachers. They're right back in school.

"The nickname and the Snapchat and all that," Riley picks up. "Could they have had anything to do with how much time Chloe was spending with you before class and at drama practice?"

"Of course," admits Cutler. "And I'm sure a lot of it stemmed from that. But I also think it had something to do with the fact that Madison felt she should have been cast as lead in the play. She was lead in the last two productions. But, to be completely honest, her performance wasn't up to snuff. And someone else deserved the spotlight."

"Chloe," says Kole.

Cutler nods, his expression somber as though him casting her as Lydia Deetz catalyzed all of this. Maybe it did.

"What do you know about Reeves Singh?" Riley flips the subject.

"Reeves?" Cutler blows out a breath. "He's a soccer star. Been dating Madison Caldwell for a while now. Or . . . he used to." He looks suddenly from Riley to Kole. "You don't think he killed Madison, do you? And Sari, and . . ." His voice falls. Axel notes how he stops before mentioning Chloe's name among the dead. Because she isn't dead and Cutler knows it. He's keeping her. This Reeves Singh stuff is all a filibuster.

"We just don't want to rule him out," warns Kole. "Guys kill their girlfriends all the time." And then, realizing how laissez-faire he sounds: "Well, not *all* the time. But it happens. Unfortunately. He and Madison could have gotten into an argument before the play that night. Maybe he didn't agree with how she was treating Chloe. She must have chastised her, yeah? Made her life miserable if she thought Chloe stole her part."

Cutler nods. "She and Sari Simons both. They were relentless from what Chloe told me. Just picking her apart." He fixes his gaze solely on Kole. "When her dad came to my house yesterday, and you found us out by my chicken coop, I was showing him one of my hens that had been pecked to death by the others. That's what they did to Chloe. They pecked and they pecked and they pecked until she . . ." He swallows. "I was worried about her, let's just say that."

"You mentioned that people with dyslexia can develop an unhealthy obsession. Was that true for Chloe?"

"Acting," says Cutler without a second of hesitation. "She told me it was her only way out of Black Harbor. And she was brilliant at it. So much so that it was a little scary at times."

"What do you mean by that?" asks Kole. "What kinds of behaviors was Chloe exhibiting?"

"She started . . . hiding in plain sight, I guess. Wearing oversized sweatshirts that she could draw her knees up into and pull the neck of it up over her chin. I asked her once about it and she said she was getting into character for Lydia. She might have been telling the truth. Like I said, she was a method actor. But I just felt, in my gut, that something was off."

Axel remembers. He'd confronted Chloe about her change of style and she'd given him the same response.

"What did they tease Chloe about, specifically?" asks Riley.

Cutler thinks for a moment. He tilts his head up toward the ceiling, eyes rolling so Axel can see the slivers of white under his irises. When he comes forward again, he plants his elbows on the table, tucks his thumbs under his chin, and talks over his knuckles. "Anything and everything," he says, "from the way she dressed to what she ate for lunch. Her name. After the prank, they called her Chloe the Hoe-y."

The investigators fall quiet and Axel knows, beyond a shadow of a doubt, that Cutler is acting. He acts and he teaches kids to act, too. To pretend. How many kids has he coached through interviews like this? Had Sari Simons been acting? All this talk about Reeves Singh and the girls . . . it's a diversion. He can feel it in his bones, in his blood that boils beneath his skin despite the chill in the room.

Cutler knew Chloe would be alone that night, going home to an empty house. He'd planned for Rowan and Axel to be gone, investigating the homicide of Madison Caldwell, because he'd killed her.

The jigsaw pieces in his head are finally fitting together. Finally, he has his answer. Cutler killed those girls, and he has Chloe.

"Can I tell you something?" Cutler's voice bears the quiet edge of defeat. His mouth is slack, as though he doesn't have the willpower to keep the words he's about to say inside anymore.

"Please," invites Kole.

"I didn't kill those girls. And I never had sex with Chloe. Sure, she was cute, but she's a high school kid."

Axel feels the blood drain from his face and pool in his chest. His ears burn. Cutler's into high school kids. He just admitted that's how he met his wife.

"I know that," continues Cutler, and it sounds almost as if he's talking more to himself than to Riley and Kole. "I know I didn't do any of that . . . but after a while, it doesn't matter whether or not you did it. You begin to wear the allegations like a stain. A stain that looks an awful lot like guilt. And do you know the worst part?"

"What's that, Mark?"

He lifts his gaze to meet Kole's. "You start to doubt your own innocence."

He's lying. He killed those girls. He fucked Chloe. He's probably still fucking her, wherever he's got her kept.

And Kole and Riley are lapping it up.

Before his brain registers what his body is doing, Axel is out of his chair and bursting through the door of the interview room. He lunges at Cutler, and crossing his forearms over each other, sweeps them under his hoodie and pulls tight. Cutler's face turns red, the whites of his eyes suddenly aflame. He tries to shout but only a gasp escapes; Axel has his windpipe in a vise grip.

Ten seconds and lights out.

"You lying son of a bitch!" he yells. "You have her! You have Chloe! Where the fuck is she?"

Nine . . . eight . . . seven . . .

Cutler punches him in the kidney, but Axel doesn't let go. He can't now.

Five . . . four . . . three . . .

The concrete is cold and unrelenting against his cheek. He cuts his teeth on it. Pain vibrates through his skull. There's pressure on the back of his neck. From his peripheral vision, he can see Kole is on top of him, an arm bar across his neck and shoulders.

Cutler is on his hands and knees, gasping for breath. "I'm gonna sue you!" The promise is ragged, tearing from his throat. "I'm gonna sue the shit out of you!"

He keeps yelling, but Axel can't make out any of the words. The floor feels good against his hot skin. He closes his eyes and lets consciousness drift away from him.

30

ROWAN

She pulls up to the curb across from Beck's bar and knows she's made a mistake. She should have parked in the municipal lot and walked over. It's only a handful of blocks, and yet, she doesn't want this to take up more time than it has to.

It's only 5:45 p.m. and the sky is already beginning to darken. This is the time of year when she feels compressed. Day and night are bookends that get closer and closer to each other, the space between them dwindling as the end of the year draws near. The birds are right to leave. If she could grow wings and take to the skies, she would be out of Black Harbor so fast.

Would she, though?

No. The thought would present itself like a spark of light, like it always does, and then she would remember Chloe, her actual spark of light. Chloe's memory is now her anchor, bringing her back down to earth. To the perpetually half-frozen soil of Black Harbor.

In her heart of hearts, Rowan knows she is a liar. She tells Axel that Chloe is dead, that she is a collection of skin and bones somewhere they just haven't thought to look, and yet, she feels Chloe's life flowing through her own veins as though they are one. It is startling how much you can love someone. She was always afraid of this. Loving someone so intensely, that when they're no longer around, you become unmade.

She is unraveled. A ribbon rolling toward her destination: a bar with a neon sign glowing in the window. She will have to get herself together. As she crosses the street, Rowan makes a point to walk taller, hold her chin higher, and wipe away the tear that has slid down her cheek.

She can't remember the last time she set foot in here. The bar opens up before her. An air hockey table glows white, waiting for a roll of quarters. There are two pool tables and dartboards to her left, pinball and old arcade games lining the wall on the right, running into the bar where people sit on top of their jackets draped over barstools. A row of red-cushioned booths divide the space. She notices Deschane in the middle one, staring at his phone. He looks up, having heard the door close, and tilts his chin in greeting.

Rowan takes a deep breath and unzips her coat.

One drink. Get the information. Get out.

"Mr. Deschane." Rowan stands at the end of his table and takes off her gloves.

"You sound like my students. Just call me Dale, please." His beer glass is filled up to an inch from the top, foam clinging to the glass from where he took one sip. He notices her looking at it, and says, "I would have ordered you something, but I didn't want to pick your poison for you."

Rowan cuts over to the bar and orders. Her poison is of the gin and tonic variety, enough to take the edge off. She takes a sip before she returns to the table and sits across from him. After being married to Axel for sixteen years, she's used to having her back to the door. It's a cop thing. While Deschane is no cop, she wonders if there's a reason he wants to keep an eye on who comes and goes from this place.

"So, you mentioned there being characters at the school." She doesn't have time or patience for social niceties. They did enough small talk behind his shop earlier.

Deschane frowns, amused. "You get right down to business, eh?"

"I'm sorry, I don't do this often." The confession is out of her mouth before she can filter it.

Adding to her dread, he asks: "Do what? Meet a guy in a bar?"

His gaze cuts to her wedding ring that shines bright under the pendant lighting.

She shrugs. "More or less."

"I don't, either. Meet men in bars, I mean." There's a flicker in his eyes, and suddenly she is reminded of the men back home. Not Black Harbor, but Saltsburg, Pennsylvania, where often enough she'd be filling up at the gas station and a guy that looked like Dale Deschane would pull up in a rusted-out truck with a dead deer in the back and go in for some jerky and a pack of smokes. The familiarity endears her to him and she hates that.

You can take the girl out of Saltsburg, but you can't take the Saltsburg out of the girl. Rowan smiles at his jest, and feels a little more at ease. She tries a new approach. "How long have you been teaching taxidermy?"

"Oh." Deschane leans back, touching his palms to the back of his skull and stretching. His flannel shirt strains across his chest. "Five, six years? My old man did it for the longest time, and then, well, he died and passed it on to me. Like everything else."

"You have any kids, Mr. De—Dale—to pass on the legacy?"

Deschane takes a drink. "'Fraid the buck stops with me." His gaze wanders from her eyes to her breasts, which Rowan knows are tucked away beneath layers of cotton and vegan leather, but still, she feels exposed. She excuses Deschane. He is simple and as far as the male species goes, not as evolved as some of his peers. Like Axel. Now that is one sophisticated son of a bitch. In the animal kingdom, Deschane would be a bear—powerful and slow-moving—while Axel is a raptor. "The women folk don't take too kindly to us Deschanes," he goes on. "My mom left me at a young age, just like my dad's mom left him. I figured I'd save myself the cost of a divorce. They're a hundred percent preventable if you don't get married."

"Now that's a fact," says Rowan. She clinks her glass against his. "So, in those five or six years of teaching at Monroe, did you ever come across anything . . . weird? I'm sure the teachers' lounge is quite the cesspool."

"It is," Deschane agrees. "That's why I stay outta there. A man knows when he isn't welcome." When Rowan frowns, he adds: "Like I told you before, the full-time faculty don't care for adjuncts."

"Because they view you as . . . unnecessary?"

"I'm the fat on an otherwise prime piece of meat. They think my lousy stipend comes out of their salaries. I don't think it does. If anything, it's probably a taxpayer thing, but . . . who knows what really goes on with all these handshake deals, right?"

"That's shitty," says Rowan. She takes a drink of her gin.

Deschane lifts a shoulder. "They're just protecting their kingdom. Can't say I really blame 'em. I learn to stay in my territory. Keeps me outta the bullshit and gives me the higher ground."

"What do you mean *higher ground*?"

"I mean when they want something, they gotta come to my turf."

Rowan pauses. She watches Deschane's Adam's apple rise and fall when he drains the last of his beer. "What kinds of things do they want from you?"

"Oh, under-the-rug things. Ms. Kazmaryck wanted the neighbor's yippy dog to disappear. Mr. Cutler had a fox stalking his henhouse. Mr. Taylor ordered a pair of glass eagle eyes . . . what the fuck for, I don't know." He sits back in the booth and offers a quick, close-mouthed smile that asks if she's satisfied.

A sudden blast of cold makes her straighten up. The hairs on her arms stand on end, and she can't tell if it's because someone has opened the door behind her to enter the bar, or because of what Deschane just said. She feels frozen in place, Deschane's eyes a pair of red-dot sights trained on her. Would he tell her all of this if he knew her husband is a cop? "You kill people's dogs?"

The flash in his eyes is back, but colder this time. Any ounce of endearment she might have had for him at the beginning of this conversation is gone now. "Sometimes dogs run off. Like kids." He adds that last part, and she'll be damned if she doesn't notice a smile tugging at the corner of his mouth, like a fish hook snagging his lip.

Rowan bites back a riposte. "And the fox?"

"Amazing what a can of tuna and a trap can get ya."

Setting animal traps within city limits is illegal. A chill slides down her throat, though she hasn't taken another drink. What other kinds of traps has Deschane set? Ones that could ensnare little girls off the walking path?

She's almost too terrified to ask about the eagle eye, when Deschane reaches for her hand. "Listen, Rowan—"

She yanks her hand away as though evading one of his traps, but it's too late. Suddenly, Axel is at their table. He looks from Rowan to Deschane, back to Rowan. She notices a bruise purpling the side of his face, a split halving his lip like the gash in their countertop.

"Axel? How—" She remembers the chill that hit her just a moment ago. It must have been from him walking in.

"I saw your car outside," he manages, before the sentence falls flat. His mouth hangs open, and Rowan can see how wrong she was about these two men. Deschane is the cunning one; meanwhile, Axel's been struck dumb. He turns to leave.

"Axel!" Rowan bolts out of the booth, her jacket catching on the corner of the table. She yanks it free and catches up to him as he reaches for the door. He pauses, and it is the longest, deadest silence of Rowan's life. His eyes travel from her face to her fingers curled around his coat. Then, he wrenches away without saying a damn thing.

31

LIBBY

That was close.

Libby sits in her window seat with her feet tucked under a blanket, book nine of the Crestfall series splayed across her knees: *Lullaby Lazarus*. It isn't her favorite one, and yet, it's a welcome distraction as she waits for courage to strike so she can reach out to Reeves.

With a sigh and marking her page with her hand, Libby flips the book over. She stares at the corpse on the cover that rises to a melody played on an ocarina, and scratches at a spot of dirt. Late last year, she'd been walking on cruise control with her nose stuck in her book, when Madison knocked it out of her grip.

"Hey! Mads, what are you doing?" Reeves had knelt and picked up the novel, handed it back to Libby.

Madison kept walking. "Lesbi-honest, Reeves, she shouldn't be reading that kiddie smut anyway. You're welcome, Libby!" Madison waved dismissively, as though she'd done Libby a favor.

"Bitch," Libby muttered. It was the first time she'd ever sworn in her life, and it felt good, the way it cut the air.

Now, over the book's pages, she peeks at the tips of her toes. Chipped purple polish. She scrunches them back beneath the fabric.

She can see Chloe's bedroom window from here, through the gnarled, naked branches of the sugar maple on which a meager handful of scarlet leaves still cling. And below it to the right, Reeves's backyard, with the soccer goal and the patio where they often barbecue and play cards.

She still hasn't responded to his message from yesterday morning. Now her phone lies beside her, faceup on a fold of blanket. She eyes it suspiciously.

It's now or never, honestly. She has to talk to him. Axel's got her pinned.

The Pumpkin Lady stuff saved her today. But tomorrow, she's sure there won't be any lucky breaks.

Warily, Libby reaches for her phone as though it might bite. She sucks in a deep breath . . . lets it out. Then, she swipes into her messages and clicks on the thread Reeves started all those hours ago.

Her heart rate quickens. A bubble swells inside her. Until this week, never in her wildest dreams would she have imagined a message on her phone from Reeves Singh, Monroe Academy's golden soccer star. He was untouchable—Madison would scare off any female who came near him like a territorial dog—but now she's dead and Libby has her teeth in a locket. Well, *had*.

Soccer star or not, Reeves could be a killer. In fact, that's the entire purpose of this conversation: to get a confession that she can show to Axel and get the cops off her back.

Her fingers are clumsy when she texts back: **Hey, it's Libby :)**

Her stomach twists. Is the smiley face too much?

A minute later, he replies: **Lol I know**

Relief spreads through her extremities, but it quickly turns to dread. Where does the conversation go from here? Should she ask him a question? Something open-ended, so he can't reply with a simple yes or no and leave her dead in the water. She's about to start typing when the little ellipses dance under his last response.

> **You lose your phone or what?**

> **Sorry. No I just—**

She deletes the second sentence and clicks send.

Another trio of dancing dots appears. So . . . are you ok?

Libby reaches back in her memory and the bubble in her chest pops. She feels empty, something unpleasant scraping at her insides as she remembers the Compound and Sari Simons. The events tangle together until they create one spiked knot that sits heavy in the pit of her stomach.

I am, she replies. And then: Are you?

Yeah. It's wild tho . . . right?

That's one way to put it, she thinks. If by "wild" you mean terrifying, then yes.

Did they grill you hard? The cops?

Oh. The interview with Axel was so fresh and frightening that she almost forgot about how she and Reeves were separated and questioned the other night outside the haunted house complex. Not too bad, she replies. You?

I think I'm their favorite. For a suspect I mean.

Libby frowns. He's her favorite, too. There's no way Chloe killed these girls on her own. She had help. Reeves's help, probably. Why do you think that? she asks.

The dancing dots appear then vanish. A minute goes by. Then finally, an explanation: Fuck Occam.

Libby squints and wonders if she read it right. Occam?

That Occam dude and his razor. The simplest answer is usually the answer, right? That guy.

Oh right, Libby texts. She pauses and then adds: So you're the simplest answer?

In their eyes.

He's lying, she tells herself. This is a game. He wants to endear her to him, get close like he did with Madison and Sari and Chloe, then he will kill her next. Her heart rate spikes again. She's talking to a murderer. The answers to the questions on everyone's minds could be within her grasp. If Reeves admits to killing Madison at least, she can clear her name with Axel.

Entrapment. It's so not in her wheelhouse. Fortunately, there's something about texting—the fact that Reeves cannot see the creases in her forehead or the way she licks her lips with uncertainty—that makes her fearless. All she has to do is sound confident, not look the part.

She starts typing. But are you sure y

No. Delete. Delete. Delete.

Hey, did you

Ugh! Deleeeeeeete.

If there was ever a class called How to Get a Boy to Ghost You 101, Libby could freakin' teach it. She sets her phone down beside her and inhales deeply. She presses her fingertips to her eyelids and takes another breath, slowly letting it out. She keeps doing that as she counts to ten. *Think, Libby,* she urges herself. *How do you get a boy to keep texting you?*

A game, yes? Boys like games.

She picks her phone back up and tries again. Have you ever . . . played Never Have I Ever? Her heartbeat thrums in her ears. She can feel her temples pounding and she's convinced that if someone were to look at her dead-on, it would appear as though there's a pair of Beats headphones screwed to her skull beneath her skin.

I'd like to be clever and say never have I ever played Never Have I Ever . . . but yes I have. You?

Libby smiles. He set her up perfectly. Never have I ever played Never Have I Ever . . . :) It's a lie, of course. She's played with Chloe, many times as they sat pretzel-legged on Chloe's bed, facing each other, like children playing patty-cake.

> Lol. Are you saying you want to play?

Yes. Conversation is so effortless this way. She can almost pretend to be someone else. Unless, maybe it's the opposite. Maybe by texting, she can be exactly who she really is, without the distraction of wondering whether or not he's staring at her bulges or her double chin.

> OK I'll go first. Wait. What should the stakes be?

Libby's brows scrunch toward each other. The stakes?

> If I win . . . you have to tell me something no one knows about you. If you win . . . I'll tell you something no one knows about me.

Deal.

> And everything is fair game.

What does that mean?

> It means we can both ask anything we want, and the other person has to be honest.

Deal.

> Alright, here goes. Never have I ever . . . shaved my legs ;)

Libby laughs. So Mr. Singh is coming in swinging. Not even to make yourself more aerodynamic for soccer?

> LOL. Now that you mention it, maybe I should.

She bites her lip. Her turn. She thinks about all the things she's never done, and realizes that this may have been a terrible idea. *Never have I ever . . . been kissed . . . gone on a date . . . been invited to a birthday party.* These things are too telling, too pathetic. They're of the caliber of secrets she would only have shared with Chloe.

> Never have I ever . . . prank-called anyone.

Reeves sends an emoji of a character waving its hand. Guilty.

LOL explain yourself. Her eyes widen at the acronym. Never has she ever used LOL, until now. Is there no limit to what Reeves Singh can make her do?

Reeves shares an anecdote of prank-calling his older cousin. I pretended to be his doctor and told him his herpes test came back positive. I never in a million years would have expected he'd have his speakerphone on, with his girlfriend next to him. Who does that?

Libby feels her face go hot and now, more than ever, she's glad Reeves cannot see her. He started a rumor. Not so different from the one that Madison and Sari started about Chloe. Chloe, who is now missing. Chloe, who is more than likely dead.

> Was his girlfriend mad at him?

> Probably. She wasn't his girlfriend much longer after that. LOL.

No. No one is laughing out loud. This is not a laughing matter. Libby swallows. Her throat is dry. Her anger has made it so raw that her own saliva scalds her esophagus as it slides down.

They play a few more rounds. Her anger over his prank-call admission simmers. It's unforgivable, as all rumors are. Sure, Libby is not the most honest person on the planet—perhaps not even in this conversation—but never has she ever started a rumor about someone. Rumors ruin lives.

Throughout their game, Libby learns that Reeves has also never cried in front of the opposite sex or stolen anything.

How long have you worked at Gallagher's? Reeves asks.

> A little over a year.

And you're telling me you never so much as picked a flower or swiped something from the cafe?

> Nope.

She's lying again. There's no reason for her to confess to pocketing the glow-in-the-dark jack-o'-lantern charm, not to mention all the latex gloves she's stolen, like the pair she had on the night she collected Madison's teeth, and all the times she's managed to sneak into Chloe's bedroom without leaving so much as a fingerprint.

She gets the feeling he doesn't believe her. Why? Because no one in Black Harbor is that *good*? But, what does she care, especially if Reeves had anything to do with killing Madison and Sari? It's her turn. Never have I ever . . . put my hands on anyone.

Umm . . . you mean in anger?

> Yes.

> There was that soccer incident.

> Besides that?

A long pause ensues. Libby glances up from her phone and conducts a sweep of her room. She imagines police tearing it apart, rifling through her things, if she doesn't get something to condemn Reeves.

Guilty, he says. And then immediately after: I'm not proud of it.

Who? she asks.

The name that appears on her screen charges her blood. She draws a sharp intake of breath.

> Madison.

How to be tactful here? This is where texting works against her. Reeves cannot see the genuine shock registered in her expression, cannot see that this isn't scripted and she's just prying information out of him. She is, but she didn't know how easy it would be.

Libby swallows and takes a slow, rattling breath. What happened? she asks.

A handful of seconds later, Reeves's reply is a block of text. She imagines him across the fence, in his own room in his house on Rainbow Row, typing furiously as catharsis rips through him. How long has he kept this secret?

> We got into some argument. She called me Voucher, her go-to for when she didn't know what else to say. I didn't hit her or anything but I sorta backed her up into a locker and held her arms at her sides so she couldn't hit me. I just wanted her to stop saying it.

Libby leans forward so her elbow rests on her knee. She chews her thumb. Voucher? she texts.

> Yeah, like as in I need a voucher to go to school at Monroe. Cuz my parents aren't rich like everyone else's.

Yes, the voucher program. Libby hardly ever thinks about it, but there are five kids who attend Monroe Academy with vouchers in lieu of tuition. At least, that's how she understands it. She's heard her parents gripe about it before, how they've sent three kids through that school now at twenty grand per year each, while some people's kids go for free. It isn't fair and yet, should Reeves be denied a quality education simply because his parents cannot pay the price?

Maybe? These are questions too big for her. Although, if he turns out to be a murderer after all, the voucher program is probably dead, too. She can see the headlines now: MONROE ACADEMY OPENS DOORS TO MURDERER—AT NO COST!

Did Madison stop after that? she asks.

> It got kinda heated. She kicked my shins. Mr. Taylor saw tho and separated us.

Did you get in trouble?

> Nope. He never brought it up. IDK I think he might've been a voucher kid too. He lives on my street.

Mr. Taylor lives on Rainbow Row? This is news to Libby and yet, she has never specifically looked for him on her walk to school. He doesn't take the trail. Instead, he drives a green Ford Explorer that sits parked all day in the teachers' lot. She wonders whether or not he grew up there. Although Rainbow Row is no longer the low-income housing it started out as for tannery workers and their families, decades later, it never shed its stigma. Most of the houses still wear garish coats of free government paint, from canary yellow to radioactive green and there's even a hot pink one with a matching giant flamingo lawn ornament. Not that she ever goes down there, but you can't miss the flamingo. It looks like it was ripped off a Vegas hotel.

Not that she's ever been to Vegas, either.

He came to Gallagher's for a bunch of roses, she says, remembering how Mr. Taylor had visited her at work yesterday before Axel.

Interesting, texts Reeves. Think he has a girlfriend? He and Ms. Kazmaryck seem friendly. Kayden told me he saw them making out in the art room once, but . . . you know Kayden. He likes to talk mad shit about people.

He said they're for his sister, she replies, and adds an emoji of a little person shrugging.

Interesting, texts Reeves again, and Libby knows that means he doesn't find it interesting at all. You can go again, btw. I can't think of one.

Libby sinks her teeth into her bottom lip and is reminded of Madison's teeth in her locket. The locket that is now in Axel Winthorp's possession. The locket he will show her parents if she doesn't turn his head toward Reeves first.

She holds her breath as she resolves that she isn't here to make friends. Then, she texts: Never have I ever . . . murdered someone.

The message goes from *Delivered* to *Read,* but there are no more dancing dots.

32

ROWAN

The short drive home is exquisitely dark. Even the stars are shut in for the night, abiding by the City's curfew not to be out past nightfall. Rowan screws a knuckle into her right eye. The wind on the walk back to her vehicle wicked all the moisture out of them. Now, they feel raw and pinpricked with thousands of perforations that sing when the cold air touches them.

She rationalizes that as the reason she isn't crying right now. Not that she is dead inside and has no emotions to pour out. She's a rag that has been wrung and hung out to dry. If only a gust of wind would carry her off, and place her on a whitecap so she could sink to the bottom of the lake and shut out all this noise. Drowning seems like a dream.

Would she find Chloe down there, she wonders. She imagines her daughter as a skeleton, scraps of her red lace dress clinging to her bones, bleached white and nibbled on by perch and smallmouth bass. Or would she be pristinely preserved, with her artificially black hair tugging languidly at her scalp like frayed pieces of rope, her porcelain skin drinking in the moonlight that permeates the crystal-clear depths? She has read articles of corpses being found intact decades after their demise, the bottom of lakes creating a type of cold chamber. Lake Tahoe in California, for instance, has a reputation as an underwater graveyard of Chinese railroad workers and Mob victims. At depths of six-hundred-plus feet, the lake maintains a temperature in the neighborhood of thirty-nine degrees Fahrenheit, which prevents gasses that lead to decomp from being released into the bodies, thus freezing them in the moment of their death. Fascinating.

She cannot bring herself to imagine Chloe's expression. Who would be reflected in the blacks of her eyes? Would it be Deschane, twirling the ends of a chain or a rope? Her mind careens to the crime scenes of Madison and Sari, and the marks on their necks. Kole had suspected ligature marks, but Rowan had been quick to dismiss that as the cause of the abrasions. Why? Had her misstep misled them down a circular path with a rising body count?

And what of the sisal fibers on Sari's body? They could very well have been from a rope, though the lab will not have the results for weeks. Rowan doesn't have weeks. She is at the end of her own rope now.

Or would the reflection be of Libby? The scorned, seemingly non-threatening social pariah, whose hobby involves taking animals apart?

Rowan allows a rare moment of feeling sorry for herself, and thinks back to when today took a wrong turn. She'd been at Beck's, peeling back the layers of Deschane's allegations—Ms. Kazmaryck ordering him to off the neighbor's dog, Mr. Cutler asking him to trap a fox, and Mr. Taylor requesting a pair of glass eagle eyes—when Axel walked in and assumed the unthinkable. Even now, her blood boils over his reaction. She would never cheat, especially with a mountain man like Dale Deschane.

She called Axel a total of nine times since he stormed out of Beck's, and sent him a text. I'm sorry.

She really is, though. For everything.

For not telling him about her taxidermist lead. For meeting another man at a bar. For never allowing herself to be fully present in their marriage—their life—because of the life she ran from.

She is sorry for being so goddamn emotionally distant. Sorry for being so *Rowan*.

She loves Axel to death; however, the simple fact that Axel's mind went there is enough to make her hate him. And yet, hasn't she stewed in the same unsavory thoughts, that he is more than work partners with

Riley? It's more than that, though. She hates him for what he is not will-ing to admit—that their daughter is innocent and probably dead.

Chloe is not a murderer because she was murdered herself. What will it take for him to open his eyes and fucking see that? And when he does, will he come home? Or will they be trapped in this never-ending cold war, him always bracing for the impact of her *I told you so.*

And then as it always does, the inevitable realization sinks in. This is all her own doing. Chloe is gone because of something Rowan did eighteen years ago.

An eye for an eye.

Her hand shakes as she reaches for the glove compartment. Fumbling blindly, her fingers find purchase on the laminated cigarette carton she returned there after her near-death carbon monoxide experience in the garage the other day. The lone cigarette rolls out and slides between her index and middle finger, begging for a final hurrah. *Smoke it and you have to leave.* That was the promise she made to herself all those years ago.

She drives as autonomously as though she's in the car wash, being pulled on a track. Muscle memory compels her to turn the steering wheel right and enter Belgrave Circle. Her house is the third on the left. She pulls into the driveway and hits the brakes.

Someone is sitting on her porch.

Dark hair. Red lace dress. White streamers drape from her arms and encircle her legs.

Chloe!

The tears she thought she'd run out of pour forth with a vengeance. She throws the shifter into park and, still gripping the cigarette box and leaving her keys in the ignition, Rowan catapults out of the driver's seat and sprints across the front lawn.

"Chloe!" Her voice tears from her throat. The frigid air sears her lungs and she pushes herself harder, faster toward her daughter, her sweet girl who has finally returned h—

What is she holding?

Raked across a piece of white tagboard in black Sharpie are three words: *Mummy, I'm Home!*

Pure, unadulterated horror spikes Rowan's blood, freezes her in her tracks just three feet away from the abomination on her porch steps. It's a dummy, a white pumpkin with a black wig. The body is stuffed with straw and shoved into a red lace dress. Dozens of feet of toilet paper mummify the thing. The face on the gourd is demonic, taunting. Rowan screams and drives the heel of her boot into it.

The pumpkin tumbles down the porch steps and rolls onto the grass. Its dead eyes stare at her. Rowan goes after it. She stomps it again and again until the thing is a mangled mess and orange guts splatter the shrubs, the solar walkway lights, and everything within a ten-foot radius. Breathless, she falls to her knees and hears the obnoxious cackle of kids laughing, then the *tap-tap-tapping* of their footsteps as they take off running down the street.

She hopes they trip in a ditch.

Time passes. She can't say how many minutes transpire between her crumpling to the concrete and crawling to the front door, but when she is back in her house, Fry scampers across the hardwood floors to greet her.

She would be alone if not for him. Completely and utterly alone.

Choking back a sob, Rowan scoops him up and heads up the stairs. She doesn't go to her bedroom, though. Instead, she turns right, down the dark, narrow hall where Chloe's school pictures watch her from the wall. She closes her hand over the doorknob and turns.

Blue moonlight filters in through the window and bathes the room in a ghastly glow. Chloe's room is just as she left it, how she fixed it up after the police tore it apart. The bed is made with Chloe's old bunny, Bubby, slouched against the pillows. Franklin the ghost's shadow twirls in front of a black-and-white Winona Ryder poster. Trinkets collect dust on the dresser. Shirts and dresses hang limp in the closet, like skins shed by something other than a girl.

She sits on the edge of the bed. It creaks beneath her weight. Tears stream down her face and melt into the fibers of the comforter. She cries hard, sobbing until she is a dry, hollow vessel. And when she finally looks up, she discovers a book knocked askew on the shelf.

Rowan reaches for it. It's thin. She turns it over and foil lettering catches the light. *Monroe Academy*. It's a yearbook.

She frowns. Has she ever paged through this? Probably not, she thinks as she recalls her own high school yearbooks with the flirty messages and phone numbers from upperclassmen. She would have been mortified if her mother read them. But Chloe is not here anymore.

Rowan flips to Chloe's sophomore class. Just to see her daughter once more, as she was before this depraved city swallowed her up and refused to spit her out. And she pauses. Because there on the first page, in the second row, is a photo that's scribbled out.

Rowan's gaze slides to the roster on the right. *Madison Caldwell.*

Her heart crawls into her throat. She swallows to tamp it down, but as she turns the page, her eyes frantically moving down the list for Sari Simons, she stops on a blacked-out square in the L's. Rowan gasps as she reads the corresponding name: Libby Lucas.

Two rows beneath Libby is a scribbled-out Sari Simons.

"No." The word is a breath, whispered from damned lips.

There, in the last tile of Monroe Academy's sophomore class, is her daughter's smiling face.

TUESDAY, OCTOBER 24

33

ROWAN

It's 3 a.m.

The chill that's threaded itself into the kitchen floor permeates the thin soles of her slippers. She stands, her hips pressing into the countertop's cold edge. It is the only thing keeping her upright as greyscale images from last night flash through her mind. Madison Caldwell. Sari Simons. And Libby Lucas. Their faces all scribbled out.

She will tell Marnie—she has to. But how do you bring up to your best friend the fact that your daughter—who might not be dead, after all—might be hunting hers?

After yesterday, Marnie is all she has left. Without her, Rowan is as alone as the day she first arrived in Black Harbor. She can't bear the thought of Marnie abandoning her, and yet, she will have to risk it. If someone had known something bad was going to happen to Chloe before it did, she would have wanted them to tell her. Maybe then she could have protected her.

Unless Axel is right.

No. No, it's all wrong. Chloe didn't do it. She couldn't have, and yet . . . no one has touched that room since Thursday night, when police conducted their search of it. Rowan reviews the mutilations in her mind. The teeth, the eyes, the word carved into Madison's lip. If Axel is right about Madison and Sari starting the rumor, then what was Libby's crime?

She hasn't decided what to do about the yearbook, but something tells her it's best to keep quiet about it for now.

A noise outside stirs Rowan from her reverie. Slowly, she slides a kitchen drawer open and grabs the largest knife she has—the one she uses for cutting watermelon in the summer. If those teenage menaces are back, she'll give them a scare they'll never forget.

The house is still pitch dark but her eyes have adjusted. Rowan creeps toward her porch, staring intensely out the skinny windows that bookend the front door. The white pumpkin she kicked off the dummy lies on its side, grimacing at the concrete. Rowan crouches, watching, as suddenly, a hand reaches for it. Knuckles glow white as the fingers flex to grip the gourd like a basketball. Rowan freezes, watching as the Pumpkin Lady cradles it in her arms, deposits it in her stroller, and begins to walk away.

When she is a good thirty feet from the driveway, Rowan stands. She grabs her jacket from the hook on the wall, and slowly unlocks the door.

The air still smells like night: dew freezing into frost, leaves sweet and curling as they decompose into the earth. The waves crash against the pier and she imagines them crawling up the shore, wanting to sweep her by the feet and pull her in. But she moves in the opposite direction. She still has her knife, she realizes, and it isn't a bad thing. Nothing good ever happens after midnight, yeah? It's an unwritten rule that Rowan has seen proven true over and over again. Pulling her coat tightly around her, Rowan follows in the wake of the Pumpkin Lady, careful not to get too close.

Black Harbor post-midnight might as well be *The Purge*. The name of the game is murder and all bets are off. People like her and Axel are called to clean up the mess afterward.

She is stealthy enough in the dark, the moonlight not bright enough behind a gauzy cloud to pull a shadow over her. The Pumpkin Lady stops at two more houses along the way, grinchily scooping up their glowing jack-o'-lanterns and plopping them in her stroller. Then she approaches the end of Belgrave Circle and turns left onto

Main Street. Rowan follows, past a rusted fence and an overgrown asphalt lot.

They take another left into the cemetery. The path is nicer here, fresh black asphalt. A breeze comes and shakes red and orange leaves from the trees. They swirl around Rowan, creating an almost magical effect, as though she's wandered into a new world from the other side of a wardrobe.

The Pumpkin Lady pushes the stroller to an area beneath an aspen tree, and Rowan sees it. Piled high like skulls on a crypt are jack-o'-lanterns. There must be dozens of them, grinning and grimacing, their faces no longer glowing.

The Pumpkin Lady takes the pumpkins from her stroller and adds them to the shrine. When she's finished, she kneels and presses her forehead to the tombstone. Her lips move, whispering a prayer. It sounds like a different language. French, perhaps? She hasn't spoken to Axel since he went to find the Pumpkin Lady at the house on Winslow Street. He didn't mention anything she said or whether or not she even spoke English.

Rowan creeps closer. A twig snaps beneath her foot.

The Pumpkin Lady doesn't startle. She turns her head, leisurely, and side-eyes Rowan.

"I'm sorry, I was just curious . . ." Rowan cautions a step, squinting to read the name on the grave. When she does, her heart plummets.

Jack Peter Cyzon
Beloved son
October 14, 2008 to April 21, 2016

Rowan closes her hand over her mouth. "Your son?" she asks.
The Pumpkin Lady nods.
To the left of his name, she reads another.

Celeste Lucille Cyzon
Loving mother to Jack
August 26, 1979 to _____

"How?" Rowan asks.

Celeste stretches her arms out, fists closed as though holding an invisible steering wheel. "Auto," she says.

"An auto accident?"

She nods. A frayed knit hat comes down over her forehead. It's oversized on her, like everything else she wears. Either her hair is all tucked up under her hat, or she doesn't have any.

"I'm so sorry." Silence hangs in the air. "My daughter is gone, too. Not . . ." What? Not dead? It would be the first time she's admitted it to anyone but herself. Chloe is not dead. She just isn't here.

Celeste reaches toward the tombstone again, her bony fingers tracing the letters of her son's name.

"I see Jack just had a birthday," says Rowan.

Celeste nods. *"Les citrouille-lanternes,"* she says. "Jack-o'-lantern. He loved." She makes a carving motion with her hand. "So, I bring." From where she stands six feet away, Rowan sees a tear glisten on the woman's cheek. It slides down her ruddy face then, disappearing into her rags.

Rowan feels her heart split open. The Pumpkin Lady isn't an urban legend like the neighborhood watch posts make her out to be. She's a real person, who once had a family—a child, at least. Now that he's dead, she wanders Black Harbor like a ghost in purgatory, bringing jack-o'-lanterns to his grave every year for his birthday.

She's a grieving mother.

Rowan's eyes fall to the space between them. There's no wall, not even a fault line separating her and this woman. How easily madness strips us of who and what we once were. It changes us into something we don't know how to navigate.

Suddenly, her phone rings in her pocket. Her heart jumps into her throat. *Axel!* Rowan grabs for it clumsily.

The caller comes up as UNKNOWN. He could be calling from the death phone.

"Hello," she answers breathlessly.

"Rowan." The voice does not belong to Axel, but to Kole. "I'm out at Forge Bridge."

"We've got a jumper?"

"We've got a problem."

34
AXEL

The body belongs to Cutler. His skin is as pale as a fish belly, devoid of blood flow. It pools in his left cheek and on that side of his body, the purple lividity disappearing beneath his clothes, leading Axel to guess that's how he smacked the water.

Rowan's joined them now. Crouching beside the corpse, she estimates out loud that he jumped around 2200 hours. He watches as her black-gloved hands lift up Cutler's collar and he knows she's searching for the marks on his neck that won't be there.

Cutler killed those girls. He kidnapped Chloe. And he knows police were closing in on him, so he jumped.

Fucking coward.

"Axel." His name from her lips brings him back to the here and now: standing on the leaf-strewn riverbank near Forge Bridge, at approximately 0400 hours.

He approaches her and, leaning in for a closer look, observes a pair of red chafe marks on both sides of Cutler's neck.

"Fuck." Kole steals the word from Axel's mouth. His voice is a sharp whisper in his ear as he comes to stand next to him. "Any mutilation?"

"None that I can see," says Rowan. "Unless it's concealed beneath his clothing." She shimmies Cutler's sweatpants off to check. Everything's intact. Shriveled, but . . .

"He got all his toes?" asks Kole.

Axel helps Rowan remove the victim's shoes. She pinches the toe of his black sock and pulls straight up. It dangles from her fingers like a deflated balloon. "Seven, eight, nine, ten," counts Kole. "All accounted for."

"Where's his jacket?" asks Rowan, and Axel knows why she's asking. For one, it's thirty-seven degrees out here, and two, jumpers always leave something behind. Cutler didn't come here without a jacket.

"Miserelli!" Riley calls. "Bring his jacket over here."

A flashlight orb bobs toward them and the titian-haired patrol officer appears, clutching a paper bag, the top of which has been scrunched into a handle. She holds the bag while Rowan extracts the article: a navy-and-grey sherpa-lined flannel jacket. She shoves her hands into the pockets wherein Axel knows she will find his keys: car, house, and classroom, probably. He can hear their metal teeth grating.

She shines her flashlight on the jacket, checking for blood. "There, on the bottom." She points to a series of rust-colored flecks.

Axel leans in. His gaze flicks to Rowan first. She looks awful, unrested. Dark circles cup her eyes and her features look as if they're being dragged toward the ground. He might have thought he'd get some sick satisfaction out of it, a little schadenfreude, but he doesn't. Seeing her like this makes him sad.

He's sure he doesn't look much better. After getting worked to the floor earlier, his face probably mirrors Cutler's with the purple bruising.

"Looks old," says Kole, and Axel snaps toward him, forgetting that they're talking about the blood on the jacket and not Rowan.

"Might be," she says. "Wonder what it's from."

"He's got a chicken coop." It's the first thing Axel's said since she arrived on-scene. "His chickens used to attack one another."

Rowan draws her head back in a suspended nod. Her gaze moves from Axel to Kole back to the jacket. "Aren't chickens illegal in the city?"

"Cutler's technically not in the city of Black Harbor," explains Kole. "His property is on the other side of the woods that surround Monroe."

Axel stares at Rowan, watching the gears turn behind her eyes, and he knows what she's thinking. That perhaps he wasn't crazy to think Cutler was guilty after all. He lives on the other side of the woods, where young girls are ripe for the picking.

Girls like Chloe, whose last known location was the walking trail.

Rowan hands the jacket back to Miserelli. Kole and Riley wander away, and Rowan and Axel are left in the shadows. "You think he jumped because of the rumor . . . resurfacing?" Rowan's voice is low.

"That would be my guess." He stops there, short of confessing that they dragged Cutler into an interrogation just hours before he jumped.

"If he's the one, Axel . . . if he's been killing all these girls, then maybe . . ."

He feels his brows knit. "You think we have a chance at finding Chloe? If we can get into his house?" They have his keys; they wouldn't even need to ram his door.

"Don't you?"

"She's dead, remember? According to you, anyway."

Steam puffs out her nose. He can see he's done it. Her wall is coming back up as visibly as the window in a limousine. He wants to ask her about yesterday, why she was with Deschane, but now isn't the time or place. She begins to walk away. "Rowan, wait." He grabs her arm at the same time Kole announces he's heading back to the bureau.

"Walk with me," says the sergeant.

Axel lets Rowan go and follows Kole up the bank. They stand at the top, overlooking the scene. Yellow placards peek through foliage, and Cutler's skin glows under the moonlight. Axel remembers when Chloe was a kid, catching frogs under the little stone bridge where Madison Caldwell's body was discovered. Hours after she came inside, he discovered a tick on her ankle, so bloated and drunk on her blood it had turned white. That's what Cutler's head looks like, or like one of those mushrooms you mow over in the yard and take satisfaction in stomping on.

Forge Bridge groans. The water is a black snake, slithering beneath it. Its waves lap the rocks like tongues, the river thirsting for another body.

"I'm gonna ask you one time," says Kole. "Not as your boss, but as your friend and your brother. And if you lie to me, I'll murder you myself."

Axel meets the sergeant's gaze. They hold hard on each other's stares.

Finally, Kole speaks. "You didn't do this, did you?"

The question smacks Axel like a bullet in the chest. "What?"

"Don't lie to me."

"No. I didn't."

Kole works his jaw. "Okay."

"You don't believe me?"

Kole narrows his eyes. He swallows, and his expression softens. "He might have murdered your daughter, Axel. Or at the very least, done something bad to her. Who wouldn't have wanted to push him off the bridge?"

Axel knows what's happening here. This is how Kole gets guilty people to confess. He aligns with them, empathizes with them. He chooses his next words carefully. "I didn't do it."

"Okay," says Kole, as though that's the end of it. His footsteps are oddly loud as he walks toward his Impala. Axel stands there, flinching when he hears the door slam. The wind comes, then, and tears at his skin, threatening to carry him off the same way as Cutler. But dread keeps him weighted down.

This is far from the end of things.

35
LIBBY

She can't believe she's here. She's on the other side of the circle. At her back is Erie Street and the thicket into which Chloe vanished. In front of her, a one-story home slouches. White paint lifts from its siding; there's a loose strand long and slender enough, she bets she could pinch it, pull, and unpeel the whole house.

The window is a dark grey, its pane reflecting the maze of trees behind her. Libby treats it like an autostereogram—one of those Magic Eye pictures where if you cross your eyes, it will reveal something hidden. Chloe, perhaps, in her red lace dress and clutching a single black rose?

She slides a surreptitious glance over each shoulder, hopeful that Reeves will suddenly appear and she won't have to knock. The Singh home has a burgundy door, pumpkins set out on the porch. Halloween-themed window clings smatter the picture window: jack-o'-lanterns and grinning ghouls, a bat with fangs, and a mummy whose dressings are in a state of unravel.

She takes a deep breath. The morning air is crisp and quintessentially autumn with its sweetness and bite. Her lungs feel frosted. Standing at the door now, Libby knocks softly. She waits.

Her ears prick to the sound of footsteps coming from inside. Instinctively, her hand reaches up toward her neck, fingers fumbling blindly for the locket that isn't there.

A high-pitched groan disrupts the quiet as the door swings inward to reveal a sleepy Reeves in gym shorts and nothing else. Libby's mouth falls open. She's sure she looks like a taxidermied fish, but she can't help it. He is a gorgeous specimen.

"Libby?" Reeves drives the heel of his hand into his eye.

"Um, hey."

"What are you doing here?"

"Did I wake you?"

"I didn't really go to sleep," he admits, and begins to retreat. Libby's heart sinks, but then he extends his arm and wiggles his fingers, beckoning her to follow.

She closes the door behind her and feels as though she's been wrapped in a hot, cinnamon-tea-infused towel. The Singh home is cozy and decorated with rich, warm tones: burgundy walls, a marigold backsplash along the kitchen countertops. Candied apples sit on the stovetop. It's the complete opposite of her house, where things are cold and clean and quiet.

He leans against a kitchen chair, and looks as though at any second, he could break into tricep dips. Libby has to fight to drag her gaze upward, instead of focusing on the light grid of his abs, the way the slightest movement sends a ripple through his torso.

"I'm actually glad you're here," he says. "I wanted to show you something."

That catches her attention. Her eyes snap up to meet his. No one, besides Chloe, has ever told Libby they were glad for her presence.

"My parents are at work," offers Reeves, "and my sisters are sleeping in there." He tilts his head toward a closed door on the left as they move quietly down the hall. A soft light spills from a room on the right and Libby slows her stride, suddenly suspicious that this could be some nasty prank.

"What's wrong?" In his room now, Reeves pauses near his unmade bed, the blanket rumpled like his hair and cascading to the floor. He is a picture of innocence, just a boy in his bedroom, standing in front of a—

"You like Crestfall?" Libby asks.

He looks at the poster on his wall and back to Libby. His cheeks pinken to the color of daybreak. "Yeah. I've read 'em all. I know it's not really 'cool,' but . . ." He smiles, a nervous non-Duchenne.

"Which one is your favorite?"

Reeves's eyebrow shoots upward. There's only one answer to that question, which is: "*Vale of the Valkyrie.*"

Libby smiles approvingly and steps over the threshold. Her blood starts to fizz again. Her fingertips *tap-tap-tap* against her thigh. He likes Crestfall, which is unexpected. But just because they like the same graphic novel series doesn't mean they could like each other. After all, he could still be a murderer . . .

And she's still . . . Neck Roll.

Keep your wits, she reminds herself.

"Listen," says Reeves, and he is so pretty and persuasive that she knows she is prey to his every command. Listening is simple. She could listen to him all day long. Especially if he never puts on a shirt. "You said something last night that . . . I don't know . . . got me thinking."

Libby is engaged in a silent civil war. Her body wants to take a step toward him, but her mind wills her to step back. So, she stays frozen. "About what?" she manages.

"You said Mr. Taylor came into your work the other day. To buy a shit ton of roses."

She nods.

"But . . . it isn't a good time to plant roses, yeah? My mom always plants them in the spring. They have to have, like, a certain number of weeks before the frost."

"They're Aurora," she remembers. "Engineered for cold weather and stuff."

Reeves's brows inch toward each other. He looks thoughtful. "Aurora," he repeats.

"His sister's name," offers Libby.

Without another word, Reeves turns to hunch over the computer. Libby counts the vertebrae that zip down his spine, distracting herself from the slow, paralyzing release of guilt. Mr. Taylor had shared that little factoid with her, no one else. Now, it's out into the world, as if she'd just cracked open a locket and spilled out its contents.

She creeps closer to him and squints at the screen. At home, her mom has a candle called *Fresh Linen*. Reeves smells like that, and a hint of day-old body spray.

"What are you looking at?" she wonders, her eyes scrolling down a list of names and dates.

"Last year, Mr. Taylor mentioned in my class that his sister died when she was young. I don't remember how it came up, but . . . it always stuck with me. Maybe because I have sisters and . . . well . . . I don't think I could ever forgive myself if something happened to them."

"Even if it wasn't your fault?"

Reeves sighs. "No, I mean. I don't think I'd be reasonable about it. I think I'd blame myself no matter what."

Libby allows her mind to drift, just for a moment, as she wonders if her brothers think of her that way, too. She's their only sister. Who they see once a year at Christmas and maybe, individually, once more in between. Would they care if she died? Would they even notice?

"So, if his sister is dead," Reeves continues. "Why is he buying that many roses for her?"

"He could have more than one sister," she reasons.

"He could. But when he mentioned her last year, it sounded like she was the only one." Sitting in his desk chair now, he tosses a glance over his shoulder. His eyes roam her from head to toe, rapid, like the puck in one of those strength tester games at the fair. A dimple dents his cheek as he doles out a subtle, reassuring smile that wills her to trust him.

Does she?

She must. That, or she simply doesn't value her own life. While Libby might be brazen, she isn't stupid. She knows as well as anyone that if Reeves wanted to pin her to the floor and cut off her airway, nothing would stop him.

"They could be for her grave," she guesses.

"Sure. If she's buried in a crypt." Reeves clicks around on the screen while Libby tries to keep up. "I figured Mr. Taylor must be in his thirties," he explains. "So, I checked the obituaries of everyone who's died in Black Harbor in the last thirty years. There were a bunch of Taylors, but they were all older women. No one was a match for his sister."

Libby's lips move in sync with his as she hangs on his every word.

"So, I switched up my search." Reeves minimizes the window of the endless roster of Black Harbor's deceased, though something tells Libby they will be revisiting this page. "I searched for accidental deaths that had occurred in the area in the past thirty years. Because, you know, if she was young when she died, there's a high probability it was an accident or something like that." He huffs out an exhale. "If you think Black Harbor is dangerous now, don't go down this rabbit hole."

"Really?"

"Oh yeah, all kinds of fatalities. People drowning, getting burnt up in house fires, guy trapped in an elevator for two weeks. He died, by the way. And then there are all the jumpers. I guess if it can't be proven as a suicide, it's ruled an 'accidental death.'" He makes air quotes. "I think I was onto something, but then . . ."

"What?"

He tilts his head so that his ear is almost touching his shoulder and swivels his chair toward her. "You knocked on the door."

Libby bites the inside of her cheek. She shrinks back, toward the wall, like she always does when wishing she could disappear. Wishing she'd never come, actually. If it hadn't been for her, Reeves might have been further into his investigation.

She's the reason he has to do this, she realizes. She dug a hole around him, pushed him into it, and now he has to claw his way out.

It was self-preservation. The cops were looking at her for having killed Madison and Sari. How absolutely ridiculous! And, like a rabbit caught in a trap, she squealed and lobbed Reeves's name out there as a distraction.

If he's innocent, she owes him. If he's a killer, she's as good as dead anyway.

"But, if you're telling me his sister's name was Aurora . . ."

The air between them is suddenly charged. They are on the cusp of finding something, a clue, maybe, to bring them closer to Chloe. Libby leans further, her eyeballs practically sticking to the computer screen. Then, she feels the soft part of her arm brush Reeves's shoulder and she backs away.

Without missing a beat, Reeves types "aurora taylor obituary" into the search bar. The first result is a baby who passed away two months ago, the second an eighty-four-year-old woman from Florida. He scrolls down the page, coming across no Aurora Taylors from Wisconsin. "These deaths are all pretty recent," he says. "When Mr. Taylor brought it up in class, I got the feeling it had happened a while ago."

A cramp needles the back of Libby's calf. She's been crouched over Reeves for the past several minutes as he searches. Finally, she gives in and kneels on the carpet. "Try 'Aurora Taylor tragedy Black Harbor,'" she suggests.

New results populate. The first few call out a mass shooting in Aurora, Colorado, but then: "What's that?" asks Libby, pointing. "Click on it."

A fresh page loads. It's a news article from almost twenty years ago. Together, they read the headline. GIRL, 15, DIES IN TRAGIC 30-FT FALL IN DEFUNCT FACTORY.

"That's the old tannery," says Libby, recognizing the ramshackle brick behemoth. "I've always heard the place is haunted. Now I guess we know why."

"And by who. Check this out." He scrolls down the page, eventually stopping on a photo of a teenage girl. She's pale with dark hair chopped into an asymmetrical bob. A small, delicate nose and slashes of black eyeliner give her a catlike aesthetic.

"'Aurora Patricia Blum fell thirty feet through the roof of a derelict building after she spent time "chilling" and listening to music before being spooked by her brother who had come to collect her.'" Libby gasps and whips around to face Reeves. "Mr. Taylor?" she asks.

"Keep reading."

She does, and they learn that Aurora Blum was described as a "quiet, contemplative" teen who enjoyed singing and writing poetry. She liked to visit the old tannery as a "refuge for her thoughts" and occasionally skipped school to go there.

"'Her brother, Edward Taylor Blum (16),'" reads Libby, "'reports finding Aurora at the tannery and calling for her to come home. He heard a noise of floorboards snapping, and a scream, and ran to her aid.

She survived for approximately ten minutes before succumbing to internal bleeding and ultimately cardiac arrest.'"

"Oh my God." Libby presses her hand over her mouth. "That's so sad."

"I know."

"So . . . Mr. Taylor must use his middle name as his last name."

"Eddie Taylor is Edward Blum," acknowledges Reeves.

There is one picture at the bottom of the page. It's a photo of an adolescent Mr. Taylor with his sister. He wore glasses, and Libby recognizes the close-mouthed smile. The girl next to him—Aurora—sucks on a red lollipop. She has black-painted lips and her neck is severed by a plastic choker.

Libby's heart pulses in her throat. A gasp escapes her lungs as she realizes she has seen this girl before.

And judging by his horrified expression, Reeves has, too.

She looks just like Chloe.

36

ROWAN

The water scalds her skin. Each stream from the showerhead is a rake down her scalp. It soaks her hair, slides down the curves of her body, and pools at her feet. She stares at the drain where long blond strands cling to the trap and it reminds her of the yellow caution tape she's seen caught in the river rocks.

She doesn't know how long she's been in here. Only that it's somewhere between a while and not long enough to run out of hot water.

The steam creates a nearly opaque vapor. She feels like she's in a scene from *Psycho*, with the bloody handprint on the vinyl curtain. She doesn't have a curtain, though. Instead, there are two glass sliding doors, the bottom half of one obscured by her towel. She can watch herself shower if she wants. Not that she wants to, but when they first moved in she and Axel used to fuck in here until they ran out of hot water, then they'd finish on the bed.

She cannot tell him about the yearbook. He will want to collect it as evidence and further condemn their daughter for killing her classmates. Chloe will be guilty until proven innocent, like Mark Cutler.

The image of his body dredged up on the riverbank haunts her more than the others. He bears all the telltale signs of a suicide, except for the matching marks on his neck.

Kole is leading a search of his residence. If they find a suicide note, then it's pretty much a closed case. But if not . . . it's probable that the same person who killed Madison and Sari killed Mark Cutler.

Which means that no one is safe.

Had his picture been scribbled out in the yearbook? She hadn't noticed, only that Libby's was. Libby, who, for all intents and purposes, should have been next.

And still, throughout all of this, Chloe is missing.

Her eyes burn but she can't tell if she's crying or not. That's the beauty of the shower. It lets you lie to yourself about things like that.

Rowan reaches for the bar of soap, finally deciding to scrub herself clean. When she straightens up, the corner of her eye catches a man in the mirror. She gasps, her left hand instinctively splaying across her throat to guard her jugular, the right wielding the soap as though it's a brick.

"Row, it's me."

Axel. Her breath escapes from her like air leaking from a balloon. "Axel, what the fuck?" Her voice is sharp, shrill. She wrenches the faucet all the way to the right, shutting the water off. She steps out onto the memory foam mat. There is nothing but vapor between them.

In a past life not so long ago, she would tuck her fingers into the crevice between his hips and his jeans and yank them down. Lift up his shirt. Press her body to his. But this is not that life. That life is dead now.

"I didn't mean to scare you." His voice is unconvincing.

"What are you doing here?" She tears her towel off the bar and wraps it around herself.

"I live here, actually."

"Oh, really? Because last I checked, that meant you actually came home once in a while and slept in bed with your wife." Venom laces her words. It catches her off guard and yet at the same time, feels like a release, like biting down on a cyanide capsule. This argument has been brewing for a long time. She can feel that now. Because it isn't just these past five days that he's been MIA . . . it's years. Work takes precedence, always. Her stomach contracts when she realizes how hypocritical she is.

She waits for his rebuttal. To point at her and tally up all her late nights at the ME's office or out in the field. Instead, he says: "Row, don't do this."

Do what? The question stays inside. She doesn't have enough energy to vocalize it.

"We need to talk. Come downstairs when you're dressed."

For a few seconds, Rowan is acutely aware of the water droplets dripping on her shoulders and sliding down her back. Rage boils beneath her skin. She follows Axel out into the bedroom, where the vapor dissipates. It's easily fifteen degrees cooler. "I don't answer to you."

"You never did. That's what I always loved about you." He keeps walking.

Loved. The sound of the past tense is a mallet to her temple. She grabs his elbow before he rounds the doorframe. He turns back into her, like this is some kind of midwestern tango and she's leading. He's hotter than she thought he would be, temperature-wise, despite the fact that he's just come from outside where it can't be more than forty degrees. Something's got him worked up.

Her mind is fucked. A moment before she hated him. But in this moment, this infinitesimal blip on the map of their lives, she wants him. More than that, she wants him to want her. Something clicks in her brain, a key turning the right tumblers to unlock the secret: Isn't that what she's wanted all along? Just for him to notice her. To put his work phone down or come home at a reasonable hour. To sit with her and talk about the future like they used to do. To give her more than a passing glance.

Perhaps that's what he's been wanting from her, too.

And was Chloe so different?

All three of them, coexisting on separate planes in the same house, wanting the same thing, but all too proud—or terrified—to ask for it. Love. A moment of someone's undivided attention.

She wants to kiss him, but knows she shouldn't. She watches his lips move. "I thought you buried her," he says. "And I thought you quit smoking."

Rowan's heart stops. Her eyes shift from his face to the paper he holds up between them, the old cigarette box pinched between his ring finger and the meaty part of his palm. How did he get the obituary? She must have dropped it in the yard last night, when she went ballistic over that dummy. "I—" Her mouth is too dry to form an explanation. It isn't an explanation, though, she knows. She was on the cusp of a lie. *I did.* Isn't that what she was about to say?

"I'll be downstairs." Axel yanks his arm back and walks toward the landing, and she knows that if he goes down those stairs, it will be the last time.

"Don't leave! Please." Her hand flies to her mouth, but it's too late to stop the words from reaching him. Chloe used to say that very same thing. Rowan would kiss her good-bye on her forehead, promise to be back in a few hours when she'd bagged up the body, and Chloe would beg her not to go, not to leave.

She never listened. She always left.

You'll love me more when I'm dead. No wonder she said it.

Because it was true. Not true in the sense that she *loved* dead people, certainly not in the way she loved her own daughter, but true in the sense that she actually listened to them as they told her how they died with the marks on their bodies, the contents of their stomachs, and the DNA shoved beneath their fingernails.

She never listened to Chloe.

Now, Rowan remembers the same sentiment falling from her daughter's lips the night she walked away from her at the play. All done up in her goth makeup, red lace dress, holding a bouquet of black roses, her lips a painted heart that split down the center as she whispered, "Don't leave. Please."

The memory threatens to turn her inside out. Clutching her towel, she sinks to the floor, her back sliding down the wall. She's eye level with Axel's knees now. His feet are planted at the intersection between their room and the hall that leads to Chloe's bedroom. His presence is fragile, she knows. She could blink and he could be gone.

She flinches, imagining the note of finality the click of the back door closing would bring.

All because of her guilt. Because of her inability to tell her husband how a mistake eighteen years ago has haunted her all this time. To speak the name of the girl she murdered, the girl whose grainy black-and-white image stares at her now. The girl she has kept hidden away in a cigarette box.

"Katelynn Diggory." His utterance of the dead girl's name chills every molecule in Rowan's body, as though that arrangement of letters and syllables has conjured her ghost. It lingers between them.

Finally, Axel sighs. He lowers himself to the floor. She doesn't realize how close he's gotten until she feels the bend of his index finger tilt her chin up. They search each other's eyes. She sees her reflection in his pupils—wilted, worthless—and wishes he would look away.

"Rowan. Why didn't you tell me? I would have gotten you help. We could have talked to someone—"

"I didn't want to talk about it anymore, Axel. I wanted to move on."

"There's no moving on, only moving forward." He recites a line she's encountered all too often at counseling sessions and in self-help books.

Rowan leans with her elbows pressing into her knees, cups her hands together in front of her mouth. When she left Pennsylvania for Wisconsin, she had wanted to move *on*. She wanted to rewire her brain into believing that it had never happened. That she had never even gone to medical school and become an anesthesiologist, where she worked at Divine Savior Children's Hospital and killed fourteen-year-old Katelynn Diggory who went under the knife for laryngeal surgery—and never woke up. Afterward, Rowan checked her charts. She'd accidentally grabbed another patient's paperwork. The weight was wrong. She gave Katelynn too much.

She wanted to punish herself. So, she looked up the worst place she could find—one that was as off-the-grid as it could get—and drove through the night. Becoming a medical examiner was perfect. She had the pedigree for it, and it allowed her to still do the things she was good at, but assured she couldn't hurt anyone anymore. They were already dead.

Axel knew this about her, and still, he loved her.

Who knowingly marries a murderer?

"This is all my fault," she says softly. Her gaze slides to her towel and she begins picking at the cotton fibers. "Karma really is a bitch."

Now, it's Axel's turn to look rueful. "What are you talking about?"

"Our daughter is dead because I murdered someone else's, Axel. The universe has finally settled the score."

She feels his breath hot on her skin as he exhales. "You and I both know there has to be intent for it to be classified a murder. It was an ac-cident, Rowan. Look at me." He tips her face up toward his again. "You did not murder Katelynn Diggory. Say it."

She won't. She can't.

"Say it."

Rowan drinks in a deep, unsteady breath. "I did not murder Kate-lynn Diggory."

"No. You didn't." He reaches up and touches a piece of her wet hair. His hand grazes her neck, sending shivers throughout her entire body. "Is there anything else you wanted to tell me?"

He's hinting at her being out with Deschane last night, she knows. Nothing happened. She wants to tell him that and she will, but first . . .

"Did you kill Mark Cutler?" she asks.

His brows cinch together, but he doesn't look away. Instead, he stares at her harder than he ever has before, his verdigris gaze piercing her to the bone. "No," he says.

The word sends a shot of relief through the back of her skull. He could be lying. Lies come all too easy and yet, she chooses to believe him on the sole basis that he chooses to believe her. If she cannot trust Axel, then she can trust no one. And that is too grim a thought to bear.

Without breaking eye contact, she reaches for his hand, knits her fingers through his. Her towel falls away and he leans in as she presses her naked body against him. Her other hand tugs on his belt. The news-print flutters to the floor as he lets her pull him on top of her.

There was a time when she wanted exile. But now, in this exact frame of her messy life, she wants connection. She wants to be crushed and cradled by the man she loves, who has chosen to love her despite it all.

37

AXEL

He plunges into her and it feels like déjà vu, transporting him to their first time, when they made love on the floor of an Airbnb in Tennessee. They'd exchanged numbers and been talking for several weeks when Axel dreaded driving alone and showing up stag to his cousin's wedding. He mentioned his predicament not so offhandedly to Rowan, who offered to be his plus one, and that was the beginning of their life together.

It's only been a few days, but so much has happened, so much has changed; they have to relearn each other's bodies, the curves and the crests and the negative spaces, and how they fit together, just like they had to learn them for the first time all those years ago.

The carnal urge is as desperate as it was, then, too, and he knows it's the state of upheaval into which their lives have fallen. Uncertainty breeds desperation. They've moved to the bed. Axel bends Rowan over the edge of the mattress and drives in deeper, making her gasp and grab the sheets.

She might hate him after this. Which would be better than how she's been toward him, anyway. To hate him means she must have loved him, once. That there were real feelings there beneath her hard, un-crackable shell. What he can't take anymore is the indifference, and the sneaking around on eggshells.

And she's not the only guilty party. He's conducted his share of confidential operations.

"Harder," she tells him.

His chest heaves. His thighs burn. He grabs her hips and thrusts. She moans and demands more. Harder. Faster.

He smiles as sweat trickles from his hairline and splashes onto the small of her back. This is them. This is the Rowan and Axel behind closed doors that he has always loved, and yet perhaps taken for granted.

Breathing hard, he leans over her, guiding her to crawl farther up onto the bed so he can kneel behind her. His hands trailing from her hips to the dip of her waist and up the xylophone of her ribs.

"Don't stop."

Her nipples stand at attention. He pinches them, feeling the weight of her breasts in the palms of his hands. Then, he paints slow circles around them with just his fingertips, kissing the back of her neck as he does so. Rowan stifles a gasp, arching her back and rising to meet him, her head falling back in ecstasy. Her blond hair tumbles down his shoulders and he knows, then, that he has brought her to the edge. Still hard, he pulls out and lies on his back beside her.

"Get on top," he says. His voice is rough, a growl. The flash in her eyes as she glances furtively back at him tells him she likes it. The friction of her hips against his is magic. He could close his eyes and be swept away into some blissful oblivion, but she's too beautiful to look away from. He holds his gaze on her as though the power of eye contact alone will be enough to keep her here with him forever. The smallest smile peaks Rowan's mouth, but then, the flash in her eyes is back. She slows her movement and reaches to touch his neck. Her lips part. "What's this?" she asks.

He frowns, and blindly presses his fingertips to his own skin. "What?"

She crawls off of him and sits on the edge of the bed with the comforter scrunched to her chest. Her shoulders hunch and she begins to sway, like a buoy in the water. "It's Riley, isn't it?"

"What?" Axel tears the covers off of himself and opens their closet door to consult the full-length mirror. "What are you—?" There it is. A few inches below his jaw, a pink eraser-sized patch of skin glows. His insides roil, and he knows it is from Riley, from when they practiced cross-collar chokes at Silva's the other night. Snatching a pair of workout shorts, he steps into them. "It isn't what you—"

"Oh, it's not what it looks like, is that right?" Rowan is throwing clothes on, too. "Can you do me a favor and be less of a cliché, Axel. This is honestly humiliating for both of us."

"Rowan, stop." He reaches for her arm, but she pulls away. And that's when the pieces begin to lock into place. The realization hits him with the force of a salt truck. Light-headed, he lowers himself to the bed. He's afraid she's gone, when suddenly, her legs appear in the space between him and the doorway. He can tell by her stance that her arms are crossed.

"Are you okay?" she asks. Irritation tinges her voice more than concern. "You look like you're going to have a heart attack."

Still trying to find his words, he nods. "I'm okay," he manages, "just . . ."

"Just what?"

He looks up at her and it's starkly different from when they held each other's gazes a moment ago. Fear and anger make her irises sear into him. "The marks on Cutler's neck . . . they're from me."

Rowan squints at him. "What do you mean?"

His memory replays the events from early this morning. Cutler's body dragged up onto the shore, his bones smashed, face practically caved in from smacking the water. Kole walking away from him after asking whether or not Axel had murdered the man suspected of taking his daughter.

"I fought him . . . yesterday. He came to the bureau for an interview—"

Something like fear twists Rowan's features. She inches away from him, and he knows he has to explain before she gets too far. "You *fought* him?"

Axel flinches. "Attacked" is more accurate, but for now, "fought" is as much as he can damn himself. "He was making horrible claims, Row. About us and Chloe, how we neglected her . . ." As soon as he says it, he wishes he hadn't. There's a darkness returned to her eyes that had dissipated if only for a few moments.

There was a morsel of truth in Cutler's accusations. How many nights had they left Chloe alone in this house so they could work a crime scene? If murder were a product, it would be a top import of Black Harbor. There's so much of it, they can't clean up one body fast enough before another one drops. At least, that's what it feels like. For years, they've buried their heads in depthless piles of other people's problems, and they failed to notice the trouble that brewed at home.

"These marks are from a cross-collar choke. Same thing I did to Cutler. Which means that whoever killed the girls . . ."

Rowan fixes him with a dead stare for several seconds. Her eyes pulse black and return to their normal shade of green. Then, she runs out into the hall.

"Row!" he calls, half-standing. His ears perk, listening intently as Chloe's bedroom door swings inward. When Rowan returns, she's carrying a thin black book with metallic writing on the cover. "I found it last night. It was on the shelf, off-kilter. As though someone might have been looking at it recently. But no one's been in her room, not since . . ." She trails off.

Together, they pore over Chloe's yearbook. The chill in the air nips at his chest, his arms, his nose, but the blood under his skin runs hot. He watches as Rowan flips the book open and skims to the first scratched-out face: Madison Caldwell.

The image steals his breath.

Whoever did it pressed hard, as though writing a message in braille. The harried lines gouge deep into the page.

"You didn't touch this?" he asks.

Rowan raises a brow, daring him to repeat the question. "Of course not."

"We can swab it for DNA. Maybe it wasn't Chloe."

"Turn the page," Rowan urges quietly.

He does, and discovers another scratched-out face, this one belonging to Libby Lucas. His heart doesn't race; it pauses for a beat. And another. He hears the blood filling his eardrums, pooling there with no current to pump it out. It starts again when he swivels his gaze to the next page. Sari Simons's face is scratched out, too.

"Fuck," he whispers.

Rowan inches closer to him. "Those are all the ones I saw. I didn't think to look at the faculty. Do you think . . ." She takes a deep breath. "I mean, if Cutler's crossed out, then we know, right?"

"Know what?"

"That our daughter did this. Killed those girls, and her teacher."

Axel is shaking his head. It's the first time he's ever heard Rowan consider Chloe guilty. Now that she's finally agreeing with him, he wants nothing more than to argue with her. Perhaps because, while some pieces are falling so perfectly into place, there are others that don't match up at all. "But we've been over this," he says. "Chloe couldn't have killed anyone on her own. She's too small."

"We've also come to the conclusion that she could have had help," says Rowan. "You think those marks are from a cross-collar choke?"

Axel sighs. There isn't a shadow of a doubt in his mind. "Yes."

"Think, Axel. Who's in your jiujitsu class?"

She keeps turning the pages, arriving at the faculty section. Warily, his eyes move down, searching like a pair of heat-seeking missiles for Cutler. He is there, smiling reservedly. He sports a suit coat and the quintessential first-day-of-school haircut. His eyes are dark, and kind, and suddenly, Axel can see why Chloe may have been drawn to him. Not as a romantic partner, but simply a friend.

He and Rowan exhale a collective breath. His photo is unmarred. It isn't substantial enough to clear Chloe of his murder, but it's something.

Cutler's death means one of two things: he's guilty and took the coward's way out, or the real killer lured him to the bridge. Axel considers the other victims. They were all young, all female. But, like Cutler, they all had ties to Monroe Academy. Axel knows he isn't responsible for the marks on the girls' necks, so who is?

His gaze pans to the window where silver, midmorning light leaks in. Riley and Kole will be searching Cutler's place now. Axel wasn't invited, for obvious reasons. Besides a suicide note, they will be looking for eyes and teeth—the missing parts of the murdered girls.

And Chloe.

If she's there, she'd better be in one piece. Alive.

And if she isn't?

He cannot think about it. Instead, something cold enters his bloodstream as a third theory rears its thorny head. What if their interrogation pushed Cutler off the edge? Cutler's monologue echoes in his memory: *After a while, it doesn't matter whether or not you did it.*

Perhaps he felt there was no way out of this. No way but down.

No matter how this shakes out, Axel is on the hook for Cutler's death. He pushed him, one way or another.

Is that what happened to Chloe? Her peers pushed and pushed and pushed an accusation on her until she couldn't take it anymore and decided to put an end to it? They should send another dive team into the river to check for her one last time, before it freezes.

And it wasn't just her peers who pushed her to disappear. It was him and Rowan, too. What had Cutler shared yesterday in the interview room? *She used to tell me the only way they'd start noticing her was when she was dead.*

If everything Cutler told them was true, he really had cared for Chloe. He'd played to her strengths and challenged her by casting her as the lead in the school musical. He'd met with her twice a week to work on her spelling before class. And how had he been rewarded for it all? By being profiled as a sexual predator and accused of murder.

"If it wasn't Chloe . . ." Rowan is thinking out loud. "Then, who would have crossed out these photos?"

"Libby." Her name is a life raft, the only thing saving him from drowning. It falls from his lips in a mumble, but he is more certain of it than he sounds.

Rowan screws up her face. "Libby? Like next-door Libby? Marnie's Libby?"

Axel nods. "All of the above." He remembers, now, what he never told her. So he tells her about the teeth she poured out of her locket.

Rowan is silent through it all, pressing her hand over her mouth.

"I wouldn't doubt," Axel continues, "that she came here after I interviewed her in my car and scribbled out her own picture as a way to divert attention from herself. So, whenever someone happened upon the yearbook, we'd think she was a victim instead of . . . a suspect."

Carefully, Rowan pinches the page between her thumb and index finger, flipping it back and forth. She leans close to the book, her nose mere inches from the grid of portraits. "You're right," she says finally. "The ink on Libby's picture is fresher. Darker. It still has a smell." She pauses. "But how would she—"

Outside, a gust of wind causes the leaves on the sugar maple to shiver. He and Rowan both turn toward it, staring at its branches ablaze with titian leaves. Back in sync with each other, he can feel a knowing settle in her as it does him, as they both note the way it bridges the distance—or lack thereof—between their daughter's window and Libby's.

"Chloe's window was open that night," whispers Rowan. "Maybe Libby was here . . ."

But her words fall on deaf ears. Because on the next page over, Axel has spotted a man with a gap-toothed grin. He tilts his head as though to better read the corresponding name: Mr. Eddie Taylor.

Only he knows him by another name.

Orca.

At Silva's, he is Gordo's sparring partner. The pale man with the sharp, spaced-apart teeth, hair buzzed close to his scalp. He wonders now . . . at the house on Winslow Street when Celeste Cyzon had pointed to her own head to indicate that a man with grey hair had strangled Sari Simons and cut out her eyes . . . what if that wasn't what she had meant? What if she had not been referring to the color, but the close cut of it? Much like her own, Eddie Taylor's hair is shaved so short, it barely stipples his skin. "Son of a bitch," he mutters.

"What?"

"Eddie Taylor," he reads. "This man is our daughter's English teacher?"

Slowly, Rowan nods. Her eyes flit to him, but his never leave the page.

"You've met him?"

She shrugs. "Parent-teacher conferences. You were working." A pause, in which he feels her eyes move from the page to him. "Why?"

On the nightstand, his phone vibrates. He reaches for it. A message from Libby Lucas floats on the screen: Can we talk? I think I might have found something.

38

EDDIE

Chloe is dead.

It happened the instant he snatched her off the trail. He likens her death to plucking a rose. Although the flower may look alive, its petals a lurid color like blood pumping through a vein, it isn't. And after a few days, it begins to wilt, the hues of life fading, dissipating into the true, monochromatic colors of death. Because, you see, the rose is dead the second you break its stem.

She'd been walking alone, still wearing Lydia's red lace dress with a leather jacket over it, and carrying a bouquet of black roses when he came upon her Thursday night. She wasn't paying attention to him, wasn't suspecting anyone might be stalking her through the trees. She stared at her phone screen, and in the faint blue glow, he saw that she was crying.

Stealth was a skill he'd been perfecting, ever since his mom had gotten sick and he had to move her bed out into the living room. It was just easier that way. She could watch her shows all day long and he could keep an eye on her while cooking and cleaning. He learned to live in silence, and he didn't mind it. In fact, he'd grown to like it. God knows he gets enough social interaction at school.

His appearance was seamless, as though he was as much sewn into the fabric of the night as the stars. It's why little Chloe Winthorp never even heard the crinkling of the leaves' curled edges as he crept toward her. She didn't hear his footfalls when he suddenly padded onto the asphalt walking trail, or his breath hitch and the name he whispered when he got a good, up-close look at her.

"Aurora."

Aurora, his dear gone but never forgotten sister. The one who fell through the cracks.

Eddie was sixteen the day death came for her. Their mom was working. He'd just returned from wrestling practice, the ends of his hair crusted to his face from walking a mile in the cold, when he realized Aurora was not at home. He knew where she was. For the past year, she'd made the old abandoned brick building of Hedelsten Hides & Leather Goods Tanning Company her retreat. It was her refuge, a second home for her whenever she and their mother weren't getting along.

Which was often.

She used to tell Eddie she wanted to leave their hardscrabble house in Rainbow Row and live there permanently, that one day, she would plant a rose garden on the roof. It was an act of rebellion, he knew. Because whenever either of them complained about the cold showers and toast made of moldy bread, their mother's response was always the same: "I never promised you a rose garden."

Perhaps Aurora would never have a rose garden on Rainbow Row. But she could have one here. "Once I buy this place for real and fix it up, you'll move in with me, won't you, Eddie? This place is so huge we wouldn't even have to see each other if we didn't want to!"

He vowed that he would, that one day they would make the place their own. In the meantime, Aurora had been hell-bent on guarding the tannery, as though possession really was nine-tenths of the law. Honestly, if some contractor ever had half a mind to tear it down, she would have chained herself to the door. She made it hers as much as she could, stringing Edison lights in a crisscross pattern from the rafters and making shelves out of old crates, wherein she kept little skull baby figurines and punk style magazines. A misshapen beanbag she'd rescued from the curb slumped in a corner, and My Chemical Romance trilled on her MP3 player. She'd hang out there for hours on end, reading and dreaming and making jewelry out of safety pins. Sometimes, she just lay on her back, staring up at the stars through the hole-punch roof. This was the only place in Black Harbor you could see the stars, she told him, out here by the lake.

His recollection of that night is as vivid as the real thing. He went to collect her, to bring her home before their mom got back from work; she hated Aurora crawling around that derelict old building. The crack of splitting wood and the burst of a scream that followed would play on a loop in his memory for the next eighteen years.

He rang for help, using the disconnected cell phone on which he could only call 911. During the eight to ten minutes it took for rescue to arrive, he discovered that the fall wasn't the worst part. Rather, the true tragedy of it all was that Aurora was alive for nearly that whole time, her eyes unblinking, mouth opening and closing like a fish out of water, blood draining from her face and darkening the floor. And he didn't know a damn thing to say to her, until at last, he knelt and pressed his forehead to hers. "Aurora," he whispered. "Aurora, don't leave me here. Don't leave me."

He started to sob.

She couldn't see him. Her gaze was faraway, lost in the stars, and her lips were grey but for the dash marks of blood where she'd bitten down on impact. He had to tilt his ear to her mouth to hear her final words. "She never promised us a rose garden, Eddie."

That was why, when he saw Chloe Winthorp walking alone with roses hanging at her side, he knew it was fate.

She was a dead ringer for Aurora. Dressed in her goth getup and skin as pale as moonlight, had he not been watching her transformation at school the past several weeks, he would have sworn she was his sister returned from the dead. He had to bring her home. So, he made a plan.

Recognition registered in Chloe's watery eyes the second she saw him. "Mr. Taylor?" Her voice was thick. As the distance closed between them, he noticed the fingers of mascara that striped her cheeks.

She was the second crying girl he'd encountered that evening. Madison Caldwell had been the first. Subconsciously, Eddie lifted his gaze to gauge the phase of the moon. "Miss Winthorp." He offered a smile, close-mouthed, like he'd trained himself to do since his middle school days. The same smile he'd given to Miss Caldwell before grabbing her by the jacket collar and dragging her down to the gully. It wasn't until they were out of the eye of the lamppost that he had bared his teeth.

Killing her had been for Chloe. Smashing her teeth out of her skull had been for both of them. He knew she teased Chloe for having retained baby teeth; he'd heard the jeers firsthand, seen the drawings that she and that wicked Sari Simons passed back and forth. Madison acted as though having perfect teeth herself gave her license to harass those who didn't. And she was exactly the kind of girl who would have teased him during his teenage years for his shark-toothed smile.

Dolphin teeth, that's what they called them at the jiujitsu academy. Only there he didn't mind so much because everyone had a derogatory nickname. A guy could do much worse than Orca, which was, ironically, the same in English as it was in Portuguese—the language from which most of their monikers originated.

He'd taken a detour onto Belgrave Circle Thursday night, where he knew Madison Caldwell would be headed to the walking trail. He circled once, then parked in front of the beach and began to walk in her direction.

"Oh, hi, Mr. Taylor." Madison's smile was bright, teeth practically glowing under the light of one of the lanterns in someone's front yard. She sounded a bit breathless. "Sorry, I didn't expect you to be out here."

Blotches bloomed on her usually flawless cheeks. She was upset. A fight with her boyfriend, perhaps?

"I was just taking a walk, soaking up some of the last nice days of the year," he said, carefully so as not to scare her off. "Are you on your way to the play?"

She nodded.

"Would you like a ride?"

He noticed it, the alert behind Madison's eyes. It's what's ingrained in us since we're children: don't take rides from strangers. But rideshares had changed all of that, hadn't they? And he wasn't a stranger; he was her teacher. He watched these thoughts roil in her mind as her lips parted to form her answer, but he was already choking her into silence.

He had to do it that way—act before he changed his mind. It was the only way to bring Aurora back. His mother would be so happy. She might even forgive him for being the one who lived that day.

Madison let out a yelp and kicked, but it didn't last. She went limp in less than ten seconds, and he dragged her down to the gully when something took hold of him. Pent-up anger and emotion from all those years of being teased by girls like Madison Caldwell. He grabbed a rock and smashed her teeth until they were sharp, broken little pegs like his.

Then he went to the play. He paid for his ticket with a faculty discount and sat a few rows behind Axel and Rowan, so he could watch when they inevitably got the call that would force them to leave.

And leave Chloe ripe for the picking.

It worked like a charm.

Thus far, police had found nothing that traced back to him. Chloe Winthorp's disappearance on the same night as Madison Caldwell's death stirred up enough suspicion, especially when it became public knowledge that the missing girl and the murdered girl had recently suffered a falling-out.

Eddie had the student body to thank for that. They could dig up dirt on anyone, and when the infamous Snapchat rose to the surface like a sliver determined to poke through the skin, it felt like the stars had finally aligned for him.

Cutler and Chloe, herself, were the obvious suspects for killing Madison. And then there was the bonus of adding Reeves Singh and Libby Lucas to the mix. A neighborhood canvass placed Reeves in the vicinity of the crime scene that night, and the collar burns on his girlfriend's neck resembled hickeys. As for Libby, she was weird and unlikeable. Lifting her taxidermy kit from Deschane's classroom was too easy. He'd seen it just lying willy-nilly on the table when he went to pick up the glass eagle eyes the great oaf had ordered for him. It was almost as if she'd placed it there expressly for him. *Take me,* an invisible note said. *Plant me at your next kill scene.*

Honestly, the muddier this investigation became, the merrier. Eddie would be lying if he said he wasn't amused by the myriad theories, his mouth quirking upon hearing whispers of what *really* happened in the hall, ears pricking anytime someone mentioned Chloe as the culprit.

But, what he really enjoyed was hearing Cutler's name entangled with it all. After killing Sari, Cutler's name started getting thrown around a lot, particularly on social media. Everyone knew the connection: that she'd sent the Snapchat condemning him of having a sexual relationship with Chloe Winthorp. He was as good as guilty. Eddie thinks that if he'd endured the same as Cutler, he probably would have jumped off the bridge, too.

Now, everything's turning up roses. He almost smiles at his cleverness. He has devoted his life to making things right. Their mother never promised them a rose garden. But nothing could stop him from creating his own.

For her. For Aurora.

39
ROWAN

The coffeepot gurgles. Droplets splash and sizzle on the warming plate as Rowan lifts the carafe and divides its contents into two mugs, leaving an inch of space at the top of one for Axel. She takes the half gallon of skim out of the fridge and sets it on the countertop for him. There's an orange Halloween bowl filled with the purple and orange Sour Patch Kids she picked up from the store the other day. What had she been thinking? That she could lure Chloe home with her favorite candy?

"Thank you." He slides the milk toward him and pours it into his coffee.

She takes a sip of her own, then, coaxing the caffeine to do its magic, and watches Axel work before climbing up on the barstool next to him. She's missed being a front-row observer into how his mind works. He's a fascinating study. His hands move gently and expertly, sorting the evidence that's spread across the countertop: photos of the victims, autopsy results, and the yearbook. He touches each piece as though asking its permission to be committed to his memory. Rowan steals a secret look at him and sees the gears turning behind his vivid blue-green eyes and the million-dollar question they churn out: How do they all connect?

Because they do. There is no way in hell these are isolated incidences.

She reopens the yearbook to the faculty page and finds Eddie Taylor's picture again. As she set to making the coffee, Axel filled her in about his conversation with the Pumpkin Lady, and how she indicated that a man with either grey or very short hair had left Sari Simons for dead Saturday night. A cold needle drills into Rowan's spine. Could he have Chloe? Could he have killed her along with Sari Simons and Madison Caldwell?

"I saw him at the grocery store," she says, her voice quiet as though she's unsure whether or not it really happened. "Sunday morning. He bought a bag of these for his sister." She points to the sweet-and-sour gummies in the bowl, and as she talks through it, the realization sets in.

"Chloe's favorite," says Axel, smiling sadly. "Of course she couldn't love a candy that was out year-round, right? Always had to have this special zombie edition . . ."

But Rowan hardly hears him. She's riffling through the archives of her mind, searching for evidence the way the police would riffle through a drawer. Had she seen Eddie Taylor the night of the play? She can't remember, and yet, it was dark and there were a lot of people. He could have been sitting behind them, watching and waiting for them to leave—

"Axel?"

"Hmm?" He's got one of the little brightly colored baggies in his hand, studying it as though the answers to this investigation could be spelled out in the fine print.

"What if killing was just a means to an end?" The revelation slips out into the universe and hangs in the sliver of space between them. When Axel regards her quizzically, she explains: "What if Eddie knew a dead body meant you and I would both respond to the scene? And he killed Madison Caldwell on the night of the play . . . so Chloe would be left alone?"

Axel drags the corner of the bag along the edge of his jaw. "But how did he know Chloe would walk home instead of getting a ride?"

She's considered this, too. Rowan remembers back to that night and the text she sent that Marnie never got. She puts herself in Chloe's shoes. Something she's never been good at doing. Not like Axel. The adage of walking a mile in other people's shoes has always been a natural response for him. She tries it on for size now. Chloe was upset. What did she do when she was upset?

She left.

Without saying a word to anyone about where she was going. "He didn't," she thinks out loud. "But he would have taken her one way or another. He was her teacher, so it's not like she wouldn't have trusted him if he showed up at the front door. He knew we were tied up with Madison's murder. Because he'd planned it that way."

"What about the window?" Axel reminds her. "It was open."

A frantic knock sounds at the front door. Rowan jumps and throws her gaze over her shoulder. Axel goes to answer it, his right hand touching the gun holstered to his side.

A moment later, Libby Lucas and Reeves Singh are in her kitchen. Marnie appears behind them. Rowan feels the sudden urge to go to her but wills herself to stay put, on the other side of the quartz countertop. What they have right now is one theory among many. Their daughters may not be entirely innocent in all of this. One could still be hunting the other.

By the way she remains next to Libby, shoulders pulled back and arms stiffly at her sides, Marnie seems to have arrived at some of the same hypotheses.

Axel steps aside and lets the kids have the floor.

"We found something that . . . well, we think you need to see." Libby's eyes dart from Reeves to Rowan to Axel. There's something pleading about the way she says it, and she can imagine it's because the girl is desperate to clear her name, and Reeves's. But Reeves wasn't the one keeping Madison Caldwell's teeth in a locket.

Reeves steps forward and extends his arm, offering up the papers they brought. They're computer printouts of articles. Rowan takes them and reads the headline at the top of the first page: GIRL, 15, DIES IN TRAGIC 30-FT FALL OF DEFUNCT FACTORY.

She recognizes the building as the old tannery, but, "Who . . . ?" Rowan is shaking her head. What can this possibly have to do with—

"Who does she look like?" prompts Libby, and Rowan flips to the next page. There, in black-and-white, Chloe stares at her.

No, not Chloe. Not quite. Here is a teenage girl with her dark hair cut in a severe asymmetrical bob, wearing slashes of eyeliner and a safety pin necklace. Her eyes are a little closer together than Chloe's, her face less heart-shaped. Still, they could be sisters.

The next page is an obituary. A different picture of the same girl looks intensely at her, daring her to keep reading. "'Aurora P. Blum,'" she reads, "'born in Black Harbor on April eleventh . . . beloved daughter of Patricia Blum and dear sister of Edward (Eddie) Blum . . .' I don't . . ." She looks up at the anticipatory faces, and then back to the printout.

"Edward Blum is Mr. Taylor," Reeves explains. "Or . . . Eddie Taylor. He teaches English at our school."

"He came to the garden center on Sunday to pick up a bunch of rosebushes," says Libby, stepping forward, and Rowan doesn't know if she's ever heard the girl string so many words together before. Apparently, Libby has the same realization, because she pauses and bites back a breath before continuing. "He said they were for his sister. Aurora."

Rowan and Axel exchange a look. "He said these were, too," says Rowan, sliding the bowl of Sour Patch Kids toward them.

"These are Chloe's favorite," says Libby, echoing Axel from just a few moments ago. "The zombie ones."

Rowan and Axel both nod.

"How do you know that?" Marnie's brows are knit. She edges forward, eager but trepidatious at being fully part of this conversation.

Libby takes in a deep breath. She lets it out slowly. "We were friends," she admits. Her gaze falls to the floor, as though she's just spilled a secret.

"You and Chloe?" asks Reeves, incredulously.

Libby nods. "I come over here at night, whenever you two are working." She looks up guiltily under dark lashes to regard both Rowan and Axel. "About a year ago, I saw her crying by her window, so I opened mine and we started talking. Then I figured I could get to her by climbing the sugar maple and . . ." She shrugs.

"Why was she crying?" asks Axel.

"That night?"

Those two words break what's left of Rowan's heart. They imply there were multiple nights Chloe cried, alone in her room.

"She was lonely," says Libby, and Rowan can tell by the cadence of her words that she is treading carefully. The girl is smart enough to know not to say too much, however, and Rowan knows better than to pry, at least in this moment. They can resolve things with Chloe later, if they ever get her back.

Rowan revisits the printout of the obituary. Aurora Blum died eighteen years ago.

Axel reads over her shoulder. "I remember her." He shakes his head. "I was on patrol at the time. God, that was tragic."

"What about him?" Rowan points to the picture of Aurora and Eddie together.

Axel works his jaw. "He would have been at the scene, yeah. But I was manning the perimeter, making sure no one crossed the tape. Even if I had encountered him, he was only sixteen. He looks different now."

Rowan does the math. Eighteen years ago was right around the time she ended up in Black Harbor. It would be another four years before she completed her training and certifications to become a medical examiner, and another twelve before she started running the show. "How do we find him?" she asks, uncertain of everything, but certain that they need to amplify things if they're going to have a chance in hell at finding Chloe, dead or alive.

"Guys."

All heads turn toward Reeves, who wields his phone. "The zombie edition of this candy didn't come out until four years ago."

"And yet . . ." starts Rowan.

"They're his sister's favorite," Libby finishes.

Rowan feels charged. She needs to move. Now. But the exhaustion of the past several days suddenly slams into her like a freight train, and she can hardly muster the strength to stand. It's too heavy—everything. "How do we find him?" she asks.

"He lives on Rainbow Row," says Reeves, his voice laced with what she recognizes as shame. "Over by me."

Marnie's voice is small and uncertain. Her composure has eroded to reveal raw terror. "Row? What's going on?"

Rowan edges toward her and slips her fingers through hers. She will tell her everything, soon, and their friendship will survive or it won't. But first, she has to find Chloe.

Marnie's question dissipates, drowned out by Axel speaking into his phone. "Activate SWAT," he says.

40

EDDIE

"Sing for me, Aurora, I know you can. What was that little 'Dead Mom' ditty you performed the other night?"

Eddie's gaze slides to their mother, who side-eyes him from her wheelchair. She's brushing his sister's hair just like she used to do when Aurora was young. The scene thaws Eddie's heart. It's almost as though no time has passed at all—if he ignores his mom's blanched hair and her crepey skin, most of which has succumbed to gravity. It's almost as though he . . . fixed . . . everything.

The thought is a bubble of happiness that bursts in his rib cage, coating his insides with gooey sentiments. In fact, he's so happy that *he* could sing! But he wants Aurora to. She is the star of the two of them. She belongs up onstage . . . in a cage . . . no longer a static picture on a page . . .

Stupid. She was always the better writer, a true-born lyricist, and yet it's funny how he became the English teacher.

Those who can't do, teach, right? It's a stubborn, derogatory proverb that clings unfairly to educators—Albert Einstein was a teacher, for Christ's sake—and yet, he cannot deny it holds true for him.

Eddie can teach English fairly fine. He can speak it. But when it comes to writing, the words get tangled up in his head and he is all thumbs. Not Aurora, though. She could speak it, sing it, ink-sling it— hey, that was pretty good—which was why she was the one destined to leave Black Harbor. She'd become a famous singer or a writer and pull him and his mother out of the rotting, ramshackle slums of Rainbow Row. That was always the plan.

Until that plan splattered all over the tannery fl—

No. Perhaps Eddie is not good at writing, but he is damn good at rewriting, if he does say so himself. Aurora is here now, isn't she? She is living proof that he has rewritten history, just like he's rewriting the future of the tannery.

He steals another look at her. She is so perfect with her pale skin and a choke chain around her neck. He was proud of himself for finding such a functional accessory that complemented her emo aesthetic. It isn't too tight for her to belt out a few notes—if she doesn't strain. Her hands are zip-tied behind her back but she doesn't need them.

"Sing for us," he says again. "You have the most celestial voice, Aurora."

Aurora sinks her teeth into her bottom lip. A single tear trails from her eye, sending a shiver down his spine. She's getting into character for them. Ever the professional, ever the perfectionist. This is why she will make it. This is why she will leave Black Harbor, and take him with her this time.

He can't wait to show her what he's done for her, as a thank-you for saving him, for getting him back in their mother's good graces. *I love you, Eddie,* she told him when he showed up with Aurora the other night. *You brought home my darling girl. You are the best son in the world.*

"I love you, too, Mom," he said, and planted a kiss on her wizened forehead.

"You can do it," he coaches Aurora now. "This is a safe space." He promised no one would ever hurt her, and he intends to make good on it, even if it means murdering girls from her class. Girls can be wicked.

Aurora lifts her shoulder, trying to catch the teardrop with the fabric of her shirt. She winces as the prongs dig into her neck. Eddie walks toward her, swipes his thumb gently across her cheekbone when his mother's voice interrupts the tender moment.

This isn't Aurora. Your sister had a scar on her left cheek.

With Aurora's face still cupped in his hand, Eddie closes his eyes for a few seconds. He takes in a breath and lets it out slowly, along with the feelings of inadequacy that seem to be building up inside him like plaque. Then, he reopens his eyes and conducts a careful search of his sister's flawless skin.

His mom is right, he hates to admit. It isn't there. When Aurora was little—about four or five—she took one of those rat-tailed combs and jammed it into her cheek, just to see what it felt like. Not great, apparently. Her cries pierced the night, and after being rushed to the emergency room, she was left with an X-shaped scar.

This cannot be. She must be perfect when she sees the surprise he has in store for her. How many times has he played the fantasy in his head of the moment when he brings Aurora to the rose garden—*their* rose garden? How many times has he imagined her falling to her knees and weeping with joy? How many times has he practically heard her say: *I can't believe you made us a rose garden, Eddie. I love you!*

He can't wait to take her there, finally after all this time, and simultaneously, no time at all. All the years they were apart are erased from her. Absentmindedly, Eddie touches his own face, feeling his stubble prick his fingertips, and wonders if the universe has been as kind to him. Is he still thirty-four? Or has he gone back in time and become sixteen again?

Eddie reaches his other hand into his pocket. "Shh . . ." he soothes when she jerks her head at the sight of a thin, silver minutien pin, one of which he stole from Deschane's classroom and used to write a slur in that pretty little bitch's lip. "I'll fix you," he promises. Aurora's eyes widen, revealing his reflection smiling in her pupils as he begins to carve.

41

AXEL

Rainbow Row is as dismal and even more decrepit than he remembers it. The houses here are old and run-down and crammed together like a mouthful of too many teeth. They wear a rainbow of heinous colors—from hazmat green to coagulated bloodred. The paint is donated to the city and free to anyone. The house Axel grew up in was chicken-fat yellow with teal shutters his mom rescued out of a used home and building supplies store. She tried to make it nice for him, his dad, and his siblings, even going so far as to tip an old wheelbarrow on its side and plant perennials in the mound of dirt that spilled from it. How did it make her feel, he wonders, when all her children ever talked about was leaving this place in the dust?

"This is it," says Kole. He's in the driver's seat, hands at ten and two on the steering wheel, though the raid van is parked. They confirmed Taylor's address in Onyx, thanks to a speeding ticket issued a few years ago.

Kole cuts his gaze over to Axel who stares at the house through the tinted passenger window. It's molting, little triangles chipped out of the siding. If it were an animal, it'd be the kind you take behind the shed and put out of its misery. A screen porch juts off the front like an underbite, waiting to swallow them whole.

A wave of dizziness rushes over him. If he wasn't already sitting, he'd probably have fallen over. This is it. It could all come to an end right here. The five days Chloe has been gone feel like five years. No.

Five lifetimes. Axel exhales. His breath creates a little cloud on the glass. He turns to his sergeant, then, his eyes homing in on the sheen of sweat that glistens on Kole's upper lip. It's stuffy in the raid van. A sweat and cologne cocktail tinges the stagnant air. Including Kole and Axel, there are nine men dressed in SWAT gear, damp from the rain, rifles ready. A patrol car pulls up behind them as well as an Impala, inside of which sit Riley and Rowan. It was the only way Axel could convince Rowan not to come on her own. At least Riley is armed and has never missed her target.

"This guy doesn't get into Halloween, by the looks of it."

Kole is right, Axel observes as he conducts a cursory sweep of the postage stamp–sized yard. There isn't one Halloween decoration. No fabric ghosts in the trees or jack-o'-lanterns on the porch steps. That fact alone makes this place a little eerie.

The plan is as follows: the four patrol officers will stage at the perimeter and watch for anyone trying to escape out a window. Sergeant Hayes will move to sit behind the wheel, leaving eight SWAT operators to enter the premises.

Kole pulls his door handle, which creates a domino effect. Axel gets out just as he hears the sliding door grate on the tracks. Fletcher and Mattox stand beside him.

"Jesus Christ." Kole pulls his black turtleneck up over the lower half of his face. "What crawled into a ditch and died?"

Immediately after he says it, Axel's eyes burn. The stench is suddenly overpowering, tenacious in the air that's thick with the memory of rain. It reeks of roadkill. He walks a few steps toward the ditch, checking for the carcass of a deer or a raccoon, but there's nothing.

On his left, Fletcher mimics Kole and tucks his chin into his shirt collar.

They execute formation. The perimeter officers move to the four corners of the house while Axel, Kole, Fletcher, and five more SWAT operators: Crue, Mattox, Jiminez, McKinley, and Whitmore approach the residence single-file.

Crue hoists the ram and punches the door. One strike busts the lock from the frame. The door swings inward. He steps aside, letting Kole,

Axel, and the rest move past. They filter into the living room and fan out.

The house is an icebox, with two bedrooms, one bathroom at most, and the smell is worse inside. It's so strong, it burns Axel's eyes. But, no matter how badly he wants to close them, he can't, because they are fixed to an old radiator on the far wall. An air mattress lies in front of it, a purple-and-black bedspread uncoiling from it like skin shed from a giant snake. Breathing through his mouth, he bolts across the room and tears through the blankets, hoping Chloe might be curled up beneath them, asleep and unharmed.

"We've got a corpse!" Kole's voice cuts through the haze of dread that's gripping his mind.

Axel's heart stops. *Please don't let it be Chloe.* The prayer is a broken record. He repeats it over and over as he turns to look over his shoulder. Then, he sees her. A woman sits on the couch, draped with a blanket as though she's just watching TV.

Kole creeps closer to it. "Female. Must be . . . sixty, sixty-five years of age?"

Wisps of russet hair do little to hide the woman's mottled scalp. Colorless skin is stretched taut over bones that have begun to shift out of place. Her lips have completely disappeared, receding to reveal a skeletal smile.

Axel squints and edges in. Is she moving?

Suddenly, a soft *plink!* disrupts the silence. A white macaroni noodle falls to the floor and begins to wriggle. Axel jumps back. Looking at the dead woman from this distance, he can see that her barrel-shaped torso is teeming with maggots. Bile surges in the back of his throat. He chokes it back down.

Her state of decomp isn't the most freakish thing about her, though. Her eyes are unnaturally round; bright gold with a black dot in the center. Looking more closely at her other parts, Axel can see that she's held together by twisted wire hangers and safety pins. Glass, amber eyes are fitted into the otherwise empty sockets.

Within minutes, the residence is cleared.

Mattox returns, rifle raised. "House is empty."

"You check the basement?" asks Kole.

"Crue just came back up. Nada."

"Where's our ME?" asks Kole. "I knew it was a good idea to bring her along."

They bring Rowan in to observe the body. Axel watches her eyes widen at the sight of the mess where Chloe must have slept with one eye open. Then, she approaches the dead woman as though she isn't disgusting and decomposing at all, but just an old woman watching her programs. If anything, she seems fascinated.

"Any idea if this was a natural death . . . or perpetuated?" Now that Rowan's here, Kole keeps his distance from the corpse.

"My guess is she was sick," says Rowan, with a nod to the prescription bottles that crowd the end table. "Judging by the state of decomp, I'd estimate she's been dead for . . . probably ten days or so."

"Maybe that's what made this guy snap," offers Kole. "Sister's dead. Mom's dead. He's got no one in this world, so he takes someone."

There's a prickling sensation on the back of Axel's neck when he considers that Kole might be right, and the *someone* he's referring to is Chloe. But where is she now? He looks at Rowan, who is still studying the corpse of Eddie's mother, Patricia Blum. "This sick psycho taxidermied his own mom," she says finally. Regarding both Axel and Kole warily, she shares what Deschane had told her about the teachers at Monroe Academy and their morbid requests. "He mentioned Mr. Taylor wanted a pair of eagle eyes. He didn't know what for, though, but . . . these look like eagle eyes to me."

Still listening, Axel drifts to the coffee table where mail and paperwork are stacked almost hip-high. The edge of a packet peeks out from near the top. He picks it up and discovers it's a bill of sale for the old tannery.

"Hey, look at this." He calls Rowan and Kole over.

"Hedelsten Hides & Leather Goods Tanning Company," Kole reads. "So this is the bastard who bought that place."

Rowan meets Axel's gaze, and he knows she is thinking about the

article they just read that told the tragic tale of fifteen-year-old Aurora
Blum falling to her death.

"Roll out," commands Kole. Then he calls to Crue, rattling off the
tannery's address: "Radio for backup. We've got a hostage situation."

42

ROWAN

Riley drives, keeping tight to the raid van as a mile of chain-link fence zips by on their left. Coils of barbed wire float on top, their tines catching the spectral light; they flash like a predator baring its teeth. This is it. Rowan feels herself pitch forward as they begin the steady descent down a road that gives the illusion of leading straight into the lake. She keeps her eyes trained on the lighthouse, her gaze zeroing in on the third-story window where she knows the Violent Crime Task Force has set up shop. She imagines Axel waking up there the other morning and peering out to discover plumes of red on the rooftop of the tannery across the expanse of frosted grass, which he'd shared with them while still at Eddie's house.

"That was fucked up . . . in there." Riley's focus is intense and trained on the road. "Sixteen years on this job and I've never seen anything like that."

Rowan pauses and knows she is referring to the DIY-taxidermied woman on the couch. She's certain that in their combined years of crawling around crime scenes, they've never encountered anything like that.

"I know that wasn't easy for him," starts Riley, and Rowan realizes she must be talking about Axel when she adds: "Going back there."

Back to Rainbow Row, she means. For as long as she's known him, Axel has vehemently ignored any connection to his neighborhood of origin, acting as though his life only began at age eighteen when he finally left that row of ramshackle houses.

A thought enters Rowan's mind, not for the first time since they got in the Impala together. Over the years, she and Riley have worked countless deaths and seen each other at different law enforcement–related events. But today is the first time she's ever been alone with the woman with whom Axel spends the majority of his time. They work alongside each other forty to sixty hours a week, spar at Silva's gym a few hours more. Amanda Riley has been tangled up with Axel in so many ways, she has become an essential thread in the fabric of his existence. If Rowan's being completely honest with herself, she feels like a fraud in Riley's presence, riddled with the fear that she'll be found out for not knowing her husband as well as Riley does.

The words come out before she's had a moment to think them through. "Thank you."

One perfect eyebrow arches. A constellation of dimples appears in the other woman's chin as she works her mouth into a discerning frown. "For what?"

"For . . . always being there for him. God knows I haven't been. I was . . . fighting my own demons, I guess." She summons to mind the obituary of Katelynn Diggory and wonders where it's gone to. Now that she's finally communicated to Axel the hold it's had on her all these years, she feels somewhat free of it. She did not murder that girl. And yet . . . if it hadn't been for her, Katelynn might still be alive, in her thirties now, with a career and maybe kids and sharing her life with someone.

Tears well in her eyes.

"Hey." The strength of Riley's voice makes her sit up straighter. "Don't apologize for how you grieve. Your daughter's been missing. That's heavy."

Rowan sets her jaw. "So has his," she says.

Riley nods. She opens her mouth as though to say something reassuring, but apparently thinks better of it. Rowan knows from Axel that a primary rule of police work is to never make promises. Still, she wishes Riley would give her a sliver of hope to hold on to, even if it isn't real.

The road curves to the right, depositing them at the base of the hill. The old tannery building fills the whole windshield. From down here, Rowan can just barely see the plumes of red.

Roses? Why would anyone plant a rose garden all the way up there?

Eddie's green Ford Explorer is parked at the bottom. They coast to a stop beside it and wait for the sliding door of the raid van to open before getting out. Rowan climbs out of the Impala and stands next to Axel, who is still dressed in his SWAT gear. The other team members regard her but say nothing. They know better than to tell her to get back in the vehicle.

Kole's voice blares over a megaphone. "Edward Blum, this is Sergeant Nikolai Kole of the Black Harbor Police Department. Please come out with your hands up. We know you're inside."

Rowan's eyes ricochet from the factory's double doors to the windows, some of which bear the entry wounds of rocks smashing through their panes. There isn't a flicker of movement from inside, and yet, all around her, the world rebels. Leaves rip from their branches and behind them, the lake throws punches at the half-sunk piers. The wind is bullish and sharp, biting at patches of exposed skin. Tendrils of hair slash across her face, and she imagines she must look like a reflection in a broken mirror. This is it—a do or die moment. Bring her daughter home, or die trying.

Life isn't worth living without Chloe. She's witnessed that firsthand these past days that she's been gone.

You'll love me more when I'm dead.

Oh no, darling girl. I need you beside me, breathing, laughing, just simply being. That is what she will tell Chloe if she is lucky enough to speak to her again, if her words don't fall on deaf, dead ears.

She takes a step forward. Axel grabs her bicep and pulls her against him. "Give him a minute," he says so quietly, she's sure she's the only person who can hear him.

"Edward Taylor Blum, this is the Black Harbor Police Department. Please surrender the girl and come out with your hands up. You have ten seconds. Ten . . . nine . . ." Kole begins the countdown.

"She's in there," she whispers to Axel. "She has to be."

"I know." He squeezes her arm tighter. A reassurance or a warning, she cannot discern.

"Five . . . four . . ."

What is that, now, that's just appeared on the rooftop? A man emerges. He's wearing a canvas jacket, no hat. He looks almost bald from down here, but for the light stubble that makes a shadow on his scalp. He reaches behind him and yanks a smaller person forward.

"Chloe!" Her daughter's name tears from Rowan's throat before she can swallow it back.

The girl on the rooftop is silent. Dressed in black from head to heel, her face betrays nothing—not fear nor recognition, not even acknowledgment of the people armed and gathered on her behalf.

She leans toward them at a forty-five-degree angle. Rowan feels her brows knit. How can this be? She almost looks as though she is floating, levitating from the ledge.

"Leave us, or I let go," Eddie calls down to them, and that's when horror takes up residency in Rowan's bones. Chloe isn't floating; she's being restrained. A collar is fitted around her neck, connected to the chain he grasps in his right hand. All he has to do is release, and she will plummet forty or more feet below.

"No one will hurt you," Kole calls to him. "We just want to talk—"

"Bullshit!" Eddie spits.

Rowan's stomach flips when Eddie jerks back on the chain. Chloe sways in the wind. How is she not crying? How is she not terrified?

"I know you've been to my house, yeah? We watched you from up here. You saw dear old Mom? The woman who promised I'd never leave Black Harbor. The woman who blamed me for living when my sister didn't." Eddie shakes his head. "No thank you, gentlemen. I don't really care to spend the rest of my life locked up in a padded room."

"Things don't have to end badly for anyone, Eddie," explains Kole. "We can get you help."

Eddie's quiet for a minute, surveying the crowd that has gathered. Then, his gaze lands on Rowan. She feels it like a barrage of termites burrowing under her skin.

"Mr. and Mrs. Winthorp," he projects, finally, for all to hear. One hand clenches Chloe's chain while the other points at Rowan and Axel. "Why don't you come up and see my rose garden."

43

EDDIE

Aurora stands so frozen among the roses, she might as well be a gargoyle. Eddie breaks one and touches it to her bud-shaped lips. "Don't they smell nice?" he asks in a quiet, nonthreatening voice. It's the one he uses with his students, fragile ones like Chloe Winthorp who often became frustrated with her reading. A soft voice is a dam for a flood of tears.

She doesn't make a sound. He presses the flower more firmly to her mouth. "Smell it."

Her delicate shoulders move beneath her oversized black sweatshirt. He hasn't seen that thing since . . . well, he's seen it, just not on a human frame. It's been in Aurora's closet among the other things she can finally wear again. He leans toward her and breathes her in. Her scent makes his eyes roll to the back of his skull, rattling loose old memories.

A small Eddie and Aurora watching cartoons together on Saturday mornings; the way she used to lie with her head on his torso, using him as a pillow. Eddie cooking macaroni and cheese for them while their mother worked her evening job; Aurora crushing up saltines and mixing them in with the cheese to make it go further. The two of them exploring the tannery for the first time, crawling through a broken window and climbing all the way up to the rooftop. Aurora standing right here, right where she is now, and proclaiming she would make a rose garden when she had the means. Then there would be a spot of brightness in Black Harbor, something beautiful.

Now, here she is, standing in the midst of the oasis he has created just for her, and what does she do? She won't even stop and smell the fucking roses.

His knuckles connect with her jaw. She falls. The wound in her cheek has opened up. It bleeds onto the concrete.

Eddie massages his hand. There's a streak of blood from her teeth having scraped across his knuckles. "You always were an ungrateful shit," he spits at her. "I'll never know why Mom loved you most."

Shakily, Aurora stands. She goes to him, untethered, her chain swaying at her back. "I'm sorry, Eddie," she cries as she hugs him tight.

The anger inside him dissipates. He's like a pot that has boiled over. Everything simmers now. "It's okay," he says as he strokes her dark hair. He sets his chin on top of her head and breathes her in. "It's you and me against the world, kid," he says.

"Like always," she agrees. Then, she takes his hand and leads him down one of the paths around the fountain. The sun piercing through the petals bathes everything in a pinkish glow. His heart swells, threatening to burst at the seams. This is everything he's dreamed of.

From below, the creak of the double doors announces Rowan and Axel's entrance. In just a matter of moments, they will be up the stairs, on the rooftop, and he will be forced to kill the last people who dared hurt his sister.

44

AXEL

He's always known that places have memories. The tannery brims with so many, it's suffocating. Folded into the fabric of its darkness, they wrap him up and corkscrew into his ears. How many hides must have passed through here? How many skins salted and sawdusted and hung to dry? How many ghosts like Aurora Blum haunt this place? Urban legends say you can still see the stain where she smacked the concrete.

He flicks on his tactical flashlight. Eddie demanded he drop his rifle and unholster his sidearm. They're weaponless; although it doesn't seem they'll have much trouble finding something to kill him with if need be, Axel notes as he conducts a cursory search of their surroundings. Old dusty hides flop over cedar drying racks, the stakes pointed. The wash bins are bone-dry, bags of salt slumped against them. Drums and cages for tumbling skins loom ominously along a wall, near a dust-covered workbench of broken taxidermy tools. Anything that was worth anything is long gone by now.

Industrial fans line sawdust-covered walkways. He steps over a cord and nudges Rowan to do the same. The hair on the back of his neck stands up when he reminds himself that Eddie has the higher ground. A bullet for each of them is all it would take, though judging by the other victims, Eddie prefers to kill people up close and personal.

He's usually good at navigating in the dark. But his mind is a melee of every possible fear, with the worst rising above: What if

Eddie has brought them here so they can watch him kill Chloe, his final victim?

A staircase zigzags to the second floor. Axel starts up it without looking back and feels Rowan closely behind him. Dust motes float down from the floorboards. The upper levels of the tannery are set up like a large scaffolding. On the far side, he observes an old elevator for carts, presumably, as they deliver freshly washed hides to cedar lockers on the second floor where the sawdust must be two inches thick. The third floor must have been used primarily as storage, he guesses when they arrive at it. His eyes scan the area for Aurora Blum's things: magazines, sweatshirts, candy wrappers—items a teenage girl might have kept in her secret hideout—and discover, instead, a figure that slowly emerges from the shadows.

Instinctively, Axel steps in front of Rowan, shielding her. "Where's Chloe?" he asks.

A humorless laugh disrupts the dust motes. Eddie Taylor smiles thinly, his sharp teeth gleaming in the hoary light that leaks through the holes in the ceiling. "Good to see you, too, Bueller," he says. "It's fun see-ing each other out of context, right? I almost didn't recognize you in this getup." He makes a vague gesture at Axel's black SWAT uniform. "And without your usual partner, of course. Hello, Rowan, how are you?" He wiggles his fingers at her.

Axel feels Rowan shift behind him, still on the staircase. She tries to take a step forward, but he forces her back. If anyone is fighting Eddie, it's going to be him.

"Let her go," he tries. "And we'll walk away, I swear."

Another smile splits Eddie's face. "Why would I go and do a thing like that? I finally have my sister back."

"She's not your sister!" Rowan screams, her voice ragged. "She's our daughter."

"Possession is nine-tenths of the law, ain't that right, Officer?" Eddie tilts his head and regards Axel with a smirk. "You let her go Thursday night. And who did she come to? Right . . . to me."

"You planned that," states Axel. "You killed Madison Caldwell. Be-cause you knew that if there was a homicide, Rowan and I would have to leave the play and investigate. You knew we'd have to—" He chokes on the last two words. They tumble out, a pair of strangled things. "Leave Chloe."

A slow clap punctuates the quiet. "You're smarter than you look, Bueller. What else do you know?"

Crime scene images flash through his memory. Madison's busted teeth. The marks on both her and Sari's necks. Like a software program, his mind matches them to the ones he is now sure he left on Mark Cutler, when, in his less-than-finest moment, he grabbed him by the hoodie and choked him out in Interview Room #1. "Cross-collar choke," he says, the name of the technique a revelation. "You walked right up to them. Maybe even spoke to them. They saw you, they just . . . never suspected you would murder them."

Eddie is swathed in a literal spotlight as patches of overcast sky filter in through holes in a pockmarked roof. He seems to be enjoying it. "There's something . . . utterly delicious about hiding in plain sight. I'll admit it's a bit of a thrill," shares Eddie. "As I'm sure it was for Aurora, too. All these years she's been under the guise of blond, demure little Chloe Winthorp. I should thank Cutler. After all, if he hadn't cast her into the role of that goth character, I may never have seen it for myself. Who she really is."

"She isn't—"

Axel bars his arm across Rowan's chest, preventing her from advancing.

"She told me all about her issues with those girls," says Eddie. "And I saw it for myself, too. The shitty looks they doled out to her, the salacious sketches they left behind for their peers to come across. 'Chloe'"—he uses air quotes—"trusted me. And when someone trusts you, there's no end to the things they'll tell you, or to what they will let you do to them."

"Did Sari Simons trust you up until the moment you scooped out her eyes?" Axel asks.

A wicked grin twists Eddie's lips. "Girls like Sari Simons don't deserve eyes," he says. "She saw the trouble Madison was causing for my sister. She could have stopped it. Instead, what did she do? She amplified it. Made it so much worse by sending that Snapchat around the whole school. She was dead before I took them, though. If that makes you feel better."

A lull settles. Axel feels himself stiffening, like rigor mortis is setting in the longer he stands here and lets Eddie suck air. Carefully, he takes a step forward. The stair creaks in protest as though trying to persuade him to come back. "I can't let you leave here, Eddie."

"Who says I want to be left?" Eddie retreats, but not out of fear. Without taking his eyes off Axel, he reaches into a cedar locker, and pulls the door toward him. Blindly, expertly, he grabs a two-handled knife with a curved blade that must be more than twelve inches in length. He's practiced this.

"Give us our daughter." Axel starts to circle him. If he can keep Eddie's attention on him, perhaps Rowan can sneak past, up one more flight of stairs, and go to Chloe. And do what with her? Rappel down the wall? It doesn't matter. She just needs to get to her. This is where they split up. He'll take care of Eddie.

Eddie snorts. "Your daughter is dead, gone the same way as the others, I'm afraid." He shrugs. "The girl in the garden is my sister, Aurora."

"Aurora fell through this floor eighteen years ago and you know it. You were there, Eddie." He can see Eddie's nostrils flare. A vein bulges in his forehead and Axel knows without a shadow of a doubt that he wants to kill him. Good. He keeps needling him, watching from the corner of his eye as Rowan slips away. "You watched the light dim in her eyes. You watched her blood soak into the pavement and what did you do? Not a damn thing. No wonder your mother—"

The air bursts from his lungs with the force of a freight train. His skull connects with the floor, catalyzing a cloud of sawdust to scatter into the dead air. He gasps for breath, one hand of his daughter's would-be murderer squeezing his windpipe, the other about to bring the rusted blade down on his head.

45

ROWAN

Rowan slams down hard at the top of the stairs. Pain shoots through her palms and zips up her spine. Her whole body hums, and yet, she scrambles to her feet, climbing out of the crater she accidentally kicked through the rotted step.

Axel and Eddie wrestle below her. She doesn't know who's at the mercy of who, only that she needs to reach this door and get to Chloe. Rowan rams her shoulder into it and practically somersaults onto the rooftop. A gust of wind threatens to rip her off, but she hunches over and grabs onto a wooden pallet. All around her, vivid blooms unfurl like blood spatter, and she is reminded of every particularly gruesome crime scene she's ever walked into. This isn't a crime scene—yet.

"Chloe?" she calls. God how good does that name feel as it pirouettes from her lips, especially when there is hope of an answering voice. "Chloe?" She runs across the roof, eyes searching frantically for her daughter.

She finds her curled up in the farthest corner. The sight of her breaks Rowan's heart all over again. A toothy collar chokes her neck; the skin of which is torn and red. A crimson X is carved into her left cheek and a bruise marbles her jaw.

"Chloe!" Rowan rushes to her. She takes her ice-cold hands into her own and warms them. "We have to go now. Chloe!"

Chloe turns her face toward her, and it is the stuff of nightmares.

Her sunken eyes swell, pupils dilating and constricting like dual camera lenses trying to find focus. But there are those turquoise irises that
Rowan would know anywhere. Suddenly, she's launched back to Thursday night, backstage at Monroe Academy with Chloe staring at her just
like this, a single teardrop cutting a trail through her pale foundation
when Rowan left her for the last time.

"Chloe." She rubs her hands vigorously, as though trying to birth
a flame. "It's me. Mom. Listen, I'll never leave you again, baby. I'm so
sorry."

Chloe's lips move slightly, almost as if she is trying to repeat Rowan's
words, but then her mouth forms the shape of an O, stretching as she
unleashes a bone-chilling scream. Rowan claps her hands over her ears.
She can feel him—someone—behind her. Her nerves prickle with warning. On instinct, she ducks, barely evading a blade that slices the air, and
when she falls backward, she looks up in time to see Axel bulldoze into
Eddie. A wooden pallet explodes into shrapnel as the two men crash onto
it. Axel grabs Eddie by the collar and throws a punch. Rowan hears the
sickening crack of his nose breaking.

"Come on!" She takes Chloe's hand and pulls her to her feet. They're
a good ten yards from the door. If Axel holds onto Eddie for just a few
more seconds—

"Aurora!" Eddie's bellow rents the air. It stops them in their tracks.
"Don't leave me!"

"Rowan, go!" Axel yells, lifting his head from off the broken boards.
Eddie has him pinned now. He sits on his chest, driving his knees into
Axel's elbows.

But where is the two-handled knife that Eddie had just a few moments ago? He must have dropped it on the stairs. Straining her eyes, she
can see the ragged edge of its blade grinning at her from the doorway
to the stairwell.

She turns to Chloe, who looks terrified and frail. But she has strength,
still. It's there in the pink hue that blooms in her cheeks, the way the fingers of her free hand curl into a fist. "I'll be right back," Rowan promises,
even as guilt churns her stomach. Chloe gives an almost imperceptible nod
and Rowan is gone, running for the stairwell. Fallen rosebushes block her

path. She jumps over them and is suddenly wrenched back down when Eddie grabs her ankle. Her chin smacks shingles and exposed boards. Her skull vibrates. Stars pop in and out of her vision.

"Mom!" Chloe's scream is shrill. Rowan can just see her black combat boots rushing toward her, into the tumult. The chain from her neck swings; she watches as Chloe grabs hold of it and draws it back like a whip, bringing it crashing down across Eddie's legs. He yelps like a wounded dog. The disruption is enough for Axel to roll out from under him, but then Rowan watches in horror as Eddie springs to his feet and clamps his large hands over Chloe's head. He shoves her into the low brick wall, where she crumples like a broken doll.

"Chloe!" Rowan shrieks, but her daughter lies motionless as Eddie advances. She has to go. Now!

"Axel, stop him!" she cries as Axel struggles to stand, the air knocked from his lungs.

"Row, where—" he wheezes.

"Just stop him!" Rowan darts past him and takes the stairs two at a time. Seconds later, she returns to the rooftop, with the two-handled fleshing knife in hand and sprints at the hulking form of Eddie Taylor. In one swift motion, she fits the rusted blade over his head and notches it in his mouth. She reefs on it, but it catches. The edge is too dull.

Eddie's hands fly up to his face, grabbing at the knife and desperately trying to pull it away. She is losing her balance. Behind her, she feels nothing but air, nothing to stop her from plummeting to her death.

Except for one thing, which is that she vehemently refuses to die.

With one final, violent burst, Rowan kicks her foot into the back of the man who killed Madison Caldwell and Sari Simons, the man who stole her daughter, and with one hard yank of the blade, she makes him smile.

TUESDAY, OCTOBER 31

46

ROWAN

Aurora Blum died eighteen years ago when she fell thirty feet and smacked her skull on the floor of the old tannery. She had a plan and a dream of leaving Black Harbor in the dust.

Most do. That being the people who reside in this bitter, crime-ridden city where morals erode as surely as the shoreline. Where everything is blackened and broken, and even something as beautiful as a rose can elicit dread. A sanctuary for some, and hell for all, Black Harbor waits with open arms for souls looking for a place to hide.

Souls like her own.

And Eddie Taylor's. Formally known as Edward Taylor Blum, he was the monster—now deceased—who murdered two girls with his bare hands and kidnapped another. Law enforcement suspected a rope might have been used, specifically in the death of Sari Simons, but the sisal fibers found on her body were later determined to be from a cat-scratching post.

An interview with Mark Cutler's wife confirmed he likely took the plunge from Forge Bridge by his own will—though it will never be proven. Rowan knows that Axel feels guilt over that one. Whenever he lies awake at night, she knows he is haunted by the episode that happened in the interview room, when he lost his mind and accused Cutler of having a wrongful relationship with their daughter.

They all lost their minds for a while. And as she's discovering in the aftermath, a mind isn't something that simply boomerangs back to where it belongs. It takes time and, perhaps, careful recalibration.

She tells herself the same thing about Chloe. She's confident her little sun-kissed girl is in there somewhere—now and again she catches a glimpse of her in the form of a wink or a laugh or a fleeting smile—but Rowan knows as well as anyone that you don't go that deep into darkness and emerge unscathed.

They're at the child advocacy center, a squat brick building with almost floor-to-ceiling windows that let in ample natural light. Chloe sits pretzel-legged on a grey beanbag, fingers worrying the cuffs of her sweatshirt sleeves. She wears a light blue hoodie and black leggings. From behind the glass in the observation room, Rowan can see the blond roots of her hair pushing the dark dye away from her scalp.

Yesterday, she asked Chloe if she wanted to go to the salon, but she declined; she's sure she must feel conflicted about this goth guise that simultaneously placed her in Eddie Taylor's crosshairs and saved her life. No, it wasn't her look, Rowan reasons. It was her act. Because for all intents and purposes, for the five days she was in his clutches, Chloe became Aurora.

"Tell me about method acting," invites Camille Mitchell, the forensic interviewer.

Slowly, as though examining each word before she speaks it, Chloe explains how, when awarded the role of Lydia Deetz for the *Beetlejuice* musical, she never broke character. "I started dressing like her. Listening to her kind of music."

"Which was?" Camille's pen is poised over her legal pad.

"Emo. Scream-o. Maybe a little classic rock now and again. I liked to think of her as having a lighter side." There it is, a hint of a smile. "Before she lost her mom, anyway."

"Your mother is alive, though, Chloe, correct?"

"Yes."

Camille leans slightly forward. Tilts her head. Bars of light from the fluorescents overhead reflect in her glasses. "How did you channel those feelings through your acting? Of missing your mom?"

Just like that, the smile is gone. Chloe's face darkens with contemplation.

In the observation room, Axel squeezes Rowan's hand. She inhales deeply and tries to steel herself for what Chloe is about to say. To their right, Kole and Riley remain silent, watching and listening intently.

"I just . . ." Her teeth sink into her bottom lip. "I thought of all the times she left for work. Sometimes I was afraid she would never come home. That maybe murderers would return to the crime scene and finish what they started. And I imagined *what if*. What if it came true and one night she didn't come home?" A tear slips down her cheek, rerouted by the X-shaped scar.

Camille hands her a tissue. "It's not easy to think about those kinds of things, is it?"

Chloe shakes her head.

A shot of salt hits her tongue and Rowan realizes she is crying, too. She wants to go to Chloe, to hug her and promise things will be different moving forward, but her livelihood revolves around the deaths of others. And in Black Harbor, it seems to be the only thing of which there is no shortage.

But . . . she can do better. She has to.

Camille pivots the conversation back to Eddie Taylor and the five terrifying days she spent with him. "Did you know that the character you were method acting and Eddie's sister, Aurora, were . . . practically one and the same?"

"They had their differences," offers Chloe. "Aurora was a bit more of a rebel, I think. Independent. But yeah, I figured it out pretty quickly. Once I saw her things."

"Did he ever tell you why he killed Madison Caldwell and Sari Simons?"

"Because they hurt me," Chloe answers. "He told me . . . Aurora . . . that he was going to protect me this time." She tells her about the rumor and the way Madison used to tease her about her baby teeth, admitting, as well, to scribbling out their photos in her yearbook with Libby Lucas.

"Did he ever mention anything about Libby Lucas?" Camille wants to know, and Rowan is impressed with how conversational this interview is, as though Camille is not armed with a list of questions.

Chloe pauses at the mention of Libby's name. She has been over twice since Chloe has come home, using the back door instead of the second-story window. Oddly enough, seeing her and Marnie's girls on the couch together is one of the strangest—and most wonderful—things to come out of all of this.

Chloe shakes her head in response to Camille's question. She also shakes her head when she asks about whether or not she had a romantic relationship with Mr. Cutler. Beside her, Axel exhales with relief. Rowan holds him up so he doesn't crumble.

At home now, red leaves roll across the walkway. Rowan recognizes them as belonging to the sugar maple tree in the backyard. Their edges are dried and curled under; they look like a brigade of canoes scooting and tumbling end over end. The wind hurries them past—a sudden breeze that whooshes in off the lake and wicks all the moisture from her hands as she wields the carving knife.

It's Halloween. Normally, their quiet neighborhood is teeming with kids in costumes, ringing doorbells and toting plastic buckets filled with candy. But not this year. The air is crisp and heavy with melancholy. Madison's funeral was Saturday; Sari's was Sunday. They didn't go to either of them, out of respect. While there certainly wasn't any love lost between Chloe and the girls, they had been her friends once, in what feels like another lifetime. Selfishly, Rowan didn't know if she could look the girls' parents in the eyes. Her daughter returned, alive, when theirs didn't.

Sitting on her front porch steps, Rowan plunges the blade into the top of her pumpkin, near the stem. She looks to her left, then, where past Marnie's house she can see the tail end of the walking trail that stretches from Belgrave Circle to Monroe Academy. Chloe's on it now to meet up with Libby and Reeves.

She's being homeschooled the rest of the semester. If counseling goes well, and if she's ready, she will return to Monroe in the spring.

"Hey, Mom!"

Rowan looks up. Chloe and Libby walk toward her. Fry pulls ahead on his leash, tugging Chloe into a jog. Chloe laughs and Rowan feels her heart swell. The sound is magic. She waves.

"I got one for each of you." Rowan points to the two pumpkins on the step. "And your mom, Libby, if she ever gets out of work."

Libby smiles. "I think she just got home, actually. I'll go tell her." She turns and jogs toward her own house.

A cobalt SUV stops at the mailbox before pulling into the drive. There's a buzz of the automatic garage door, then the sound of an engine shutting off.

"There's my girls. And my Fry guy," Axel adds when the dog barks. He's dressed for the detective bureau, wearing a dark grey suit and polished black shoes. In his arms, he cradles a paper bag that Rowan can smell is filled with Chinese food, and an assortment of mail.

Of course, she knows it could be that she's under the spell of the sweet and spicy aroma of crab Rangoon and kung pao chicken, or the fact that she almost lost him forever—Axel on one side of a rift and she on the other—but one thought is clear in Rowan's mind: God, she loves this man.

He walks up the front porch stairs and leans down to kiss her. She closes her eyes and allows herself to melt a little at his touch. He plants a kiss on Chloe's forehead next, and hands her an envelope. "Something came for you."

Chloe frowns at it, then her eyes widen. Rowan snatches a glance at the return address before Chloe tears it open.

THE JUILLIARD SCHOOL
60 LINCOLN CENTER PLAZA, NEW YORK, NY 10023

"It's the Juilliard School," Chloe gasps. Her eyes scan hurriedly as she reads. "They heard my story and they want to invite me to their summer acting camp!"

"That's fantastic!" exclaims Axel. He pulls Chloe into a one-armed embrace. Chloe hugs him back, then throws herself at Rowan.

"We're so proud of you," Rowan whispers into her daughter's hair.

And it's true. This could be the beginning of the life Chloe's always wanted for herself. And even though this dream will take her far away from here, Rowan wants her to hold on and let it take her as far as she can go.

She and Axel will be fine.

Axel sets his hand on Chloe's shoulder. "You're gonna knock 'em dead."

Chloe smiles. Tears stream down her cheeks and disappear into her flannel. "I have to show Libby!" she says as she races next door.

A moment of silence descends and Rowan feels like it is the dust settling all over again. But in a good way.

"Wow," Axel breathes. "Well, that's something. Isn't it? New York." Mirth dances in his blue-green eyes. A shadow darkens them, though. "She'll be okay, there, don't you think?"

Rowan looks over at Marnie's house, where through the window, she can see the Lucas family celebrating with Chloe as though she is one of their own. "No," she says. And when she turns back to Axel, she draws him close. "She'll be extraordinary."

Axel presses his thumb to her cheek and swipes away a teardrop. "So will we," he promises.

They kiss again on their front porch, in their little crescent-shaped neighborhood of Belgrave Circle, where the waves of Lake Michigan crash against the broken pier, and one more thought rings true to Rowan: Black Harbor is no longer her exiled purgatory; it's home.

"Are you coming inside?" Axel waits by the front door.

"I'll catch up."

He takes Fry in the house while Rowan stays to carve a smile in her jack-o'-lantern and add a few finishing touches. Then, she sets it on the bottom step, comforted with the knowledge that it will be gone by morning.

ACKNOWLEDGMENTS

"Save the girl. Kill the bad guy." If anyone has a knack for simplifying plot problems, it's my editor, Leslie Gelbman. I'm so grateful for the opportunity to publish a third book together, and I couldn't be happier with the entire team at Minotaur and Macmillan Audio. Leslie's assistant, Grace Gay, has been instrumental in keeping things on track; my publicist, Kayla Janas, and marketing director, Stephen Erickson, are two of the best people on the planet; and David Rotstein killed it with the cover design . . . again!

Thank you to Sharon Pelletier for finding an incredible home for this book, and to Stephanie Rostan for championing it to the finish line. I am so grateful for both of you! To my author friends, if you crafted a quote, recommended my books, or tag-teamed an event with me, know that I am so appreciative. Special shoutouts for Elle Cosimano, David Ellis, Stacy Willingham, Vanessa Lillie, Riley Sager, Hank Phillippi Ryan, May Cobb; and my "dirty work wives," Tessa Wegert and Danielle Girard.

Booksellers, bibliophiles, book lenders, and bookstagrammers: you guys are awesome! Thanks especially to my friends at B&N and Blue House Books for getting my stories into the hands of readers, Gare @gareindeedreads for his dreamy dreamcastings, and my dark and spooky friend, Abby @crimebythebook for all the book love. I promise you'll be on my murder board someday. P.S. The MCR reference is for you.

Speaking of murder boards, I talk about mine a lot in regards to writing process, but something I love (almost) as much is connecting with real humans. My good friend Becky Porcaro was imperative to nailing down my medical examiner, Rowan, as well as any scrap of medical knowledge that appears on these pages. I remember the first time we met up at a bar off the beaten path. People were practically falling off their stools trying to eavesdrop on our conversation. I'd also like to thank my friend Andy Lueneburg for the jiujitsu knowledge that helped inform Axel's character; my brother-in-law, Peter Delzer; and Elenna Garrett for filling me in on what the kids say these days.

My police friends and family are endlessly helpful when it comes to answering the gamut of weird, morbid, or procedural questions. Honestly, with all the resources I have, it would be a crime for me not to write crime fiction.

To all of my friends and family, whether you've read snippets of my works in progress (Alissa Stormont and Nikki Sharon Schultz) or you've come to my book events or recommended my books to others, your support means the world to me. Thank you especially to Mom, Dad, Grandma, April, Miranda, Elizabeth, and Lily. Whenever I want a break from Black Harbor, I know someone will always leave the porch light on for me.

Bringing it home, there are a million and one reasons why I'm lucky to have Hanns as my ride or die. From plucking a "what if" out of the air to doing mock interviews, or telling me what Nikolai Kole absolutely would or wouldn't say, he's always here for me. Finally, to my three little pigs: Griswold, Muffins, and Kevin. These early mornings would be awfully lonely without you. Thank you for keeping me company. Banana loves you.